Hello, Gorgeous!

A NOVEL BY

Marcia Lewton

© Copyright 2006 Marcia Lewton
Cover Art by the author, photographed by Eric McRea
Author photo by Kathy Walker
Book design by Valerie Brewster, Scribe Typography
Thanks go to the Centrum Foundation and the Indiana Arts Commission
for their support of this work.

Note for Librarians: A cataloguing record for this book is available from Library and Archives Canada at www.collectionscanada.ca/amicus/index-e.html
ISBN 1-4120-9543-3

Printed in Victoria, BC, Canada. Printed on paper with minimum 30% recycled fibre. Trafford's print shop runs on "green energy" from solar, wind and other environmentally-friendly power sources.

PUBLISHING™

Offices in Canada, USA, Ireland and UK
This book was published *on-demand* in cooperation with Trafford Publishing. On-demand publishing is a unique process and service of making a book available for retail sale to the public taking advantage of on-demand manufacturing and Internet marketing. On-demand publishing includes promotions, retail sales, manufacturing, order fulfilment, accounting and collecting royalties on behalf of the author.

Book sales for North America and international:
Trafford Publishing, 6E–2333 Government St.,
Victoria, BC V8T 4P4 CANADA
phone 250 383 6864 (toll-free 1 888 232 4444)
fax 250 383 6804; email to orders@trafford.com
Book sales in Europe:
Trafford Publishing (UK) Limited, 9 Park End Street, 2nd Floor
Oxford, UK OX1 1HH UNITED KINGDOM
phone 44 (0)1865 722 113 (local rate 0845 230 9601)
facsimile 44 (0)1865 722 868; info.uk@trafford.com
Order online at:
trafford.com/06-1298

10 9 8 7 6 5 4 3 2 1

In memory of my husband, Vance Lewton,
whose love and support made this work possible.

HALLOWEEN, 1984

Darkness was falling on Clover Street as the first trick-or-treaters approached the parsonage. The old neighborhood streetlights shone round in the magnifying wetness of a just beginning rain. Some houses had a stay away look, where people hid behind dark windows because they were afraid of children, while others had been spooked up for the occasion with skeletons and sheeted ghosts. Jack-o-lanterns grinned from brick porch railings. They looked much alike with their ragged teeth and triangular eyes, except for the one by the parsonage door, which was clearly a pumpkin in distress with straight-across slits for eyes and a hole of a mouth crying out.

Three children crunched through piles of wind-gathered leaves whose dusty odor was changing now with the dampness. "Hurry up, slowpoke," said one of them, a Bo Peep of about nine wearing a bonnet and a long skirt over her wraps. She poked her crook at a smaller child, a boy on all fours who was costumed in a black-nosed mask and two sheepskins fastened at the shoulders with diaper pins. The ends of the rope that held the skins around his middle dragged the pavement.

The third child, a girl, was dressed as Red Riding Hood in a cape and sweet-faced mask. On a leash beside her a wolf-like German shepherd lifted his leg at every tree, every lamppost.

"She'd better be ready," said Bo Peep. They turned up the parsonage walk to where the yellow leaves of a maple tree caused the light suddenly to intensify, where the floor of bright leaves on the ground mirrored the yellow ceiling still hanging on the branches.

But a few steps later the gloom settled again and here, seeing it head-on, they got the full effect of the jack-o-lantern. "Ugh," said Red

Riding Hood. "Sicko." Up on the porch the dog sniffed it, jerking back suddenly when his nose got too close to the candle in the hot mouth.

Then Bo Peep and the sheep began scuffling over who would get to ring the doorbell.

PROTECTION FROM PREDATORS

A few blocks away, another child, who had hoped to be part of the group, lay across her parents' bed watching TV and eating store-bought popcorn. Positioned carefully on her belly to protect the cardboard wings of her costume, she wore black tights that encased her chubby legs but did not quite meet her hooded black sweatshirt at the waist. Every so often she hitched and tugged, trying to cover the uncomfortable roll of bare flesh.

Her wings ended with long swallowtails that drooped because they were made of thinner paper. Higher up, colored in iridescent crayon, were conspicuous eye spots copied from the science book picture on "Protection from Predators." The wings were held on with straps cut from a daypack. The daypack had been ruined, of course, and her father had smacked her, but the wings were worth it. At least they were when she had still had plans.

"You're not going out, no matter what your mother told you. You're in enough trouble already."

"Going trick-or-treating isn't trouble! And they hardly ever invite me. Please, Daddy!"

Duncan's look had hushed her up.

Her mother had tried to comfort her by praising the costume and getting the camera out. "Suck in your stomach, Josie Honey, and stand a little sideways." That was supposed to make her look slimmer. "Pull your hood back so your hair will show." Josie's hair was her good feature. People even stopped her on the street to exclaim about it.

"I want my antennae to show." She was pleased with the antennae, pipe cleaners dyed with shoe polish. The tips curved backward, like in the picture.

"Well now, which is more important?" said Eve impatiently. Josie sighed. She already knew which was more important. She pulled the hood back to display her hair. Eve snapped the picture and said, "He's just trying to protect you." Josie swallowed hard. Why didn't she feel protected then?

Now she was upstairs hiding to escape the humiliation of being found at home by other kids out trick-or-treating. The TV volume was turned up. Even so, she heard the click when the doorknob turned. She quickly stuffed the popcorn bag under her wing.

"Get on downstairs where you can answer the door." Duncan flipped on the overhead fixture. In the too-bright light, his red hair flamed like her own.

She hesitated, wiping her buttery fingers on the spread. He took a threatening step into the room. She slid off the bed sideways to keep the popcorn hidden. On the way out she made a face in the mirror and slipped past him, still protecting her wings.

No trick-or-treaters had arrived yet. She turned on the living room TV to finish watching her program and stashed the popcorn bag behind the couch. Then she switched off the porch light and drew the drapes so that no one would knock.

A little later the sound of her parents fighting came from the kitchen. Eve hissed, "I *never* should have told you. I knew it! It would have been better to let it go. Just said nothing and let her forget about it. If this is what you call protecting her, making her miserable, ruining her social life. A girl has to have a social life!"

"Shut up. I've got all I can handle at the shop. If I have to step in here, then I'm going to do it my way. *Your* way certainly hasn't worked."

"You won't *let* me do it my way."

"You're damn right. You want to set her up. Well, let me tell you one thing. She's *my* daughter too, and if you let anything else happen to her, you're damn well out of here!"

Josie turned up the TV until the volume filled the living room.

COSTUMES AT THE PARSONAGE

Inside the parsonage the four inhabitants still sat at the kitchen table, which was cluttered with pushed-aside chili bowls, slaw plates and cornbread crumbs. At one end of the table the Reverend Corcoran Pearlman held up a long-handled mirror to admire his handiwork. He wore a long black cassock, which added bulk to his thin body, and his face was sculpted with actor's putty into the features of a witch. Wisps of hair sticking up from his cowlick detracted from the menace, however, and not even the deforming makeup could alter the effect of his lively, sand-colored eyes.

At the other end of the table Corky's round little wife Claire was busy stapling wads of frowsy black yarn around the brim of the pointed black hat that would complete the costume. Claire was short enough – not quite five feet tall – that the table was a little high for her. She stood up periodically to get enough leverage behind the staple gun to make it hold the thick yarn hair to the hat. Claire's own hair, dark brown and laced with white threads, curled all over her head. The hairline dipped into her forehead in a widow's peak. Her skin, fine-textured and firm in spite of her years, was the plain, healthy color of milk. She worked with efficient movements, quickly, her dimpled hands making up in dexterity what they lacked in reach.

Claire was used to mothering Corky. Tonight her mothering took the form of helping him prepare himself for an evening of play. He surely needed it, after an afternoon making the rounds of the nursing home. Four frail members of his congregation were confined there, one in a fleece-padded bed on the dismal floor everyone called "the last hurrah." This bedfast woman had sent flowers home to Claire, an outsize bouquet of spicy-smelling carnations that now cast forth their perfume from a mason jar on the drain board of the kitchen sink. "You know where all these flowers come from, don't you?" the old woman had whispered to Corky, with a certain good humor. "I'm not ready," she said. "I've got another couple of weeks of dandelions left in me before they bring on carnations."

Claire knew, of course, that Corky didn't mind visiting the nursing home, in spite of the atmosphere. The people there were among the few in the congregation who had not turned against him. Even so, he had come home relieved to be free to spend the evening with children. The very old and the very young were the ones he still got along with, but of the two he preferred the very young. With them he could let his hair down and play, and if he made a mistake, there would be time tomorrow to correct it, whereas the very old might die between one visit and the next.

At the side of the table sat Claire's niece Romy. She too would have unburdened herself for Halloween if she could have. But Romy was in misery, and she was not able to ignore it. Her compact body under jeans and a turtleneck was held unnaturally stiff by a back brace that bit into the flesh above and below it. The discomfort, along with the occasional stabs of pain, made her awkward at her chores, even easy ones like now, brushing rouge on her little girl Nancy's pretty, heart-shaped face.

"The Witch of the Flattened Hemisphere," said Corky in his deep ministerial voice, admiring his reflection. "I feast on roasted children." He practiced a cackle, "Yaaahahahaha," which revealed his doggy smile that was attractive against all odds, with teeth that looked like little unmatched pebbles tossed carelessly into place along his gum line. Then, having assured himself that he was menacing enough, he winked over the mirror at Nancy. "Hello, Gorgeous."

Nancy hesitated, then winked back. Made up as she was, she looked older than nine.

"What if somebody from Freethinkers sees you dressed up like this?" said Romy. Her tone scolded Corky. "You don't need any more trouble, do you?"

"No, of course not, but who's going to see me? The neighborhood kids aren't going to think there's anything so terrible about dressing up for Halloween. They never mind my being Santa Claus at Christmas. And besides, it's not the costume that folks object to."

"That's because they haven't seen it. They haven't even *dreamed* of seeing it. And the minister as Santa Claus is a far cry from the minister as witch."

Corky shrugged. With the help of a padded costume he had been Santa Claus time after time over the years, but this was the first year he'd tried his hand at being a witch. The congregation would just have to get used to it. He had believed, back in the sixties when he'd helped create the Freethinkers' Meeting, that this congregation would be less contentious than the Unitarians he'd served earlier, and the Methodists earlier still, less prone to see the minister as an authority figure to be placed on a pedestal – and then brought down. But no. People were people, and a church was a church, even if its members insisted on calling it a "Meeting."

He sometimes used the hands-and-fingers game as a model: "Here is the church, here is the steeple, open the door and see all the people." And where was the minister? On the floor being kicked around.

Romy tried once more. "It still seems to me that a person in your position ought to keep a low profile."

Claire glanced quickly at Corky's profile, hag-like, the nose and chin pointing to each other. "You're good, Romy," she said. "We can count on you for the right word every time." Dimples appeared on Claire's face in unexpected places, a deep one in front of her right ear, as she gave her niece an affectionate look that took note of the unwanted advice but forgave her for it.

Romy shrugged. "Have it your way." She held Nancy's chin high and applied a little more rouge. "The Snow Queen has pink cheeks from the cold. Let's get this right."

Nancy's own skin was not very pink. She was one of those pale-haired children who tan in summer, but last summer she hadn't had the opportunity to spend much time at the pool. What tan she'd gotten was now faded out. Her costume was a white fur coat of Romy's gone bald in patches, and a gilded tiara studded with glass diamonds. Under the tiara were curls, pale blonde, the kind of hair beauticians call "perfect" because scissors and comb are all it ever needs.

"I know what's missing," exclaimed Corky. He pushed back his chair and went to the drain board to the bouquet of carnations.

He selected the largest carnation, a red one, then dug into the catch-all drawer for a pin. "Here," he said, moving back to the table. He fussed with the flower, holding it first to Nancy's hair, her throat, then pinned it to her coat as a corsage. A fallen petal stuck to the white fur like a drop of blood in a "Save the Baby Seals" poster. Corky sat back down at his place and picked up the mirror. "No one would recognize me anyway."

Claire dimpled. "What if they did, and thought it was a change for the better?"

Then the door chimes sounded: ding dong. Everyone began to hurry. Claire added three more staples to the hat: bang, bang, bang. Nancy pulled away from Romy's grasp. "They're here." Corky laid the mirror on the rim of his chili bowl. "Wait for me." He stood up quickly. Above the evil nose and chin, his sand-colored eyes gazed at Nancy.

"I hope I made this big enough," said Claire. Corky bent his head and she covered his disorderly hair with the hat. "It needs more yarn."

"It'll do," he answered impatiently. He grabbed Nancy's hand. They hurried, swinging arms, down the hall made narrow by bookcases on either side, to the unlighted living room where there were even more books.

"You stand behind the door when I open it." he said. "They have to see me first, or they won't be scared." In the darkness he bumped his shin on the coffee table. "Hairballs!" he exclaimed.

Nancy giggled. "Hairballs!" she echoed. She pressed her back against the bookcase behind the door.

CANDY

Corky turned the knob and opened the door a crack, then swung it wide and gave a loud, falsetto cackle, "Yaaaaahahahahahaha."

The children on the porch backed up. The police dog backed up too.

"Come into my parlor, tender morsels!" Corky's deep voice was now high as a soprano.

"Let's get out of here," said Bo Peep. The children scrambled. The pumpkin was knocked askew, its face now turned to the household.

Nancy dashed from behind the door. "Don't let him scare you," she called. "It's just Uncle Corky."

The children, at a safe distance down the walk, stopped. "He didn't scare me," boasted the sheep. His rope was loose again. He looped and twirled it like a lariat.

"Come on in a minute," said Nancy. "I have to get my sack. Where's Josie?" she asked.

"I'm not supposed to run around with her anymore," said Red Riding Hood, while Bo Peep said, "Her parents wouldn't let her out."

Inside, Corky maneuvered through the crowded room and snapped on the ceiling fixture, then squatted on his heel. The full black cassock puffed around him. His tall hat pointed to the light. He offered his hand to the dog to sniff. "I certainly recognize this one," he said. "I'd know the Big Bad Wolf anywhere."

"He's not the Big Bad Wolf. He's not from 'The Three Little Pigs' at all. He's the wolf that ate grandmother." The girl's costume was a hooded cloak made of plastic that had not been smoothed out after being unpacked. It crackled every time she moved, and the folds left windowpane lines that made it look plaid.

"Of course," said Corky. "I should have known."

The sheep moved in close. "Why are you dressed up like that?"

Corky tilted his head back and stuck out his sharp chin. "Because it's Halloween."

"Are you going to a party?"

"No."

"You're not going trick-or-treating, are you?"

"No I'm not." Off balance on his heel, Corky stood up. "Would you like some candy?" he asked.

The candy was piled loose in a long wooden bowl. Claire had bought Corky's two favorites, candy corn and malted milk balls. "Take all you want," he said.

The boy started to pick malted milk balls out from the candy corn, but as soon as she saw what he was doing, Bo Peep shrieked at him, "You can't have those. We're not supposed to take anything unless it's still in the package." The boy pushed up his sheep mask quickly and stuffed a handful of candy in his mouth. She pounced and shook him, but he stood firm and chewed, his determined little jaws busy between the mask and the sheepskin.

Corky edged the bowl toward the girl persuasively. "Go ahead, I can keep a secret," he said. He winked at the boy. "We men know what's good, don't we?" He picked out a malted milk ball and held it to the girl's lips. "Here's the best one in the whole bowl."

She shook her head. "No thanks."

He dug in his pockets under the robe. "If they won't let you take any candy, how about these?" He handed the girl a quarter, then found two dimes for the little boy. She quickly pocketed her own money and worked on her brother's clenched hand to get his. "Give me that," she said. "You don't have any pockets. You'll just lose it."

Corky moved close to Red Riding Hood and offered her the bowl. "Don't I know you?" he asked affectionately. He put his arm around her shoulders. "Aren't you Heather Merchant?" Both of these girls were in fourth grade with Nancy, but this one had also been over to play after school.

Her voice was artificial as she answered, "I'm Red Riding Hood." She helped herself to candy corn with no qualms.

"That's funny. I'd have sworn you were Heather Merchant. Could you be her twin?"

She took another handful of candy without answering, but her lips pressed together to hold back a smile.

Corky went into one of the flights of fancy that had become less and less appreciated by his congregation in recent months. "Have you ever thought you might really have a twin? A Heather-Red Riding Hood twin? Someone just like you, only the opposite, like the person in the mirror?" He slipped into his storytelling mode, a favorite. "Up in the farthest north, there's a tribe of Indians who believe that everyone is born a twin, only at the moment of birth, one twin vanishes to go and live in the spirit world."

Behind him he heard Nancy come back. He moved the story along. "If you have light skin, your spirit-twin is dark, and vice versa. If you're a good girl, your twin is the bad one – and has all the fun, of course. Everything about your twin is the opposite." Corky's voice was a natural for story-telling, deep and persuasive, one that people could listen to endlessly.

The children, however, had their own plans. "Come on," said Nancy. "Let's go."

"How about a kiss for your Uncle Corky?" He gave her a compelling look. She looked embarrassed, holding her face up.

But the sheep was still eyeing him. "That's not even a mask, is it?"

Corky knelt to show him. "No," he answered. "But it's not my real face either. It's actors' makeup."

Nancy said, "Uncle Corky, we want to go now."

"Of course," he answered, standing up. He adjusted her corsage and tucked two more malted milk balls in Red Riding Hood's bag. "One for you and one for the wolf."

"And sixty hundred for the sheep," crowed the little boy, grabbing a last handful and moving to put Corky between himself and his sister. His mouth was so full of malted milk balls and candy corn that he could hardly speak, but this did not stop him from delivering his opinion. "You're too old to dress up for Halloween."

"Spoken like a true Port-Villain!" exclaimed Corky. "This city has a pernicious effect on children!"

From the doorway came Romy's mocking comment, interrupting his tirade: "The neighborhood kids won't think there's anything wrong with your acting like a weirdo, now will they?"

Nancy opened the door. "Do you want to trick-or-treat Josie?"

"No," said Heather. "My mother doesn't want me to play with her any more."

But the children had not yet made it out when Claire came bustling in, wearing a quilted khaki coat too long for her. She pulled a flowered headscarf over her curly hair and grabbed some umbrellas. "I'm going with them," she said to Corky. "I'll worry the whole time if I stay here. With all the meanness, you never know what might happen."

"I could go," said Corky.

"No. You want to be here for the children. I'll just stay in the background and see to it that nothing happens." She reached up to kiss him, then changed her mind. "You did a good job with the makeup." Then the door closed behind them.

Corky stood still for a moment, as though he didn't know what to do with himself now that the children had gone. He took a handful of candy corn and sized it up, opening his lips tentatively. But the makeup that had altered his gaunt cheeks into a mass of wrinkles also restricted the wideness of his mouth. He couldn't stuff it with amoral abandon, the way the little sheep had done. He nibbled a kernel and wandered toward the kitchen.

Romy was washing dishes, moving gingerly, her shoulders painfully straight, her pretty mouth drawn small. Even her hair, which was actually thick and blonde and luxuriant like Nancy's, looked sparse and miserable. Although she was young, her face was more creased than Claire's.

"Shouldn't you be lying down? Someone else could do that." He stood in the doorway hag-like and exuberant. "Go lie on the couch and be the Sleeping Beauty."

"The couch is too soft. It would kill my back." Her words were tight little explosions, popcorn without the butter. "Besides, Aunt Claire shouldn't have to come home and do dishes after standing around in the rain all evening."

Corky's makeup precluded a chastened face, but he did say, in a more subdued voice, "Of course she shouldn't. I hadn't thought of it that way." He went to the counter and picked up a sponge to wipe the table, but before he could begin, the doorbell rang and he hurried to answer it.

"Yaaaahahahahahah!" The cackle rang out. "Come into my parlor, tender morsels!"

Romy cleaned the table herself, with severe little rubs and a soapy rag, like a mother who washes her child's face to keep from smacking it.

PORTVILLE POLICE

Cigarette smoke filled the front seat of the police car, while the rain, picking up now, shone in wet streams under the Euclid Avenue streetlamps, which were higher and harsher than those on Clover Street. Claiborne and Tibbs, the two policemen in the car, had orders to make an arrest. Both policemen smoked. From time to time the dispatcher's voice came on the radio, bringing static with it.

"Do it after dark," the Chief had said. There was no use riling up the neighborhood. The Chief had even talked with Prosecutor Bayer about phoning the suspect to bring himself in, which was how they'd handled it six months ago when he was arrested the first time. Such a practice was not unheard of in cases like this concerning a community leader.

But the Prosecutor had thought otherwise. "On a second offence? You want to call this pervert up and invite him to tea?"

The Chief reminded the Prosecutor that he hadn't been able to make a case last spring and might have trouble again this time. But Bayer insisted that he had a lot more to go on now, so Claiborne and Tibbs were sent on their assignment.

The car stopped at a red light, then continued toward the library. There Claiborne, the driver, slowed down. A spotlight hidden in a clump of junipers played on the front of the building, highlighting the quotation carved deeply into the limestone lintel above the door: "A GOOD BOOK IS THE PRECIOUS LIFE BLOOD OF A MASTER SPIRIT." The spotlight also showed a man sitting on the floor of the entryway, leaning against the wall. He was wrapped in a piece of carpet.

The police car pulled into the parking lot. Tibbs left Claiborne to radio the dispatcher while he walked across the plaza with his head bent against the drizzle. "Hey Hugh, want to sleep in a bed tonight?"

"Nah," was the answer, spoken in a harsh, Indiana twang from the southern part of the state. "S'long as I can keep dry I'm fine right here. Last time I slept at the shelter, the sons of bitches stole the socks right off my feet."

"That's what comes of wearing those gold toe jobbies. Listen, Hugh, you'd better go around back if you don't want to get picked up. Some big shot drives by here and sees you, he'll call in."

"Beautification, eh?" Hugh stood up slowly. "I was hoping nobody would notice. It's not as nice back there." He was bundled in several layers of clothing, and in addition to the piece of carpet, he lifted a peeling, round-shouldered case. "Okay," he said. "Thanks."

Back in the car Tibbs said, "He'd freeze to death before he'd give up his turf."

Claiborne nodded. "Funny how they act. Just like a homeowner."

The dash lights glowed red. On the radio the dispatcher was talking. When the radio was quiet, Claiborne stretched his chin to ease the flesh above his collar. "They ought to throw away the key when they get this one."

Tibbs rocked his open hand, yes and no. "Sometimes it's the other way around. What are you going to do? They don't have to be grown to act like whores. Some of them solicit you on the street. I've seen full-fledged whores twelve and thirteen years old, even younger. They've got themselves a pimp and everything."

"I know, I know. I'm not talking about whores. I'm talking about kids."

"Sure, but it's not always easy to tell which is which. Sometimes you've got a real short-eyes, and sometimes you've got a little liar." The wide avenue had given way now to a narrower street with old store fronts and boarded windows. "Well, Bayer's cracking down. He's after the female vote."

The dispatcher's voice came over the radio again, this time for them, a burglar alarm nearby. They turned the car around. The arrest was put off a little longer.

A BATHTUB IN THE KITCHEN

The trick-or-treaters were now several blocks from the parsonage. Their candy sacks were filling up. The dog snuffled the wet leaves. Nancy, the Snow Queen, and her friend Heather walked arm-in-arm under one umbrella, while Little Bo Peep and the sheep fought over the second. Claire walked behind them under the third. In time with her footsteps, Claire sang under her breath, "Tramp, tramp, tramp the boys are marching." She managed a military beat on the first two bars; after that the melody floated like a love song.

There were not many trick-or-treaters out tonight. The neighborhood, old but comfortable, included families with children, but only two groups of assorted ghosts and monsters had appeared and one lone alien, more interested in tricks than treats, running across the yards with a bar of soap, house to house, pane to pane.

Although she had thought to bring the umbrellas, Claire had not worn boots, and her feet in loafers and thin socks were getting wet. Her song changed to "trampling out the vintage." Singing kept the circulation going and made her feel warmer. Well, she could have a hot bath when she got home, she thought, and at least she didn't have to get herself ready for work tomorrow. Being unemployed had benefits if you looked hard enough for them. "In the beauty of the lilies, Christ was born across the sea." Her mind's voice was now a French horn instead of a trumpet.

It occurred to her to wonder why *she* was the person accompanying the children rather than one of their parents. Romy, of course, was in no condition to be out. But what about the others? Didn't these other kids have parents? These two who had been fighting ever since she'd laid eyes on them, didn't they have parents?

"Come hold my umbrella, Leslie, while I blow my nose," she

called. Leslie was Bo Peep's real name, and Claire's intent was to end the bickering.

But instead of letting her brother hold the umbrella they'd been using, the girl folded it up and brought it with her. The boy stomped viciously in the next puddle.

Thinking quickly, Claire closed her own umbrella, slipped it into its skinny sleeve and handed it to Leslie to hold while she blew loudly into her handkerchief. Then she said, "Umbrellas *do* spoil all the fun of walking in the rain, don't they?" She put her arm around the little girl's shoulders. She was skilled at such maneuvers, which were aimed at changing the situation. She held her own face up. "It's raining pennies from heaven for you and for me," she sang.

Leslie's jaw hung as she peered from under her bonnet brim at Claire.

Ahead, the others turned where a porch light signaled that children were welcome. Claire waited while Leslie and her brother joined the ritual at the front door. After a moment they were back, Nancy and Heather inseparable under one umbrella, Leslie alone, the other two umbrellas in her treat sack.

Claire exhaled a sudden sigh. Another pathetic brat to worry about. Her thoughts went to the children's shelter, closed now due to President Reagan's drive to shift priorities. It was not unusual there to see children like Leslie cling to anything they could get, even an umbrella that they couldn't use. She didn't know this girl, her family, their circumstances – anything about her really except that she lived next door to Heather and was in Nancy's class at school. For all Claire knew, Leslie might have been a candidate for the shelter herself.

She hoped there was nothing to be concerned about here. She was worn out from worrying. Even before the shelter had closed, she'd been daydreaming about doing something different. Something that didn't involve worrying about children, didn't involve social services at all. She wouldn't have quit, of course, without another job in hand. Not with Corky's pay as lean and precarious as it was. But now that the freedom to choose something different had been dumped in her lap, all she could think about was finding another social service job, because social service work was all she knew.

Leslie's little brother had dropped back and was now walking with

Claire. His sheep mask was off, his face up and his mouth open to catch the rain. Claire's hand went out in an automatic gesture. She hugged him against her for a moment. Her body was aware of the act, but her mind went right on with its thoughts of a life without concerns about children.

What would she *like* to do, now that she had the time? Useless things. Quilts, maybe. She had been wanting to make her daughter Elizabeth a quilt. But living in the tropics as she did, Elizabeth did not need a quilt, at least not now. In addition to making quilts, Claire wanted to build trellises and espalier a plum tree. Landscape gardening. Work with her hands. But these wishes seemed frivolous to a person whose conscience had always insisted on service. Even since she'd had the enforced freedom to choose how to spend her time, she still found it taken up with children, for it if weren't Nancy staying at the parsonage, it would have been another foster child, and there was always the Meeting school needing help.

Suddenly she stopped humming. "Let Mother Theresa do it if she wants to, but I'm tired!"

"Who's Mother Theresa?" The little boy was now holding Claire's hand.

"She's a wonderful old woman who keeps on working no matter how hopeless it all is."

"She ought to move to Florida if she's old."

"She should," agreed Claire. "We all should."

Ahead, the girls turned in at a tall old house set back from the street. "Wait for me," said the boy. He put his mask on.

But this time Claire went up to the lighted porch with them. She wanted to inquire after old Mr. Rochester, the druggist, who lived here with his daughter. She hadn't seen him since he'd retired.

She glanced around the L-shaped porch with its painted wood floor that sloped off toward the yard. A swing and several chairs were clustered at one end, and near the door one armchair was draped with a blanket and pushed against the house backwards, making a sheltered bed for the cat curled up in it. Disturbed by the visitors, the cat stood up and stretched. Then, seeing the police dog, it doubled in size, gave a long growl, and streaked off the porch into the dark, wet yard.

The door was answered by a woman so small she looked like a

pipe-cleaner doll. Her pompom of hair was frizzy and short and very white. She wore maroon corduroy slacks and a pink sweater, and she peered at them through the round lenses of wire-rimmed glasses.

"Trick or treat!" the children chorused.

"Oh do come in!" The woman stepped aside for them all to file in.

The room was large and comfortable-looking in a sloppy way, as though it had not actually been decorated, but put together by someone who liked to read novels and talk and eat. There was a fire burning in the fireplace and a big old yellow dog of indeterminate breed lay in a battered armchair in front of it, soaking up the heat. Seeing that another dog had come inside the room, it struggled to its feet, still in the chair, with a raised scruff and a breathy but brave volley of barks.

"Freddy," called the old woman. "Come see to Marigold, would you?"

The police dog strained on his leash, sniffing and cautiously wagging his tail.

There were footsteps in the hall, and a compact, smooth-headed man of about fifty, in baggy trousers and house slippers, a gray wool cardigan buttoned over his seal-shaped middle, went to the dog's chair where he held her collar and stroked her ears. "There, there, Marigold," he said in a gravelly voice. "You got a visitor. Be a nice girl, now." He nodded to Claire and the children. "How do you do?" he said. "I'm Fred Bekin and this is my Aunt Jenny, Jenny Cavendish. Do I know you?"

The children shook their heads, but Claire said, "You may not know them, but you know me. I worked with you at the park." She waited for his recognition. Volunteers for this project had cleaned up the neighborhood park two summers ago, and she was sure he hadn't forgotten. "I had the easy job. I drove the truck back and forth to the dump, but you guys had to load and unload it." She smiled at Fred. Her dimples popped out, and her generous smile transformed her into a woman who might still make a living with her face.

Fred pushed with his forefinger on the nose piece of his sliding trifocals and looked at Claire again. "Of course I do." His cheeks mottled with pleasure. "Mrs. Claire. Aunt Jenny, this is Mrs. Claire, the truck driver. I want you to meet this lady. She talked her way into the city dump at closing time, just as they were pulling the gates together, and not only that, but they stayed open while we went back for another load. She's the Freethinker minister's wife."

Jenny was passing an orange-colored basket filled with candy bars to the children. "Now that's a lively-sounding group. The paper never has a kind word to say about them. I can always tell that something's interesting when *The Clarion* sneers."

"I'm glad somebody feels that way. We certainly attract a lot of sneers." Claire shook her head at the candy when it was offered. "Mr. Rochester. I heard he'd moved here to live with his daughter. Am I at the right place?"

"He's in the back of the house watching TV." Behind his glasses, Fred's lizard-like eyes indicated the direction. "You wanna see him?" The dog Marigold exhaled one more disdainful woof, then settled back down into the soft armchair and sighed. By closing her rheumy eyes she signaled that she was not going to defend her household against the wolf that ate grandmother. Fred's thick fingers stroked her head.

"No, no, don't bother him," said Claire. "I just wondered if he was still alive. It's your wife, then, who runs the drugstore now?"

"She runs it in body, if you know what I mean. He's still the head."

"She's doing a heroic job. And she looks so beautiful, so statuesque, up there in the pharmacy cage in that old-fashioned green coat and the wonderful blonde braid swinging down her back. Every time I go in, she's up there working."

"I know, I know. She's got more help now, though, and a pharmacist that works the whole evening shift, except when he doesn't. I mean because he's sick or something, like tonight. She's down to fifty hours a week instead of eighty."

"Her father's reputation would be hard to live up to," said Claire. "He was legendary, very stern and no-nonsense, but absolutely reliable."

Fred's eager friendliness was giving way to a more reserved tone as he talked about his father-in-law. "Yeah, well, he's got the palsy. Otherwise he'd still be there. His right hand shakes so much he can't pour pills."

"I'm sorry to hear that. Your wife followed in her father's footsteps. That's a nice women's movement story."

Fred's chuckle was a short bark. "Maybe. But you gotta realize that things aren't necessarily what they seem."

Claire could tell that the drugstore was a sore point with her host, so she changed the subject. "This is quite a house. You have enough room for the generations to spread out and not get in each other's hair."

"The house helps. We got the room all right, but the generations got a lot of hair too. You wanna see the kitchen? You'd like that. We got an unusual kitchen here. You can say hi to Mr. Rochester, but I warn you not to mention the store or he'll talk all night."

Claire left the children with Jenny and followed Fred through a hall with several doorways and a row of pegs on one wall holding an assortment of coats and jackets. She could hear, coming from a TV set somewhere ahead, the unmistakable voice of a televangelist.

The kitchen was warm. It smelled spicy, as though the dinner might have included a cooked apple dish with cinnamon. "Umm," said Claire. "Now I know where to come when I'm down on my luck."

She would remember these words later, when she was down on her luck.

They continued through the room into a summer kitchen still farther back. Through a hall door to the left Claire glimpsed the object of her visit. The druggist sat sleeping in a high-backed leather Supreme Court Justice chair near the TV. He was a tall man, very thin, with immaculately trimmed white hair, and he wore sharply creased, severely tailored slacks and a tie under his sweater. His head leaned to one side, and his jaw was relaxed. The exhortations of the evangelist surrounded him as a river surrounds a rock.

"Don't wake him. It's not worth it for the little time I have to spend."

"Smart lady," said Fred.

Then Claire saw what her host had been referring to when he said the kitchen was unusual. Along the inside wall opposite the windows was an old claw-footed bathtub. Above it hung a braided string of onions.

Claire's laugh pealed out. "But this is wonderful!"

"Isn't it!" Fred answered. "Very handy. I figure this house didn't have indoor plumbing when it was built, so when they put it in, they put the bathtub right where the Saturday night washtub had stood."

"Does anyone ever use it?"

"Sure," said Fred. "We got a shower upstairs, but anyone wants a bath has to take it here. It's a good place to wash the dog, too, or soak the broiler pan that's too big for the sink."

"I wouldn't have believed it, something like this right here in the neighborhood. Most people would have taken it out when they remodeled the kitchen."

"Yeah, well, Sara keeps at me, but I tell her we got a prize antique here."

Back in the living room the sheep was putting on a display of rope twirling for Jenny. "Ready to go?" asked Claire.

Jenny told the children to stop in after school on chilly days. "We can make a fire and have some cocoa." To Claire she said, "I taught school for forty-five years. I miss the children now that I'm retired."

After one more passing of the candy basket, Claire left with the children, but the warmth of the house and its inhabitants stayed with her. As a minister's wife she was used to being offered hospitality; even so, the difference between this open, rambling household and the dark porches down the block made her feel a little sad, reminded her of something good that seemed gone forever. During her own childhood, almost every house had been open that way on Halloween, and it had been safe to enter.

"I need my umbrella again, Leslie," she said. "It's raining a little too hard now, even for me." When she raised it, the sheep crowded close to her.

At the corner the group turned and headed for a cluster of houses with their lights turned on. This time Claire waited again at the sidewalk, humming, while the children claimed their treats. Ahead was the end of a block. She would suggest that they head for home when they reached the corner. "Just singin', just singin' in the rain." It wouldn't be long.

THE ARREST

The burglar alarm had gone off accidentally. They did that all the time and, according to Tibbs, every nervous Nellie owned one. After making sure the alarm was false, the two policemen continued on their way.

Clover Street was in an old Portville neighborhood with alleys in the back instead of driveways at the front. Claiborne parked on the street in front of the parsonage. He radioed the dispatcher their whereabouts. Then he and Tibbs walked toward the house through the yellow maple leaves still bright in the evening wetness.

On the porch, the jack-o-lantern, now turned to face the street again, gave its wounded, slit-eyed cry.

Tibbs said, "Good God, if my kid carved a pumpkin like that, I'd chop it up for pie."

"Makes you wonder, doesn't it?"

Tibbs rang the bell while Claiborne rapped the doorknocker. Each man was alert. It was easier to act as if there might be trouble, even when they didn't expect it, than to have trouble when they weren't prepared.

After a moment the door opened a crack, then swung wide to show the witch. "Yaaaahahaha," the falsetto cackle rang out.

It ended with a sudden indrawn breath.

Then Claiborne spoke. "Is this the Pearlman residence?"

There was a long, long silence. "Yes," answered Corky, using his own voice, which was now dry and papery. "It is."

"We'd like to speak with Reverend Pearlman."

"Yes, here I am."

It took a moment for this information to register. "You're under arrest." Claiborne showed Corky his identification. Tibbs moved closer while Corky backed into the house. When they were all inside, Corky fumbled with shaking hands to turn on a lamp.

"May I see the warrant, please?" He almost whispered the request.

Claiborne handed it to him with a Miranda card. Corky took them to the lamp to read, then handed them back. "It'll take me a few minutes to get this makeup off." His voice was still powdery.

Tibbs and Claiborne exchanged glances. There was no requirement that they wait for a perp to clean himself up.

At this moment Romy's oddly erect figure appeared in the hallway. She stared at the two officers, at Corky, and back at the policemen. "What's happened?" Her voice rose almost to a scream as she spoke. "It's Nancy, isn't it? What's happened to her?"

Corky answered. "It's not Nancy, it's me. I'm being arrested again."

She looked with amazement at the two policemen, first one and then the other. "But this is hysterical." She started to laugh, then stopped with a wince. She held the doorframe for a moment. "Well?" she asked. "What pot are your Freethinkers setting to boil for you this time?"

Corky's slight shrug was his answer.

"Is it a secret what he's being arrested for?" asked Romy. "Is this Secret Policeville?" She addressed Claiborne. "You can't just arrest somebody without even telling him what for, can you?"

"Let's go, Reverend," said Tibbs, jerking his head toward the door. "Get a coat if you want to."

Corky was the one who answered Romy. "It's the same thing as before." He sounded like a ghost talking, his voice empty as a paper cup rattling down the street in the wind. He made no move to get his coat. "Have Claire call Neil for me. Tell her I'm all right, not to worry. Tell her I'll be more careful this time." He put his arms behind him and waited.

Tibbs gently lifted the sleeves of the cassock and snapped on the handcuffs.

As the two policemen sandwiched Corky out the door, Romy called after them, "I can tell you this: he's not a child molester, he's a *child*."

"The worst kind," muttered Claiborne under his breath, so low that Corky, close behind him, was not even sure he'd said it.

On the porch there was the pumpkin again. "You got kids?" asked Tibbs.

"No."

"Who made that thing?"

"My niece Nancy did."

A moment later the patrol car pulled away. The smoke from Claiborne's newly-lighted cigarette joined that from Tibbs' half-smoked one and swirled around Corky in the back seat. His eyes watered instantly. His nose ran. He hunched a shoulder to wipe his lip, but try his best, he couldn't make it reach.

He thought about sin crying out to heaven for vengeance. He thought about trading places with his black twin in the spirit world. With his eyes defocused, he thought about manhole covers and succulent plants. Anything to take his mind off the humiliation ahead of him, humiliation that might well be worse this time, because of the way he looked. He did not expect to be treated well, a man disguised as a witch. How much easier this might be if only it were Christmas and he were dressed as Santa Claus! But this was more than he could stand to think about, so he took a deep, centering breath. Almost immediately his mind, having practiced for years, went to the still, black place he called, for lack of a better term, the arms of God.

Then they turned off Clover Street, and Corky fell from the arms of God back into the real world. There on their way home were the trick-or-treaters: the wolf, the sheep, the three lovely little girls, and Claire, his wife, Claire. Corky closed his eyes and bent his head. His nose dripped in his lap, making a slimy spot on his black cassock. When he opened his eyes again, the patrol car had left the neighborhood and was on its way downtown.

SCANDAL RIGHT HERE IN PORTVILLE

When Sara and Fred Bekin left for work shortly before nine the next morning, November 1st, the *Portville Clarion* had already been in the vending machine in front of Rochester's Drugstore for more than two hours. A number of copies had been purchased by Osborne Avenue commuters from the south suburbs, who found it convenient to turn off the high-speed artery and leave their engines running on Brewster Street while they grabbed a paper, then hurried on to work. A few more copies had been taken leisurely, by local people, who noticed the small "Minister Arrested" column blocked into the front page, read it and, with heightened interest, realized, as Sara and Fred would soon realize, that another juicy scandal had broken out, this time right here in the neighborhood.

Portville, in days past, had been the scene of several such scandals, though few people remembered the ones that had surfaced before the tide of consciousness was rising against child abuse in the early eighties. Back in the thirties, a "dangerous sexual psychopath," who lured two little girls from a playground and raped them, had been sent to the insane asylum in Indianapolis. And in 1954 a "sexual deviant" had been convicted for the act of sodomy against a little boy, but he had gone free. His successful defense had been based on unconstitutional self-incrimination during a psychiatric interview. He also claimed that his rights were further abused when his young accuser was not present for confrontation.

But by the mid-eighties, hardly anyone in Portville remembered these cases. Most people were just thankful that the goings on they were hearing about on network news had not been going on at home.

There was no picture of Corky Pearlman in *The Clarion*, and very few details. There had not been time last evening to get the whole story in. But almost everyone who took a paper from the box at Rochester's Drugstore knew who the Freethinker minister was, and many of them looked forward to the next issue without realizing that what they looked forward to was the little buzz they would get from further information about the scandal.

A BETTER MAN BY FAR

Sara worked at the drugstore longer than Fred did. Because of that, they drove separate cars to work, one following the other. They parked his Pinto and her Toyota one behind the other well down Brewster Street, saving the closer spaces for customers.

They lived only a mile from the store and often resolved to begin walking all the way, but time was so scarce for Sara that she never seemed to have the extra twenty minutes at either end of the day. She would have enjoyed a little frivolous consumption of time: a walk to work, a few minutes with the newspaper. But no, she had to rush here and rush there, help her father get his breakfast, get herself showered and dressed for work, urge Fred away from the breakfast table where he and Aunt Jenny would linger over toast and more toast all morning if she'd let them, and all for the sake of managing one dull crisis after another at the store, then rushing home again to see that her father was given the attention he had to have in the evening.

Until Fred had lost his job at Powkin last March and joined her at the store, Sara had not noticed that the various crises were dull. Nor had she felt put-upon because her workweek was long. Rochester's had been part of her life from her earliest memory, and the life of the neighborhood druggist, with its endless hours, its routine chores and inconvenient emergencies, had the same familiarity as the onset of a head cold, annoying but known.

Thirteen months had gone by with Sara as manager of Rochester's. She was now seeing the end of the store's second Halloween. This season had been different because Fred was there with her. Last year she had simply stapled up the orange and black cutouts and ordered and sold the monster and Muppet masks and the bags of trick-or-treat candy without paying attention to the fact that it wasn't pharmacy she was doing, but now that Fred was at the store looking around, she could see the whole operation through his eyes.

Fred was happier, Sara knew, when his gaze rested on books. He had liked his job at Powkin, had been happy in his snug little office working on books, albeit how-to manuals. She had watched him go to work without complaint in the morning and come home at night in a good humor. What more could a person ask?

By the same token, she knew that he did not like the drugstore. "A natural habitat for ailments," he said. Pushed by a takeover from the chair at Powkin that he'd sat in for so long, he viewed Rochester's as a campstool to occupy temporarily. Pharmacy was her job, not his; he was just helping out. He spent as little time there as he decently could, usually leaving around noon to go downtown to the library, where he maintained that he was doing some freelance writing, but actually, as Sara saw it, where he could again be in the company of books.

All the flaws in the operation became evident to Sara as Fred noticed them. The hypochondriacs. The sick people. The old people from the housing project who needed expensive medicines they couldn't afford. The kids from the junior high school at the age when even the best of them dared each other to shoplift. The deteriorating building and the run-down block of stores on Osborne Avenue. The customer complaints about the merchandise: why they carried No Nonsense instead of L'Eggs, Olympia instead of Bud.

This morning the air was damp and chilly with a wind blowing scraps of paper over yards and along sidewalks like news from the Yukon about the weather to come. Fred had remembered Sara's scarf and gloves for her; in fact his pawing through her drawer to find them had caused her to be a few minutes behind schedule. When her father glanced pointedly at the clock on the mantel, she had called out, "Oh Fred, come on, will you? We're late and there'll be someone waiting, I know there will." She felt sorry as soon as she'd said it.

As Sara drove to the store, warm in the scarf and gloves, she could see, through the back window of Fred's car ahead, the outline of his sleek head and wide shoulders, so familiar, yet separate and strange as only another motorist can seem. He looked like a man in a movie, the shorter, stockier one who turns out to be a better man by far than the handsome but faithless charmer. She parked behind him, unbuckled the seat belt from around her beige raincoat, pulled her heavy blonde braid to the front, and waited for him to come to her door. In that moment while she watched him approach, she felt a surge of good fortune that it was this man and not some other who was her husband. Then, guarding herself against too much feeling, she opened her own door and snapped the lock before he could do it for her.

They had left their cars down Brewster and were walking hand-in-hand toward Osborne, Sara tall and slender, Fred a little shorter and thickly built, when she felt him tugging on the fingertips of the glove he had taken time to find for her. She started to draw her hand away, almost as a reflex, but he held it tight and pulled the glove off.

"I wanna feel skin, not glove, when I hold hands with my wife."

Fred's voice had gravel in it, and his accent and diction made him sound more like a Chicago tough than an educated man, a book person.

He gave her long, slim fingers a squeeze.

She squeezed back. His hand was meaty and warm, unfailingly warm. He never wore gloves, and often didn't even wear a coat. "You certainly do have good circulation."

"Yeah, me and *Gone With The Wind*."

She waited a moment to think what he meant. When she had figured it out, she said, "You're going to ditch me and go to the library, aren't you?"

"You know I turn into a pair of crutches if I stay at the store too long. But I'll wait till Christabel comes before I leave. How'll that be?"

"What good would Christabel be in a hold-up?" Christabel, the afternoon/evening clerk, was a talker and would be more likely to strike up a conversation with the robber than to fend him off.

"What good would I be? I'd be on the floor so fast they wouldn't even know I was there protecting you." He wouldn't let Sara keep the pistol that her father had always kept in the pharmacy cage but insisted instead on having an alarm button installed at the cash register that would alert the police directly when pushed. "Besides, with Ben in and out, there's not going to be a holdup. Nobody in his right mind would tackle Ben." Ben, the traffic guard at the school down the street, worked at the store part time when he wasn't guarding traffic. His Sumo wrestler build and terrifying glare were of inestimable security value in an old city neighborhood where a certain amount of crime was taken for granted.

Fred started to explain what he was doing at the library. "I got a new article I'm working on I think New York'll like: 'How to Structure Your Time When Unemployed.' That ought to be a winner, don't you think, the way things are?"

Sara recognized this as an opener, leading to Fred's favorite subject, The Way Things Are. She answered, "You're not really unemployed."

"Of course I'm unemployed. 'Early retirement' is a euphemism. And helping out at the store doesn't count. I'm not on the payroll, am I?"

"You could be, if you would."

"Not on your life. It's bad enough having you on the payroll. I'd take a job busing at McDonald's, if it came to that, rather than report to your father."

Sara wished she could say the same.

They were nearing the store. While the houses at the far end of the block were tidy, their leaves raked, their paint kept fresh, those closer to Osborne Avenue had begun to deteriorate, as though the owners were expecting a zoning change that would allow them to tear down the houses and put up another fast-food restaurant or another self-serve gas station. Fred and Sara swung their arms wide to step around the mess of a jack-o-lantern that had been smashed on the pavement.

"Brats!" muttered Fred. Then he modified his judgment. "At least it's kids doing the meanness, not adults."

Now they came to the rear of the store building. The sidewalk was cracked, and dead plantains and foxtails with heavy seed heads crowded the strip of soil between the walk and the building. Where once the store windows had looked in at the soda fountain, there were now large rectangles of newer brick that didn't match. Still holding Sara's hand, Fred stooped swiftly to pick up an empty Jim Beam pint, then a soft drink cup from the Steak & Shake, the straw still poking through the lid. Sara was looking ahead, to where the drugstore door was set into the cut-off corner of the old brick building. "Look," she said. "There's someone waiting. She pulled away, and Fred dropped the trash through the swinging cover of the trash can that stood next to the newspaper vending machine.

Sara spoke immediately, reassuring the customer, a regular from the senior citizens' housing project nearby. "You're not too early, Mrs. Worrell. We're running late this morning. Just a minute now until I get us in, and I'll take care of you." She rummaged through her purse, then felt in each of her coat pockets. "Fred, do you have the keys?"

"I don't think so." He felt his coat pockets and slipped his hands inside to check his pants pockets as well. He shook his head. "I'll go back and get them. Just relax. It won't take long."

She threw out her hands impatiently. "If you hadn't spent so much time," she started to say, but he was already gone, running surprisingly well for a heavy man who avoided exercise whenever possible.

Sara turned again to Mrs. Worrell and slipped into her role as reassuring pharmacist. "Why don't we sit here on the urn and wait for him? It's not far. He won't be long." She smoothed her immaculate raincoat behind her and sat down on the chilly concrete of a large planter filled with chrysanthemums, some dry and brown, some still the colors of October.

The customer, Mrs. Worrell, wore a slick gray quilted coat and held a canvas bag stenciled "Sail Lake Michigan." Perhaps she really had sailed Lake Michigan in her day, who could tell? She eased herself down, then withdrew a folded newspaper from the bag, held it out to Sara and said, "Isn't this the limit?"

Sara glanced at the paper. "I haven't had time to read it yet." Her father had asked her to make French toast for his breakfast; she hadn't even seen the headlines.

"It's that Mr. Pearlman, over at the Freethinkers. They arrested him last night."

"Really?" Mr. Pearlman was a customer. Sara's mind immediately skipped to the thought that she should install one more aisle mirror. You could never tell.

"They say he molested some little girl. A little Freethinker girl."

Sara's breath suspended itself in her chest and her face assumed a mask over the stinging in her cheeks. She couldn't think of anything to say.

"If you ask me, I'm surprised anybody complained," said Mrs. Worrell. "Those people are secular humanists. They don't believe in God. They don't know any difference between right and wrong. Them and their free thinking, I'm just surprised anybody even noticed."

Sara took the old woman's paper and started to read, shaking her head and hiding her expression. She finished the article. It didn't give much information, only that the minister had been wearing a witch costume when arrested. She felt uncomfortable; her cheeks stung as though she were turning red. This was one of those subjects that other people seemed able to talk about freely, while she could not utter a word, so she went on to read the Kroger ad and an article about the mayor's plan to revitalize the Port of Portville. Then, believing that Mrs. Worrell was waiting for her to respond to the newspaper article, she muttered, "You never know, do you?" She hoped Fred wouldn't take all day. She had work to do.

A HOUSE TO SPREAD OUT IN

Ten years earlier, when they were first married, Fred and Sara had bought their present home, a house much older than the others on the block: a sprawling, added-onto farmhouse, with a shaggy windbreak of pines by the rutted driveway and a back yard that sloped down through the woods to Sweetwater Creek. The house stood gray and tall as a clapboard wraith with its attic window gazing over its newer, smaller neighbors. There were two outbuildings on the property, a fair-sized barn with the stalls torn out and an old two-hole outhouse that had been converted into a shed to hold the lawnmower. An addition off what had once been a summer kitchen stretched to the south with another three rooms downstairs, used now as a study for each of them and one for Mr. Rochester. Above these rooms were three more bedrooms that were kept closed off to save heat. The house was too large for them when they bought it, but they had been thirty and forty then instead of forty and fifty, and they had thought it would be a good place to spread out and raise children.

Fred left the Pinto in the driveway and hurried across the yard. Today he would do what he'd been meaning to do: get another set of drugstore keys made to keep on his own key ring.

At his heels came the cat, an orange tabby named "Duck," a stray that had figured Fred for a soft touch a couple of months ago. So far Duck lived outdoors, where she guarded the yard against birds and chipmunks. She would come as far as the porch, but at the threshold, Marigold's threatening presence scared her off.

When Fred opened the front door into the living room, an odor he knew all too well hit him. "Marigold!" he roared, but the dog was nowhere to be seen. Fred held his nose and detoured to the coffee table, where he kept a roll of toilet paper handy for such occasions. He tore a length of paper, scooped up the reeking pile and carried it down the hall to the toilet under the stairs. When he reached the kitchen to look for the keys, there was Marigold, lying under the porcelain-topped table, flopping her tail against the floor. With a mighty effort she heaved herself into a sitting position and looked away from him, her face a study of embarrassment mixed with reproach. "See the disgusting lengths to which I have to go," she seemed to be telling him, "to show you how much I dislike being left?"

"You oughta be ashamed," Fred told her, knowing it would have no effect. She had been well behaved for years, but after the old people had moved in, she began to object to being left alone with them. She now dumped out wastebaskets, nosed into purses after gum or pills, chewed up matchbooks, devoured any food left out in the kitchen, and held back doing her business when Fred put her out mornings, waiting to deposit it on the rug after he and Sara had left.

Fred was convinced that her objection was to being classified as one of the old folks and left alone with Aunt Jenny and Mr. Rochester. If she had been left with children, he was sure, she would have acted differently.

There were still no children. Fred had been married once before and, for the short time the marriage lasted, was a stepfather to his wife's two sons, so the matter was not urgent for him. But Sara had agonized over the decision for years. She wanted a baby, but not right away. Always not right away. Something held her back. She liked the practice of pharmacy and didn't want to give it up. Or, she believed that a child needed care, a lot of care. Her own mother had been sick and hadn't taken very good care of her; it might turn out that she would do no better. She had so many reasons that Fred couldn't tell what the real one was, and he had long since lost patience. He wished she'd make a decision and be happy with it, though he refrained from saying so because he knew she would if she could.

But now that she had taken over the drugstore and the care of her father, the issue seemed to be resolving itself. "Not right away" was changing to "probably never."

The keys were not on their hook.

They were not on the table, either, nor on the catch-all counter by the back door. Fred retraced steps, looked on the floor, looked on tables and chairs, the toilet tank. He even glanced into the dining room, though it was rarely used. He went back to the kitchen and searched it and the adjoining summer kitchen thoroughly, thinking the keys might have fallen and then been kicked under a radiator. No luck.

He put off going down the hall off the summer kitchen from which he could hear the hyped-up voices of television. His father-in-law spent much of the time he was downstairs sitting in his study, in his leather-covered Supreme Court Justice chair, listening to the televangelists as though he were taking a Berlitz course in a language he was going to need soon. Fred avoided the room as much as possible.

Instead, he went up the back stairs and searched the floor of the upstairs hall. Passing Jenny's room he glanced in to see her asleep, lying small on her tidily made-up bed with a maroon and orange zigzag afghan drawn over her.

When he looked in Mr. Rochester's room, Fred wished his father-in-law were less a creature of habit and would leave his key ring lying around on the dresser, so that he could borrow it without making an issue of it. But even though the old man rarely went to the drugstore nowadays, he kept his keys right where he always had, in his pocket, as though having them on his person were part of his identity. He still shaved every morning, too, got his hair cut every week, and wore a tie from morning till night.

The house was very large. Fred continued down the long hall, not bothering to look in the wing with the unused bedrooms, and searched the spacious double room at the front of the house that he shared with Sara. Still no luck.

Going down the front stairs, he had one more idea where the keys might be. He crossed the living room and went again into the hall, where one wall held the row of hooks that served as a coat closet.

Sara was wearing a raincoat this morning, but yesterday she had worn her suede jacket. Fred dug in the pockets. The keys were not there.

Back in the south wing off the summer kitchen, he walked quietly past Mr. Rochester's study and looked in his own. He hadn't been in there for several days. A quick glance was all he gave to Sara's; she hadn't had time to enter it for ages.

He gave up.

Mr. Rochester sat sleeping in his chair a few feet from the television. Fred switched off the plea for "just one hundred of the Lord's dollars." At the sudden quietness, the old man opened his eyes. He looked at Fred for a moment, drawing his head back against the white linen towel draped over the chair back, then glanced at the schoolroom clock on the wall. The time was nine twenty. Mr. Rochester's thin nose pinched even thinner, and a look of distaste came over his face, as though Fred had brought in something foul-smelling on his shoe.

"What can I do for you?" he asked formally, managing, by half closing his eyes, to look down from a seated position on Fred, who was standing.

"I need your keys, sir," said Fred, matching the old man's formality. He refused to implicate Sara; her father never lost an opportunity to criticize her, and Fred did not like hearing it. He waited a moment, then said, "There's a customer waiting to get in."

Mr. Rochester grasped the arms of his chair and stood up slowly. "Customers give up on places that don't keep regular hours."

Fred didn't answer.

Mr. Rochester's hand went into his pants pocket. "I found these in the bathroom." He held out the lost keys.

Fred remembered that Sara had stopped there on her way out. "Thank you, sir," he said, taking the keys. Then his anger mounted and he added, with as much courtesy as he could muster, "You'd have saved five, ten minutes if you'd left them there."

The old man's nostrils pinched again. "It's asking for trouble to leave pharmacy keys lying around."

Fred controlled himself and backed out of the room. When he was all the way out of the house, he said aloud, "Not once. Not one god damn time." Never had he heard his father-in-law express any appreciation of the sacrifices Sara made for him.

Fred roared the Pinto back to the store at forty miles an hour, which, on quiet residential streets, seemed more like eighty.

DRUGGIST IN A GREEN SMOCK

Sara's discomfort over the newspaper story had subsided by the time
Fred returned. Nevertheless she was glad enough to see him to be lenient
about his taking one of the customer parking spaces instead of leaving
the Pinto down the block. "Here he comes," she said to Mrs. Worrell.
She folded the newspaper and tucked it neatly into the old woman's
bag, the minister's unfortunate scandal already put behind her.

"Where did you find them?"

Fred gave her a look and unlocked both the upper and the lower security locks before answering. "In your father's pocket. After searching
the house." He handed her the keys.

"I can imagine what he had to say."

"You imagine right."

Sara went to the pharmacy cage and unlocked it while Fred hung
up coats, switched on lights, and adjusted the thermostat. "Now," she
said to Mrs. Worrell, who was fingering through her purse, "let's get
you taken care of." She suspected that she already knew what the
woman wanted.

"I seem to have run out of these." Mrs. Worrell held the bottle at
arm's length and adjusted her plastic-rimmed glasses. "Yes, these are
the ones." She handed the bottle up to Sara in the pharmacy cage.

It was the same bottle she had already brought in twice since August,
when Sara had labeled it "No Refills." Couldn't the woman read, or
wouldn't she? But of course she could read; she bought magazines and
sometimes checked out books from the store's little lending library.

"I'm sorry, Mrs. Worrell, but I can't refill this. These were the pills
Dr. Fanchon gave you for postoperative pain last summer, remember?"

"Yes, of course I remember, and I still hurt." The old woman held
up her left hand. "Look at that crooked finger. A pain shoots through

that joint every time I move and sometimes when I don't move. And that's not all. My operation still hurts, too. When I get up in the morning, I'm just one mass of aches. I was feeling so much better when I was on those pills, it seemed like I was getting somewhere, and it's a shame the doctor didn't give me any more of them."

"I'm sure you did feel better. But those are too strong for everyday aches and pains. If you kept on taking them, pretty soon you'd have to take so many that you wouldn't be able to function. But you sit down there and let me call Dr. Fanchon. He may be able to prescribe something that will ease things for you."

She looked up the doctor's number and dialed it, hoping he was in, and hoping he could find a way to keep Mrs. Worrell from continuing to present her with a problem she couldn't solve.

As she waited first for an answer, then for connection with the doctor, she looked from the cage out over the store, at the crowded gondolas that held the bulk of the merchandise, at the counters and cases around the perimeter that attempted to maintain the period atmosphere of the late thirties. The period image was furthered by the floor, covered with old white hexagonal tiles and bordered in blue.

Rochester's looked more spacious than it actually was, due to the reflection from a long mirror left on the wall where the soda fountain (gone for years now) used to dispense after-school snacks to most of the neighborhood's children. Lesser reflections from the mirrored tiles that covered four large, weight-bearing pillars added to the illusion as well. These, along with two angled mirrors attached to the ceiling, provided visual access to most of the store, and Sara, from her high spot in the pharmacy cage, used them to keep tabs on whatever might be happening. Looking out, she thought again of installing one more mirror.

Fred, bless his heart, after moving his car back down the block, had gotten busy with the chores that would be heavy today because it was the first of the month. Her father had always stuck to an exacting schedule, and Sara had found it easier to continue it than to explain any reason she might have for changes. There were, of course, reasons, good ones. Delivery schedules had changed, and it might be easier, for instance, to defrost the ice cream case just before instead of just after a delivery. It wasn't as though Sara hadn't thought of it. And Fred too.

When he had begun helping at the store, she expected him to want changes just to make it clear that her father was no longer in charge. She had dreaded the pressure she felt he would put on her, but he had surprised her by making it his business to ease rather than increase tension.

The doctor came on the line now. She explained the situation and listened to his answer, then stepped out of the cage to Mrs. Worrell. "Dr. Fanchon says he could prescribe some medicine for you, but it costs $30 a bottle, and it's no more effective than aspirin. He's recommending that you be sure to take the aspirin every four hours and chew up a Tums at the same time. Also, he wants you to call him to talk about a water exercise group at the Community Center." On the wall behind Sara was a rack of pamphlets. She selected one and handed it to Mrs. Worrell. "Here," she said. "You may find some tips on pain relief in this. Oh, and this too." She riffled through a sheaf of computer printouts that drooped from the pamphlet rack. "Here's a list of everything the public library has on arthritis."

Mrs. Worrell was looking outraged. "He's not getting me into any swimming pool," she said. "I haven't worn a bathing suit in years."

"I don't know," said Sara. She sized up the woman's lean body under the quilted coat. "It looks to me as though you've kept your figure. You might find a swimsuit you'd like." Behind her in the cage the phone was ringing again. "Excuse me, dear. I have to answer that. Let me know how you get along, won't you?"

With Mrs. Worrell gone, Sara attended to the other demands of the morning. Leonora, the early shift clerk, came in, apologizing for being late. The UPS man came and the Weideman truck. Ben, the school guard, arrived and mopped the floor. Fred finished defrosting the ice cream case and the other coolers and began wiping down the display cases. Customers came in, most of them regulars, some with prescriptions to fill, others just wanting companionship and willing to buy a pack of gum or a magazine from Leonora to get it. More than one of them brought up the subject of Mr. Pearlman's arrest.

"It's got to be some kind of a set-up," said Fred, when he heard the story. "Mrs. Claire was at our house last night. I showed her our bathtub."

"That hardly qualifies as an alibi," muttered Sara to herself up in her cage, where she could hear what everyone said but was not obliged to answer. It was just like Fred to say something like that, she thought. He never believed how bad people could be. But then neither could she believe that Mr. Pearlman's oddness might include odd behavior with children.

Even so, with the magazine rack right there in the drugstore, she could not help being aware of the new assessment of child abuse, its harmfulness, its frequency, the ordinariness of its perpetrators. Almost every magazine that Rochester's stocked had recently carried a lead article on the subject, usually with a headline on the cover.

A new wrinkle for the porn market, was how Sara thought of it. That's how they sell magazines. People who wouldn't dream of buying real porn were glad enough to choose the magazine with the sex headline over the one that proposed to discuss affairs of state. Even the upcoming election could not compete with the excitement of some new nursery school scandal.

To be perfectly honest, Sara had to admit that she herself read the articles, took magazines to the cage and skimmed them to give herself a momentary break in the continual work. She excused herself for reading on the grounds that she didn't smoke. Other people take a cigarette break every so often; she picked up a magazine instead, read a few paragraphs and got back to work. A person has to cultivate some little vice to break the monotony, she thought. Her father, of course, would have criticized the habit on several grounds: primarily that the magazines were filled with useless trash and that they took her attention from watching the store. But he was not here, and when he did come in, she made sure there were no magazines in the cage.

Shortly after Ben left for his noontime shift at the school, a customer came in with the news that Mr. Pearlman was not in jail. "I saw him in his front yard staring at a mess of pumpkin that the kids must have smashed last night. He looked like death warmed over."

Sara refrained from pointing out that he always looked that way. He was thin to the point of gauntness, with wisps of hair going every which way on his large head as though he had too many cowlicks. Sara had seen him looking lively only once, when he was engaged with someone who was going along with his antics. Then his pale, sand-colored eyes took on a light of their own and an elfin smile came over his face and showed a mouthful of funny-looking little teeth. Oddly enough, this smile had been attractive; it gave him the look of an Irish terrier that might jump up and lick noses, given half a chance. But the expression had been fleeting. It took over his face for a moment, then disappeared, leaving him looking worn out from the weight of that heavy head.

"If I'd been arrested last night, I can tell you that I wouldn't be thinking about cleaning up my yard," said Leonora. "I'd be thinking about talking to my lawyer, wouldn't you?"

"I don't know what I'd be thinking about," answered Fred from the floor behind a glass case that held electric shavers, hair dryers and curling irons. He sprayed cleaner on the shelf, wiped it and moved the merchandise to spray the next area. "It would depend a lot on what I'd done or hadn't done to get arrested."

Sara was not entirely happy with Leonora as the clerk, but her unhappiness lay, not in dissatisfaction with the work the woman did, but in a self-disparaging comparison of Leonora, who was pretty and outgoing and relaxed, with herself, whom she considered to be none of those things. When Leonora blew in the door as she had today, breathless from running, with cheeks red from the wind and hair becomingly mussed, Sara felt older, less healthy and far more tightly constrained that she had only moments before.

I should jog, she told herself without going into the matter of when. I should cut my hair and get a perm.

"Oh good," Leonora had said, when she saw what Fred was doing. She called up to Sara, "I was hoping Fred wouldn't skip out of here and leave the dirty work for me."

The Walgreens drugstore eight blocks farther out on Osborne hired stock boys and janitors and clerks and pharmacists, but at Rochester's, everybody did everything except handle drugs and fill prescriptions, jobs in the cage left to Sara and Charlie, the pharmacist who worked evenings.

Sara held back giving instructions to Leonora, not wanting to sound like an old grouch, then saw that the woman had gotten busy dusting in spite of her noisy talk and her lazy manner.

I should laugh more, thought Sara. I *am* an old grouch.

Fred soon finished what he was doing and came to give Sara a goodbye kiss before he left for the library.

"Why would you show Mrs. Pearlman our bathtub?" she asked. She didn't care about the answer; she just wanted to engage him for a few more minutes.

"No reason," he said. "I just thought she'd appreciate it."

"I wonder if she appreciates her husband's activities."

"Wait a minute," said Fred. "He hasn't had a trial yet."

"You'd stand up for Charles Manson himself, wouldn't you?" said Sara, feeling unreasonably peevish. 'Oh I don't know,' you'd say. 'His parents were probably hard on him and he was having love troubles or something.' You'd excuse him. You won't believe anything bad about anybody, will you?"

Fred looked bewildered, as though a sunny sky had started to rain down on him. Then he said, "Of course I believe bad things about people if they deserve it."

"Name one," she said. "Name one person you'd believe bad things about."

He leveled a look at her and answered without hesitation. "Your father."

"You're crazy," she said. "My father is an absolute stickler. He wouldn't do anything wrong if his life depended on it."

"Your father's mean," said Fred. "He's mean to you, and if you could get that through your head, you'd be better off."

"He isn't trying to be mean," cried Sara. "He's just trying to see that everything is done right."

Fred lowered his head and stared at her over the tops of his glasses. It was the look he sometimes gave people, a look that meant: Think about what you just said. Then he stepped out of the cage and went for his coat. Before he left the store, however, he came back.

She bent over her counter without looking up.

"Take it easy this afternoon, baby," he said. He stood behind her high stool with his coat open and his chest against her shoulders. He wrapped the two sides of the coat front around her and kissed the top of her head. "Give yourself a break now and then. See you at supper."

She half turned and moved him into hugging range. "It's your night to cook," she said. "Make it something good." She had cooked last night's meal, put a stew in the slow cooker before leaving for work, but had come home too late to want any. She had eaten the last piece of apple crisp and gone to bed.

"Pork chops and gravy," he answered, the gravy simmering richly in his voice. "Mashed potatoes, lotsa butter. Chocolate pie."

"Go on," she said. "Kill us with fat." But she knew he was kidding, at least about the pie. He didn't like bakery pies, and he didn't know how to make his own.

She and Fred were still working on some kind of schedule for getting the chores done. It had been easier before Fred left Powkin, before she left the hospital pharmacy and took on the store, before her father and Aunt Jenny came to live with them. They had eaten out more often or had brought barbecued chicken and pasta salad home from the deli. Under the present circumstances they felt pressured not to be extravagant. There hadn't actually been any more money then, but it had been their own, while now, although both Fred and Aunt Jenny had pensions, most of the household income came from the store – through its owner, her father. And her father did not approve of convenience foods; he had always gone to great lengths to cook for himself. Therefore, home-cooked meals were important, and a schedule had to be arranged.

It was almost two before Sara had time to take a break for lunch. Leonora was at the cash register helping customers, giving them the sociability they'd come for, ringing up sales. Sara slipped out to the magazine rack and brought back the new *Deeper Story*. She took out her peanut butter sandwich and her apple and began to read the lead article, which was about still another daddy who'd molested his daughter.

At first Sara read casually, with Mr. Pearlman in the back of her mind.

It was the story of B, with photographs. B's father had built her a playhouse when she was seven years old, then, while his wife worked evenings, played "Daddy" to her "Mommy" in it. Sara felt a moment of envy; her own father had never played anything with her, not even checkers.

No, it was more than that. "You don't really get the picture from that kind of description," wrote the reporter. "It sounds harmless.

Innocent. But it is neither harmless nor innocent." *Deeper Story* went in for looking behind what was usually printed about a subject.

Most such articles use legal or therapy language that dulls the reader's perception of what really went on, but here the reporter would not permit any dulling. She translated.

What Daddy did was trick B. He offered to play with her (a lonely child who needed playmates) then tied his tie around her doll's mouth and laid the doll (named Kimberly) in its cradle with its face to the wall. "So Kimberly won't see anything or tell on us."

Then he initiated oral sex with her. This was how the therapist being interviewed put it.

The reporter probed. "That means…?"

It meant that Daddy taught B how to do a blowjob. "Like mommies do."

Sara bent over the magazine and chewed her bite of sandwich as though it might never wash down.

With a little more probing the reporter got the therapist to admit that even the slang did not adequately express what had happened to B.

"He put his penis down her throat and gagged her. He told her it was a game grownups played and that she was special, getting to learn it. He told her it was good for her and she would like it when she got used to it."

There were no pictures of the blowjob, only family snapshots of the playhouse, and of B (with her face blacked out), older now, and her mother, wearing winter coats and standing outside the shelter they had stayed at for a while. The picture was not very good. Just one more awkward snapshot of a little girl and her mother standing on the steps of a brick building.

They sometimes played that Kimberly told. Tattletale Kimberly. Bad doll. Then Daddy laid Kimberly on her face in the doll bed with her dress up and her panties down. He took off his belt and wrapped it around his hand to make it small enough to use on a doll. And then Kimberly got a hard, hard whipping with the belt for telling.

B herself was never whipped.

When she was eight she started to stutter. She also murdered her doll. "That means," wrote the reporter, "that she enlarged Kimberly's mouth with a steak knife. Then cut her arms off. And then her head."

Now she was ten. Her mother had come home from work sick one evening and caught her father in "the act of sodomizing" her.

Sara closed her eyes for a moment, then opened them to read the reporter's translation.

Mrs. W, with a fever and a strep throat, did not call out when she entered the house. She had stopped to see the clinic doctor and had received an antibiotic. She was supposed to rest and avoid any more exercise than she could help. So instead of doing any work when she came in, she went right upstairs to go to bed. B's door was closed. She could hear her daughter crying behind it. She opened the door to find out what was wrong.

What she saw was her daughter crouched on the bed with her rear end in the air and her husband on his knees behind her. There was a bottle of sun tan oil on the bed. "Sun tan oil," she said. "Can you believe it?"

"It was a sight that'll never be erased from my eyes," said Mrs. W. "I looked at him holding B's skinny little bottom and thrusting, thrusting. And her crying like she'd never stop. Then he saw me. And he didn't even stop. He just gave me a look, a kind of sick look like he wasn't quite there, and then, then I could tell he was ejaculating.

"I closed the door and went downstairs and called the police. I didn't hesitate a minute. I know some women try to defend their husbands, but it didn't happen that way with me. It was like everything had become clear to me right then. The way she'd been acting, the bloody stools, the vomiting. She was so skinny she looked like she'd blow away in a hard breeze. And when I worried, the pediatrician just told me it was better for them to be a little underweight than to get fat as children, a great help he was."

The father, Mr. W, now in treatment, had been interviewed too. There were no photographs of him, and Sara saw him as thin and large-headed, like Mr. Pearlman. His perception of the case was quite different from his wife's. "B and I were both very needy individuals," he said. "We had certain needs that were not being met. It wasn't just me taking advantage of her. The relationship benefited us both. She got a playmate and I got the sex I needed."

What about the infections? Didn't that bother him?

"All kids get sick," he said. "Show me a kid who isn't sick half the time. Hell, when I was a kid, I never made it to school the whole week running."

The treatment of Kimberly?

"I'm not the kind of father who beats his kids. I've always been good to my daughter. A doll's a doll, for Christ's sake."

Mr. W's molesting had been confined to his daughter, which made him fit into that group of offenders that statistics showed were most likely to be rehabilitated. Thus he was in a treatment center instead of a state prison.

Mrs. W was not doing so well. Laid off from her job and no longer living with her husband, she was forced to accept public assistance. Working at whatever low-paying job she could get would have made her ineligible for help to pay for B's therapy, yet would not have provided enough income to pay for it herself.

According to the article, B's therapy, three times a week, was aimed at convincing her that she was not to blame for what happened. Sara choked. Not to blame. She herself had always been to blame. Again she felt a flash of envy. Then, "God," she murmured, and thought, "this is sick. I should be pitying this poor little girl, not envying her."

She could finish neither her sandwich nor the article. With her mouth full of peanut butter, she choked again, trying to be absolutely quiet. She felt as though she were flying apart. Then she heard someone at the entrance to the cage. Her father! He had walked to the store for exercise as he sometimes did, and now he had caught her. In a panic she shoved the magazine under her jacket.

Leonora was speaking to her. "What's wrong, Sara? What's wrong?" The woman's voice was alarmed. "Are you sick?" In another moment she had taken the liberty of entering the pharmacy cage.

Sara tried to answer, but couldn't. She shook her head. Leonora went away for a moment, and by the time she came back with a wet washcloth from the restroom, Sara had managed to swallow. "Are there customers out there?" she asked, her mouth still sticky with peanut butter.

"It's okay," said Leonora. "There's nobody here."

With a great effort Sara explained that she had choked on a bite of sandwich and that she was fine, just fine, and thanks very much for the concern.

When Leonora had gone back out on the floor, Sara wiped her face. She slid the *Deeper Story* out of her jacket front and tucked it in the outer pocket of her purse to dispose of later; it was too mangled to be saleable.

For the rest of the day, even while she did the work that needed to be done, tears slid from Sara's eyes occasionally, and she affected a cough to go with all the nose blowing she had to do. The feeling of being about to fly apart would not leave her, nor would an even less comfortable feeling – one of guilt because she was so depraved as to envy a poor abused child. From time to time she remembered Mr. Pearlman, and each time he came to mind, strands were added to his connection with Mr. W. Soon he was guilty in her mind of a far different crime from the one he'd been accused of.

LIAR, LIAR

At the school crossing big Ben staved off the Osborne Avenue traffic to let the afternoon kindergartners cross, then waited on the sidewalk for the wave of older children.

The redhead was running, heavily but fast, chased by several other girls some distance behind her. "Liar, liar, pants on fire!" The girls' voices rang out.

As she pounded closer Ben bellowed, "Walk!" She glanced behind her. The others were far enough behind that she slowed down, but she did not walk.

Ben favored this one. He liked the red hair, that glowing flame, and the purity of the skin that went with it. You didn't see it often, but when you did, you couldn't help noticing, and if she was tubby, well, it was just baby fat, and there was nothing wrong with that. She was going to be a looker one of these days.

There was a break in the traffic flow. Ben stepped in the street with his sign and waved her on. "Hurry," he growled. "And then "WALK!" She broke her stride by adding an occasional hop. When she reached the far corner, she dashed down the side street out of sight.

By the time the others arrived at the crossing, he was back on the corner. Cars again streamed past. He chided the two ringleaders. "How come you're picking on her? What's she ever done to you?"

Their voices were almost feverish. "She's a liar!" The blonde girl said, "My uncle got arrested last night because of her and her lies."

Ben did not take this story seriously, but he kept the crowd waiting until the next natural break in the traffic before he held up his STOP sign and let them cross.

THE SECOND EARTHQUAKE

At the parsonage on Clover Street, Claire Pearlman sat with her eyes closed, rocking, in an alcove formed by a large bay window in the living room. This part of the room was Claire's, sacrosanct, where Corky was not allowed to pile books or scatter papers. A three-section window seat held in its recesses some of her own books, some music tapes, miscellaneous drawing pads and charcoals, and several bags of scraps she had been saving for years for the day she would have time to make her daughter Elizabeth's quilt. Within the alcove, there was room for a large Boston rocker as well as her own smaller, more cozy Tell City model. Claire was not asleep, but she wished she were, and she was trying to pretend that she was, to keep from having to talk with Romy about Corky's arrest.

She couldn't, however, keep from thinking about it. Wiped out, was how she put it. We're wiped out. After what had happened last night, she was still trembling inside. A first earthquake makes a shambles of a town, but the second one destroys security itself. This was Corky's second arrest.

Claire had not slept at all. She and Corky were late going to bed, of course, after getting home from the police station. As soon as they lay down, Corky sank immediately into a bitter sleep from which he groaned and twitched until daylight. He was turned wrong in the bed, with his back to Claire, rather than curled around her the way they usually slept. She had made the best of it without waking him to change position, but her eyes had flowed all night even though she didn't stir. While trying with her body to contain Corky and comfort his unconscious suffering, Claire had all too consciously reviewed their years together and the prospects ahead.

The years had gone quickly, as years do when the number remaining starts to dwindle. Although she had been acquainted with Corky since the inception of the Freethinkers' Meeting, she had been married to him for only thirteen years, a short time, really, and now these horrible people were going wreck the rest of their time together. A minister spoken of in the same sentence with a sexual crime against a child sees doors slamming shut everywhere he looks. The only thing worse would be if he were guilty, and she was indeed thankful that such a possibility was unthinkable.

And if Corky's career was ruined, how about his health? What physical toll does it take when the police knock, and the knock is for you? A month off your life, a year? Where would this particular event fall on the list of major life stresses? It was not the worst thing that could happen, perhaps, but it had to be higher than simple "false arrest" and certainly higher than mere "loss of job."

Through the fringe of her eyelashes she could see out the window to where Corky was puttering in the yard. He had gone out to clean up the pumpkin that had been smashed on the concrete walk, but he seemed to be raking leaves instead, or at least standing with the rake in his hands. Since Corky wouldn't be doing yard work for its own sake under the present circumstances, she assumed that he too wanted some time to himself.

She wondered what he was thinking, out there in the yard. Claire had often known what Neil, her first husband, had been thinking, had checked it out by guessing silently, then asking. But as close as she felt to Corky, she did not know what he thought. When she guessed and asked, she always found her guess to be far off the mark, for he never seemed to be thinking about the matter at hand but rather about some interesting tidbit from a book, or a quote from an ancestor, or an item of history.

He looks so vulnerable, she thought. Dressed as he was, Corky looked much younger than his sixty-four years. He wore a long Aran sweater of heavy wool, so close-knit that the sharp November wind could not penetrate it, and a pair of Army surplus winter pants, both garments already old when Claire first saw them nearly sixteen years ago. His green cap with the stumpy peak protected his ears and covered his straw pile of hair. His shoes were a battered version of the plain black pair he preached in. Corky did not buy himself different shoes for different purposes; he simply moved his worn-out preaching shoes down one category to "sportswear" and then to "dirty work."

No wonder the crazies are out to get him, Claire thought. He doesn't know how to blend in. Maybe that's the whole trouble. He's an affront to them, showing up their vanity. Maybe the whole episode could be ended if she could just get him to look right. She sighed, knowing it wasn't going to be that easy. Half way through the sigh she remembered to make it sound a little like a snore.

Claire could hear Romy at the other end of the room, where she had been clicking softly at her computer, working on a program application that would allow her employers to track expenses even more closely than before. It amazed Claire that they would pay the cost of this information, but Romy had assured her that Omni was not the only corporation willing to spend more on keeping track than they saved by doing so. "That's what they all do now," Romy had said. "They never know what they might need, so they want it all. I'm willing. It puts bread on my table." The phone had rung a moment ago, and Romy had answered it with the message that neither Claire nor Corky could come to the phone. Now she was tentatively moving through the closely placed furniture and stacks of books to where she could hover close enough to Claire that her breathing was audible. The breathing sounded angry, as usual. Claire kept her eyes resolutely closed. "Go back to your computer," she silently willed Romy. "Your aunt is sleeping peacefully, and you wouldn't want to disturb her."

Romy's anger had been a burden on Claire for the past few weeks and was even more of a burden today. It was hard enough to keep her own anger chained down where it belonged. The two of them, Romy and Nancy, had come to Portville in August at Claire's insistence because they were in need of a haven for a while, but Romy's temperament made the role of haven-hostess difficult.

The downward slide toward Romy's needing a haven had begun early last spring when her husband, Frank, who had taught history at Indiana University, had been denied tenure. (Claire thought it began much longer ago, but Romy always started the story there.) To comfort himself, he had spent money even more lavishly than before, and

Frank had always been a big spender. He bought another television set, a camcorder, a rowing exercise machine. A Jenn-Aire range and copper-clad cookware, with which he concocted gourmet dishes in large quantities. Since he came home for lunch and Romy didn't, Frank ate all the rich gourmet leftovers by himself, then cooked still another buttery sauce for dinner.

After a heart attack had killed him, one of Romy's guilt trips was the trip to the kitchen, where she had accidents with the equipment (pounding her fingers with a mallet, shredding them on a mandoline, even breaking a toe when she leaped for a box of coarse sea salt on the top shelf and came down too hard) while telling herself that she might still have a husband if she'd watched his diet and kept him from gaining so much weight so fast.

But she hadn't, and Frank had died, suddenly, right in front of her eyes, on a sultry June evening in Bloomington, had leaned forward in the porch swing and kept on leaning until he collapsed on the fiber floor mat like a pile of old clothes still sheltering a body. He was only thirty-seven years old.

Romy had been left with a daughter to bring up alone and the debts of a man who spent money without restraint. She was not without income, of course. She worked as a programmer for Omni in Bloomington, made thirty five thousand a year with a raise coming up. But this salary couldn't begin to pay off the bills she owed as Frank's widow.

Neither widowhood nor indebtedness, however, had triggered her back's giving out. It had taken the smallest of straws to break it down, a problem that wasn't even a problem. Nancy had been playing with friends one evening a little too late, a little too far away, and her absence had sent Romy into a panic that the child, as well as the husband, might now be dead, lying murdered in a cornfield or drowned in Lake Lemon. When Nancy finally came dawdling home that evening, Romy was sitting on the porch giving the sheriff's deputy information for a lost child report. She stood up, and then it happened, the pain seized her upper back and telegraphed its message down her arm. She clutched the chains that held the porch swing to the ceiling. She apologized for taking the deputy's time. She sent Nancy to bed. Then she took to her own bed and wailed, with a corner of the pillow in her mouth to keep from waking all of Bloomington. Nothing was safe for her now. She had no husband, no money; her body was not reliable. How could she take care of herself and her child?

This had happened in mid-August. It was not the first time Romy's back had caused her trouble; she was a hard worker, and there was a quirk in her spine that made it susceptible to stress of any kind. Thus she knew immediately what she was in for. But how could she rest her back, do her exercises, work, and take care of Nancy?

Claire, of course, had been keeping in close touch with Romy since Frank's death, and at this point had taken a truck down from Portville and moved the two of them, Romy and Nancy, into the parsonage before Nancy's school started in September. They had been there ever since. It was not what Claire or Romy or anyone else wanted, but it was the best they could do. Claire could see to it that Romy and Nancy were fed, housed, comforted, and above all, safe. Romy had been able to keep her job by working at home, with the understanding that she would return to Bloomington as soon as she could. For the time being Claire had been able to arrange some breathing room for her.

But as her burdens lightened and her back began to heal, Romy changed from being pathetic to being enraged. The widows' support group she attended encouraged her to express how angry she was at Frank for getting into debt and then dying on her. And express it she did, along with how angry she was about everything else as though, once angry, she discovered how ultimately rotten the whole world was. While Claire understood that being angry was better for Romy than being pathetic, it amazed her how far-reaching the fury was. The very sound of her breath indicated ash and hot lava. The amount of listening Claire could do was limited. The limit at the present moment was zero, and Claire kept her own breathing as slow and even as if she were deep in sleep.

But Romy was a heavy presence still standing by her chair. "Aunt Claire," she said, finally. "Neil just called. I told him you couldn't come to the phone right now and he said he was on his way over."

Claire gave up the pretense and opened her eyes to the uncurtained windows where she could see Corky moving leaves around with the rake. "Damn," she said. "I swear it's easier to deal with the trouble than it is the help." But she would have to deal with both, she knew, and she could choose neither the time nor the place. She picked up the muted plaid mohair that had slid to the floor, then stood up and got her balance.

"You could walk out on the whole mess," suggested Romy. "He's no more worth it than any of the rest of them."

"I could indeed," Claire answered, "but I don't want to."

Romy had been leading up to an attack on Corky all morning, and Claire decided to decoy her by giving her a new target. "I'd better tell you this so you won't be too surprised," she said, "but Neil doesn't look the way he used to."

"So who does?" answered Romy. "I haven't seen him since I was a teenager. How does he look different?"

"He's been going the other direction from the rest of us. While the rest of us have been aging, Neil keeps getting younger." She glanced out the window to where Corky, in his shabby outfit and schoolboy cap, was standing in the yellow leaves under the maple tree as if in a trance. Corky appeared younger, too, but while he sometimes seemed to Claire to be going for early childhood, Neil kept himself at the youthful middle-aged executive look. "He has a power haircut," she said. "But that's the least of it. You'll see."

"It's none of my business," said Romy, backing out of the way to let Claire past, "but why do you still have anything to do with Neil, anyway? I was really surprised when Corky told me to have you call him last night."

"I'm stuck with him," said Claire. "Till death do us part, and all that."

"Come on. You've been divorced for ages. You've been married to Corky for how long? Over ten years, I know. And with Elizabeth living in Mexico, you can't be using her as an excuse." Claire and Neil's daughter, Elizabeth, had been working out of the country for the past four years.

"Okay," said Claire, "you're right. The connection with Neil is unusual. But when we were divorced, we wrote up a property settlement that gave me a lifetime share in the law practice instead of trying to balance out our two contributions with what was available at the time. And given the fact that we're going to be connected, it's only a matter of whether it's going to be cordial or spiteful."

Romy followed Claire to the kitchen. "That's amazing," she said. "I didn't know you could make up a property settlement like that."

"There's nothing illegal about it," Claire answered. "And both of us thought it was the fairest way to go. Who's to stop it?"

"Well, Neil's a sharp lawyer. He could have seen to it that you got alimony for a year and then nothing. That's what most of them do if they can get away with it. A lot of men would give up law and dig ditches just to keep you from having your share."

"Romy, you may be right about men, but I just don't see things your way. I wouldn't have married Neil in the first place or lived with him all those years if he'd been a scoundrel." Claire could hear her own voice sounding irritated, but she was glad to be talking about Neil. It kept Romy from pouncing on Corky. "It was Neil's feeling for justice that turned him toward law in the first place. And there was no other fair way to compensate me for my contribution those years when I had the home and the family and his mother, and he had the career."

Claire pulled a chair to the kitchen cabinet, where she climbed on it to reach a high shelf. She pushed aside some blue mason jars and a chafing dish. "Here." Turning around, she felt suddenly dizzy, but she sucked in her stomach and defied the feeling. She couldn't fall apart. She couldn't fall off the chair. She was needed. She handed Romy the coffee-grinder, an old square wooden one with a drawer at the front and a grinding handle on top. "Neil likes good coffee." She stepped down. "And I just happen to have some."

Romy blew air through her lips, making a snorting noise like a horse.

"Neil's doing us a considerable favor." Claire let a little acid leak out in her voice. "Is there anything wrong with acknowledging it?" She took a brown sack of coffee beans from the freezer and measured them out by rounded scoops into the grinder cup. "Shall I make enough for you?"

"Might as well," said Romy. "I like good coffee too."

The grinder jumped around when Claire turned the handle; her small hand did not reach far enough to hold it steady. But before she could ask for help, Romy saw what was needed and took over.

Neil arrived before the coffee had finished dripping through the pot. Claire heard his car and got to the living room in time to see him come in the front door. She also saw Romy's reaction at the sight of him.

Neil looked and moved like the leader of an expedition. He was the one who would reach the South Pole or climb the other side of Everest first, and right now he was leading his host, who had come in with him, through the maze of books in the host's living room.

The deep blue eyes and the strong features had always been there, but some time after Neil and Claire had split up, he had learned even better how to use them, how to turn the head just so, how to intensify the blue of his eyes. He was lucky: his hair had stayed thick on top, and it was just gray enough to look mature without looking old. It had surely been trimmed and blow-dried within the last few hours; it was in perfect order without being stiff. Whatever scars were left from the two face lifts he'd had in the last ten years were not visible, and while his suntan didn't look like August, it didn't look like November either, thanks to the tanning room at his health club. He used the club's weight machines and the track as well. Thus he was still lean and muscular.

He entered the kitchen followed by Corky, who, next to Neil, looked extremely shabby and odd. With his green wool cap gone, his hair stuck out in all directions.

Claire's feelings rushed to Corky's defense. But it was Neil who had to defend him, and Neil liked to develop his own cases. Neil has to be enjoying this, she thought. He can subtly point out how right he was about Corky's worthlessness.

Neil greeted her with a hug and several comforting pats on the shoulder blades. "I knew you wouldn't let Corky come downtown to the office alone, so I thought it might be easier on you if I dropped by here."

Claire did not believe that story. His pride would keep him from parading her through the office with Corky, his ex-wife with her down-at-the-heels husband.

"It was good of you to come," she said, swallowing her feelings. "And heroic of you to go to the police station with me last night."

She refrained from smiling at him, however. Long ago, during the heat of battle, he had accused her of using her dimples to manipulate him, and because the accusation was true, she had stopped. That was what led to the divorce, she thought. Being cut off from her smile kept her from seeing anything to smile about. She poured his cup of coffee.

"Good of you," echoed Corky, his timing just a moment off, leaving a short wedge of silence. "I certainly didn't think I was going to sleep in my own bed last night."

Claire poured Corky some coffee too and added the cream and sugar he liked. Both men sat down with Romy at the table while Claire filled two more cups before joining them.

"You were lucky it was Halloween." said Neil. "There isn't always a judge down there at night to set bail."

Last night Claire had called Neil immediately when she arrived home to find Corky arrested. As it happened, Neil had just come in the door from taking his eight year-old twins trick-or-treating. He picked up Claire in his little Mercedes in less than half an hour, and the two of them arrived downtown before Corky had even been booked.

Romy spoke now in a husky voice. "What he was lucky for was to know somebody who could write a ten thousand dollar check without having to sell something."

There was a noticeable silence, then Claire said, "You won't lose anything, Neil. Except for your time."

"I know." For the first time Neil really seemed to notice Romy.

"This is Claudine's daughter Romy," said Claire.

"Of course," said Neil. "I could tell by looking that you were someone in the family. I just couldn't tell who. You were here last night?" He still looked puzzled. "I didn't see you."

"You didn't come in last night, remember?" said Claire.

"Romy is staying with us for awhile," said Corky. "Her husband died last summer. We brought her and Nancy here to look after them."

"Ah," said Neil. "Tragic." He frowned and shook his handsome head. "And Nancy is who?"

"Nancy's my little girl. She's nine."

"All right. Now I've got you straight. I do remember you, but you were a lot younger then." He leaned on the table and let his blue eyes twinkle at her.

"So were you," answered Romy coolly.

Claire saw Neil flush into the still more congenial look he was able to summon to cover unpleasantness, and she couldn't help mentally scoring one for Romy. Neil's second wife, Francesca, was about Romy's age. About Elizabeth's age, as a matter of fact. It wouldn't hurt Neil a bit to realize that not every woman his daughter's age would fall all over herself for him.

The perfect lines of Neil's power haircut took on an energy now, and he transformed himself into an attorney who could save the damned. "It'd be great to sit here and bring ourselves up to date," he said gallantly to Romy, "but I'd better hear from Corky what we're up against. We need to get started."

Corky didn't say anything. He stirred his coffee and frowned. After a moment, the silence was too much for Claire, so she answered Neil herself. "It looks like we're up against a repeat of last spring." Her own words struck her like a blow and brought tears to her eyes. Her voice swelled. "And who knows where it's going to end?"

The rush of words seemed to take everyone by surprise. Nobody answered.

She went on. "This whole thing reminds me of a flock of crows I saw once that had a thrush, pecking it to death." She had rescued the thrush, had taken it to the bird woman for care, but not until one of its eyes was gone.

"One thing's different from last time," said Neil. "He doesn't have any cuts and bruises."

"Only because we got him out of there."

Corky's bruises from the first experience were long gone, and Claire had thought she could put the whole thing behind her, but since last night, she had suffered another painful squeeze inside her chest whenever it came to mind. She felt that they were safe from nothing, that not even the police who were paid to protect them would bother to do so.

But Neil had turned again to Corky, who still sat staring into his cup as though there were readable tea leaves in it instead of coffee. "If you could tell me who these people are and what might have led up to this accusation, it would certainly help."

Claire willed herself to keep still and wait for Corky's answer. A careful speaker at the best of times, Corky could ponder interminably when an answer was not clear enough to document. Oftentimes he never got a chance to answer at all, for the wait was hard on the people waiting.

Neil sipped his coffee, looking urbanely out of place in the cluttered kitchen. He belonged where there was hand-rubbed walnut instead of Formica, plush carpet instead of linoleum. Romy breathed, with nostrils opened, pulling in extra oxygen. Claire waited.

Corky still stared at his coffee. He shook his head. He frowned. Then his expression changed slightly. "The Flannerys are basically decent people," he said. "We've known them for years."

At this, Claire could stand no more. "They're horrible people!" she cried. "They want you out, and they're willing to put their own child through this to get you out."

"I said 'basically'," answered Corky. "I admit that they're not acting very well. But they're doing the best they can." He addressed Neil directly. "The real mistake I made was in staying on at the Meeting." His thin smile was pained. "It's hard to gather the energy to move on when you're not ready, even if other people are pushing on you."

Claire could not argue with this. They should have moved as soon as the strife between the church members became apparent, and certainly should have gone when Corky had been fired last spring after the first arrest. It was humiliating to be allowed to stay on provisionally, week by week, this way. They should have gone long ago.

But where?

Corky's path had led him out of mainstream Christianity, out of the Methodist church where he'd preached until the sixties, had led him through a brief stay with the Unitarians, and into the forming of the Freethinkers' Meeting with a group of people dissatisfied with the stand their own churches were taking on Vietnam and civil rights. This progression was common enough. For the church attendee, the next step after being a Freethinker could be in almost any direction, including staying in bed on Sunday morning. But the minister's career was involved. Where does the minister go when the Freethinkers won't have him any longer? Some would leave the pulpit for the marketplace. But Corky was not made for the marketplace. Claire wondered if he was made for this earth, otherworldly as he was.

"What I'm driving at is how to combat this particular outburst," said Neil. "It's not going to be relevant to the court that people in the Meeting would like for you to go somewhere else. The question we're faced with is a Class C felony charge of molesting a child under twelve that could put you behind bars for more years than you'd care to contemplate."

Corky shook his head again as though in amazement. "I can't even believe it, that word "felony," let alone fight it." He sighed. "I've always tried so hard."

"You'd better believe it," said Neil, beginning to sound exasperated. "The situation is not the same as it was last spring. Bayer would not have brought charges unless he had good reason to think he could make a case against you. He's up for reelection, and he's not wasting his time. This is hardball, Corky. Your case is just what he needs to get the women's votes."

Romy, who had been listening intently, now flipped her spoon over the table and into the sink. It clattered for a moment, while everyone looked at her. "Wouldn't you know?" she said. "Wouldn't you just know they'd find a way to twist a women's issue to their own advantage? And the women and children once more get screwed!" She pushed back her chair. "Excuse me, folks, but I'd better get back to work."

As she left the room Neil gave Claire a look that said, "You do harbor some strange ones."

"She has a point," said Claire, defying Neil. "We all know very well who does the child molesting in this society, and it's not Corky. It's the fathers. The fathers and stepfathers and grandfathers. The uncles and the brothers. I saw too much at the Center not to understand. They don't prosecute the fathers because the prisons aren't big enough to hold them all, and because they don't want to support all the women and children who would be on welfare if the fathers did go to prison. They can make a big splash over one minister or one teacher and avoid the expense of cleaning up the real problem."

"I'm not going to argue with you," said Neil. "You may be right. But the real problem here and now is what happened last summer and how to keep Corky out of prison."

"Well, how, then?"

Neil launched into an explanation. "A child molesting case is different from other cases in several ways. Since you're not going to have witnesses to the actual event, and since a jury is often loath to take the child's word alone for what happened, the prosecution has to build up the case some other way. They'll be soliciting statements that

Corky molested other children. This provides them with the evidence that, yes, he is indeed the kind of person who does things like that, and yes, they can believe the child since others agree with the character assessment." Neil looked inquiringly at Corky.

"Well they won't get any," burst out Claire. "No one could be any better to children than Corky is. I think that's what prompted this thing with the Flannerys. Evie Flannery was jealous that Corky had become Josie's friend instead of hers. She was jealous of her own daughter. And Dunk is a redneck bully. It's no wonder the poor girl needed Corky as a friend, with parents like that."

"What I don't understand," said Corky slowly, "is where they got a story to take to the prosecutor. I had no idea she was upset. But I'm sure I can straighten it out when I see her."

Neil broke into Corky's sentence, "You can't see her. Don't even think about it. You'd better not have any contact with her at all."

"How can he defend himself if he doesn't even understand what brought the charge about?" asked Claire.

"He doesn't defend himself. I defend him. I'm the one who asks the questions, not Corky. If this comes to trial, which I hope it doesn't, he may not even be in the courtroom at the same time she is. It's too easy for a child to be intimidated by an adult. That's the reason Indiana law can deny a person accused of a sex crime against a child his usual right to confront his accuser."

"She's been intimidated, all right," said Claire. "Her father's good at intimidation. How do we counteract that?"

"One way is to get the case into court as quickly as possible to keep them from having time to build a substantial case. Another is to wait and hope they'll get tired of it. And either way is to find every way possible to show the girl up as a liar."

The skin under Corky's eyes looked ashen above the bluish, unshaven line of his jaw and chin. "I don't think she really is a liar," he said. "Something must have upset her, and I feel terrible about it. She's a high-strung girl, not many friends, a difficult family. I wouldn't have anything bad happen to her for the world."

"The issue is not what you think of her," said Neil. "It's whether the court believes her or not. And it would help if you could tell me what did happen that afternoon."

Claire started to explain, then stopped herself.

"I don't even know for sure what happened that afternoon," said Corky. "She frequently stopped in after school, when I was in the office, sometimes just to say hello, sometimes to talk for a while or help Marge, she's the church secretary, with odd jobs. Several of the children did. Sometimes Josie had another girl with her, Heather Merchant, a girl who lives near her. I think Josie was a little hurt that Heather hit it off so well with Nancy – our niece, Nancy. They're together all the time now and Josie's been feeling left out."

While Corky seemed to be warming to his subject, Neil was looking impatient. "Well, were you in the habit of rubbing them around on your lap and kissing them? That's what this is all about, not their helping Marge run the copier or whatever they do."

Claire could not wait for Corky to answer. "Of course he was. It takes a pretty cold adult not to be affectionate with children who need affection. And if anyone needs affection, it's Josie. She was crazy about Corky. She even told me she'd like to live with us."

"Did you keep your office door open? The church secretary would know, wouldn't she, if anything funny were going on?"

"I think so," answered Corky. "Sometimes it was open, anyway."

Neil heaved a sigh. "Oh brother," he said. "Well, I can talk to her." He scooted his chair back. "I'll have a little more coffee if there's any left." There was, and he poured himself half a cup and brought the pot to the table.

Then the front door opened and closed, and Corky stood up. "Nancy's home," he said with obvious relief, as though he had been waiting for that moment. "I'd better talk to her. She's upset about all this." He left the room hastily and could be heard, after a moment, in conversation with the little girl in the front part of the house.

Neil stared at Claire and slowly shook his head. "I hate to be the one to tell you this," he said, "but there's something damned peculiar about a man his age who likes kids that much. I hope you're preparing yourself to find out some very ugly truths."

"Be careful, Neil," said Claire, feeling dangerously near hysteria. "Don't say anything you'll regret. You know as well as I do that people in our society pay lip service to their love of children but actually value them very little. Just look at how upset people get if they're asked to pay enough taxes to educate them. It's no wonder it seems unnatural when once in a while there's an adult who takes them seriously and treats them with affection and courtesy." She stopped speaking when she felt her voice going out of control.

"You're tired," said Neil. He reached across the table and stroked her hand. "Forgive me. I should have given you a chance to rest." He drank the last of his coffee and stood up to go.

Claire watched him take his cup to the sink and rinse it out. Of course he wouldn't want to discuss the real issues. He never did. Unfortunately, she was indeed tired, too much so to fight his condescension. It was the same old story.

Well, if he would use his talents to help Corky, she was willing to let him lord it over her all he wanted. If that's what it took, that's what she could provide. "I appreciate the help. We couldn't possibly pay an attorney to do what you're doing. I don't know what we'd do."

"Glad to help out," he said. "I'll get out of here now so that you can rest. The next thing will be the arraignment, but that doesn't mean much, so don't worry."

Claire followed him into the living room and opened the door.

"It was a pleasure to see you again," he said to Romy, who was back at her keyboard working.

Romy gave him a long, bored look over the monitor.

Claire stood on the porch and watched him go down the walk.

"It looks like somebody tricked instead of treated last night," he called, guiding his meticulously shined shoes around the smashed pumpkin that Corky had not yet cleaned up.

How like him to notice! Claire felt herself enter his classification: People Who Live in Squalor. She retaliated by placing him squarely among People Who Care About The Wrong Things.

He bent to unlock the door of his Mercedes. Be careful, Neil, she thought. You're not in suburbia. This is the inner city. Lock yourself in. She remembered the care he took to separate himself from his clients so that no sleaze would rub off. She had always maintained that he did good works, not through love of his neighbor, but rather to prove himself better than his neighbor.

When he had driven away, Claire started in to get a pan to put the pumpkin in, but Romy was already on her way with a plastic garbage bag.

"I'll take care of it," Romy said. Claire watched from the porch as Romy squatted carefully to protect her back while she picked up the chunks and little gobs of mashed pumpkin and put them in the plastic bag.

What Claire didn't know was that the jack-o-lantern had been smashed last night by Romy herself.

THE PORTVILLE LIBRARY

Downtown in the library parking lot Fred sat in his Pinto eating a sandwich. He too had brought peanut butter, but his was more carefully put together than Sara's. Not just any bread would do for him; he liked a thick-sliced wheat berry that he refrigerated to keep fresh. And grape jam, because it spread more evenly than jelly. And a thin coat of margarine applied before either the jam or the peanut butter so that the bread would sustain its character.

As he munched the sandwich, part of his brain thought contentedly that nothing could beat peanut butter done right. With another part he watched a man carry a small suitcase, not much bigger than a briefcase, across the wide plaza that separated the library from the parking lot. Under a neat gray topcoat left carelessly unbuttoned, the man wore a business suit. He walked slowly. The sight seemed anachronistic to Fred. Men in business suits no longer carried suitcases out in the open with nothing but sky above them; they drove or they flew. Could he be going to the Greyhound Station? Surely not. This man wasn't Greyhound, he was TWA.

Fred felt the urge to question him, go up to him and say, "Hey, buddy, need a lift somewhere with that bag?" just to find out. He had always been curious about people. Now that he was trying to freelance, he needed to overcome his natural reserve and ask the questions. You could never tell when you'd find out something you could use. A story about changing modes of travel, perhaps.

But the man reached the sidewalk and crossed the street then disappeared between two buildings. Fred was left with a feeling of sadness, as though he had witnessed a crucial downward step in a stranger's life. Suddenly he knew exactly what the man was doing: the same thing he himself had done last spring. He didn't need to do the interview. He already knew the answers. It was the poor slob's last day at the office. He had cleaned out his desk and was carrying things home: his clock, the framed pictures of his wife and kids, the onyx holder with the fancy pen that didn't write, the date books that kept track of how he'd spent his quarter-hours for the last eight or ten or twenty years. Someone else would use his desk now, set out pictures, and assign time that clients or customers would pay for.

Fred peeled his banana to eat between bites of sandwich and thought grimly that now there was one more reader for his article on "How to Structure Your Time When Unemployed." Maybe there was even one more patron for the library.

The library did not have many patrons. The whole demeanor of the place discouraged entry. The expanse of flat, clipped plaza created a no-man's-land between the library and its parking facilities. Readers couldn't just duck in, grab a few books and duck out. They had to cross that plaza and expose their whereabouts, knowing that if they were seen, they would be dismissed as persons with nothing better to do than sit with their nose in a book. And once inside, those who braved the plaza would be stared at by a uniformed guard as though they wouldn't have come unless they were planning to steal or deface something. Built of smooth gray limestone from the quarries in southern Indiana and situated six blocks from downtown, the building was thus quiet and underused except by a few furtive readers and researchers who shared the place with street people coming in out of the weather and unemployed men who needed somewhere away from home to spend the day.

In spite of its inhospitable face, however, Fred loved the library. He loved it even more than he had loved his office at Powkin. The high ceilings and wide halls gave him a feeling of wealth, of generous space, while the typing cubicles and carrels provided cozy places to work or read. The quietness seemed profound. These rooms had never been filled with the sound of Howard Cosell or a studio audience. And the smell, the mixture of books and floor wax, was something you couldn't duplicate anywhere else.

Because there was a rule against food inside the building, Fred couldn't eat while he read as he used to do at Powkin, but he frequently ate lunch in the parking lot. He would linger in the breeze on the plaza in nice weather and sometimes even in the rain or snow. He bravely tried not to care who saw him or what they thought. So what if successful people were too busy to read. He was now a failure and could read as much as he liked. He had long since made friends with the guard and discovered that his overdeveloped stare compensated for the foot trouble that kept him from chasing wrongdoers.

The only problem with the library, as Fred saw it, was the books, or rather the lack of them. The library did indeed capitalize on the fact that it held a fine old collection from Slater College, which had gone under seven years ago. But the budget's being what it was, fewer and fewer books had been added each year since then. Although there was much concern in Portville about the literacy problem, and campaigns were undertaken every year or so to make sure that everyone was able to fill out a job application, the *Clarion* advised that throwing money at the library wouldn't make anyone literate. The city fathers agreed. They allocated less and less, then, to books, and now the budget was such that only best sellers or near best sellers had a chance of being selected. The law of the marketplace was Portville's law. Books that didn't sell were probably not worth having anyway.

Fred had written several letters to the editor deploring the scarcity of new books, and on one occasion had drawn a response from another reader. "Books are on their way out, man," the writer had explained. "Spending money on books in the age of TV is about as smart as buying fountain pens in the computer age." Fred did not respond to this. He loved books. He also loved his silver fountain pen. But how could you justify spending money on something just because you loved it? The bottom line was the bottom line in Portville, and Fred had been living in Portville for a long time. He felt so angry and frustrated that he couldn't even get a grip on what was wrong.

One thing the city fathers were willing to buy for the library, however, was a computer system. To automate the library would bring the city up to statewide standards of efficiency, and keep track of who read what. Even this long after the McCarthy era was over, there were still some who thought it might be well to know who took out books on communism, as well as devil worship and the building of bombs. The system was duly installed, and one day last summer it was ready to use.

On the day of the changeover from card catalog to disk, Fred noticed a library assistant, wearing the stony expression of a man who has to shoot his dog, taking a box of heavily reinforced trash bags to the balcony. Sniffing trouble, Fred followed him to where the card catalog was housed in polished walnut cabinets. There, before the horrified gaze of half a dozen patrons, the man pulled out each drawer of each cabinet, unscrewed the brass rod that held its contents in place and dumped the cards into a trash bag. After the job was finished, one of the other onlookers said, with tears in her eyes, "I know how people felt when the Arabs burned the library at Alexandria."

That night mischief was done. The next afternoon Fred saw that the carved quotation, "A GOOD BOOK IS THE PRECIOUS LIFE BLOOD OF A MASTER SPIRIT", which graced the lintel above the main doors, had been spray painted out with a fluorescent red slash, above which was the word, "ON-LINE!"

The card catalog was still mourned. The red paint had been sandblasted away, but the computer did not catch on. Some patrons couldn't learn to use it; others wouldn't. They wanted to browse. They wanted to open drawers, touch cards. The librarians grew so tired of listening to complaints about the computer that they set up a bulletin board where people could post their gripes. Fred's gripe was this: "More and more goes into useless information about less and less."

Today, when Fred finished his lunch, he went inside, talked to the guard, Mr. Phillips, for a few minutes, then visited his locker to put on his library sweater. A dark-green cardigan frayed at the elbows, the sweater came together as far as the zipper worked, about six inches. It was a sweater that Sara disliked intensely. It made him look twenty years older and ten thousand dollars poorer, she said. In fact she had once hidden it in the trash. But Fred went more by comfort than looks, and when he saw his favorite sweater in the can by the curb, he rescued it and took it to the library, where he kept it in his locker. Also in the locker was a pair of comfortable old ankle-high shoes with soft soles and matted fleece linings. It was no longer warm in the library. The heat that had built up over the summer was gone, and so he brought clothing that would keep him warm even with the thermostat set low. The library was where he worked now, and he wanted to be comfortable at work. He proceeded to his favorite typing cubicle to get started on his article, nodding and saying hello along the way to some of the regulars and to the librarian disassembling the Halloween exhibit in the upstairs hall case.

Seated at the typewriter, however, Fred discovered how depressing his subject was. Structuring time when unemployed was not much better than marking time or killing time or passing the time away. The problem was that nobody wanted to pay you for your time. But you'd better structure it, or people will notice that you're unemployed and will find things you can do for them without being paid.

This was where Fred learned how hard it was to continue writing an article when he no longer believed its premise. What he was coming to believe now was this: that if he wasn't being paid for his time, it belonged to him, and he could do whatever he liked with it. Who was to care? If anybody cared what he did, let them hire him.

Except for the drugstore. Sara's claim on him was legitimate. He agreed that if he wasn't working, he ought to help her in the store. It was only fair. *If* he wasn't working.

Which meant, then, that he'd better work if he wanted out of the drugstore. He'd damned well better write his article and then another and another, or his tail would be tethered forever at the corner of Osborne Avenue and Brewster Street with the Pepto Bismol and the diaper rash cream.

As he worked, Claire Pearlman kept insinuating herself into his thoughts: the way she had charmed the men at the dump; that smile of hers. That smile must have made life different for her than it was for ordinary folks. There's a lady, he thought, who oughtn't to have troubles like a husband with a yen for the kiddies. It was a damn shame. The reverend would be fired and there she'd be with a money problem as well as a sex problem. Another one unemployed.

"Shave every morning just as though you're going to work," he wrote dutifully. He thought of his father-in-law and the difficulty he had shaving. Maybe shaving wasn't such a good idea, he thought. But he left the line in. It was the kind of thing New York would like.

What I need is something hot, he thought. Something like the Pearlman story. With a minister that's innocent. Or even if he's guilty, he's got a story people would pay good money to read.

He felt the little hairs along his spine tingle the way they did when an idea crept up the ladder of his backbone. That's it, he thought.

That's the project for me to work on. The untold story: the whole thing from the molester's point of view. He wished he knew whether Pearlman was guilty or not.

But Fred did not rush to start the new project. Instead, he continued to fill in the details of how unemployed people should structure their time. "Finish what you start," he wrote. "You finished the boss's projects; finish your own." Idea by idea he filled in his outline.

Late in the afternoon, his rough draft on paper, Fred went to a phone carrel near the main doors of the library. He braced the white pages against the slope of his green-sweatered belly. His meaty forefinger walked the P's while he tilted his head to get the name he wanted lined up in his trifocals.

Although he had spent enough time on his outline to be sure he could write the "structure" article, had disciplined himself to work when he didn't want to, he was less and less sure that New York would actually want it. It was neither upbeat nor sensational, and while the "how to" element was saleable and the idea of "structure" popular, "unemployed" was a loser concept that was not likely to sell magazines. The public didn't like to think about "unemployed." Fred would query, but he was glad he'd come up with something else. That was the hardest thing about freelancing. You couldn't settle in and get comfortable. You had to keep thinking of something else, the next idea, the next story.

He had already found the last name, "Pearlman," and was zeroing in on "Pearlman, Corcoran, Rev." when he noticed the caller in the carrel three down from him. Youngish. Chapped face. A corduroy jacket with flaps that wouldn't lie flat. Fred heard him whisper into the mouthpiece but couldn't make out the words. Then he heard him exhaling like a runner settling into distance. After a few moments of breathing, he whispered something else.

Fred listened. The whispering and the breathing continued. He could hear just enough to catch on. He moved two carrels closer. The caller hung up.

"Wait a minute," said Fred, sure now that he had something interesting. "Hold on. You were making an obscene call, right? I could use an obscene phone caller. Human interest. How would you like to give me an interview?"

"What the hell?" the man answered. "You some kind of pervert?"

Fred drew himself up with dignity. "I'm not a pervert," he answered. "I'm an author." Here he stopped for a moment. It was necessary to substitute mentally the words "would-be author." Then he thought, what the hell am I apologizing for, this guy's an obscene phone caller, for Chrissakes. "You give me an interview and you get to be in a magazine. Everybody wants to be in a magazine. How about it?"

The other man shook his head in wonderment.

Fred leaned toward him persuasively, like a salesman with a lot full of used cars. "You'd like it," he said. "You get to tell it like it is, see, and that's rare on this earth, somebody willing to listen to it like it is. I'm willing." His voice lowered. He was beginning to enjoy being outrageous. After all, what did he have to lose? "You gotta have your hardships, calling from a public phone like this. You come in your pants and hafta go out in the cold. Life's tough for you too, isn't it?

"How many times did you ever get to tell somebody what it's really like to be an obscene phone caller? I'll bet the breathing makes your mouth dry, doesn't it?" Fred pulled out his appointment book. "How about Tuesday afternoon, three o'clock? We meet here and go up to Science and Technology. I got an office up there. One of the typing cubicles. Very private. Just you and me. If the tape recorder bothers you, we don't use it, I'll remember what you say without it. What do you say? Tuesday afternoon, right?"

The man looked hesitant for a moment, then shook his head. "No way," he said. "Fuck off, pervert."

Fred grabbed his sleeve for a last try. "You better take me up on this," he said. "If you don't, you'll read in a book some time about a guy like yourself, only there'll be things wrong, it won't be the way it really is. You'll throw the book across the room and the pages'll all fall out. If you want me to get it right, you better tell me."

"I don't care if you get it right," was the answer. "I don't read books."

"Don't read books?" Fred felt suddenly hot, his chain pulled, as though a furnace door had opened nearby. "Then what are you doing in the public library gumming up the phones with your filthy curbreath?" He turned. "Mr. Phillips, come down here. We got an obscene phone caller here."

The man dashed for the exit while the guard left his magazine and lumbered to the row of carrels. "We can't keep them out," he said. "They're a fact of life." He headed on into the men's room across the hall.

Fred collected his train of thought. The fun was over. He had to be serious again. His belly rumbled, suggesting an early dinner that he knew he couldn't have, as late as it already was. He wished he could go home right now without making his call. But he couldn't. If he wanted out of the drugstore, he had to do work of his own, and interviewing prospects was part of that work. He wished he were back at Powkin secure on a payroll, instead of here in the public library learning how hard it is to freelance. He looked gloomily at the phone book, so heavy, so worn. Walking the pages chasing prospects day after day would give his fingers fallen arches. The sudden temptation came to invent the interview, make up his own answers to the questions and sell the piece as genuine. Then, ashamed, he closed his eyes for a moment, braced himself by whispering like a mantra, "You wanna eat, you gotta hustle," and found the number he needed. The mantra wasn't quite right, of course. He would eat whether he worked or not, but he couldn't help associating work with food, and he did love food.

The voice that answered was deep and cultured. "Hello?"

"Hello," said Fred. "My name is Bekin, Fred Bekin. I'm a friend of Mrs. Claire. Is this Reverend Pearlman?"

"Yes it is." Again Fred noticed the deepness of the voice. He was surprised that it didn't sound especially upset, no jailhouse pallor of the voice, so to speak. It was just right for a reverend, someone who needed a voice deep enough to support talk of serious matters.

"I'm pleased to find you home this afternoon, under the circumstances."

"I'm pleased to be at home."

"Yes, well." Fred shifted his feet nervously. "Look, I haven't had the pleasure of meeting you, sir, but as I said, I'm a friend of Mrs. Claire. I'm an author." Again he mentally inserted the "would-be." "I write a lotta stories, see, and I got something in mind right up your alley. I thought you might like to be interviewed."

The reverend took his time speaking. "Interviewed?"

Suddenly the whole promising idea struck Fred as bizarre. Why on earth would the man allow himself to be interviewed? He closed his eyes and thought, oh God, and then went on. "For an article. A magazine story." The request sounded unreasonable and his voice sounded lame, even to him. He tried to make it as attractive as he could. "It might even turn into a book, maybe, but I can't make any promises except that from what I read in the morning paper about what happened to you last night, I think there are definite possibilities." When he realized he had almost mentioned *In Cold Blood*, he began to sweat.

"Just one moment, please." Fred heard a noise that sounded like a hand over the mouthpiece. Then the reverend came back. "I'd better let you talk to my wife," he said.

In a moment Claire was on the phone. "Yes?" she said. She sounded tired.

"Look, I'm sorry, Mrs. Claire. I read in the paper about your husband and I had an idea of something I could do, but I shouldn't have bothered you with it. I apologize."

"What was your idea?" she asked. "We need all the ideas we can get."

"It was nothing. I shouldn't have called. It was just that I've been doing some writing and I thought maybe his side of all this was something the public ought to hear." Fred was torn between his desire to get off the phone and his desire to go on talking to Claire.

He had to squirm through a long silence before she responded. "You're exactly right, of course," she said. She no longer sounded tired. "It's a scandal, a travesty. To have an innocent man ruined by a false accusation is something the public ought to know about. But what can be done?"

Fred took heart. "I thought I might interview him and write it up. Or maybe even do some investigative reporting and find out what all the parties have to say and write the whole thing up."

"That's the ticket. Get the whole story. You'll see, then."

"You wouldn't mind?"

"Of course we wouldn't mind. It's probably our best hope. When can you get started?"

Fred couldn't believe his good fortune. "Right away," he answered. "If I could talk to the reverend again, I'll set up an interview."

In a moment Corky was back. "Claire tells me you're going to arrange my deliverance."

"That's a big order, but I'll sure try, Reverend, I'll sure try. When can we get together to talk? Tomorrow?"

"No, tomorrow is All Souls Day and there's a service at the Meetinghouse. I haven't written the sermon yet. I think we'd better wait until some time next week. I have an idea these next few days are going to be difficult."

"Maybe I could come hear the service?" Fred did not want to lose momentum, now that the project was under way.

"Of course. It's at seven thirty tomorrow evening."

Finished telephoning, Fred went to his locker. He was elated. "You've done a real day's work," he told himself, "even if nobody paid you for it. Maybe you don't hafta be a failure after all. You disciplined yourself to do something you didn't want to do. That's what it's all about, isn't it? And now it's time to go home." He hung up his sweater, put on his coat and jiggled the locker handle just so until it clicked.

Maybe Lady Luck and his Muse were going to get together, he thought. Maybe this was going to be his chance. A hot topic, plenty of cooperation, what more could he ask? New York would love it. He thought about calling Sara. It was often the easiest way to have a talk with her, the most private, given the presence of her father at home. But he didn't have another quarter and was too impatient to change a dollar bill, so he decided to wait.

On the way home, he tuned the car radio to *All Things Considered* to hear "the news of this day, November first." He was a little in love with Susan Stamberg, whose beautiful sunlit voice made news of the Way Things Were less enraging. He often used her sweet reason to gear himself down for a respite between the anxieties of the day and the anxieties of the evening. How would she handle the reverend's story? With courtesy and mercy for all. He hoped he could do half as well.

Tonight, however, on the eve of the election, Susan had nothing to talk about but politics: Democrats blaming Republicans for the poor getting poorer, Republicans blaming Democrats for the *rich* getting poorer; liberals blaming the deficit on the arms race, conservatives blaming the arms race on the liberals. Not even Susan Stamberg could make this palatable.

He turned off the radio and dictated into his tape recorder, taking notes toward the big book he hoped to write someday. He had not yet settled on a title for this work. Sometimes he called it *The Anatomy of Blame* to make it sound like criticism. Sometimes it was *Blame and Responsibility* to give it a sociological slant. When he was thinking philosophy, he favored *The Denial of Blame*.

Responding to what he had just heard on the radio, he began to speak. "Nowadays," he said, keeping his eyes on the freeway narrowing to a single lane ahead, "the bigshots wanna keep their ass covered above all else. Unlike Harry Truman, who said the buck stops here, the president of today avoids taking responsibility so's to avoid taking blame. And likewise everybody else. There's nobody in charge, ladies and gentlemen. They're all busy pointing the finger and patting themselves on the back and sitting on their hands and keeping their nose clean. Everybody's left hand knows that the other guy's right hand is in the till, but nobody can lift a finger to make any progress. They say they have no choice but to *this*, and they have no choice but to *that*, and they say that their hands are tied, ladies and gentlemen, but the truth is that there are no hands on board."

He slowed to avoid a road crew. Then, realizing that he was no longer geared down to enjoy his respite, he switched off the tape recorder, abandoned *The Anatomy of Blame*, and thought instead about a nice moist meatloaf with a thick slather of ketchup baked into the crust. New potatoes. Lotsa sour cream. The good thing about being the cook was that the cook got to choose the menu.

JOSIE'S GOLD COIN

At Osborne Elementary, the fourth grade's Homeroom period was over and it was time once again for Language Arts. Josie Flannery's eyes came into focus and her back straightened out of the slump that Homeroom always inspired. Reading was fine with her. She read all the time anyway and liked not having to do it on the sly. Writing was fine too, one of her best subjects. She opened her notebook and lined up her pencils, three of them, freshly sharpened and only slightly tooth marked. She hoped Mrs. Babcock would not make them write about whatever they wanted. That was the hard part, figuring out what it would be okay to want. She hoped there would be an assignment. If everybody wrote about the same thing, then no one could laugh at her for what she chose. Now she waited while chair legs squeaked on the old wood floor and books fell and papers rustled as the class quieted down.

Osborne Elementary had celebrated its ninetieth anniversary in September. It was such an old school that several pupils' grandparents came to the party hoping to find initials they had carved or gum wads they had left there. The rows of old bolted-down desks had been removed, of course – gum, inkwells, initials and all – and replaced with moveable tables and chairs, but the wooden floors were still waxed and buffed, the water fountains still ran warm, and the T.C. Steele autumn landscape still hung in its gold-leafed frame at the end of the upstairs hall. Ninety years of history provided the children with a background for the personal dramas being acted out at the present time.

Josie, of course, like all children, had no idea that the dramas were much alike or that suffering was universal, with only the particulars and the degree being unique. She had started the day the same way she did every school day, assembling her outfit, vetoing the worn-too-often, the unfashionable, and the ludicrous, and wondering how she could dress and what she could do to avoid humiliation. Her father had the idea that getting good grades and following the rules were what school was all about, and her mother imagined a social whirl. Both had mercifully forgotten the realities of childhood, but Josie was there every day and knew how things were. Her parents helped support the Watchers, who patrolled the school and the surrounding area. They told her how lucky she was to go to a school where the kids were safe from drugs and guns. But they didn't understand how little it mattered to be safe from drugs and guns when what you wanted was some ordinary respect. In fact, she often daydreamed about lethal weapons, especially axes and machetes that made use of a person's own raging force. She daydreamed about razors that could leave a bully bleeding before he even knew he'd been cut. Guns were not as attractive, though a gun could be useful to take out an attacker too big to slash or chop. Josie's reality was much different from what her parents imagined.

Mrs. Babcock's full red-flowered skirt swirled above her ankles as she made her way through the maze of tables checking to be sure everyone had a fresh page and a sharp pencil. Josie admired that skirt and the red blazer that went with it. Mrs. Babcock was tall and slender, with crispy-curly black hair that grew close to her head like a cap, and she was one of those teachers everyone wanted to have nearby, both because she was pretty and smelled like Roses Soap and because she would help when you got stuck, instead of making a click with her tongue the way the third grade teacher did.

Now Mrs. Babcock reached in the pocket of her blazer and took out a gold coin. She held it up. "I want you to use this in today's writing," she said. She handed it to a boy at the nearest table. "Pass it around."

As the coin was handed around the room and inspected by each of the children, Mrs. Babcock talked to them about the value of gold and about how people could use money. "We don't know the exact value of this coin," she said, "so we're going to imagine that it's worth whatever you need it to be."

Brian Waters, whose teeth were always stained from chewing crayons, bit the coin ostentatiously. "You're supposed to check if it's real," he said.

"Is it real?" Mrs. Babcock asked. He nodded. "So pass it on."

He handed it to Nancy, who just as ostentatiously held it by the edge and wiped it on her skirt.

Mrs. Babcock continued with the assignment. "I want remind you of what we talked about yesterday, the things you can do with money. Can anyone tell me?"

Several voices replied: spend it, save it for later, invest it, blow it, give it to someone else, hoard it, throw it at problems.

"And do you remember the difference between spending and investing?"

Josie knew, but she did not raise her hand. She heard it often at home. Spending was what her mother wanted to do, but her father always said they couldn't because they had to invest in the shop. Flannery's Import Station ate up all the extra money it produced. Spending was foolish and wasteful, but fun. Investing was virtuous, but boring.

"So what we're going to do now is imagine that this gold coin is yours, and that you are free to use it however you want to: spend it now, save it for later, invest it, give it away, whatever you want."

Josie tried to fix her attention on Mrs. Babcock. But Jeffrey, the boy sitting at the near corner of the next table, had an unsanctioned project going on that drew her gaze as well. He had pounded a nail point-down through the edge of his shoe sole and was engaged in using it to dig out the cracks and grain in the old floorboards near his seat. When Mrs. Babcock was looking toward him, Jeffrey took part in the lesson like an exemplary student, but when she turned her back, his foot would seek a groove, and he would peer down to check his progress.

As Josie watched, the pressure of digging pushed the nail to where it fell out of his shoe. It rolled across the floor toward her. Her own foot reached out quickly and took possession, drawing the nail under her chair where she could pick it up. Jeffrey whispered furiously, "You give that back!" Without acknowledging him, she put the nail in her pocket.

"The question you have to answer for yourself is what's important enough to use your gold coin for," said Mrs. Babcock, shushing Jeffrey with a keep-it-down motion of her hand.

Josie fingered the nail, thin and sharp, with an almost nonexistent head. She started worrying. This was going to be one of those assignments that could really trip you up.

"It's a question for you to ask yourself over and over again all your life, but for now I want you to write about how you would use your gold coin today."

Josie drew a continuous-line star where the first word should go, then erased it. What if what you wanted was something that a gold coin couldn't buy?

Or could it? If she had a lot of money, would people still make fun of her? Maybe not to her face, but she knew how things got said behind people's backs. Would people like her enough not to torment her if she were rich? They would like her money, that's for sure. But that wasn't what she wanted.

What she really wanted was a place in the sun, like a blessing. A place where she fit, where good things happened to her, where people liked her and treated her well.

It had started out like a blessing when Corky first invited her to stop by at Freethinkers on the way home from school. He had singled her out to be especially nice to. That's probably what was happening with him and Nancy now.

Her feet had been light-hearted, going to the Freethinkers. Corky gave her the good parts in all their games, changed the princess from a blonde to a redhead so that she fit the part, let her be the leading lady. He made up singing games because he liked to hear her sing. He preferred her to all the others.

She drew another star and erased it. Thinking about what she wanted would be okay if there was any chance of getting it, but there wasn't, no matter how many gold coins she had.

And now he had Nancy. He would like Nancy even better, because she was pretty. And because she lived right there at his house, where they could play any time they wanted, not just for a little while after school. Thinking about Nancy being Corky's girl now made her feel like she might throw up.

She reached in her pocket for the nail. The point was not as sharp as a pin, but when she pressed it, she could feel it start a little hole in the web of skin where her thumb joined the rest of her hand. It hurt, but not a lot. Concentrating on the little hole the nail was making steadied her thoughts, and the slight pain steadied her stomach.

After a few moments with her focus removed from the classroom and centered on her own hand, she roused and noticed that all around her everyone was busy writing.

So what could she write? What good was a gold coin? It couldn't take back what she had said. It couldn't make Corky her friend again. If she hadn't told, there would still be a place there at Freethinkers where she fit. If she had kept her mouth shut, Corky would still like her, and she wouldn't be in so much trouble, and people wouldn't all hate her so much. No gold coin in the world could swallow up those words and make things right again.

Here she was in Language Arts, learning "communication skills," how to write and speak, but what she wanted was a Pac-Man that could gobble up what she had already said. She had learned the real truth about communication skills: that once spoken, words don't disappear. They hang in the air like sticky shreds in a horror movie. You can't move without getting them on you, and no matter how you scratch and claw and wash, you can't get them off.

If she hadn't told, all hell wouldn't have busted loose. Yes, there would still be the problem of how Corky acted. But maybe by now Corky would see her in a different light. Maybe he wouldn't keep mentioning how sexy she was. He had said he couldn't help noticing, but maybe he would be noticing something else by now.

Or maybe that was what he really liked about her, her sexiness that no one else seemed to see. Except her father, of course, only he didn't admire it. He wanted to uproot it completely so as to keep her out of trouble.

Her left hand was slippery now with blood, but she didn't stop digging with the nail.

What could she do with a gold coin that would get her out of the mess she was in and give her a better life?

Money would not help, but nobody said she had to use the coin as money.

In desperation to have something to turn in when the class was over, she put the nail away, balled up a tissue to stop the blood, and began to write:

"I would not spend my gold coin or invest it either. I would put it in a giant roller machine and roll it thinner and thinner and bigger around. Then I would make it into a big gold umbrella. I could use it a lot of ways. When it was dark and rainy and mean outside, I could hold it over me and I'd feel like the sun was shining. When people gave me dirty looks or attacked me or thought ugly thoughts about me, I could put it in front of me like a shield, and its brightness would change their minds. When good things came my way, I could use it for a net to catch them, like cherries from a cherry tree. When I needed to move fast, the wind could swoop under it and lift me out of trouble. When I wanted to slow down, I could hold it behind me for drag. I would never have to be alone unless I wanted, because who could resist an invitation to walk under my golden umbrella? And under it, I could say whatever I wanted and people would understand. There would always be a good place for me. I would carry it with me all the time, just like the turtle carries its shell."

When she finished writing, she read it over to herself, nodding. Then she thought of how the class would act if Mrs. Babcock read this out loud or put it up on the cork board. She could hear the laughter, imagine the endless umbrella jokes. No matter what she wrote, someone would make fun of it. Heat scalded her face. She folded her paper and hid it in her pocket with the nail and the blood. She put her head down and took deep breaths to keep from crying. When Mrs. Babcock came to her table and asked her what was wrong, she said she felt sick.

"Maybe you'd better go see the nurse," said the teacher. Josie nodded. "I'll get you a pass." Mrs. Babcock went to her desk, Josie following. "I hope you'll feel better soon," she said, giving the little girl's shoulder a squeeze.

But on her way to the hallway door, Josie heard Nancy whispering to Heather and Heather giggling in response. They were looking at her. She heard the words "morning sickness."

At this moment she would not have hesitated to destroy the whole class with a machine gun or a bomb, her tormentors because they were picking on her again, and the rest of them because they didn't come to her defense. For a moment she wondered why *she* should be the one to have to leave the classroom and go to the nurse instead of Nancy and Heather being sent to the principal. Everything was upside down. Why should *her* writing about the gold coin be blood-soaked in her pocket while theirs would be given stars and praise? It wasn't fair, and even though she was only nine years old, for a moment, at least, she *knew* it wasn't fair.

Then things went right side up again and she was back in the real world, where *she* was the guilty party: guilty of a sexy streak; guilty of telling secrets; guilty of getting Corky arrested; guilty of being a laughingstock; and now guilty of wanting to kill people.

Nausea and dizziness overcame her before she reached the nurse's office. She vomited on the shiny hallway floor.

GHOULISH

That afternoon, Friday, All Souls Day, Fred was too badly needed at Rochester's to leave at his usual time for the library. Sara seemed inexplicably fragile, with the look she sometimes had of being just on the edge of tears. Fred didn't inquire. Sara would tell him when she could – if she could. He had learned that Sara was not like his first wife in wanting to be questioned when something was wrong. Rather, she needed time to find words. He made himself useful at the cash register and in the stock room. When Christabel, the second-shift clerk, and Charlie, the evening pharmacist, arrived, he offered to do the grocery shopping on his way home.

Sara gave him the list. "Romaine," she said.

"Romaine," he echoed. It was all the same to him, that funny stuff Sara wanted instead of the plain old head lettuce you could slice and spread with a quarter inch of Miracle Whip. "What are you trying to do, eating that stuff, become a yuppie?"

Sara's eyes narrowed. "I've given up on 'young' and 'upward.' Just trying to fight 'old' and 'downward.'"

"Don't fight so hard. Moving downward isn't the worst thing that can happen."

"Romaine," she said. "Pay attention. It's my night."

He saluted. "Yes'm."

At dinner he found Sara's salad tasty, and he congratulated himself on butting out while she was making it.

"Go watch the news or something," Sara had said, stepping around Marigold, who was giving her resentful looks about the dearth of scraps. "And take your damn dog with you. I like an empty kitchen when I cook."

He had gone, but reluctantly. "Come on, Marigold. We know when we're not wanted." The kitchen was his favorite place. He felt forlorn when banished. He found Aunt Jenny on the living room couch watching the news. Marigold jumped heavily into the wing chair.

"Sit down here, Freddy. You can have the tail of my afghan." She was wrapped in zigzags of red-orange and maroon.

He let her fumble a corner over his knees, and he stayed there until he heard Mr. Rochester in the kitchen. He and Marigold could be kicked out, but Sara wouldn't banish her father. She didn't have the nerve.

He pushed off the afghan and started back to the kitchen, then paused, noticing the tone of their conversation. He couldn't hear the words, but he knew they were talking about the store. They were *always* talking about the store, Sara telling what had been happening, Mr. Rochester giving instructions. The voices were what struck him: Mr. Rochester's dry monotone growl, like one of those deserts where it never rains; Sara's liquid voice filling in what was missing, with her subdued flow of verbal tears.

This painful conversation was still going on when Sara called them for dinner, and it continued through most of the meal. Fred finally put an end to it by asking who wanted to go to church with him.

There was a silence. Then Sara asked cautiously, "What church are you talking about?"

"The Freethinkers. They're having an All Souls Day service."

Instantly Sara's face was transformed. A red splotch spread over her left cheek as though from a hard slap. "That's the most ghoulish thing I've ever heard of. Besides, he won't be preaching. You know they won't let him preach."

Fred sensed that the less said right now, the better.

"Count me out," said Mr. Rochester. "I've never been a churchgoer, and I'm not going to start now. Tonight's Friday and the talk shows are on."

Fred felt his eyes roll from left to right and down behind the mask with which he hid his pleasure. He hadn't figured the old man would be interested, but there was always a chance he'd surprise you.

Then Jenny spoke up eagerly. "I'd love to go, but I look a fright. Would there be time for me to bathe? But I guess not."

"You won't look a fright if you wash your face and get dressed." She was wearing a quilted robe with something spilled on it and little flat slippers.

But Jenny had already left the table. "My hair looks terrible. I'll have to wear my tam." She could be heard telling herself what to wear and why as she hurried up the back stairs.

Fred smothered a twinge of guilt that he'd forgotten how lonely Jenny was.

Mr. Rochester excused himself, leaving almost as much food as he'd started with. When he had gone, Fred slipped the plate down to Marigold, who was lying in wait under the table. The dog's legs churned as she hastened to her feet and began gulping the food with convulsive jerks of her head.

Sara made a tsk with her tongue. "She could at least chew it."

"Her teeth aren't so good." Fred carried two plates to the sink and began to scrape and rinse them. Sara followed with the salad bowls. The red stain had faded from her cheek, but she was angry, he could tell, with her back ramrod straight like her father's and her gaze directed anywhere but at him. He left the water running and the garbage disposal on while he went to the table for another load. She turned them off.

"Sara," he said, "I'm not just being ghoulish."

"You'd better shave if you're going to church."

"How can you tell if you won't look at me?"

She glanced his way, surprised. "I can't believe this. I just can't believe it. I've never known you to go to church before. If that's not ghoulish, what is it?"

"It's business. I'm going to write something about the reverend."

She stepped backward onto Marigold's paw. The dog stopped eating to yelp. "For God's sake, get out of the way!" Sara hissed. Marigold moved her rear end back under the table but did not forsake the plate. Then Sara opened the dishwasher and impaled two water glasses on the plastic prongs. "I can't stop you, can I?"

Fred came up behind her and put his arms around her. He nuzzled her hair aside and kissed her neck. "I'm already committed. Mrs. Claire's counting on me."

Sara's still stood unnaturally straight. "I don't want to hear about it. Just go, will you?"

He backed away. Sometimes there was nothing he could do. He went quietly around the corner into the little half-bath to shave. With the door closed, he caught himself exhaling with relief. Usually a home-body, he was glad tonight to be going out. Sometimes it came to that.

THE CONTINUUM OF SOULS

Fred had finished shaving and was starting upstairs to change clothes just as Jenny started down. He made way and watched her progress down the stairs. She wore a gray coat and a scarf that looked quite nice, but on her head was the tam, knitted from a pastel rainbow of yarn. Large and loose, it had a heavy pompom on top that made it hang to one side, and it covered her hair, except for a frizzle over one eye.

"Ready to go," he said, trying not to seem put off by her appearance. "I'll be down in a minute." Good God, he thought, if I don't get her out of here more often, she's not going to be *able* to go out. He changed from his baggy house pants into a decent pair of slacks and met Jenny in the living room.

The Meetinghouse was only two streets over and a mile down. Fred drove part of the way on Adams Street, his car lurching in the grooves where trolley tracks used to be. This was a neighborhood of cold-looking houses, their roofs peaked and pinched, their shoulders huddled side by side, some of them already wearing plastic wraps over their windows and protective tents over their foundation plantings.

Jenny shivered. "Winter's on its way. Don't those places look bleak?"

Fred had often noticed the same thing about this particular row of houses. "It's because there's not one porch on the whole block. A house with a porch looks forward to summer. These houses think about snow."

The corner of 53rd and Plainfield Blvd. was crowded, the parking lot almost full, significant for a Friday night service that certainly didn't sound very important to Fred: a memorial service for All Souls Day. He assumed that "all souls" were miscellaneous dead people, not anyone's specific parent or spouse. Surely this flock didn't care any more for their miscellaneous dead than other folks did, he thought. But the arrest of their minister would have brought the whole congregation out.

"You know anything about All Souls Day?"

"Not really," said Jenny, "except that I think the souls are dead ones, not live ones. Why? Is today All Souls Day?"

"Yes, and we're going to an All Souls Day service."

"Think of that! Well, I suppose that's as good a reason to have church as any other."

"That's not the reason we're going. I'm maybe gonna write something about the reverend here and maybe his congregation."

"Oh." Jenny seemed unaware of the scandal, and Fred did not fill her in. If she had missed it in the paper, so much the better.

Fred parked on the street rather than pulling into the crowded lot. He crooked his arm for Jenny. She took small steps.

Although it was dark and not all of the building was visible even with the outdoor lights on, Fred knew what it looked like, for he often went past it on his way to the warehouse supermarket farther out on Plainfield. It had been built about ten years ago in the mid-seventies. At the time, the *Clarion* had quoted someone who called it the "Free-thinkers' Barn" because of its exterior of unpainted, fast-graying boards. Now it seemed to have inhabited the corner forever, a weathered church in a weathered neighborhood.

There had been coverage of the building's dedication ceremony and an interview with Corcoran Pearlman, which yielded the fact that the Freethinkers' Meetinghouse was not a church. "Ninety-five percent of the members voted not to call it a church," said Pearlman, "so it's not a church. We are not a part of any denomination. We believe in the democratic process."

And what else did the, ah, Meeting believe in? "We believe in the right – even the duty – of a person to ascertain his own beliefs and live by them the best he can. We Meet to help one another."

Pressed to explain, Pearlman told the reporter that the group had come together from various churches during the previous ten years, after discovering that their own denominations were not taking a strong moral stand on the social issues confronting the nation.

The group espoused many of the tenets of the Human Potential Movement as well, said Pearlman. "We're eclectic."

What about God? "Well," answered Pearlman, "we take the approach of the old Vermont farmer who, when a stranger remarked about what wonderful farm land God had blessed him with, said, 'Feller, you ought to have seen it when God had it to himself'."

Inside the building, the din of people talking hit Fred. There were people everywhere: in corners, by the coat racks, at the water fountain, out in the open. People in groups of two or three or more, all of them talking, everybody talking. Talking all at once, it seemed to Fred, and each person louder than the other in order to be heard. It sounded more like a cocktail party than a memorial for the dead.

He took Jenny's coat and tried to get the tam as well, but she clung to it. "My hair's a fright," she whispered. "I couldn't go into church like that." But no one paid any attention to them. He added their coats to the row of hooks. They proceeded unobtrusively past conversations, past a large fieldstone fireplace, and through a glass door into the quiet, empty sanctuary, in which there was another fireplace back-to-back with the one in the entrance room. The sudden absence of voices was almost as startling as the noise had been.

"Where would you like to sit?"

Jenny surveyed the room. "You choose."

He chose seats near the back but in the center of the row. There were no pews, no fixed seats at all, but rather stackable padded chairs set neatly in semi-circular rows divided into thirds by two aisles.

"More comfortable than they look." Jenny closed her eyes. Fred could see that she'd daubed on a little blue eye shadow. "I'm not going to sleep. You won't have to be ashamed of me."

Fred was helpless against a fierce wave of love that fought his criticism of the way she looked. She had helped his mother bring him up, had made French toast and taught him his times tables when he couldn't learn them at school. She had told him that no matter how big the dog in his nightmare was, he could call a bigger dog to protect him.

Music came from speakers near the carved wooden pulpit, which stood on a raised platform at the front of the sanctuary. Behind the pulpit was a semi-circle of glass in an irregular pattern of beveled panes that looked out onto spotlighted grounds spectacular even this late in the year.

From inside, it was not possible to tell that the church was within a city. A grove of tall pines formed a backdrop to the landscape, looking as dense as a forest that might have gone on for miles. In the foreground were holly trees and birches whose white bark in the light of the spotlights contrasted with the dark boughs of several small evergreens.

Fred was alert. He wanted to find out anything he could about the reverend's stomping grounds, and what he noticed was an atmosphere of beauty that seemed in keeping with a church, yet was unlike any church he had ever seen. The walls and ceiling were painted in a pale sand color with a grainy texture. The soft lights were recessed, and the interior of the room was subdued, drawing attention to the outdoor scene through those shard-shaped glass panes. As they waited, organ music began to sound from speakers mounted on the wall. Recorded music, most likely, since there was no organ in evidence.

They had been seated for only a few moments when Fred heard the doors open behind him, and the uproar from the entrance hall began to pour into the sanctuary. Jenny gave a start, opened her eyes and sat up straight.

As people came forward in the room, their voices dropped, but they did not stop talking until they were seated, and even then a few people continued to whisper.

Finally the music came to an end. The doors at the rear of the room closed when Corcoran Pearlman appeared. He walked to the pulpit down the left aisle while everyone watched him pass. He wore a too-short black gown over pants that were also too short over one navy and one black sock. His straw-like hair was mussed and his face blue with hours of beard, but he walked with a dignified step that carelessness of grooming did not affect. He climbed the platform and stood behind the pulpit facing his audience without speaking for a moment so long that Fred wondered if he might be in some kind of trance.

"I have an announcement to make," he said. The voice was deep and cultured, as Fred remembered it. "I have been instructed by the Board to advise you that on Sunday morning, instead of the service, there will be a meeting of the congregation. You are all urged to attend." After he had made the announcement, he stopped speaking. His gaze seemed to search out each person there.

"We have come here tonight to put our burdens down for a time, while we remember the burdens of the past and those persons who bore them."

Fred wondered if the people in the sanctuary would be able to concentrate on past burdens with a present scandal on everyone's mind. But the reverend's demeanor did not admit scandal.

"It is easy to forget the dead. They cannot tug at our sleeve or send us a card that says, 'Thinking of you.' They cannot visit our space and leave flowers or a wreath. Yet even to make this declaration implies that we believe the dead want us to remember them. But who knows? Many of us in this room – perhaps most – do not believe the dead want anything, know anything, even exist in any way other than in the works and memories they have left behind. So we are not here to do any favors, wanted or unwanted, for those who have gone before us. Rather, we are here to remind ourselves that we too struggle and die, just as they did. This is a memorial service for all souls, especially our own."

"I guess I was wrong," whispered Jenny.

"And yet we have specific people to remember tonight. Four years ago a car carrying five members of this congregation home from a Halloween party was struck broadside by a truck. Everyone in the car was killed. We lost in a moment's explosion of metal five people who had given their talents to this Meeting since its inception. We cannot forget this event or those persons.

"Let us take time now in the spirit of meditation to recall our friends who were so vividly with us only a few short years ago." He read their names slowly, like a roll call to which no one answered, "Here."

Heads bowed, and Fred took the opportunity to glance cautiously around. Jenny's head was down, her eyes closed tight, her pompom hanging.

Fred did not think of himself as religious, had never joined a church, although his mother had taken him to Sunday School at the neighborhood church wherever they lived. Because they had lived several places, Fred had learned how to act in a number of different churches, but he had never been in one like this before.

The only time in his life he had even known anyone who called himself a freethinker was back in college when his roommate took

"Introduction to Philosophy" and suddenly burst from his Methodist background into full-blown atheism. "God didn't create Man," his friend insisted. "Man created God."

Fred had wondered, "So what?" How could anybody know whether the egg preceded the chicken or not? Maybe it alternated, with God creating man for a while, then hibernating while mankind took on the job of creating God. What difference did it make, anyway? God was there, whichever way it went. Fred knew of God's presence, no matter who had done the creating. A situation would come up and he would feel his edges stretched; he would have to make some new accommodation for the good of his soul. It was God yanking on his corners again, he knew it, and he was in for a hard time.

But this didn't have anything to do with church. With being nice to people and smiling false smiles. With repeating the Apostles' Creed and the Lord's Prayer and sometimes even the Pledge of Allegiance, depending on how separate the church wanted to be from the state. With listening to the wheezing of an out-of-tune organ played by someone who had taken a few accordion lessons.

Now he was surprised to hear the Freethinker, Corcoran Pearlman, whom he supposed to be an atheist, say, in his lowered meditative voice:

"May God work His miracles within us and guide us back to the path of goodness and peace as long as we live, amen."

Fred could see the reaction that rippled through the congregation as heads raised and people shifted their weight and looked at each other. A delicate-looking lady in long gloves in the row in front of him muttered "Bullroar!" amusing Fred and making his nostrils quiver as he sensed discord even beyond the present scandal.

Jenny poked him with her elbow. "Did you hear that?"

"I sure did."

Then music came from the speakers, hymnals opened and people sang a tune Fred remembered from childhood. The words, however, were unfamiliar. At the end of the hymn, the reverend asked that it be sung again, "this time using the traditional words on the opposite page." Fred hadn't sung the modern version, and he didn't sing the old one either. Neither did many of the other people near him, except Jenny, who seemed to be enjoying herself greatly.

"Those of our members who died are missed, as we shall all be missed, but the work of our Meeting and the world goes on. Nothing fills their places. Nothing ever fills the places occupied by those who have lived before us, because places exist in time, and their time has passed. All we can do is fill our own places in our own time with deeds that will make us feel at the hour of our death – if indeed we are given the strength then to reflect on the past – that we have used well and not wasted our place in our time.

This is what I have to say to you tonight. That our lives rest upon the lives of those who came before us. That our existence would not have been possible without theirs, nor will the existence of those to come after us be possible without ours. We are part of a continuum of persons, a continuum that came about so long ago that we can only speculate about how it happened."

Nothing bored Fred as quickly as speculation about the origin of the continuum. He let his thoughts rest again on speculation about the man in the pulpit. The molester of two children, both members of his congregation. Fred wondered if they were here now. He imagined them sitting, one on each side of the room, while the minister's eyes focused on the fireplace at the back.

Glancing again at Corky Pearlman, Fred noticed that his eyes were not focused on either the fireplace or the congregation but rather to be seeing something that hung in the air above the rows of people. Fred looked up. Nothing was there but the grainy sand of the ceiling.

"The souls of the dead are imprisoned," said Corky, "waiting for us to find and free them."

It was as though he had begun to speak from a different text, from some other sermon. In fact it was almost as though some other minister were speaking. Rather than the hollow, solemn face Fred was growing used to, he was now seeing a face filled out with delight, a face that had evidently forgotten his present status as the scum of the earth.

"The souls of the dead are imprisoned in trees, in the weeds of the countryside, in the plainest of household objects. You will find them when you least expect it. You will fix upon some everyday object from the past and will find in it the soul of someone from long ago."

The reverend's voice was no longer the level voice of good sense. Instead it sounded like some mischievous prophet passing along a message from a mischievous deity.

"Take up that object, listen to it speak, and it will open itself to you. A lost treasure will be restored to you, a parent, a grandparent, a friend. By caring for the house of their prison, you can release their soul."

And with that the reverend's face changed again into solemnity and he continued speaking in the same style as his earlier remarks.

"How can we best remember our dead? By envisioning those yet unborn who depend on us. By remembering that even as our iniquities shall be visited upon the third and fourth generations, so shall our goodness trickle down unto the thousandth. By giving thought this day and every day to how our present action appears in relation to what has brought us here and what is to follow us.

We must remember our dead, their selfishness and wrong-doing as well as their generosity and goodness. Only by holding the balanced consciousness of the lives and deeds that prepared the way for us can we judge the goodness of our present actions.

Let us pray for the sense of our place in the stream of souls connected to this physical world we call our earth." The room became very still.

Fred had not noticed whatever had led into the reverend's digression, but the transition back to his main sermon was abrupt. Was this the way he always preached?

People were standing up now. The service was over. Music to exit by was coming from the speakers. The din of talk was coming from both aisles.

Fred looked around for the delicate little person who had muttered "Bullroar!" She might have something interesting to offer.

Just outside the sanctuary he left Jenny to her own devices and found the woman warming herself at the fireplace. He nodded to her and said, "Interesting sermon. Does he always preach like that?"

She stared at him as though he were speaking in a foreign language. Then she answered, "Pretty much. He's been on that tack for quite a while now." She moved to make room at the fire. "This can't be your first time here?"

"Yes it is. That bit toward the end where he started talking about souls hidden in trees?"

"Oh that. You never know when he's going to go off like that. His wife calls those episodes little nuggets of inspiration, but a lot of us here call them little nuggets of something else. This one probably harks back to the time he heard his mother's voice coming from the rolling pin."

Fred didn't know how to take this woman. She sounded completely matter-of-fact, as though she were telling the truth, but he couldn't imagine anyone telling a newcomer such a story. He decided she must be putting him on.

"Of course," he answered. "And was delighted to hear from her again after all these years."

"You got it." She was moving away from the fire now toward the coat rack, and Fred moved with her. "Come back again," she said. "This isn't a bad place. It's really a great place, in fact. It's just that in being attractive to offbeat characters with minds of their own we're also attractive to the truly weird, and right now the truly weird happens to be in the pulpit. But come back. We're working on the problem."

"What's this about no service on Sunday?" asked Fred. "I planned to come back on Sunday. I haven't heard much from the truly weird in my life. It's fascinating."

Instead of stopping at the coat rack, she went on and stood at the door of the women's rest room. "You probably heard the last sermon this one's going to preach, at least in this building," she answered. "In addition to being weird, which we tolerate, he's perverted, which we don't. At least where our children are concerned we don't." She eyed Fred. "Are you from the paper?"

"Certainly not," he answered, acting offended even while wishing he had the snug security of a reporter's job. "Why?"

"This is a strange moment to show up here. We're in turmoil. Our minister's been arrested. We can't possibly keep him here any longer. But do come back. There'll be some kind of service a week from Sunday, I'm sure."

Fred thanked her politely without telling her that he planned to be in attendance this Sunday too, even if it meant crashing a party.

Fred found Jenny socializing with a woman about her own age. "Here's my nephew now," she said. "My only sister's only son. He's very good to me." She grabbed his arm and gave it a squeeze.

"You must come back," they were told. "Don't mind the trouble. All churches have trouble, and I must say this is getting more and more like a church every day."

Corky Pearlman was at the outside door standing in the cold, his black gown fluttering in the breeze. He did not look any more like one of the truly weird than he looked like the scum of the earth.

"I'm Fred Bekin. The one who talked to you on the phone. About getting your story."

"Thank you for coming." Corky shook Fred's hand soberly.

Jenny took the minister's hands and patted them. "My, what fine words," she said. "I haven't heard such an inspiring sermon in years."

Corky brightened. "I'm glad it spoke to you."

Then an old man with a walker approached. "Come back Sunday," said Corky quickly. "That'll fill you in on things."

"Yes sir!" said Fred, elated. An invitation helped.

From the street corner, he noticed that most of the people were streaming out a different exit. Avoiding the reverend, he thought. Not wanting to touch a sullied hand. Immediately he liked the Freethinkers less than he had a few moments earlier.

In the car Jenny bubbled. "What a treat," she said. "If you decide to go back, let me know. That woman I was talking to, that Frances whatever her name is, we hit it off just fine. She used to teach in New York State too. I thought I recognized the accent, and sure enough." And so they continued all the way home.

NEW YORK, NEW YORK

Although Jenny went up to her room with the fullest intention of tucking herself into bed, once there with the door closed and her purse put away, she found herself wide awake. She stood in the middle of the braided rug and thought about the intellectual poverty of her present life.

What a pleasure it had been, Jenny thought, going to church. Listening to a preacher talk about contributing to the continuum of souls.

It pleased her to think of it so, as a continuum, instead of each individual soul snapping on like a light bulb for a while and then burning out bang! with nothing to show for it. That was what was wrong with the American spirit of individualism, she thought. No sense of the third and fourth generations, let alone the thousandth.

And she had liked what the preacher said about the souls of the dead inhabiting the familiar places where they had lived. That was so, she knew it! No one who had ever been born and lived a life was truly dead, Jenny believed, and wouldn't be until the earth crashed into the sun or otherwise became unfit for life. That thousandth generation wasn't a cut off point; it was a figure of speech meaning "so long as the generations go on." There was a great difference between being unconscious, as one surely was when dead – when one's molecules were being redistributed – and being truly dead at the end of the earth's life.

Jenny took off her coat and started to hang it in the closet, then remembered that a coat brushed after wearing is ready to wear again. She found the celluloid-handled brush that had been her mother's in the top drawer of her high carved dresser. She laid out the coat on the bed and brushed it vigorously.

Through the faded, cornflower-papered wall she could hear the television in Mr. Rochester's room next door much more plainly than she liked. Those voices had to be television because no real voice got that fired up over nothing. How the man could sit there staring at nonsense hour after hour, day after day, upstairs and downstairs in both bedroom and den, she couldn't understand. When he had first moved in, she had tried to be gracious, to make him feel welcome, even though she too was a newcomer to the house. She had offered to converse, to loan him books, to prepare his lunch. But he seemed to have only three interests: television, the store, and his opinions, which he was ready to dispense like pills and powders, no prescription needed. He chewed on his grudges for nourishment instead of food, and in time she began to see him as a long, narrow grudge, like a bitter Tootsie Roll. You become what you eat, she thought. Which is why I like to eat a variety. If you eat a variety, no one thing will show on you. Thank God for Freddy, a Cavendish, in this house of Rochesters, she thought, then remembered that her sister had been married long enough before the man walked out to give Fred the name Bekin. Oh well, she thought, he's really a Cavendish. He knows what good food is.

The tam went in the next-to-top drawer, which held her woolens and some moth crystals, a new kind that didn't stink. Her hair was a fright; she knew it. I must get to the beauty shop, she thought. But it was hard to get around here, the house several blocks from anywhere, and not having a car any longer. She didn't like to put Fred out by constantly asking to be driven places. That was a sure way to wear out her welcome.

Jenny finished undressing and put on her robe. A glass of milk would be nice. Calm her down. She switched on the nightlight and went down the front stairs, which were wider and safer than the back ones.

She was midway through the dark dining room when the telephone rang in the hall alcove behind her. She jumped, startled. Footsteps sounded from the kitchen down the hall. Fred answered the phone.

Jenny waited. She did not want to go into the kitchen with Sara. Being alone with Sara affected her mind in a way that she didn't understand. It became hard to speak, to give Sara coherent answers, her words tumbled over themselves, and she sounded to herself like a very silly woman. So she sat down in a high-backed chair against the dining room wall to wait.

It was none of Jenny's business, of course, but stuck there, she couldn't help but hear.

"Not bad," said Fred. "How about you?"

"Yeah, well," he said, "I'm still writing on my own. I hafta say I got more respect now."

Then he said, "I finished one today. Very timely. How to structure your day when you're outta work. There oughta be a market."

The schoolteacher in Jenny cringed. Fred never sounded more Fred-like than he did when talking to New York. She knew he was talking to New York, someone he'd met at Powkin. This was how the conversations went, talk about how Fred was doing. Maybe New York was trying to help him get work, she thought.

"No," he said. "I don't have. Not at present."

What didn't he have? A job. But he was writing. She was proud of him, a boy who had trouble in school now smart enough to be a writer.

"Well one thing," said Fred. "But it's only in the beginning stages. I don't know if it's going to work into anything. It's about a preacher, see, and he's accused of molesting two little girls in his congregation."

Jenny listened more closely.

"You think so?"

"Wait a minute, let me copy down the names. You say *Jet*, and *Ladies Home Journal,* and *Time.* Hold on, you're going too fast, I can't keep up. *Newsweek,* and *Peoples Weekly,* and *U. S. News,* and *Christian Today,* and *Glamour.* Good heavens, it's Watergate all over again."

"Yes, I got a real live reverend's been accused. I'd say I got a real live reverend child molester, but I'm not absolutely sure whether he's guilty, I hafta find out more."

"Well, I'm pleased to hear you say that. Very pleased. I'll work on it and let you know something maybe next week."

Jenny continued to sit in the dark dining room after Fred had hung up, not wanting to admit that she'd been there all along. She wished that she could un-hear what she'd heard. It wasn't true, of course. You could tell by looking at that minister and listening to him that he wasn't capable of nasty business like that.

But the accusation meant trouble anyway, she knew. She'd been reading all those articles in *Newsweek* about how there was an epidemic.

An epidemic makes a perfect climate for people who want to do their mischief under cover. She'd seen it happen too many times. But why on earth would anyone want to do such a terrible thing to such a fine man?

Sara's voice rose in the kitchen. Jenny didn't like that either. Sara was not very bright about what a good husband she had. "It's that pervert, isn't it?" said Sara. "We're going to be eating and sleeping child molestation from now on, aren't we? Just the subject I'm most interested in. Guaranteed to enhance our style of living."

"Sara, what possible difference can it make to you what I'm working on, whether it's time structuring or child molesting? I'm always gonna be working on something. How can it matter what it is?"

"It matters because you get too involved. When you were trying to write that book about baseball, we lived and breathed baseball, you know we did."

"I won't talk about it," he said. "You won't hafta know."

"Not talking doesn't mean not knowing. You'll be following that pervert around hanging on his every word. You'll be singing in the choir, taking communion every Sunday."

"Not at Pearlman's church I won't."

"See, you're already involved! Well, I can tell you one thing. You'd better never bring him here."

Chair legs scraped on the kitchen floor. Sara blew her nose. Jenny had given up on her glass of milk. Now she was just waiting for a chance to get back upstairs without being noticed.

"I'm sorry, Sara. I wish you didn't find my work so offensive. You didn't hate it so bad that I was a writer before."

"You weren't a writer. You did user manuals for Powkin. There's a world of difference, in case you didn't know it."

"You think I'm happy I lost my job?"

"Quit trying to tell me there aren't jobs. I know better. With all the books being published, there have to be editor jobs."

"Not for me there aren't. I may never get another job, Sara. You talk about reality; well that's one of the hard facts of life. The word nowadays is 'dynamic.' 'Aggressive.' 'Go-getter.' All of these words translate into 'young.' And I'm not young."

"They can't know how old you are. It's against the law to ask your age on an employment application."

"They don't have to ask age, Sara. Use your head. You think a guy thirty's gonna have a military record from Korea? That's why I'm working so hard to make the writing pay off. It may be the only thing I'll be able to do for the next however many years I got."

That was one thing Jenny had never had to face: losing her job. Even during the Depression they had kept on sending children to school.

Suddenly there was a new dimension to the activity in the kitchen. Jenny heard the back stairs creak. In a moment Mr. Rochester's growling monotone began. Isn't that just like him, she thought, to walk right into a room and start talking without any thought that he's interrupting?

"I need a haircut, Sara, and I wonder if you could run me over to the barber's tomorrow morning? He opens at eight on Saturday, and if we were the first ones there, you could still get to the store by nine."

Jenny bristled with dislike. Tell him no, Sara, she thought. Tell him he doesn't need a barber to cut a quarter of an inch off six hairs. Tell him to braid it. Her anger was all the hotter for having done without the beauty shop so long herself.

"Wait till afternoon and I can take you," said Fred.

"I'd prefer morning. There's a crowd in there later in the day. Sometimes you have to wait for an hour or more."

"All right." Sara's voice was lackluster. "Just be ready. You know what happens when you're late opening the store."

"No, I don't know," came the cold-voiced answer. "I was never late opening the store."

There was a silence in the kitchen. Jenny screwed up her face in the dark of the dining room and stuck out her tongue.

Then Mr. Rochester spoke again. "Could you give me a hand up the stairs? I'm feeling a little shaky tonight."

Then do what I do when I'm shaky, thought Jenny furiously. Sit down and scoot up the steps.

There was a general scuffling around in the kitchen and the light went out. "We'll go around the front way," said Fred. "The steps are wider."

Jenny sucked in her breath and made herself small on the high-backed chair, but they went through the hall and did not pass beside her.

NOT SO HOT LOVERS

Fred helped his father-in-law gently up the stairs. He had heard the unkind crack at Sara, of course, but he was too intent on his phone call to be much bothered by it.

It was Sara's help that the old man had been asking for, not his. Fred knew that. But Sara would not touch him. Any help he got had to come from Fred. After having had him here in the house for the last year, the helping had become automatic.

"I'll take him in," Sara had told Fred bleakly when the old man's doctor informed her that the trembling would get worse instead of better and that further work as a pharmacist was out of the question. "I'll provide a home for him. But I can't touch him. Not if it were to save his life. I don't think I've ever touched him. I just can't do it."

Fred, of course, could help. Much as he disliked Mr. Rochester, he could help with buttons; he could tie a tie for him. Sara put up with Aunt Jenny; he could reciprocate.

So he steadied the old man up the wide front steps. Mr. Rochester did not lean, only locked arms, but through the straightness of his posture and the tremor in his arm Fred could feel his dismay at his own helplessness. As soon as they reached the top, he let go.

"Did you talk to Dorothy today?" Fred asked as he followed him into the bedroom to help unfasten his buttons, not because he was interested in Dorothy, but to keep him from talking any more about the store.

"Today was her bridge day," he said. "She was in a hurry." He stretched up his chin for Fred to take off his tie. "Here, let me put that away." Fred gave him the tie and waited. "She did tell me that Calvin and his family are coming for Thanksgiving."

"She'll be happy to see them, won't she?" Fred unbuttoned first the sweater, then the shirt, and then unfastened his belt buckle, hurrying to get it all done before the old man could insist on taking off and putting away each piece in turn. "There," he said.

"I'm not so sure," said Mr. Rochester. "Dorothy likes to have her own way, always did. With the children around it interrupts her schedule."

The woman he was talking about was the widow of the owner of the hardware store near the drugstore, someone Mr. Rochester had known for years and now talked with on the phone every day. Fred did not like the woman, who was extremely vain, and boring, as coquettes usually are, yet he found himself inquiring about her health, her activities, her family as though he had some vital concern – as, actually, he had: to give Sara's father a topic of conversation other than the store.

"So is Dorothy gonna cook a turkey?" he asked as he knelt to untie the old man's shoes.

"Not if she can help it," he answered. "That's enough. I can manage the rest." He stepped back from Fred.

Fred went to the bed and pulled off the spread. "Sure there's nothing else you need?"

"Thank you, no, not tonight."

Fred closed the old man's door behind him and went to the bathroom to shower.

He was happy, partly because he was Fred and found himself happy more often than not, and partly because he had something to be happy about, for a change. It was possible that this story would sell, and if it sold, he'd have a start. That was all anybody needed, a start.

He let the water pour on his head and sluice down his body. It made him feel like an aquatic animal, and he suddenly longed for a swim. His Powkin membership in the Athletic Club had ended with his job, and he wanted to swim too rarely to pay the fee himself. He stayed in the shower a long time. When he stepped out, the room was full of steam and the mirror was clouded over. He let his belly go slack, one of life's little luxuries that was hard to enjoy in front of a working mirror.

Fred was used to the way he looked by now, and although he tried not to be a slob around Sara, he tended usually to accept the body he had: his sleek head with stubbly hair that he kept clipped very short, almost shaved, his thick shoulders and spacious torso that gently tapered out at the middle. Wide, sensible feet under muscular legs.

He had never been one to enjoy exercise, and when he'd tried to write a fitness book, he had decided that if it ever got published, he'd have to get a model for the cover picture. Someone who supposedly got his build from reading the book rather than from good genes and pumping iron. But the book was never published, never even finished. It had threatened to force him into locker rooms to do his interviews, and he stayed away from locker rooms as much as possible, out of loyalty to his body.

It had always been a comfortable body to slouch around in, if not handsome to gaze upon, with very few aches and pains, and it held up well under the stress of sitting. It was, in fact, just the kind of body Fred needed, and he knew it. Thus he didn't pay much attention to Sara's sporadic attempts to shape it up with funny food and talk about jogging.

He found Sara in bed, curled up tightly. He sat on the edge to touch her rounded back. Through the blanket her vertebrae were soft little knobs; even so, he could feel the tension in her muscles.

"Want a nice backrub?" he asked. "You feel all in knots." Maybe they wouldn't have to fight any more tonight.

"I *am* all in knots." Her voice, partly absorbed in the pillow, accepted the offer. "I think I need new glasses. I was working on the books today and caught myself hunching over."

He pushed the covers down. Let her go on thinking it's eyestrain, he thought. She couldn't do anything about the real cause anyway. Patricide wasn't her style. "Maybe we could find a bookkeeper." He ran his hand lightly over her back, marking off the territory to rub. "Somebody part time who keeps books for a lotta little companies. You shouldn't have to worry about it."

She rolled over and reached for his pillow to stuff under her middle to make her back just so for rubbing. "Daddy would never accept that. He was able to keep his own books."

"He wouldn't have to know."

"He'd know. How could I explain the figures for the bookkeeper's fee? No, it's easier to do it myself."

He straddled her legs and knelt, tugged at her nightgown until she raised herself, then pulled it over her head and tossed it aside. "It's always easier to do things yourself," he said. "But you sure get tired."

Her head on the pillow nodded. Fred could not see her face for the mass of warm hair on the beige pillowcase. He gathered it up and laid it to the side, the better to reach her shoulders. "Pretty," he said.

He massaged her shoulders. "I been thinking about your body." With his thumbs he excavated her vertebrae, working down from the neck and massaging her flesh as he went along. When he reached her tailbone, instead of stopping, he continued rubbing down her long slender legs, first one, then the other. After massaging her feet, the heels, the arches, each toe, he started back up, then stopped for a moment.

"More," she said. "That was like just one potato chip."

He continued to work his way upward. Again at her head, his fingers separated her hair as he worked on her scalp. Then he moved down again and allowed his cock to nudge her buttocks with growing interest.

"Turn over," he said. "Get your belly rubbed." He got out of her way while she moved, then straddled her thighs and began to massage the front of her body, gathering up what fat he could find on her abdomen and squeezing it gently, adding kisses to nipples and bellybutton, and finally ending by massaging her face, where his thumbs sought out and cured small patches of tension.

When he finished, she gave a deep, contented sigh. "That was the best ever."

He kissed her mouth, wondering if either of them was really in the mood for sex. Sometimes a body rub turned her on, sometimes not. Then he realized that unless she gave him some pretty strong sign of interest, he wouldn't pursue it.

She opened her eyes and read his mind. "Do you think we'll ever be lovers again?"

"We're still lovers," he said. "Just not very hot ones."

"Maybe we ought to watch sexy movies."

"Why? When we wanna screw, we screw. When we don't wanna, we don't. It seems to me we got it made."

"We're supposed to want to more than we do."

"Don't tell me 'supposed to want.' I already want what I want. I don't need to add any 'supposed-to-wants'."

"What do you want?"

"Work, for starters," he answered.

"We're okay," she said. "We're not really hurting for money."

"*We* may not be, but I am. I don't like living off my wife and my wife's father and my aunt's pension. And don't tell me I'm drawing a pension myself. I don't like to think about that."

"Were you serious about maybe never having a job again?"

"You bet I was. Very serious. I been doing everything in my power to get a job and nothing's happening. Over two hundred résumés and not a nibble. I know you think I'm loafing, but I'm not."

"I don't really think you're loafing. It's just hard to reconcile all the trouble you're having with the upturn in the economy and all the jobs out there."

"Maybe there really are jobs out there," he said. "Maybe the politicians aren't lying. But there are lots of bright young bushy-tails out there too. I see the people my age, the older people, every day. Some of them come in the library to look through the Help Wanted, some of them have given up and come to pass the time away, and some of them sit there with a book upside down just to keep warm. I resent the gratuitous kick," he said. "When a guy's out of work because there aren't enough jobs to go around, he doesn't deserve a kick and an insult about being a bum."

"What do you think ought to be done?" She had turned and was propped on her elbow.

He smiled. "I think I oughta rub your back more often," he said. "Then you'll ask me how to run the country."

She swiped out at him.

He ducked. "I don't have an answer," he went on. "As long as people need to keep making more and more money so they'll know how great they are, we'll have one guy making a killing instead of two guys making a living."

"But when the one guy gets rich, doesn't he put his money into something that gives three guys a chance to make a living?"

"That's what they say happens," he answered. "But if that were true, we wouldn't be in the mess we're in. I think too many of the guys who get rich are putting their money into deals that have nothing to do with the public good."

Sara had started smiling at him as he talked, and now she said, "Doesn't it seem strange to be lying on the bed naked talking about economics?"

"Not a damn bit," he answered. "Not the way things are." He reached over and cupped his hand under her breast. "Not with the problems we got." He rolled off the bed and went to the closet for his pajamas.

LOVELY YOU

Portville's LOVELY YOU franchise had a comprehensive program that included not only liposuction and contouring but also food management classes serving two clienteles: women not yet ready for the final solution to the fat problem, and post-surgery Lovelies who wanted to keep the solution final.

Josie and her mother were among the former, but only because Duncan wouldn't hear of liposuction. Eve had been longing for it, both for herself and for Josie. "It makes sense, doesn't it, to take care of things once and for all?" But Dunk didn't like it that Eve took Josie to LOVELY YOU at all, let alone thought about liposuction for her. "She's only nine years old!" he yelled. "Can't you leave her alone?"

"A girl needs to feel good about herself," Evie maintained. "A fat girl *never* feels good about herself."

"Then run her around the block a few times," said Dunk. "That'll get the lard off her."

Josie tried unsuccessfully to block her ears to this talk, which was one more skirmish in the ideological war her parents had been fighting for control of her body and her upbringing, a war that had heated up in previous weeks.

Because of Dunk's emphatic *no!*, Eve had to trim her hopes for liposuction. Instead, she took Josie to food management classes, which met on Saturday mornings. Today, as usual, Eve stopped for a moment with Josie in Young Lovelies.

"Were you a good girl this week?" Betty, the instructor, wore a wide red belt that cinched her tiny waist and a pair of enameled slave bracelets on her upper arms over the puffed sleeves of her blouse. She took Josie's card from the box and beckoned her to the scale. "Hop on, and let's see how well you did." Her fingers sliding the weights were like delicate bird claws with diamonds. "Oooh, not so good. Up three ounces. Well, you'll do better next week, I know you will. We're here to help you. We want you to feel good about yourself."

Eve gave a huff of exasperation. "If you're going to cheat, you'll have to stop coming here, and then where will you be?"

Josie looked at the floor. "I won't cheat."

"That's a good girl," said Betty. "Now go sit down and we'll get to the lesson shortly."

Josie passed several tables where other girls were gathered and sat alone. She watched her mother leave the Young Lovelies room to go to her own adult class.

Her mother was right, of course. Where would she be, indeed, without the help to get rid of the fat? She hated coming here, but it was her only hope. Being fat was the worst thing that could happen to you, she thought. It made everybody hate you, and it made you hate yourself. It put you out of the running for the good things in life. It had to be fought tooth and nail with every bit of strength. You couldn't control everything that happened to you, but if you really tried, you could control being fat. That's what LOVELY YOU was all about.

She hadn't always been fat. Only last year, when she was eight, she'd been tall, but not fat. This visitation, this curse, had befallen her suddenly, in a few months' time.

It was just last Christmas that Dick Dobyns in her class at school had thought she was pretty. He had given her the Christmas card he made in Art, a big Santa Claus with eyes that knew everything. The verse on the inside was from *Santa Claus is Coming to Town*: "He sees you when you're sleeping. He knows when you're awake. He knows if you've been bad or good, so be good for goodness sake!" Whatever made Dick Dobyns give her that kind of Santa Claus? What did he know about her? Dick Dobyns too had eyes that seemed to see things, like the Santa Claus. Tucked into the card was a private note that said, "I love you because you're so pretty."

But now Dick Dobyns was just like everyone else. He no longer loved her. She wasn't pretty, she was fat. He hollered "Fatty Fatty Two By Four" right along with the rest of them. She wished she had a bomb that would wipe out Dick Dobyns with his knowing gaze. Wipe out the whole class. Or better still a pit trap with sharp spikes and fishhooks and broken glass where she could lure her classmates one at a time and laugh while they suffered, the way they laughed at her.

Betty had finished weighing everyone in and was now rapping for order. At one table the older girls were whispering smutty things. They were giving hot little screams. Josie hated them. It was bad enough to be fat; it was even worse to be fat and smutty. She hated smutty girls. She also hated nicey-nice ones.

Actually there was no one here that Josie didn't hate. Some of the girls were fat, quiet, and pathetic: the ones who looked soft and hopeless, as though they could be hit without the hit's making a sound, and she hated them too. They sat together but didn't talk. Josie thought of them as "the pillows," and she imagined hearing the soundless thwacks as blows landed on their pillowy bodies.

Another group talked in an affected way about clothes, just as though they could wear nice clothes and get away with it. Josie hated them for trying, and for simpering, but she heard what they had to say about skirt length and the right kind of shoes. They all wore earrings. Eve had promised Josie she could get her ears pierced, but Dunk put his foot down, and now Josie no longer wanted earrings. They just called attention to the fact that you were a girl, and then everyone knew you wished you were pretty. If you tried to be pretty, you were just setting yourself up, asking for it. What you get when you're asking for it is never good.

When Josie looked at last year's dresses in the closet, she could almost remember being pretty. Eve kept telling her, "Josie, hon, you used to be so pretty, and you could be again if you'd just watch what you eat." But she did watch what she ate. Only sometimes she found herself eating things she shouldn't, and she couldn't stop, no matter how much she hated herself for doing it. Sometimes there was a bad taste in her mouth and she wanted something good, ice cream or a Twinkie. She'd give in and eat it, and the bad taste would go away, but then she'd think about the pistol in her father's nightstand. About putting it to her temple and pulling the trigger.

Betty rapped again. "Girls!"

The giggles and screams stopped.

"Today I want you to think about your favorite food. What is it?" She looked at the "smutty" table and pointed to a girl wearing crimson lipstick.

The girl pouted her red lips and thought. "Olives," she answered. "Green olives." The others at her table laughed.

"Who likes chocolate?" asked Betty.

"Yeah!" People clapped.

Josie listened. She couldn't help being interested. She wasn't about to tell what her favorite food was – she'd already decided to say it was liver if Betty called on her – but she couldn't help thinking about it, running through her mind over all the things she liked, and coming to rest, finally, on rich, dark brownies with brown sugar and pecan topping.

"I want you to really experience this food. Imagine that you can see it there in front of you. Close your eyes and look at it. Bring it closer. Now you can even smell it, can't you? Imagine that wonderful smell. Now I want you to take a bite of it. Put it in your mouth and hold it for a moment, then chew. Really chew, but don't swallow it yet. Think about what you're chewing. Imagine what it looks like now. Not so nice, is it? Imagine that you spit it out in a dish and look at it."

There was a chorus of groans. "Ewwwww!"

"Keep your eyes closed, girls," Betty said sternly. "We're not finished yet. Now really look at that food and see what it looks like, what color it is, the consistency. Now pick up the dish and put the chewed bite back in your mouth."

The groans were much louder.

"Swallow it," said Betty. "Everybody got it down? Now go back to that delicious food you've chosen. How does it look to you? Still good? Take another bite. Don't swallow yet, girls. What we're doing here is important. I want you to chew this bite up just like you did the other. This time you don't have to spit it out, you can just imagine what it looks like and what it would taste like if you spit it out and then put it back."

Josie opened her eyes a crack and peeked. The faces she could see had a sick look.

"Eat up all the food you've chosen. Chew it slowly, imagine what's happening to it, and then swallow. Now it's in your stomach. Feel it there. Feel full."

She paused to give them time to feel full. "Okay, now think about how it looks there in your stomach. You know your stomach is full of acid and it sloshes around like a washing machine. How does your cupcake or whatever it is look now? Pretty bad, huh? Well, we're not going to dwell on where it goes next and how it looks when you see it again, after your body's through with it, but you can imagine, can't you?" Betty clapped her little claws. "Now open your eyes."

The girls were all quiet now.

Betty leaned forward. Her bracelets had slipped down and were clattering on the table. "You don't want that nasty stuff inside you, do you? The very idea makes you feel kind of sick, doesn't it? You think about that this week. Think about it when you sit down at the table. When your friends offer you a piece of candy. When you're tempted to cheat. Think about that bite you chewed and spit out and put back in your mouth. Think how much worse that bite gets as it moves through your body. That's your assignment for the week, girls, and I guarantee that if you do it faithfully, you'll all weigh less next Saturday than you do today."

Josie felt confused, as though she'd been given the kind of gift you have to be grateful for, even though it isn't what you wanted. When her mother asked her later what the lesson had been about, she wouldn't tell. "Just the usual stuff," she said. "You know. The usual."

THE NEWS

Duncan Flannery would often notice himself expelling breath in sharp little bursts. It was something like panting, but not quite. When this happened, he would correct his posture and breathe resolutely, with straightened shoulders and a strong chin, only to find himself, moments later, once again hunched and receding, as he exhaled discrete puffs of air. An image would come to him, a cur dog dumped on the highway, running between cars, its exhausted tongue hanging out, no better sense than to get itself hit. In his mind he yelled at the dog, then pulled off the road and shot it to put it out of its misery. The dog's owner, the scumbag who dumped it instead of taking care of it, was really the one he wanted to search out and destroy, but since he couldn't, he had to content himself with shooting the dog every time the image came to him. Carcasses piled up on the roadside and stank.

Ever since August Dunk had been desperate to crack down on the female element in his house, while Eve, instead of cooperating, fought him every step of the way. That was what he called it to himself, the "female element." He couldn't have defined what he meant, but he knew it when he saw it. It was what they did to get themselves raped.

It had to do with short shorts, lipstick, bare midriffs, the high heels Eve wore every waking moment, even the jelly shoes with the little transparent straps that Josie liked. "Earrings on a nine year old?" he had yelled at Eve when he caught her on her way to get Josie's ears pierced. "Next thing I know you'll have her displaying herself around the neighborhood in a string bikini."

It had to do with jiggling, also.

How could he protect what he couldn't control?

At his place of business he had a chain link fence and a padlocked gate. He deposited the day's receipts at the bank each evening. He understood how to manage the work, the timing, the money, even his personnel: when he had to kick butt, he did it. But he couldn't put in the hours it took to run the shop and see to things at home as well. If Eve had been taking care of Josie, being there when she got out of school afternoons so she didn't run wild, instead of insisting that she had to have a goddamned job, none of this would have happened.

And what *had* happened? He still didn't know the whole story.

Not knowing the whole story was the problem. Weeks had gone by. The set, blank, sullen look on his daughter's face told him there was more that she hadn't disclosed. It was a look that provoked him. Every time he looked at her he felt like hitting her. And he chewed over the problem constantly. At work he could be a good mechanic and concentrate on the repairs at hand, but between the closing of one car's hood and the opening of the next, he would be faced with the fact that he couldn't even estimate the damage where he was affected the most.

When he had come home on the evening of August 29th – he'd spent half an hour on one of Eve's interminable and confusing errands, looking unsuccessfully for the house to leave off donations for a yard sale – he found Celia Merchant's Volvo in his parking space. At first, angered, he thought she'd brought it around to the house because the shop was closed, rich bitch entitled to service any time of the day or night. Then he realized that her visit had nothing to do with the car, that she was inside talking with Eve.

He parked down the block and walked home, scowling, wondering what was going on. Josie played with the Merchant girl, the parents brought their cars to him to work on, the families saw each other at Meeting, but the Merchants moved in a different circle. So what was Celia doing paying a call on Evie?

Inside, she was already standing by the door, leaving, car keys in hand. Duncan spoke to her in the cordial manner he used at the shop, waited until the Volvo pulled away, then went back out to move his Mustang into the space in front of the house.

He found Eve in the dining room running a dust cloth over the table. "What was that all about?" he asked. Leave it to Eve to clean house at night when he was home.

She pushed the rag around the polished wood and up under the doily, leaving the bowl of glass fruit unmoved in the center. She didn't answer his question. "I never notice how dusty this is until company comes," she said.

"What'd she come here for?"

The light glared down from the chandelier. Too fancy for Duncan's taste, the table with its curved legs was part of Eve's attempt to have things nice. The bowl of glass fruit, part of the furniture store display, had come as a package with the dining room suite.

Eve finally had to answer. "It's about Josie," she said.

"What about Josie?" More trouble. As if he didn't have enough to do. Evie ought to keep better track of her. She was out running around the neighborhood at this very moment, and it was already starting to get dark. "What about Josie?" he repeated. "What's she done? And where in the hell is she, anyway?"

"If you're going to be mad before I even say anything, I'm not going to tell you."

"I'm not mad," he said, impatiently. "I'm not mad *yet*." He managed a conciliatory smile. Dealing with Eve and her feelings was a never-ending shovel-out-the-stable job. It made it next to impossible to even find out what was going on around his house.

Celia Merchant had phoned earlier to ask if she might drop by. There was something Eve needed to know. Eve had understood right away, of course, that she'd better send Dunk out on an errand to a wrong address. Nobody ever says "There's something you need to know" unless there's trouble. And Dunk's reaction to trouble was to amplify it.

The doorbell rang all too soon, giving Eve no more than enough time to fly through the living room dumping ashtrays and picking up newspapers. A comb through her hair and a quick dab of lipstick, and there was Celia at the door, the kind of woman who could chop her hair off straight and hook it behind her ears, wear camp shirts and wrap-around skirts and no makeup, and still manage to look privileged instead of dowdy.

"Come in." Eve tried to seem relaxed. "Can I get you a Diet Coke?"

"Thanks, no," Celia replied. "I can't stay. I'm on my way to a meeting."

Of course. Her "civic duty." Running things. What people have time for if they don't have to work. "Well, at least sit down and make yourself comfortable."

When they were seated, Celia in the armchair and Eve on the couch, Celia gave a quick little frown and said, "I really hate this, and I hope it doesn't mean anything, but if it were my daughter, I'd want to know."

Stillness settled over Eve. "What is it?" she asked in a calm voice. "Has Josie broken another window?" She knew, of course, that it was much worse than that. The window had been broken when Josie was still a little girl, high-spirited and impulsive. She was neither of those things now, no longer little but suddenly carrying an alarming amount of weight, no longer full of high jinks but moody and morose. Eve had tried to halt the weight gain and coax Josie into a better mood even while putting aside the worry that something was seriously amiss. Now she could ignore her intuition no longer.

"It's about Corky Pearlman," said Celia.

Eve's calmness stayed in place.

"Last Saturday night, when Josie was sleeping over, I heard her tell Heather that she was *like this* with Corky." She held up two fingers twisted close together.

Something had prompted Celia to stop in the hall by Heather's doorway to listen, maybe the pathos of the girl's voice making a claim to having special favor with the minister. Why would a child that age even care about the minister? But of course Celia understood that the Flannerys didn't offer much at home.

"He made up a special ending to *The Sleeping Beauty* for me to act out with him. I was supposed to be singing in my sleep, which was how the prince found me. He always wants me to sing."

Josie did have a beautiful voice, but Celia couldn't help thinking that Eve pushed her too much. Piano lessons. Singing lessons. Recitals.

The girls lay sprawled on Heather's peach-colored carpet, cutting pictures from a pile of magazines they had brought home from somebody's curbside. They were making collages, pasting pictures on large sheets of cardboard.

"Did he kiss you?" asked Heather.

"Yeah," said Josie. "That was supposed to wake me up, and then we waltzed around the castle...."

"Corky kissed you?"

"Yeah."

"He's pretty old."

"Yeah."

"He doesn't smell too good."

"No he doesn't." Josie's voice had lost its pleasure. She was quiet for a moment. Then she said, "He was acting kind of weird."

"Corky *always* acts weird."

"I mean *really* weird."

"What'd he do?"

"Well, he said there was another chapter to the Sleeping Beauty story and we could act it out too. You know how he gets all excited and keeps going and going with something like he's the biggest kid of all, and how hurt he gets if you want to quit and go home."

After a while Heather said, "Well, what?"

"Oh well," said Josie. "Hey, look at this one."

How much could she tell Heather? It was so confusing, what had happened. Josie felt torn in two, wishing she could talk to somebody about this, and being afraid for anyone to find out, both at once.

She knew her parents would not want her to play these games with other children, but Corky was a minister, after all. He outranked her parents for knowing was right and what was wrong.

Besides, Corky had told her she was his special girl. "People get very jealous when other folks are special to each other," he had said. "They might even send one of us away."

And she certainly didn't want that to happen, not to be sent away herself, and not to have her friend Corky sent away. So what if he acted weird! A friend was a friend. Sometimes a friend did things that made you feel uncomfortable, but you stood by him anyway. Telling Heather was probably not a good idea .

"Can I have the long red slinky one for my picture?" asked Heather. Then, "Thanks. So what's the other chapter about?"

"Oh well, not too much. The prince just carries Sleeping Beauty to his castle and then he takes off his suit of armor and they're married."

"Does that mean they're going to do it?"

Papers rustled for a while. Then Josie answered. "They have to show each other their appendicitis."

Celia heard Heather giggle. She held herself back from marching into her daughter's room and breaking up this conversation.

"Does Corky have an appendicitis?"

"Yeah. He has a puckery one."

"Ew, gross!"

"Yeah."

The talk about Corky ended here, as a choice magazine was unearthed from the pile and the girls went after it with their scissors. Celia tiptoed away and seated herself rigidly at the kitchen table with a cup of hot, sweetened tea to process the shock. Her first concern, of course, was Heather's matter-of-fact question about doing it. It was too late, she realized, for the mother-daughter talk about the birds and the bees. The talk would have to be much more advanced and realistic than she had anticipated.

And what about Corky? So could it be true, the business with the Skinners when Corky was arrested last spring? Nothing had come of it, and the Skinners moved away, but still…

But Celia just couldn't imagine it, couldn't imagine a man with Corky's gifts playing disgusting games with little girls. It was beyond the realm of the possible. He did play with the children, that was something she admired, a minister who was accessible and playful. But it could be taken wrong. People weren't used to adults who really connected with kids.

She set her teacup hard on the table. Hot liquid splashed out. Heather was going to have to find some different playmates. Celia had been thinking for some time that Josie wasn't the best companion, that she seemed to be growing into a sad sack kind of a girl. All that weight! Even if Corky *were* attracted to little girls, it wasn't likely that it would be Josie Flannery.

It was Celia's private opinion that there was a different twist to the Beth Skinner story than was generally known. Liz Skinner, Beth's mother, had hung around the meetinghouse volunteering her life away for years. She'd served on every committee the meeting had, then took her turn on the board. It looked to Celia as though Liz might have been throwing herself at Corky and been rejected, then accused him of funny stuff because he played games with Beth and the other children instead of with her. Celia had not mentioned this opinion at the time, but neither had anything about the investigation convinced her that she was mistaken. Anyone could be accused of something awful, and how could he prove he was innocent?

Now it was Josie making the accusations.

"I just thought you ought to know," Celia told Eve. "Josie probably needs a change of pace, something more constructive to do than hang around the meetinghouse." Her hand smoothed the faded chambray of her skirt. "It's been my experience that when children start making up stories like that, it's because they need better things to do."

Eve, having listened to this much, heard Celia out. She felt shut down, almost numb. "I'll have a talk with her," she said. "And I appreciate your letting me know." But of course she didn't appreciate it, not really. Knowing was going to make it necessary to act.

Whatever Celia Merchant had to say about his daughter, Duncan Flannery wasn't going to like it. He didn't want Josie discussed. Being discussed cheapened a girl. If a girl acted the way she should, people wouldn't have anything to talk about.

"You set her up for this." Light from the chandelier showed the flush of anger darkening his face below the waves of red hair. "You've been painting and powdering her, haven't you, dolling her up like a harlot, making trash out of her, that goddamned sleazy red dress you bought her, and now look what you got her into." He took a step, his hands balling into fists. Eve retreated. With the next step he reached one end of the table, she the other.

There she stopped and leaned, with her hands spread out and

pressed onto the tabletop, and gave him such a look of hatred that he stopped where he was. Her gaze went to the bowl of fruit, the heavy glass apples, the bananas like boomerangs, the grenade of a pineapple, and back to him. He unclenched his fists and exhaled. When she turned and walked to the kitchen, her hands left damp little prints on the tabletop.

"We have to do something about this, Duncan," she said. "We have to find out what's going on." Dealing with her husband required her to maintain dignity and never, ever, to fight. In a fight she was lost before she started.

"You're goddam right we have to find out what's going on!"

"Celia thought she was just bragging, you know, trying to puff herself up a little to the other girls."

Duncan's tone was as sharp as his face. "What's to brag about?"

"Being special. Being somebody. Somebody special. Being seen as desirable. That's the most important thing to a girl." Eve could remember her own pre-puberty years, practicing with her mother's makeup. Nowadays they started with Barbies in nursery school.

"At nine years old?"

"They start young, Duncan. Josie's beginning to develop. You have to try to understand."

"So what are you telling me?" His anger needed something to focus on. "I *don't* understand. Are you telling me our daughter is being molested by the minister or that she's making up stories? Which is it? What are you trying to say?"

"That's what I want to find out."

Eve had not told Duncan the whole story, not the part about Corky Pearlman unzipping his fly to show their daughter his lower belly, nor the corresponding view of Josie's body. She wanted a chance to sound Josie out. She was not convinced that Josie was making this up. But she would not get the chance to speak privately with Josie, for the screen door opened and here the girl came, flushed and sweaty, steering her bicycle through the kitchen to park it safe in the utility room.

Josie stopped when she saw them. Her body tensed, taking in the battle scene in the kitchen. Then she moved carefully past the stove, the refrigerator, the table, guiding the bicycle, negotiating the turns without bumping anything, under the gaze of her parents. Duncan's arms were folded, his face sharp and accusatory. Her mother looked small and anxious, her fluffy prettiness insufficient to the matter at hand.

What were they mad about now? Something to do with her, of course. It was always something to do with her.

Always, when they looked like this, she had to wrap a shell of carefulness around herself, create a bunker into which she could retreat in safety, lest she be torn apart in their struggle.

She looked down. There was the cracked place in the linoleum and the chair leg her dog had chewed. Seeing the chair leg with its tooth marks reminded her again that Scratcher had been dead for a long time and they still didn't have a new dog. She wanted a dog so badly! Now wasn't the time to bring it up, though. Now was the time to keep still and hold herself together.

Her father broke the silence. "What's this I hear about you hanging around the meetinghouse?"

The bunker door crashed shut. Her shoulders shrugged. Inside she crouched with her arms folded around her head.

"Answer me!"

Her voice said, "I don't know what you mean."

"Let me talk to her," said her mother in a pleading tone.

"All right then, talk to her. Let's hear what she has to say."

She didn't have anything at all to say.

"Josie, hon," began her mother. "Josie, hon, we've heard some rumors that you've been saying things about Corky."

She didn't have to answer yet.

Duncan took a threatening step toward her.

She pushed the bicycle a little farther. The air in the room seemed less plentiful.

"I want to know what kind of lies you're telling," said Duncan. "If I have to go to him cap in hand, I want to know what to apologize for."

"I haven't told any lies." She was on safe ground here.

"Then what the hell's been going on? What kind of funny stuff's going on over there?"

Her shoulders moved up and down. "It's fairy tales. It's not funny stuff."

"What about all the kissing and dancing around and holding you on his lap? Are you saying that's what he's doing?"

Josie's bunker thickened to include a mask over her face.

Eve said, "Now don't try to protect him, hon. It's not right what he's been doing."

"*If* he's been doing anything," said Duncan. "I'm not at all convinced she's telling the truth."

Stung, Josie cried, "I don't tell lies!" But she knew she was cornered. She flung the bicycle down and made a dash for the staircase in the living room.

Duncan was right behind her. When he caught her, he yanked her around to face him and shook her hard. "All right now, let's hear the truth. How long has this been going on?"

Tears sprang from her eyes. She willed them to stop. "Since last Easter vacation."

He shook her again. "You mean to tell me you've been letting him slobber all over you for months? And you didn't do anything to stop it?" He pushed her away, the grabbed her again.

"He doesn't slobber!"

"He kisses you, doesn't he?"

She nodded, her eyes closed, determined not to cry yet. "I'm Sleeping Beauty," she murmured. If she cried too soon, he would accuse her of manipulating him. She could feel the bruises forming under her father's strong fingers on her shoulders.

"And rubs you around on his lap?"

She nodded again. How much more did they know? And how did they find out? Could someone have been watching?

Her father flung her away from him. She let herself hit the wall and drop to the floor. It would be okay to cry now. He would stop without whipping her, if the crash was loud enough and her fall convincing....

FEVERISH FRED

Fred spent Saturday waiting for Sunday. Oh, he helped at the store, and he took Jenny to the beauty shop, and when she came out with her white frizz tamed, he took her with him to the library, but his thoughts were elsewhere. "Umhumm," he answered when she talked about how her taste in books had changed as her eyesight got worse. "I remember," he said, when she told him she hadn't always read mysteries.

"I used to read poetry," she said, "but when your eyes don't work as well as they should, you need plot to keep you going."

Fred was thinking about the way he wanted to approach the Pearlman project. First, gather information. Second, gather more information. He needed to know what had happened. But instead of setting up interviews and asking questions, he decided to make the acquaintance of the group as a whole first. A time would come when he would question the wisdom of this, even question his own motives, but now he had no doubt of his course.

Claire phoned him Saturday evening. "Are you serious about writing up this mess?"

"Never more so," he answered. "I gotta tell you, Mrs. Claire, that my interest is not altruistic. You wouldn't trust me if it was, right? Never trust a do-gooder. But you gotta know, if you think about it, this is a hot topic. There's quite a bit in it for me."

"That's good. Listen, if you come to Meeting in the morning, you'll get an earful."

"Your husband suggested I come. It's gonna be about him, right?"

"Right. They decide whether to let him go on preaching. You know, or maybe you don't, that they officially fired him last May. That was when the Skinners started the whole thing. Oh, there've been people who've been trying for years to oust him, but they couldn't get enough support. Until they thought of this. I suppose that from their point of view, it was brilliant, but you'd think they'd care more for their children than to use them in such a horrible way, wouldn't you?" She told him how they'd been strung along, with Corky preaching week by week, hoping to be back in the congregation's good graces when it all died down.

"That hope's gone," she said. "It doesn't matter that they can't possibly have a case. People are worried about scandal. The Meeting can't afford scandal. If we were Methodists or Lutherans, the congregation could gather round their minister and people would think how *Christian* of them, but with us, they'd just think we'd gone completely over the edge."

She was so voluble that Fred got worried. "Look, Mrs. Claire, I hope you understand that what I do isn't gonna help. You do know that, don't you? For one thing, I'm not a big name writer." He could only go that far. He couldn't bring himself to tell her he was only a would-be writer. He was too sensitive on that point. "For another, whatever I write wouldn't be allowed in court. What you need is a lawyer."

"We have a lawyer," she said, shortly. "A good one. But that's not what I'm worried about. I can't believe they could send him to prison, even if he did exactly what they say he did. It's just not a big enough thing to send someone to prison over. What I'm worried about is his good name, our future, where he's going to get another church. What you write could help there. There are always congregations in search, and some of them are idealistic. If people know he's being persecuted, someone will step forward. He isn't young, he can't start a new career, and he doesn't have much in the way of a pension coming. He needs to work, and so do I, for that matter. We need the work because we need work, you know, but we also need the money."

"I know what you're talking about," said Fred. "I know exactly what you're talking about. I'll be there tomorrow with my eyes and ears wide open."

But when the next morning came, he woke up early with hot eyes and aches under his skin. Oh no, he thought. What's happening? I can't afford to come down with something.

Leaving Sara making the little noises that meant she was awake enough to feel the bed sway, he went downstairs to ignore his illness. Properly ignored, maybe it would go away.

The first step was to bring in an armload of wood. A Sunday morning fire was part of the ritual, and he would let neither Meeting nor illness interfere with that. He and Sara had spent time together by the fire on chilly Sundays ever since they'd bought the house, and doing so had become so important that not even Mr. Rochester had been allowed to break it up.

It was light when he and Marigold went outside, but barely – a November morning with rain clouds at treetop level. His orange cat, Duck, leaped to the porch rail, arched her back, and hissed at the dog. Down the hill in back of the house, fog hid Sweetwater Creek. Too bad this house wasn't close to the lake, Fred thought, so that he could hear the foghorn. Hearing a foghorn occasionally was good for the soul. "Be careful," it hooted. There was always something to be careful about.

The wood was stacked between two trees. Fred selected the pieces he wanted, piled his left arm to the shoulder, tucked two more pieces under his right arm, carried them all in through the kitchen and unloaded them on the hearth.

Marigold acted frisky on stiff legs. "Cool it," he said. "We don't need any broken bones. The vet's closed on Sunday." He went back to the kitchen and dished her out a cup of dry dog chow. She sniffed it and gave him a dirty look. "And don't shit the floor either," he said. "I'm watching you." He carried the cat's water and her dish of kibbles out to the porch.

The vet might be closed on Sunday, but the drugstore was open, though for three hours only. The home phone number was on the door, too, and in the book, so that Sara could be reached for emergencies. Sometimes there were emergencies, and Sara went quickly to the store on Sunday evening just as her father had in years past to refill somebody's pain pills or take a phoned-in prescription for something to tide a sick person over till the doctor's office opened in the morning.

Fred put the coffee on and went back to the fire. By the time he had coaxed the two main pieces of wood to catch, the coffee was ready to drink.

The house was quiet except for the hiss and pop of wood burning. Only Marigold joined him. Her toenails clicked over the painted plank floor to the hearthrug where she stood for a moment trying to unlock her joints, then she sank all at once, releasing a cloud of dog dust that shimmered in the firelight.

After drinking the coffee that Fred hoped would cure whatever was ailing him, he lay down on the couch. Maybe he was really getting sick. While he didn't exactly feel good lying down, he felt better than he did sitting up.

If this went on, he might not get to the Freethinkers' Meeting, and the Pearlman project would be no further along than it had been yesterday. He lay, half-dozing. Claire entered his mind, then exited without speaking. He would have to get himself up, he thought. He was never sick; he never even thought of being sick. He especially couldn't afford to be sick today. A real live reverend child molester was too good a prospect to let slip away.

And slip away he might. I'd sure disappear, Fred thought. Vanish. Go to Canada. Live in the woods. I'd never in the world let myself be put in jail on a charge like that.

He dozed. At one point he heard Jenny come downstairs. He felt her presence near the couch but he didn't rouse. "Freddy," she whispered. "Are you going to church?" Asked baldly, he knew he wasn't. He shook his head without opening his eyes and felt her disappointment join his. After a moment she went on down the hall to the kitchen. The next time he woke up, he heard voices. He listened, hoping Sara was up, but it was Mr. Rochester and Jenny, their dislike for each other contained in a conversation about what constituted a good breakfast. "If eggs are so harmful," asked Jenny, "then how is it that I'm as healthy as I am?"

A little later, when they had gone, Fred went back into the kitchen. Maybe he would feel better if he had something to eat. Something good. Food might make him feel enough better to go out. His sausage patties were done and his eggs frying when Sara came yawning into the kitchen wearing a robe over her gown. Her thick blonde hair was tangled and her eyes were puffy with sleep.

"I must have needed that," she said. "What is it, eight thirty?" She squinted at the clock. "I slept for ten hours."

"There's a fire in the fireplace. Wanna take your coffee in there?"

She nodded and poured and disappeared down the hall while he waited for his toast.

The fire needed tending again. Fred stirred the coals and pushed the logs closer together. Then he sat with Sara and ate. They were quiet, watching the smoke rise between the logs.

Even near the fire, however, Fred felt cold. He went upstairs to find the ratty quilt he liked to wrap up in. "Where's my quilt?" he called down the stairs. "You didn't throw my quilt out, did you?" Sara had once threatened to–it was awfully ratty–but she surely wouldn't, would she? At the moment he couldn't be sure. All he could be sure of was that he could hardly wait to lie down again. Damn, oh damn, he thought.

"Try–oh, it may be in the cedar chest." The hesitation in Sara's voice provoked him to a peevishness that added to his misery. Won't she even help me when I'm sick, he thought? It's not like I'm sick all the time. It's not like I enjoy being sick.

Wrapped in the quilt with his feet on the hearth, he forgave Sara. She had pulled the wing chair up beside the couch to give him room to lie down if he wanted and had gone to make herself some toast.

He listened and shivered and tried to feel better. But then his face got cold and began to sweat, and he had to hurry to the toilet under the stairs where he regretfully vomited the breakfast that had turned, now, to a vile wash. He leaned on the cold rim and cradled his head. "Sara," he croaked, knowing she couldn't hear him. "I'm sick."

"I can tell," she answered from behind him. She stroked the back of his neck with one hand while flushing the toilet with the other. "Did that help?"

"I don't know yet." He raised himself to a standing position and wiped his sweat-streaked face with a damp washcloth. "I gotta brush my teeth. I can't stand teeth that taste like puke." He slathered his teeth and tongue, and felt a little better. At least the acute nausea was gone. But he didn't feel good, for the sore flesh and the hot eyes were still with him, accompanied now by an uncertain emptiness in his middle. His quilt was lying on the hallway floor where he'd dropped it, Marigold stretched out on it asleep.

He lay down again, this time under Aunt Jenny's afghan.

Sara appeared. "Do you want me to put some more wood on?"

"If you want to. I don't care." Nevertheless he listened to find out what she would do, and he was glad when he heard the fire screen being set aside and the solid thud as she added a piece of firewood. Then he fell asleep.

Time passed. He drifted awake, heard voices, and went back to sleep. Later he heard Sara leave to go to the store. He told her goodbye in his mind but did not rouse enough to say it aloud. I'm sorry, he thought. I'd come with you if I could. Then he remembered he'd planned to go to church, and this time he was *really* sorry.

Still later he felt Jenny's hand on his forehead. "Go on back to sleep. That's as good for you as anything." His father-in-law's voice came from the hall where he was talking on the phone to his lady friend, Dorothy. Fred pulled the afghan over his head to smother that monotonous voice. "It's raining," said Jenny. "Good thing we didn't go to church."

Finally after a long time dozing and waking, he awakened to the sound of the front door closing, Sara returning from the store.

It was still raining. Sara unbuttoned her coat and took out the Sunday *New York Times* from where she'd been sheltering it. "Hi," she said. "I brought you some aspirin. Sorry we were out." He hadn't noticed. She brought him some water with the aspirin and started a new fire, then sat down in the wing chair to read.

"What's that you're reading?"

"I'm reading how they have to set off rockets to keep birds out of a bird sanctuary."

"Come on."

"It's true. The water's poisoned with selenium from irrigation drainage. They're trying to keep the birds out of it."

In his mind's eye Fred could see flocks of waterfowl circling the refuge, stretching their webbed feet down for a pontoon landing, then rising in hasty confusion as rocket bursts exploded amongst them. "The light's in my eyes," he said.

"Sorry." She adjusted the lamp.

"That can't be all the news that's fit to print." He tried to make his voice jovial instead of fretful, but it didn't come out very well.

She continued reading. "I suppose not."

He got up. Sara had the main news section. He picked up the "Week in Review," but dropped it when he saw that it was going to be full of the election. A real statesman wouldn't have a prayer in this country, he thought.

Wishing he were hungry, Fred went on wobbly legs to the kitchen and opened the refrigerator. It looked bleak: a monstrous head of cabbage, a paper box of skim milk. Sara's ironing, to keep it from mildewing. Tomato juice. In the vegetable drawers everything but the good things. Bicarbonate of soda in a paper cup on the top shelf, and a covered plastic box with a big cube of something slippery and white swimming in cloudy liquid. Ugh, he thought. I'm sick for one day and the refrigerator's lost.

He wrapped back up in the afghan. The aspirin wasn't doing any good. He felt like a toxic dump waiting for help from the EPA. "Sara," he said, "what the hell good did pharmacy school do you?"

"None. Why?"

"I didn't mean it that way," he said. "I just meant I wondered why you couldn't cure a little cold or whatever I've got."

"I didn't go to medical school," she answered. "And even if I had, there's no cure for flu. You just have to wait. If it's the easy, pseudo kind, you wait a few hours, if it's the real flu, you wait three weeks. That's if you don't die."

"I'm gonna die waiting." As soon as he said this, he knew it was the wrong thing to say.

Sara put her paper down and looked at him.

"I'm sorry," he said. "I'm acting like a spoiled brat. I'm just bored. Being sick is boring. My inner resources are on strike."

"Would you like some of the paper?"

"My eyes hurt too much. Maybe you could read me some tidbits."

"An awful lot of it is about the election. You said you didn't want to hear about that."

True. Two guys spending millions on advertising. That was what really irked him. "The trouble with this country is advertising," he said. "Somebody invents toothpaste and sells it, and then a whole flock of people want to horn in. People that used to be satisfied making tires want a share of the toothpaste market, so they set up a toothpaste plant. Then they have to spend untold millions to advertise why people ought to buy Brand A toothpaste instead of Brand X, when they're practically the same."

"What's that got to do with the election?" Sara was still reading, but she responded to Fred automatically, the way a mother cat flicks her tail to entertain her kittens while she thinks her own thoughts.

Fred considered his idea, hoping to phrase it brilliantly enough to lure Sara away from the paper. "Reagan's making it the same way toothpaste makes it. He gets associated with prosperity by talking about prosperity all the time. No matter what he's been *doing*. What matters is what he's *saying*. But Mondale is stupid. He talks about everything that's wrong. You never see toothpaste ads showing people in agony at the dentist's office, do you? No. You see them flashing their choppers at the opposite sex. That's how we elect presidents. The advertising mentality."

"Stop raving," said Sara. "You're going to make your fever go up."

"Have I got fever?" He hadn't been sick enough to have fever for at least twenty years, maybe thirty.

"Of course you have fever. What do you think makes your eyes hurt?"

"Sara, I'm cold. I haven't got fever."

She put the paper down. "You may *feel* cold," she said, her eyes warming up one of their stale arguments, "but actually you're quite hot. Just rest assured that fever is the best thing you've got going for you."

Listening to her read about the election would not be as bad as having another round of the old argument about whether how you feel is how you *really* feel, so he said, "I wouldn't mind hearing what you're reading."

"Right now I'm reading about a little tribe of Indians in Nevada who want to open a whorehouse on the reservation to bring in the Las Vegas clientele and make ends meet," she said. "The government, of course, says no."

"Where's the free enterprise spirit?" said Fred, raving again. "You'd think the government would applaud. You don't see the government wanting to make donations, do you?"

"No," she answered. "They don't. You'd like this part. It says there's a legal battle, and attorneys for both sides are arguing the case."

"My point exactly!"

"What point was that?"

"The point I made the other day. About how the lawyers siphon off the money. Lawyers, management, expensive experts with corner offices. The vultures. Consultation fees. You know who's going to benefit from all this, and it's not the Indians."

"Honey, you'd be better off if you'd just close your eyes."

He settled himself obediently into the hollows of the couch and waited for the lullaby.

She read to him.

Drought and starvation in Africa. The wrath of mobs in India. Indira Gandhi's funeral pyre. Security measures for heads of state. Government no longer liable. Sara read slowly, her voice quiet and restful.

"No longer liable for what was that?" Fred pawed his afghan and sat up.

"Cancer," said Sara. "The cancers they caused when they tested the Bomb."

"If we had universal health care like other civilized nations, we wouldn't have to fatten the lawyers deciding who's to blame for every cancer that comes along. We'd take care of sick people instead of paying lawyers to dicker over blame."

"You tell 'em. We'd have an even bigger bite out of the paycheck. Why should I have to take care of people who drink and smoke and eat nothing but junk food and sit on their butts all day drawing money from the government?"

"You make it sound like having a paycheck is a virtue."

Sara folded the paper and laid it on the floor. She started to get up.

"Wait," said Fred. "Read some more."

"Only if you keep quiet. Foaming at the mouth isn't good for you."

"Yes it is," he said, smiling. "It keeps my disposition sweet and baby fresh." He breathed a deep sigh and let it out his mouth, knowing from the taste that he smelled like a swamp. "Don't come near me."

"I wasn't planning to." She read, and in between the lines he dozed again.

Famine, euthanasia, brain death, abortion, inflation, gonorrhea, crisis, intimidation, passive smoking.... Sara read on, her voice like apricot marmalade: sweet, tart and fuzzy, telling him the news. Rebels execute villagers; villagers hack rebels; students hack police; hackers hack the system. Feud, privacy, Down's Syndrome, taint, the homeless roaming homeless roaming homeless without shelter.

"Sara," he groaned, "I wanna hear what's happening out there in the world, not what's going on in my gut."

"Hush," she said. "It's all the same." She read on: vital decisions and critical roles; virile assassins; fetal emissions; shady transactions.

"How about child molestations?" he asked. "We're supposed to be getting a lot of those." She didn't respond, so he asked, "How about the election?"

"I don't want to make your fever go up."

"You're not exactly reading Anne Morrow Lindbergh."

"Hush," she said. "Listen to this." And she read him about the Chinese-American writer Henry Liu, who was murdered for publishing a biography critical of the Taiwanese president.

"Sara," said Fred, struggling to free himself from the afghan. "The one plus I've been able to see about a writer's job is that it's safe. Now you tell me I'm in the actuarial tables with steeple jacks."

"You're impossible." She gathered up the paper, turned out the light and left the room.

He settled back and dozed again, the ingredients in his mind heated up by fever… *He is walking down a corridor, the floor glossy underfoot. The sound of rubber soles. Whiteness. Beside him a nurse speaks. He follows her to the door of the hospital chapel. The sign on the door says "Brain-Death Ward."*

He half-roused, turned over and slept again… *The door opens. Inside the Brain-Death Ward a line of men snakes down another hall and doubles back on itself. He hesitates, then stands at the end of the line. "It's better here," says the man in front of him. "They feed the ones who don't work."*

Fred awakened, soaking wet. He changed the dream around so it would make better sense. They feed the ones who *do* work. You wanna eat, you gotta hustle. The fire was out, the room dark. He realized that he felt human again. Thank God. He put his feet on the floor. To his surprise he could walk. He made his way down the hall.

Sara was sitting at the kitchen table, crying. The newspaper was strewn around her. "What is it?" He'd thought she was in a pretty good mood. He went to the table and laid her braid gently down her back. "What is it?"

"I'm just disgusted with myself." She took a paper napkin from the holder and blew her nose. "I don't have any fellow feeling."

"So who does? What kind of a thing is that to cry about?"

"I spent the whole afternoon reading about the terrible things that are happening to people all over the world and none of it really bothered me until I read this." She tapped the magazine section that was open to a picture of some items of clothing and jewelry.

"Of course," he said. It made no sense to him why scarves and stockings would make anybody cry, but he comforted her anyway, massaging her shoulders and easing his thumbs around each vertebra the way she liked. "Tell me."

"Those spotted stockings cost $30 a pair," she said. "The article is advising that we buy an extra pair so that when they go out of style, we'll still have some left."

He kissed the top of her head. "What else?" There was more to it than stockings.

She looked up, her eyes leaking. Then she riffled a few pages of the Sunday magazine and pointed. The title of the story was "A Mother's Son."

"I'm never going to have children." She clutched his middle.

He could feel her face against his belly, her mouth against the knotted drawstring of his pajama pants. He thought of sex, of her mouth moving downward, but of course it would be boorish to suggest it now. "I'm sorry," he said. He could feel her bones under his hands as he rocked back and forth holding her. "So sorry."

After a moment she took a breath and straightened herself. "You're all wet. Would you like me to get you some clean clothes?"

"I'll get them," he answered. "What's for dinner?"

"Soup. You must be feeling better."

"I am. I got knees like gum drops, but I feel better. I need to take a shower and put on something that doesn't feel slimy."

When he was clean and dry, he came back to the kitchen and found that by some miracle Sara had managed to make a meal. "When I looked in the ice box, I thought maybe we weren't going to eat anymore," he said. "This looks wonderful."

All during dinner Fred smiled the smile of the newly-recovered, ate gratefully, chewed his food carefully. He was gracious to his father-in-law and courtly to Jenny and he thought about its being Sunday evening and looked forward to watching Masterpiece Theater. When he started to take another helping, Sara shook her head and he put his soup plate down.

"Eat light," she said. "You're probably okay now, but you'll feel better if you give your body a rest." She went to the cupboard for Marigold's food.

Seeing a dipper of soup being poured over the usual dry food, the dog was on her feet acting ten years younger, and when the doorbell rang, she didn't know whether to run to the door and bark or stay in the kitchen with her food.

Fred grabbed his bathrobe from the hall floor where he'd dropped it earlier and tied it closed over his clean flannel pajamas. He turned on the porch light and opened the door.

It was Claire Pearlman.

NO SOLID FOOTING

A case could be made that following characters' dreams could tell a reader more about them than following their daily lives. It's all there, no question, laid bare for the seeing. But most of us have eyes somewhat like Jenny's: we need plot, not just images. We need to trudge along behind as our characters muck through their scenes, only occasionally dipping into the vividness of the dream world.

> *The river. No bridge, no ferry, logs tumbling in the current on their way downstream to the sawmill. Claire finds a place to cross where the logs are jammed together. They boom and jolt as a new log joins the jam. She steps from one to another. Then, because she's wearing her mother's shoes to make her taller, one high spindly heel catches in a ridge of bark and the shoe comes off. Now she steps unevenly, one shoe on and one off.*
>
> *The noise becomes louder, booming all around. The jam breaks up, and the log on which she stands begins to pitch and roll.*

Claire carried that frightening dream with her all day, a tape on a player with a short in the switch. It turned itself on for a moment in the morning as she went down the front steps on her way to Meeting. She would have fallen if she hadn't been holding Corky's arm—holding it, actually, to support him, not herself. And again inside the jammed Meetinghouse she felt herself unaccountably pitching forward into Darla Wilson's arms when Darla thrust a small paper bag into her hand.

"I know this isn't the time to give you something to keep track of," she said, "but I thought it might let you know how much I care about you and Corky."

Claire, falling forward on the logs, reached up for Darla's substantial cable-knit shoulders and hung on. Darla hugged her.

"It's for your quilt. A piece leftover from my wedding dress."

Claire stepped back, her footing firm again, and looked in the sack at an egg roll of ivory satin, tied around the middle with a raveling, like a rolled-up parchment missive. Wordless, she pressed her cheek against Darla's woolen shoulder.

"It wasn't just Corky at the wedding, it was you too. You did everything to make it happen just right."

Claire nodded. That was what she always did at weddings: picked up where the caterer left off, remembered what the bride's mother forgot, hemmed drooping skirts, curled drooping hair, wiped up spills, taped cards to gifts, made peace between florist and janitor, singer and organist, bride and photographer. Her wedding gift to the couple.

"Don't be surprised if you get more quilt pieces. I've mentioned it to people." Darla chewed the inside of her cheek. "I'm on your side, Claire."

"Thank you, Darla. The support means a lot."

More pieces did come. As they were pressed into her hands by women, some of whom had cried in her living room over their men in trouble, Claire was comforted, but nothing was solved. In the end she forgot to take the quilt pieces home with her. Mr. Sullivan, the custodian, finding them under her chair after the Meeting, put them in the Lost and Found.

Earlier, while she was still in bed, the logs had stopped rolling only when she fell into the river of Corky's silent misery. She cooked him Cream of Wheat for breakfast, food for a sick child, and peeled his orange.

He fumbled with the sugar and spilled it. Claire left it lie rather than disturb him. He sat so silent and looked so vague and lost, however, that she finally did disturb him. "What are you thinking about?" she asked.

"What?" He misjudged the distance and set the sugar bowl down too hard. "Oh, I was thinking about my great-great-grandfather, Justin LaMar, walking the Wilderness Trail. That's how he got to Kentucky, you know. He didn't have the money for a horse. And his brother

Julian walked with him. Only Julian was the faster walker and got ahead, and Justin LaMar found him bloody and dead on the trail with his scalp gone." Corky looked livelier as he told this story, and when it was finished, he half-chuckled and said, "I used to shudder when my mother read me 'The Tortoise and the Hare.' Even at an early age I understood that the Hare got off much easier than my great-great Uncle Julian did."

Claire had stopped moving as Corky talked. She felt like flashing out and scolding him for not worrying, for making her do all the worrying, but what was the use? Corky was making her do no such thing. Worry was something she brought on herself. His thoughts were his own, and if she asked him to share them, it would be bad manners to carp at what he told her. If he could escape into genealogy or fable, so much the better for him.

Nancy came into the kitchen, stylish in a striped wool dress and slim pumps.

"There's no Sunday School this morning, dear," Claire told her. It would be better for the girl to stay home and watch cartoons than to hear what was likely to be said at the meeting.

Nancy looked at Corky. "Then why are you wearing your preaching suit?"

"Because there's a meeting," he answered. "A long, boring meeting. I have to go, while you stay home and read."

But Nancy knew. "Are they going to fire you?"

"I don't know," Corky answered. "I really don't know."

"Let me go too," Nancy said. "They'll be nicer to you if you have a child with you. They'll know you're not mean to children."

"Better not," said Claire. "You'd rather not hear this. I really think…"

"Oh, please," said Nancy. "You always say children have to live life too. This is part of life, isn't it?"

If Claire's energy had not been so depleted, if her thoughts had not been on Corky, she would have taken charge of the situation and seen to it that Nancy stayed home.

ORDEAL BY MICROPHONE

"Here is the church, here is the steeple, open the door and see all the people."

Picture the Meetinghouse, its unpainted siding gray in the gray rain. The seating in the sanctuary has been reversed, with the chairs turned inward, the semi-circle of faces looking toward the dark cavern of a fireplace with no fire. In front of the fireplace is a microphone stand. At the rear, on the windows, raindrops stream in interrupted pathways down the leaded shards of glass, and in the garden beyond, wet evergreens droop to the ground.

Some faces are angry, others just sad; no face is happy. Very few people talk, unusual, the Freethinkers being a talk-struck group.

In another part of the building the library is dark.

The kitchen is dark, too. Cake platters lie empty in the cupboard. Cookie trays stand on end against the wall. The coffee pot is cold.

The people who usually have jobs to do, the church school teachers, the library assistant, members of the Coffee Hour Committee, are the most uncomfortable, because they are not used to having idle hands. But everyone is entitled to take part in the meeting. No one is doing chores today.

Claire, Corky and Nancy are sitting very close together between David Mendel, past president several times over, and Amos Grant, current president and most generous contributor. Corky looks as odd and disheveled as usual in spite of Claire's help with his clothes. Small Claire beside him has a baleful look, like a mother wolf who will kill for her pups. Nancy, on his other side, stands up from time to time to make her presence noticeable, while she waits for something to happen.

Although the fireplace is dark, a fire has been laid. There is talk about lighting it, then someone says maybe the chimney is acting up and suggests finding out from Mr. Sullivan. No one knows where Mr. Sullivan is, and the fire stays unlit.

It was Corky's idea in times past to seat the group this way, facing inward, toward the center of the Meetinghouse, and toward the fire. "We're outward-looking people," he said, "and it behooves us to turn around from time to time and look into ourselves." He offered meditations suggesting that the source of human good was to be found by moving inward, not simply *to* the self but *through* it and *beyond* it. For many people, being part of a semi-circle facing the fire enhanced such meditations. For others, this was too woo-woo, but because they loved the Meeting, they tolerated it.

Today, however, it is the microphone that people face, and a procession of speakers.

"Testing." Amos taps the microphone. "Testing." People in the audience nod. "The meeting will please come to order," he says tersely. "We all know why we're here. Anyone who wants to speak may do so. Please be polite. Please speak for no more than two minutes. In order that we give the justice system a chance to work, please do not discuss the matter that is the subject of criminal proceedings. Thank you."

One person after another takes the microphone and speaks about how well Corky has served, or about how poorly.

A gray-haired woman in a rust-colored suit: "When my mother was in Portvillage before she died, Corky was the only person outside the family who took the trouble to visit her. And not just once, either. Several times a week. Now you may think that's not worth mentioning, but I was glad to find that not all intellectuals have given up visiting the sick and comforting the dying. I think we have a minister worth supporting. Thank you."

Another woman, this one nervous at the microphone: "You all know this, but just for the record I want to say that Corky ruined our daughter's wedding. Everyone was here and the guests were all seated and waiting and Ellen was playing the music over and over again, and he didn't show up. He didn't show up. We had to go find him. You can say all you like about his kindness, but someone as scatterbrained as that shouldn't be allowed to be a minister. And it would have happened to the rest of you, too, if you'd had your weddings and funerals on a day when Claire was out of town. I don't think we need a scandal to fire him. We should fire him for incompetence. Thank you."

A white-haired man who walks jerkily, nursing a bad leg: "This is going back a ways, before some of you joined up with us. The Peace March. When a bunch of us went to Washington to be in the Peace March. We wouldn't have done it if it hadn't been for Corky. He knew it was something we'd kick ourselves later if we didn't go, and he did the organizing. Did a good job too. I don't think you can talk about incompetence after that. Anyone can take an afternoon nap and not wake up on time. Let's put first things first. Thank you."

A middle-aged man wearing a sweater over his shirt and tie: "I know that my wife and I are not the only ones in this congregation that Corky has helped at a crucial time. Remember when your teenagers were picked up by the police? Corky went downtown for them, and to court too if needed. Where are all of you in his hour of need?"

A young man whose rectangular glasses lend him a look of solidity: "The most important service a minister performs is delivering a sermon every Sunday morning and not boring his audience to death. Corky Pearlman has never bored me, and I'm here every week. He doesn't mouth platitudes or spout a party line. He's an original thinker well worth going to bat for, even if we have to take flak from the *Clarion* for doing so. There'll be plenty of people who come to hear a controversial speaker, and I believe that once they hear him, they'll stay. So if we want to increase our membership, which the Board constantly touts, keep Reverend Pearlman in the pulpit."

Another young man, early thirties: "He doesn't bore me, either. He amazes me. He has a colossal nerve to stand up here and deliver irrational, pardon me, bullshit to people who wouldn't be here if they wanted to listen to that kind of stuff. We all come from somewhere else to be here, and I don't like it one bit when Neanderthalism is indulged in this room. That's exactly what I wanted to get away from, and thanks anyway, but no, I don't want to try tasting it again."

A silver-haired man: "Now that the subject of attracting new members has come up, I just want to point out that many potential new members have children. Need I say more?"

Several people stand up; a woman in front takes the microphone while the others sit back down: "Our religious education is the best I've ever seen, anywhere. People who have children often come to us specifically because of it, not in spite of it. And without the constant encouragement and sometimes even pressure from Corky to find teachers, and solicit the money for books and equipment, and strong-arm volunteers who have special talents to contribute – what I'm saying is that a school like ours takes vision and personal commitment, and we can thank Corky for providing it. Thank you, Corky."

Passion is palpable in the room. No one slumps or dozes. There have been muffled claps and occasionally a laugh as speaker after speaker has made points. Corky does not speak. Neither does Duncan Flannery, dapper and flame-haired, seated on the other side of the room between his petite wife, Eve, and his overgrown daughter, Josie, where he mirrors Corky's protected position between Claire and Nancy.

A slight man with a grizzled military haircut and steel-framed glasses reads from a small notebook: "We have a committee in this organization to select guest speakers. The minister has only one vote on the committee, the same as everyone else. We have twelve guest speakers a year. All of the committee members describe their religious beliefs as either humanist or earth-centered rather than mystical or theistic, yet in the last three years seventeen people have been guest speakers about the soul, about reincarnation, about extrasensory perceptions, about various notions of God, about conversations with the dead, and even about incursions into the science of physics by spiritualist superstitions. I believe these numbers signify a corrupting influence in our midst, especially when you add what we've been hearing week after week from our own minister. I didn't believe what was happening at first, so I didn't start keeping track right away, but since I've been counting, Mr. Pearlman has referred to God ninety three times from this pulpit, not to mention all the uncountable references to other superstitions. Most of us are here specifically because we don't want to be crippled by these ideas. If Mr. Pearlman wants to preach about God, I say let him go back to the Methodists where he came from."

A woman in a slate blue knit dress approaches the microphone slowly. Her face is solemn and her eyes magnified by the lenses of her glasses: "I have a letter here from a woman many of you used to know as a child in the Sunday School. She asked me not to reveal her identity for reasons which you'll understand in a moment. I know we agreed not to discuss the elements of Corky's currently upcoming trial, but this, while relevant, does not deal with that particular matter. I'd like to read you a paragraph from a letter I received from her last summer in the wake of the Skinner episode. I had written and told her what was happening, and she wrote back: 'I'm not surprised at your news concerning Corky Pearlman, and I'm glad that someone has had the courage to finally come forward. This is not by any means the first time he has behaved in an improper way toward children. I myself, when I was in the Sunday School there, was a recipient of his advances, carefully disguised as play acting, of course, which is, as you know, the way he operates.' While we must not judge anyone guilty until he's been tried, it certainly makes sense for us to protect our children."

Claire does not blink, does not move a muscle, as this blow hits her. Only later does she release her suspended breath slowly.

At last, after a great many opinions have been delivered, slips of paper are handed out and the members vote.

The outcome will not be announced until the bulletin is mailed out on Tuesday. Someone earlier foresaw that an announcement now, with tempers high, might result in the group's ruin. But, because the talk against Corky has seemed to weigh so much more heavily than the talk for him, the outcome is not really in doubt.

People find their coats. Still quiet from catharsis, they begin to leave the building. For the first time in years, Corky is not at the exit shaking hands. He is in the minister's study with Claire. The door is closed.

ANOTHER SHOE COMES OFF

In the white-tiled girls' bathroom in the church school wing Nancy has encountered Josie Flannery, who, in Nancy's mind, is entirely responsible for the morning's events and for her Uncle Corky's grief. Josie is in one of the stalls crying. Her sobs echo wetly in the hard-surfaced room.

Nancy knows who it is by the pink plastic jelly shoes she sees under the stall door. "Come out of there," she says.

Hesitantly, Josie comes out.

"You hypocrite!" hisses Nancy. "You nasty lying hypocrite. What do you have to cry about, anyway? You ought to go to jail for this."

Josie edges toward the exit away from Nancy's fury, then changes her mind as the door swings open and Heather Merchant comes in. Heather used to be Josie's friend, but no longer. She is Nancy's friend now. Josie stares at Heather, then makes a little "hunhh" noise and runs back to the toilet stall, where she slams the door and locks it. The bang echoes against the room's hard walls.

"Coward," says Nancy, her voice rising. "Crybaby coward."

"Let's drag her out," says Heather.

Nancy catches her glance in the mirror and nods. The two of them crouch in front of the locked stall door and reach under it for Josie's ankles. A foot kicks out wildly, grazing Nancy on the wrist. She grabs and catches the shoe. Then both feet disappear, as Josie climbs up on the edge of the toilet seat out of reach.

"Just wait," Nancy calls to her through the door. "The police know how to do things to people. You'll get yours." She and Heather leave the restroom then but not before she drops the pink plastic jelly slipper through the swinging door of the waste bin.

CLAIRE TAKES ACTION

Claire tromped the distance to Fred's house straight through the puddles, needing to move, to cut through opposition. Needing not to tiptoe, not to say, "Excuse me," when she bumped into a lamp post. Needing wet leaves shining on the pavement, the astringent air on her face and the hiss of her own breathing: all these to remind her that she was still Claire Pearlman active in the world, and that as long as Claire Pearlman had breath in her lungs, she would stand up and fight.

The log rolling had switched on again late in the afternoon. The phone rang; she answered. A man's voice, muffled and disguised: "And what do *you* like to do to little *boys?*" The floor under her gave way. She hung up.

Corky was sleeping again. In a chair. Shoes off, feet on a hassock, a hole in the toe of one sock. With his mouth open, he looked forsaken, as though his spirit had escaped through the opening.

Nothing had surprised Claire at the Meeting except the letter. She knew how much store some people set by tidiness and reliability. Corky was always up against that particular mind-set. Usually the ones who appreciated his originality managed to win. But the letter was different.

Why on earth would someone from the past bear such malice as to write that letter? Of course his style was play-acting. Everybody knew that. He treated all the children that way. He played with them. Kids loved him. How could this woman put such a bad light on it as to bring it up again years later?

It could only make sense if it were true, she thought. It could only make sense if it were true.

Maybe he did go too far in his playfulness. She could imagine a girl taking it wrong when he fell into one of his story roles. His "Bluebeard" grabbed and gathered up long hair in a display of menace. His "Prince" dropped to a knee and kissed a hand. He made no secret of acting this way. Not everyone liked it.

The letter had evidently come from someone who didn't. Claire had no idea who. This too bothered her. Someone, anyone, from the past, possibly someone they couldn't even remember, could send off an anonymous accusation that people would actually believe.

As Corky slept, Claire sat nearby, forcing herself to stay in the chair. He had been sleeping endlessly the past few days, the same way he had before, when it all happened last spring. Perhaps it was a blessing that he could escape this way, but his sleep left Claire at loose ends. Trouble stirred her up, made it necessary for her to act. Or at least talk – and of all things, on such a horrible day, one of the worst of her life, there was no one around to talk to. Romy was no help. Her boss needed a new application, access to data, always more data. Romy was erect at the keyboard, tap tap, tap tap tap, making strings of green symbols across the black screen. Even Nancy was away. She had gone home with Heather after Meeting and phoned for permission to stay for dinner.

For Claire, it was like being alone right after a funeral when a person needs company, needs the lights turned on, needs chicken casseroles and baked beans and zucchini bread: all the foods that are brought when people gather in times of trouble.

But even an ordinary Sunday afternoon would have been okay. It wasn't that Claire had to have visitors. Usually Corky was at his best right after preaching, and they took a walk along the lakeshore. He would tell her the ideas that had come to him while giving his sermon. That was his best time for ideas. They would talk, as excited as college students trying out new thoughts.

Today she could endure the strain of inactivity no longer. She went out in the car. Belted into the front seat, driving around Portville where only the shopping centers were alive, she still felt helpless, like a ticking clock with hands hanging loose over the six. She couldn't even tell an obscene phone caller to go to hell. Then she realized that driving wasn't going to help either. She had to move under her own power. She had to act. She drove home and parked the car but did not go in the house.

Fred Bekin had not come to the Meeting. A disappointment, but who knows what might have prevented him. Claire refused to assume that he had lost interest. Maybe what he could do wouldn't accomplish much, but at the moment his story was the only effort she could think of to make. Steps in the right direction are better than putting your feet up and napping.

As she walked, another quick squall blew through the neighborhood, dumped its bucketful, and sighed away. She had forgotten to bring her umbrella from the car; her hair and her rose-colored raincoat from League Thrift were wet when she reached Fred's porch.

But her coat was handsome, silky and fine, (at least $250 new, though she had only paid $10 at the thrift shop) a muted, dusty shade of autumn rose that was her color if anything was. She had good hair that curled in the rain. She shook off the droplets and prepared her appeal.

FRED LISTENS; CLAIRE TALKS

"Mrs. Claire!" Fred was wearing a plaid bathrobe with blue flannel pajama legs showing underneath. "Come inside." There was relief in his tone as well as surprise.

Claire stood back for a moment. "I don't mean to intrude. I should have phoned instead." She hoped her wish to charm was not too obvious. "But I really wanted to see you."

And also to be seen by me, Fred thought, holding the door wider, reading her mind and letting its thoughts flatter him. "You're wet," he said. "Come inside. Don't let the bathrobe fool you. It only means I'm comfortable."

As he held the door open and she passed close by, each caught a whiff of the other: Claire smelled the wood smoke that permeated his bathrobe, which she associated with competent manliness. Fred smelled the dampness in her hair, and another odor–so faint he was barely aware of it–from long ago. The odor was just a trace of Claire's powder, L'Origan, an unmistakably feminine scent. Now, of course, the connection, whatever it was, was not conscious. Claire relaxed a little, in good hands; Fred felt rejuvenated after his sick day.

"Let me hang up your coat." He held the shoulders of her silky rose-colored coat while she slid out of it. "Please sit down. I'll get the fire going again. Sara," he called toward the kitchen, "we got company." He took Claire's coat to the hooks in the hall and made room by dumping his old Boston Braves jacket–his perfectly good work jacket that Sara had better never throw away–on the floor.

Claire's boots had left wet footprints and a pin oak leaf on the plank floor. She went to one end of the couch where Fred had spent the day. The zigzag afghan was on the floor. She picked it up and folded it automatically before sitting down, then noticed its colors, noticed that it was hand knitted and wondered if Fred's aunt had done it, or perhaps his pharmacist wife, and if so, why she had chosen such violent hues. She looked around, remembering nothing of the room from the other night except the fire.

The windows were not exactly covered, but were decorated by faded net curtains, loosely woven from blue cotton string, that looked old and well-made, like curtains from a summer home of the twenties, used three months a year for ten years, then stored carefully for another fifty.

Most of the furniture was wood; the couch and wing chair were the only upholstered pieces. There was a Boston rocker haphazard in the middle of the room as though frequently moved around, and another rocker even smaller than her own at home. An unvarnished table was covered with papers and magazines with a ladder-back chair nearby. Another table, a low round one, held more magazines and a roll of toilet paper. A grandchild? Near this table was a small, threadbare, Oriental rug. It and the hearthrug were the only floor coverings in the room.

Several windows, three doors, the fireplace and an open staircase left little wall space, but what was available was filled with pictures that looked acquainted with attics and flea markets. The heads and necks of three white horses with wild eyes and flaring nostrils. A Venetian canal scene colored mostly orange. A grouping of someone's ugly ancestors. A thatched cottage with a flower garden in faded colors, and a Norman Rockwell print of the corner druggist in his green coat dispensing pills to a little old lady, prim in a hat.

Marigold had come into the room to get her bony head stroked. What could Claire make of the people who had put this room together? They didn't spend much money. They didn't go in for show. And because of the dog, she knew that Fred was not mean. A mean man, even a not-so-mean one, would have long since had this ancient dog with its senile grin and its reeking breath put down. But where was some evidence of aesthetic feeling or scholarship? It did seem to be an odd living room for a writer. Those pictures, for instance. Wouldn't a writer want something more sophisticated on his walls?

"Marigold, lay down." Fred's slippered feet had made no noise. "Please excuse Sara. She has some things she has to do. Maybe she'll come in later." He squatted on one heel at the hearth and poked the ashes until a few red coals appeared. Claire noticed the economical movements he made, the decisive hands, hands that looked capable instead of needy. Perhaps a man with hands like that could afford horse heads with flaring nostrils. He laid two small logs on top of the grate and stuffed some kindling underneath with the coals. "Burn," he said, and waited for a moment. When there was no sign of a quick blaze, he added two newspaper pages of stock prices wadded into tight horns. They flamed up immediately.

"One more minute. Let me fix things just so." He pushed the armchair into a right angle touching the couch and sat down. "Now," he said, leaning back with his arms laid out on the chair arms and his lizard-like eyes attentive. "You didn't come here to pay a social call."

Claire shook her head. Marigold nudged her knee. She resumed stroking.

"Tell me."

"It was the meeting this morning." The memory took shape as a knot in her throat that threatened to choke her.

"I meant to be there, but I got sick." When she didn't say anything, he added, "I'm okay now. A new man. Tell me about the meeting."

She swallowed past the stricture in her throat. "The whole congregation was there. The faithful, the unfaithful, the curiosity-seekers, everyone." The faces rose in her mind's eye: people who had nothing at stake, nothing to lose, deciding her fate. "Corky doesn't get to preach any longer."

Fred nodded. Just what he had expected.

"It was terrible. He looks so bad with the whiskers he can't shave off and leaving his food untouched and sleeping all the time with it not doing him any good."

"I can imagine." Rumpled clothes. Worms in his brain. "Were you both there for the whole meeting?"

"Yes. We're members of the congregation. They couldn't keep us out."

"I'm surprised you'd want to be there."

"It wasn't to have a good time, let me tell you. But when your future is at stake, you like to know what's happening."

"What did happen?"

"The sanctuary was packed. They ran out of seating and the last to arrive had to hunker down on little blond kindergarten chairs. The place was eerie. The ceiling lights are awfully harsh compared to the side lights we usually use, and a couple of them flickered off and on, off and on, the whole time. It looked like night even with the daylight, such as it was, out the window. You know the trees out that front window, did you notice them?"

Fred nodded, remembering.

"Well, sometimes you see cardinals and jays and juncos in those trees on Sunday morning during Meeting, and how beautiful it looks with the life of the earth going on right along with the life of the spirit. But this morning there was a flock of crows out there and not another bird in sight. They cawed so loud you could hear them through the thermo pane.

"The president of the congregation had people take turns talking, each one coming up to the microphone, even the little old ladies with their canes and their walkers. Some of them wouldn't look at us at all and others looked as though we'd just been hauled out of a pool of stinking slime. As though they might ruin their clothes by being in our presence.

"But we do have friends there, and there were people who spoke for us. It was good to find out that there even people who appreciate Corky's theology."

"Did anyone bring up the possibility that the accusations are false?"

"No. Far otherwise. Some of them edged close to saying they were true, even though the subject was out of bounds."

"Was the little girl there for all of this?"

"Josie. Yes she was. And that's a crime. Can you imagine, letting a child cause this much havoc and then allowing her to watch the adults quarrel over the mess she's made? Just think what she's learning about her capacity to make trouble. Mind you, I don't mean she did it on purpose, she's too crazy about Corky for that, and I wonder if we'll ever learn just how Dunk Flannery got her to tell such a story."

Claire was so persuasive that Fred had to make an effort to remember that all the havoc she was talking about might well have happened because the reverend didn't keep his hands to himself. "So he doesn't preach any more," he said.

"That's right," she answered. "And preaching is like breathing to

him. Without preaching he turns blue in the face and loses consciousness. It's a death sentence. In fact it's already happening. He's
been sleeping all the time since this started. He's asleep right now. It's
like having your husband in the chair dead, only you're supposed to
pretend he's alive."

But Fred was thinking not about the death of the spirit but about
the starvation of the body. "What about the economic prospects?" he
asked, as delicately as he could.

She wavered her hand. "We won't starve," she answered. "I have income from my first marriage. And we don't have to move until they
find another minister. They don't want the parsonage uninhabited
over the winter. So it could be worse. But one or the other of us –
probably both of us – need work."

Fred felt easier. A reprieve. He had pictured furniture on the sidewalk.

"What I'm thinking about your article is this," said Claire. "If it's
made public that Corky's been unjustly accused and ruined in this awful way, he'll be invited to speak places. You know how curious people
are, and how they come forth when *Sixty Minutes* points out an injus-
tice. And speaking could lead to something better." She smiled at Fred
tentatively. "Do you think you could get it out right away?"

Fred's face knotted. "I'm sorry, Mrs. Claire, but I'm not Dan
Rather. And I'm not gonna be doing it for television. A magazine story
doesn't have the same impact." He rose from the chair and busied himself with the poker and tongs. Recognizing this moment as a water-
shed, he thought about what to say, while he pried up one of the burning pieces of wood and turned it over.

"Look," he said, finally, "I got a confession to make." He examined
the word "would-be" in his mind, but he could not bring himself to
use it. He sat back down, this time on the couch beside Claire, facing
the fire.

"I'm a guy outta work, too," he said. "I found myself on the side-
walk outside Powkin when it got gobbled up by the International
Amalgamated Blah Blah Blah, and I'm trying to use what I know
something about to make a new career. Only cobbling up books like
'How to Fix the Air Conditioner,' is not the same as being Harrison
Salisbury. Nobody at the magazines knows for sure whether Fred Bekin

can produce the story or not. Even Fred Bekin doesn't know. I don't have much of a portfolio. A few contacts, a few clippings. It's not automatic that I get a contract. You have to get yourself a credit rating, so to speak."

The confession was over. He faced Claire. "I'll do the best I can."

Listening to him, Claire sorted through possible responses. She could cry with disappointment like a five year-old, and disgrace herself. She could say, "There, there, it's going to be all right," like a mother, and have Fred cuddled in her lap instead of her being cuddled in his.

"Well, join the crowd," was what she finally said. She gave him a smile with as many dimples as she could muster. "We'll all do the best we can, and maybe Corky will get his reputation back and you'll get a platinum card."

Fred's sigh of relief was audible. "I was afraid you were gonna write me off."

"I'm in no position to write anyone off."

"So tell me more. I better get cracking."

Her head went back and her eyes closed as she thought. "I don't know where to begin. There's so much going on and so many people involved and it's such a disaster that I don't know how to think about it." She opened her eyes and leaned toward him with a sudden movement. "Do you remember Emily Dickinson's poem that starts out, 'After great pain a formal feeling comes'?"

When he shook his head, she shrugged. "No matter. Anyway, the last stanza has been going through my mind all afternoon. Corky quoted it on the way home from Meeting. It goes:

'This is the hour of lead, remembered if outlived,
as freezing persons recollect the snow,
first chill, then stupor, then the letting go.'

"That's what this latest event has been like for him. Chill, then stupor. He's stunned. New things keep happening but none of them hurt anymore. Or rather, I know they're hurting him, but I don't think he feels the pain."

He nodded, watching her. He would really rather this were a social call after all. It was work, paying attention. It was work, feeling sorry for somebody. He didn't like feeling sorry for her. All this misery, all this concern. Why didn't she just dump the bastard? With all his ministerial polish, there was something not-right about him. She was wasting her concern. The man wasn't worth it.

"One of the reasons it hurts so much is that this is a child we've known since she was born. The other one, the one last spring, was too. Corky did both of their naming ceremonies. We've babysat with them countless times. I ran a Mothers' Morning Out at the church for several years and the little one was there every week. The older one went to camp with us three years in a row. They're like family."

All the more reason to suspect your husband, thought Fred. He didn't say it. That was another hurdle coming up, bringing up the possibility that he was guilty. "Who are these people?" asked Fred. "The same thing happened last spring, right? Is this all one family?"

"No. The two little girls are not related. The Skinners moved to Des Moines in the summer. Not because of what happened; they were going to go anyway."

"How old are these kids?"

"Josie's nine and Beth's, well Beth would be about twelve now."

"Look," said Fred. "I don't know enough yet to know what questions to ask. How about you start with the first you knew of it."

Claire settled back. "Last spring was the first I knew about it. Last spring was when it all started." There was no point going into anonymous accusations from long ago. "Corky was saying goodbye to people as they left the church one Sunday last spring, the first Sunday in May, and when Liz Skinner got to the door, she wouldn't shake Corky's hand. She said Corky was going to hear from the prosecutor, that she had reported Corky to the police and that there was a warrant out for his arrest. She wouldn't say anything else, not what it was all about, not boo. We had no idea. I called her after we got home, and she hung up on me."

Claire gave Fred a quick look. "Understand, now, that this is a woman who used to adore Corky. She took him goodies at the church when he'd be working there, she typed his sermons for him when he didn't have a secretary, she did all kinds of extras around the church. And then she got soured on him. We weren't sure why, though it's possible it was the same thing that turned everybody else against him too, his change of heart about religion."

Fred interrupted. "You're talking about the first little girl now?"

"Yes. Beth Skinner and her mother, Liz. Anyway, we thought we'd better get an attorney quick, so I called my ex-husband, who specializes in criminal cases. He talked with the prosecutor's office and found out what was going on and arranged it that Corky would go in on his own instead of being dragged in by the police. He was supposed to go in the next week on Monday morning."

Here Claire stopped for a moment. "Only it didn't happen that way," she said. "On Friday evening the police came. You've never heard a knock like that in your life. You know exactly who it is, and no matter if you're pure as the driven snow, you're scared to death. Because they have the power to ruin your life, even when you're innocent.

"Well," she said. "They took Corky downtown while I tried to get enough money together to bail him out.

"Up until then we hadn't felt too much afraid. After all, we knew there was nothing to it, and we thought everyone else would know it too. You like to think that a person can't really get into serious trouble through false accusations. You like to think that justice prevails." She shook her head. "Let me tell you that it doesn't necessarily prevail. That case never went to trial, but Corky is out of a job and it's certainly not going to be easy to find another one with this hanging over his head."

"Whoa. Back up. What happened the night he was arrested? Did he spend the night in jail?"

"Not quite. They took him to the lockup where he was beaten up." She gazed at Fred as though daring him to deny that this could happen.

"He was beaten up," said Fred. "Who beat him up?"

"Not the police," she answered. "They didn't have to do it themselves. All they did was put him in a room with some criminals and no guard. Corky doesn't have any sense about how to protect himself, so when somebody asked him what he was there for, he told them. He didn't have the sense to say he'd been arrested for something innocuous like pouring acid in a swimming pool or burning down a hospital. No! He says, 'Child molesting,' big as you please, expecting them to see how ridiculous it was, and two of them jumped him."

A picture of the reverend's skinny frame flashed through Fred's mind. He wouldn't stand a chance. "I don't suppose he's much of a fighter."

"Hardly. Fortunately I didn't know this was happening at the time, or I'd have been even more frantic than I was. I was busy with my own problems. It was a Friday night and the bank had just closed. I got what money I could from the machine, a drop in the bucket. My ex-husband was out of town. I started calling people, but the ones we know well enough to borrow money from were already out for the evening. It took almost four hours and seven different people to get together the bail money. And then I went downtown where they tell you to wait. And wait. I had a friend with me, thank goodness. In fact it was my friend's employer who loaned us most of the money we needed. The manager at K-Mart. Don't ever say anything against K-Mart; there's at least one good person in the organization. Anyway, here we are downtown late on a Friday night. I'll tell you, the people you see around the jail at that time of night don't make you feel too easy about having a wad of cash in your purse. We had to wait and we had to wait, so we went to a sleazy little bar and sat around all hunched down hoping nobody would notice us."

"But did they let him go?" asked Fred.

"Finally. It was about one-thirty in the morning. We went back home and took sleeping pills. We knew we needed some rest so we just took a couple of pills apiece and blanked it all out for a few hours. But we didn't get to rest for long. There was a reporter at the police station. There always is. You know how they're always on the lookout for some scandal involving a minister. After the paper came out and the TV news, we started getting phone calls. Threats. Hate mail. There was a congregational meeting after church on the Sunday, a lot like the one today, and we had to listen to people discussing Corky's potential for damaging the church. The only difference is that now they have their speeches polished."

"Is that when they fired him?"

"No, they waited a few weeks for that. It's written into the by-laws that they can't fire a minister without at least two meetings of the congregation and a two-thirds majority." Claire's face became amused for a moment. "They didn't have any trouble getting the two-thirds majority to fire him," she said, "but they couldn't get the three-fourths majority they need to call another minister, so they've been stuck with him because of their own contentious ways." She smiled outright. "That's the only justice in the whole mess." Then she frowned. "They still can't get together enough to find someone but they've decided that it's better to have none at all than to keep Corky in the pulpit."

Claire's words reminded Fred of the outspoken little lady who had talked to him at the Freethinkers' Meeting. "Let me ask you a question. Does the reverend really hear voices?"

Claire stared him, her train of thought derailed. "If you mean is he psychotic, no. Let's just say that his mind's ear has twenty-twenty hearing."

"How about his mother's voice coming from the rolling pin?"

"Where on earth did you get an idea like that?"

"From one of your parishioners," he answered. "Did you hear the sermon Friday night when he appeared to leave his prepared text and started talking about spirits inhabiting animals and trees?"

"He does things like that. It shakes everybody up. Something reminds him of a bit of ancient wisdom that he believes is worth paying attention to, and he puts it in whether it fits or not." Suddenly Claire yawned. "This may be enough for one night," she said. "But I have a suggestion. You need a broader picture than I can give you, prejudiced as I am."

"And what's that?"

"That you get involved with the Meeting," she said. "I don't know what your religion is, and I'm not trying to push mine. But if you're going to write about Corky, you'll need to write about the Meeting too; they're inseparable."

The crease in front of her ear appeared again, the one Fred had already begun using as an indicator of the amount of charm she was turning on.

"I been planning to come to your Meeting." He avoided the word "church" as they did. "But I want to come incognito. I want to talk to people. What I don't want is to take sides."

"I don't mean take sides. And being incognito is excellent. Who knows, maybe people will act a little better because there's somebody new around. You know, be ashamed for a new person to see how petty they can be. But no, that's just wishful thinking. They're letting us stay in the parsonage, partly because they want it occupied, and partly because at least some of them would feel bad about putting us out, but they're still making it difficult."

She went on. "They voted against roof repairs because they're going to put on a new roof next summer, and today they voted against installing a new dryer. The one that's there burned out and we have to hang the wash all over the house or else go to a Laundromat. That's no enormous problem, really. It's just hassle. But I'm afraid the furnace is going to go, and we can't get through a winter on a space heater."

"Is there something wrong with it, or is it just that you worry?"

"The repairman who worked on it last winter said they'd better get a new one in the summer. Of course they didn't. The congregation has chosen this issue to be perfectly horrid about. But this isn't your problem."

"So how do I go about getting involved?"

"Come to church and volunteer for committee work. There's a drive on now to get people to help with everything that needs to be done."

"Tell me another way."

"You could donate a lot of money. That would make you Mister Big right away."

"That's what I was afraid of. What kinda work needs to be done?" As he spoke the mantel clock struck the half hour.

She looked at the clock and stood up without answering. "I'm going to go now. I don't want Corky to miss Masterpiece Theater. He'll sleep right through it if I don't wake him. We need to get our minds off our troubles for a little while, and the king's about to put down the uprising. We've watched every episode of this one. I know it sounds silly to want to watch TV at a time like this, but life does go on."

Fred smiled broadly. "Tell you what. I'll come to your church, your Meeting, next Sunday and keep my eyes and ears open for opportunity. I would have been there this morning only I got a touch of the flu and spent the day sweating it out." He rose. "It wouldn't kill me to do a little church work. I could be an usher or something. Pass the collection plate."

"It's the Building Maintenance Committee that needs the help. They're looking for people to do plastering and painting."

"Oh Lord." Fred let his eyes wander around the room and notice all the plaster cracks and the dirty smudges. Sara would never let him live it down if he painted and plastered at church instead of at home. "I'll be back in a minute."

He left the room to bring Claire's coat. In the hallway he took off his bathrobe and slipped on a pair of overalls and his Boston Braves jacket. He couldn't let Claire walk home alone.

When he returned to the living room, she said, "There are discussion groups you could join too. They help new people get acquainted. If you were just an ordinary newcomer, I'd say to get in a discussion group and leave committee work until later. But if you really want to speed the process up and find out what's going on, you'll have to do something to make everyone think you're a fine fellow with excellent judgment and all kinds of talent. You know what I mean."

"I'm afraid so." Fred saw himself spending hours on end refurbishing the Freethinkers' Meetinghouse, then more hours on end doing the same at home. He would have to match the effort he put in for others with effort he put in for Sara. He saw himself with less and less time for anything but work.

But what could he do? He couldn't write without information, could he? "I'll be there next Sunday," he said. "You wanna eat, you gotta hustle."

"What?"

"A figure of speech."

Claire opened the door and stepped out on the porch. "I believe it's stopped raining," she said. "Good night."

"I'm coming with you. I don't want to read in the paper you got mugged on the way home from my house." At her gesture of demurral, he closed the door behind him. "No argument, please."

They went down the driveway to the sidewalk that wound around the neighborhood. The parsonage was six blocks from Fred's; he could make it back by nine.

It was no longer raining, but everything looked shiny and slick. The streetlight at the corner put their two shadows on the walk in front of them, stocky Fred and short Claire.

"This reminds me of when I noticed I was taller than my mother," he said. "We were walking home from the show one night and my shadow was longer than hers."

"That's an nice thing to remember," said Claire. "Odd, too."

"Not so odd," said Fred. "There was always just the two of us, unless Aunt Jenny was with us. When I saw that shadow, I felt like I might finally grow up enough to take care of her."

Claire's laugh pealed out. "I thought you were going to say you realized she couldn't boss you around any longer."

"I don't remember her bossing me around," he said. "She didn't have to. She really needed me, needed for me to act right, so I did."

"Is your mother still alive?"

"No. She died in 1953 while I was in Korea in the Army. I never got a chance to take care of her."

"And your father?"

"I never knew my father. He left before I was born, just disappeared. My mother never even got a divorce from him."

"That must have been rough."

"For her it was. I didn't know. I had what I needed and didn't miss what I didn't know about. Oh, of course I thought boys who had fathers were pretty lucky, but I didn't know what it meant."

The sky overhead was clear as a black crystal dish, with stars. Fred took Claire's elbow to steer her around puddles, but that was awkward, so she put her hand through his arm, which he promptly bent, and they walked for half a block silent, each one too much aware of the closeness to say a word.

Then Claire took her hand away to step around a puddle and didn't put it back. "Growing up with your mother, or your mother and your aunt, how did you learn how to be a man?"

"Ha," Fred said, almost in a bark. "My sergeant in basic training put it different, but he was asking the same thing. I guess at first I grew up to be the kind of man my mother wanted, and in the Army, I learned how to be a soldier, and between the two, I got to be me. Not much soldier, probably."

"That's good."

"Also, I started to work when I was ten years old. A kid learns a lot, working." It was a pleasure, remembering, and telling Claire. He and his mother had lived in a neighborhood of small, dilapidated houses in Buffalo during the winter he was ten. Within a three block area were five women who lived alone and were happy to pay him a quarter a week to tend their furnaces early each morning. Making the rounds had been his first job. "I used to start out at five in the morning, in the dark. There'd be new snow, up three, four feet deep, with new soot on top. It was always light enough to see, even that early, because of the snow." He could smell the cold winter odor of coal furnaces, and he laid footprints up each woman's front walk as he went.

"I had their keys, five of them, on a ring, and I was proud like you wouldn't believe." Indoors, a floor of worn linoleum might sag under his steps as he went first into the dining room to turn the crank that opened the damper. Then he would tiptoe quietly across the kitchen to the trapdoor in the pantry, lift it and attach it to the wall with a hook, and descend the steep stairs sideways to get to the furnace.

"It's different now. People got gas and oil furnaces. Then it was still coal, right before everybody converted. You had to shake and shake to get the ashes down into the ash pit," he said. If he was lucky and the lady had banked the fire right and closed the damper, there would be red coals left from the night before; if not, he would lay a bed of twisted newspapers and some kindling. The worn metal coal shovel would scrape and clang on the concrete floor of the coal bin beside the furnace. A few scoops of coal, a short wait to be sure the fire had caught, and he'd be on to the next house with the next key ready on his ring.

Sometimes the lady would be up, wrapped in a faded robe with her hair on metal curlers under a hair net, brewing coffee in the cold kitchen. There would be a light, and occasionally he was given a cup of hot chocolate.

"The money, that's what I liked," he said. "I made $1.25 a week, and my mother let me keep fifty cents. I'd go downtown on Saturday morning and buy something, anything, to spend my fifty cents."

From the furnace-tending job Fred had graduated to carrying newspapers. He had pushed lawnmowers, wielded snow shovels, walked dogs, painted porches, and delivered Christmas wreaths. Watered plants, beat carpets, weeded gardens, and raked gravel driveways. He fed a canary once while its owner was in Florida, and helped nail shingles on a roof. From the time he was ten he had worked.

They turned onto Clover Street now, and the parsonage was just ahead.

Claire took his arm again. "This has done me good," she said. "Got me through a bad couple of hours. I'm grateful to you."

"How about advice?" Fred asked her. "Is there anybody special I ought to look for when I go to Meeting?"

"Good thought. Dunk Flannery is on the Maintenance Committee. If you do any work with them, you'll be working right alongside him."

"One more quick question. I just wondered what kind of minister the reverend is. I mean, there's no Freethinker Theological School, is there?"

"No there isn't, more's the pity. Corky was a Methodist minister when I met him. That's how he grew up, that's where he got his training. And he preached in Methodist churches for almost twenty years, then in a Unitarian church for a while. But that's another story."

"And maybe I'll hear it one of these days," said Fred.

They had reached the parsonage. Claire turned in. "Goodnight now." When she was a few steps away, she said, "Do me a favor. Stop calling me Mrs. Claire." She hurried to the porch.

He had no answer available. He waited until she was inside, then ran home. He too wanted to watch Masterpiece Theater.

A NEWCOMER AT THE PARSONAGE

A few days later, Corky, who had been reading quietly with the others in the living room, suddenly broke the silence with an explosive laugh that startled Claire out of her cauldron of thoughts and broke the rhythm of Romy's keystrokes. Claire's mouth worked, chewing something that wasn't there. By dint of effort she held her mouth still and set her chair to rocking again.

Romy turned away from the green gobbledygook on her black screen. "Well?" she asked. "Where did you lay the egg?"

Corky shushed her with a raised palm and continued to read, chuckling.

Romy wore a thick wool coat-sweater with a shawl collar buttoned high under her blonde hair, the sleeves unrolled so that only her fingers peeked out. A blanket was wound around her legs like a thick straight skirt.

An hour earlier, the increasing chill had made it evident that Claire's fears had come true. Adjusting the thermostat did not turn the furnace on. She called the heating service and was put on hold. Finally she was told, "I'm sorry, ma'am, but we have a notice that the Freethinkers won't pay any more bills from the parsonage."

"We'll pay for it ourselves," Claire answered. "Send someone over as soon as possible."

To Corky she said, "This is the shabbiest trick yet. If the house were empty, they'd have to keep the furnace working, but as long as we're here, they know we'll do it whether we have the money or not."

"That can't have been a Board decision," he answered. "Somebody took it upon himself. As soon as they find out, there'll be a fuss."

"And in the meantime we're cold."

Claire's anger had kept her warm for a while, but then turned into a sour cold lump, like a black hole, that drew warmth into it.

Corky finally answered Romy, "I didn't lay an egg, but listen to this." Again snorting with laughter, he read aloud: "If a book makes my whole body so cold no fire can ever warm me, I know it's poetry." He directed his charming doggy grin at her. "Emily Dickinson. See how the poet has to work to accomplish what a broken furnace can do just-like-that."

"You're not really reading that," said Romy. "You made it up."

"I swear it's right here," exclaimed Corky. "It's in Emily's letters." He held up the book, holding his place with his thumb.

"Convenient," answered Romy.

"You wait, there'll be a cluster of references to warmth and cold now." He nodded to Claire. "Won't there?"

"My cold is like a wet wet nose," she answered, still rocking. As their circumstances became more desperate, so did their play.

"Have you caught a cold?" asked Romy.

"No, why?" said Claire.

Romy bent over her keyboard. Then she looked up again and asked, "When did the furnace man say someone would be here?"

"Shaaad–rach," sang Corky, doing trombone motions with his hands. "Dah-dah dah in de fiery furnace."

Hastily, before Corky could improvise another bar, Claire answered, "They're all out on calls, but he'll send us the first one who comes back in."

Romy raised her sweater sleeve and looked pointedly at her watch. "And since it's three-thirty on a Friday afternoon, you can be sure that no one will be available until weekend rates are in effect."

"Yes, Romy," said Claire without spirit.

The phone rang. They all sat still. It rang again. Claire got up, mentally toughening her defenses. Not all the calls were insulting, but there was always the chance, and she had to protect Corky. She had taken over answering the phone after the most frightening call of all. On the other end had been a friendly voice offering Corky a list of children for rent. The list cost $100, a subscription $200, and a child of either sex could be rented for as little as $150 a night, guaranteed clean, no whiners or problem children, and you could pay with plastic. The contact point was Chicago, only a little over an hour away.

It just so happened that Claire had picked up the upstairs phone and heard this horrible sales pitch too. She came running down and flew to where Corky was sitting. "We've got to let the police know about this."

Romy had been impatient at her dismay. "You can't tell me this is the first you've heard of these people."

"It's the first I've heard directly. And now they think we're in sympathy with them!"

Romy challenged Corky. "I'd think this would be right up your alley as a minister. You could start a crusade."

He lifted his head, which had been buried in Claire's bosom. "Crusades have a lower success rate than weight loss diets. And you're forgetting that I no longer have a pulpit."

"But isn't there virtue in taking the right stand, even if you don't succeed?" Her attitude was not serious, but mocking.

But Corky did not accept the mockery. "Romy, in my position, taking a public stand on this would be not only useless but ludicrous." His voice was harsh. "I must lend you the tape of my sermon on virtue. Virtue is scarce and costly. No one is allotted very much of it. A person should use his pittance of virtue on his own behavior, which he can at least affect, if not control."

Romy's comeback was quick. "That sounds like a Freethinker sermon."

"It is, because I made it one, but the idea's been around since the primordial ooze began to give off gas and preachers followed suit."

Corky did put the sermon tape out for Romy, and she did listen to it. "That wasn't half bad," she told him grudgingly.

This time the phone call was not an intruder but Claire's friend Alfreda, whose shift on the admissions desk at Portville General had just ended. "Claire, honey, is there any room at the inn?" Alfreda's rich loud voice sounded good in the cold room.

"It depends," said Claire.

"There's a young man here whose car was wrecked last night, and he needs a place to stay."

"I don't know, Alfreda," said Claire. "We're not very cheerful."

"His name's Wolf," said Alfreda. She waited a moment, then urged Claire further, "It wouldn't hurt you to have something different to think about. He's upset about what happened and needs some TLC. That's why I didn't just send him to a motel to wait for his insurance to come through. And with Romy at your house and all."

Claire held back a laugh. Alfreda didn't know Romy's brand of TLC. "Let me ask the others." Claire put her hand over the phone and said. "Alfreda has a young man who needs a bed for a night or two. What do you think?"

"Why not?" said Corky. "This is still a parsonage even if I'm no longer a parson."

Romy shrugged. "Who am I to complain if you take in strays?"

"Send him on over," said Claire. After she hung up, she said, "I didn't think to tell her it was cold here." She opened her little Rolodex, then said, "Oh well, what difference does it make? Maybe the furnace man will get here."

"Sure," said Romy, without raising her eyes from the screen.

Claire went upstairs, glad for the push out of inertia. She would have to make up the spare bedroom for the guest. Finding a burned-out bulb in the bed lamp, she returned to the downstairs utility cupboard for a new one. There were none left. We're getting poorer and poorer, she thought. This brought to mind the fact that she had been putting off getting her résumé out. Next week, she thought. Next week for sure. She took a bulb from a little-used lamp and went back upstairs.

Nancy arrived home from school with Heather. Claire shifted one last stack of Corky's books from the reading chair to the floor in hopes of making this catch-all room with the worst of the furniture into a place that offered some comfort. She could hear voices from downstairs and the girls' laughter. What a blessing that Nancy was living with them. Corky gathered up jokes like delicacies to present to her; the little girl's arrival home in the afternoon was all that pulled him out of profound torpor.

Claire's older sister, Claudine, who was also Nancy's jealous and protective grandmother, had phoned as soon as she heard of Corky's arrest. "Let me talk to Romy," she said. Romy, reluctant as always to talk to her mother, came to the phone to be told that it would be her own fault if Nancy ended up raped like Corky's other victims. Claudine even threatened to sue for custody. "I'm not one to run to lawyers," she said, "but it may be my duty in this case. With my own granddaughter. Romy," she pleaded, "use some sense. Get her away from that man." But when Romy was in need, she had not bypassed her own mother and come to Claire for reasons that were trivial, and she was not amenable to her mother's advice now. "So he's a screwball," she answered. "That doesn't make him dangerous." It didn't please Claire that Romy was so resolutely blind to Corky's qualities, but at least she wasn't buying Claudine's scare story, and Nancy was here, where she was not only being well-treated but was performing a valuable service.

Soon the girls clattered up the stairs to Nancy's room. "Hi," said Nancy. "Can I turn up the heat?"

"Put on something warmer," Claire answered. "The furnace isn't working."

"Bummer," said Heather, affecting the stylish, washed-out tone so cultivated by the older girls. Her low, hoarse little voice mimicked the sound so convincingly that Claire felt like shaking her.

"Did you have to stay after school? It's almost four thirty."

A careful look passed between the two girls. "We stopped at Rochester's for some Milk Duds," said Nancy. "See?" And she held out the box as proof.

Claire knew that something was being concealed. She knew also that backing Nancy into a corner would induce her to compound whatever lie she was telling. So she only gave the girls a quizzical raise of an eyebrow to let them know she wasn't completely fooled.

Although Nancy and Heather tried, every afternoon, to catch Josie after school, they did not always succeed. Sometimes Josie escaped by being the first person out the door. She would run, then, in spite of Ben's bellowing, "WALK!" Sometimes she escaped by being last, by going to the school library or by helping the teacher tidy up. But today the girls had caught her, and it was worth the effort, because between the two of them, they got in some punishing pinches and a stomp on the toes before she broke away and ran. "Liar, liar, liar," they sang in unison. "Yeah," Nancy yelled down the street after her. "Nobody believes you." "Nobody would kiss those big horse teeth," Heather yelled louder. Josie's permanent teeth were still too large for her mouth, giving her accusers a focus for their attack. "Elephant teeth." "Rhinoceros teeth." "Hippopotamus teeth." Even after Josie was out of earshot, they continued to scream insults, albeit mixed with giggles: "You couldn't sit on his lap, you lard ass; his knees would break down."

Although the girls' punishment of Josie had begun as retribution for the damage done to Corky, it was now becoming an absorbing pursuit in itself, elevating moments of the school day above the humdrum of arithmetic, social studies, and language arts. In the midst of a boring recitation all Nancy need do was raise her upper lip and show Heather across the room her perfectly shaped little teeth for both girls to collapse into laughter. Outside of school when a game began to pall, there was always The Cause: Josie. Everyone needs something to be outraged about; otherwise the molecules go to sleep. These girls were learning young.

Now Nancy offered her Aunt Claire a Milk Dud, then took Heather into her room and closed the door.

A little later Alfreda arrived with Wolf Rausch, a well-built, clean-faced, blond young man with wide-set blue eyes and a bandage on his forehead. He shook everyone's hand and repeated everyone's name before he accepted a seat.

After introducing Wolf, Alfreda went to the kitchen with Claire, who wanted to fetch a bottle of wine to make it seem warmer in the house. "I don't really mean to dump a problem in your lap," said Alfreda, "but you'll know how to handle him."

Claire crouched to reach into the dark cabinet under the big old kitchen sink. "I'd like just once to meet someone I didn't need to know how to handle." A quick vision of Fred Bekin flashed through her mind, sleek and solid on his feet. She pulled out a jug of ammonia, then bleach and then vinegar before finding the greenish glass gallon of burgundy.

"I'm going to let Wolf tell you his own story," said Alfreda. "He's not hurt badly. It's just that he's been though a horrible experience and I thought he needed people around, someone to talk to. You know, a steadying influence."

"So you brought him here." They carried jug and glasses into the living room.

Claire, remembering that she had to be getting a job, took her friend aside again and said, "Listen, Alfreda, keep your eyes and ears open for me, will you? I need to find a job."

"Of course. I don't know of anything offhand, but I'll ask around. Your degree is in social work?"

Claire nodded. "I have a good résumé. The six years at Porthaven was a good as anything of its kind."

"But if not even Porthaven could renew its funding," Alfreda said, "that means…"

"Exactly. There's not much in my field out there. I can't afford to be choosy, and I'm not going to be. I'll take anything within reason."

Alfreda turned down the glass of wine, but she went back to the living room to say goodbye to Wolf. "I hope the rest of your trip is downright boring," she said.

"I hope so too." He stood up and took Alfreda's hand in an easy way that made Claire think his manners were of long standing.

The wine was poured and handed around. Claire toasted: "Here's to the furnace man."

Wolf Rausch sipped his wine and took note of everyone bundled up. "Are you having trouble with your furnace?" Claire nodded.

"I'd be happy to take a look at it," he said. "I can't guarantee that I'll know what to do, but I'd be glad to try."

"Wine before work," said Corky. "Cheers."

"There's a Freethinker toast for you," said Romy. She was still sitting at the table with her monitor, but she had darkened the screen.

"A Freethinker toast. Is that some special kind of toast?"

"My uncle is the minister of a church that calls itself the Freethinkers' Meeting."

"Was," said Corky.

But Wolf didn't notice Corky's correction. "That sounds like a flock that wouldn't want a shepherd."

"You got it," said Romy.

Claire intervened here. Wolf Rausch would certainly come to learn of Corky's position, but it didn't have to happen this minute. "Tell us about yourself, Wolf. Where did you come from and where were you going when your car was wrecked?"

"I was heading in the direction of home," he said. "To my parents' home, that is. In Flagstaff. I've been away almost two years, and my father is ill. It's not a 'come right now' thing, but it makes me aware that he's getting on, and I want to be sure to see him again."

"That's good." Claire nodded. "That'll please him."

"I'm not so sure," said Wolf. "He doesn't approve of the way I've been living. I think he would rather I had such an important job that I couldn't get away to come home."

Claire's automatic mother-antennae switched on and waved in Wolf's direction. "Oh yes, parents feel that way," she said, "when they're worrying about your future and whether they did all the best things that will help you have a good life. But when they're thinking about how much they love you, they just want to see you." Claire smiled at Wolf, wishing to give him the gift of knowing how it is with parents. She knew exactly: wasn't she pleased that Elizabeth was making her own way in Panama so courageously, even while wishing she would come home more often?

"You're not talking about parents, Aunt Claire," said Romy. "You're talking about yourself. You can't even apply that to your own sister."

Claire thought for a moment about Claudine, who was the one person on earth she was least able to understand. Romy was right. Claudine would not want her daughter hanging around her sickbed. She had never enjoyed Romy's presence, and she would probably find it particularly offensive when she had an important event like illness on the agenda. On the other hand, she would be furious if Romy put her job ahead of being a good daughter. Claire nodded sheepishly. "I stand corrected."

"So you were on your way to Flagstaff? Where were you coming from?" asked Corky.

"I've been all over. I was actually driving from Rochester, but I've been going from one place to another for quite a while. I wanted to see the country, and I thought the best way would be to stay awhile in a place and get to know it and then move on to somewhere else."

"That doesn't sound like a bad thing for a young man to do," Corky responded.

"It's out of date. It's more of a sixties' thing. What you're supposed to do now is have a list of goals that you accomplish one by one."

"That's not such a bad thing either," said Romy.

Corky said, "Goal number one, see Montana. Goal number two…"

"By a certain time, don't forget," said Wolf, with a wide smile. "See Montana before the end of the year. Make your first million by the time you're thirty five."

"This, to me, is one excellent argument in favor of keeping God in existence," said Corky, taking the floor as though mounting the pulpit. Neither Wolf nor Romy challenged him, so he went on. "When God was in favor, there was some other standard than current public opinion by which a person could live with self-respect. But now, if you're not doing something that's approved by at least one of the groups you belong to, you have no support. You can't say, 'Well, no one understands what I'm doing, but God told me to do it and that's important.' Now you can only say, 'No one understands and maybe no one ever will, and there isn't going to be any tallying up at the end.'"

"You run your own tally," Claire said. "You'll know."

He shook his head. "Who am I to know? I'm as apt to be deluded as the next man. I could pat myself on the back and say 'Well done, fella,' till hell froze over and all I'd get would be a dislocated shoulder and a trip to the mental ward."

"Uncle Corky, you're not supposed to be saying these things to *us*. *We* say them to *you*, and then you tell us everything's going to be okay."

As though prompted by some unconscious cue to keep the corner brightened, Claire stood up to take the wine bottle around again.

Wolf raised his hand no and said, "Maybe you should show me the furnace now that I've had some wine."

"Ah, yes," said Corky. "It's time for me to be the man of the house, isn't it? The one who at least knows where the furnace is, even if he doesn't know how to make it run." He drained his wineglass and rose from the table. "I warn you, you're going to see what most folks keep from public view. The basement is where we keep our might-have-beens."

The two men went to the cluttered basement. Romy brightened her monitor and returned to work while Claire started dinner. A few minutes later, Heather left for home and Nancy came downstairs to the kitchen.

"You can set the table for me," said Claire. "Put on an extra plate. We have a guest."

"What kind of guest?" asked Nancy. She had changed into big furry house slippers with rabbit ears on them, and she made her way across the room in long, dish-rattling, rabbit hops.

When Claire told her what little she knew about Wolf, Nancy asked, "How old is he?"

"Well, I don't know, but he's somewhere near your mama's age."

"Good," said Nancy, hopping to the silverware drawer. Her pale curls quivered. Then she stopped almost in mid-hop. "Is he fat?"

"What a question! No, he isn't fat. You'll see him in a few minutes."

Nancy continued hopping. It seemed that she would surely get tired, but no, she kept it up, thumping to the table in the dining room, then thumping back, while Claire put together a meal from what she had on hand.

Finally Nancy said, "He's probably married."

Oh, thought Claire. Oh. "I don't think he's married," she answered, "but he's just passing through, honey. He isn't going to stay."

Nancy nodded with her head down.

Claire thought quickly. "I'll tell you what let's do this evening," she said. "Let's make popcorn. You know, Nancy, there are some things a person can always do to turn a place into home. One of them is to light a fire in the fireplace—only this house doesn't have a fireplace. Another is to make popcorn." She glanced quickly at Nancy, whose impassive look told Claire that she was covering up feelings. "I'll bet Wolf is homesick."

That was better. "He probably is." The little girl folded the paper napkins and placed them beside the forks.

Claire said no more on the subject, but gave it time to sink in, and after the meal was finished, it was Nancy who asked, "Is it time to make the popcorn?"

"That's a great idea," said Corky.

Wolf had not been able to do anything to the furnace. He knew what the problem was, but a new part was needed. However, the repairman finally came – with the needed part on hand – and was working on it now, which added to everyone's cheerfulness.

"I'll clean up," said Romy. "Nancy, you can help me, and then we'll have some popcorn."

The group at the table broke up, and the furnace man appeared with the good news that the repair had been made and it would soon be warm. The bad news was the prognosis. "You don't see many of these converted oil burners anymore," he said. "I'd replace the whole thing if it was mine. Gas is the way to go. A new gas burner would be a lot more efficient."

"We're not the people you have to sell," Claire answered, a little tartly. She didn't even try to be grateful that she was able to pay the bill, since she had to use money that was supposed to buy groceries through the end the month.

"I'm awfully sorry," said Wolf, his sunny expression gone. "I feel like a schnook that I wasn't able to patch it together until we got the part."

"In this house you're not a schnook until you've done something worse than make an unsuccessful attempt to do a kindness."

Soon warmth spread through the house, and a good smell emanated from the kitchen, where Romy and Nancy were popping corn. Both of them were wearing dark blue sweaters; they looked even more like mother and daughter than usual, with their pale blond hair and heart-shaped faces, Nancy's fair skin showing the approach to beauty, Romy's the consolidation of it. The kitchen was now as tidy as it would get, dishes washed and put away, the table brushed clean and the floor swept, these being the household's concessions to cleanliness within a more pervasive disorder that stemmed from keeping too much stuff in too little space.

Back in the living room, Romy moved her straight-backed chair away from the computer. The screen was dark, but she had turned the modem on in case something came in from Omni over the data line. It could happen, Friday night or not. There were always people there working; some of the programmers had been known to stay over and sleep on the office floor when something hot had to be done in a hurry. Since the spasm in her back had eased, Romy had been acting like a programmer again, working every possible moment. This was the first time she had taken time away from the application she was working on. She took her chair to the other end of the room where the rest of the people were sitting.

Corky gave her a fatherly, approving look, but said nothing. Nancy brought the popcorn from the kitchen and placed it on the coffee table in front of Wolf.

"We've all been polite, now, and let you have a meal and catch your breath," Romy said to Wolf, "but I'm dying to hear about your wreck. What happened? Do you mind telling?"

"Oh, I thought you knew," he answered, looking at each one of them in turn. "It was bizarre."

Claire shook her head.

"Well, I was driving along the interstate that by-passes the city and a man fell on my car." He stared off into space as though recreating the scene. Then he repeated, "I was driving along the interstate, and a man jumped off a bridge in front of my car. With a rope around his neck." He reentered the present and looked around. Everyone was watching him. "I hit him. He was dead when the ambulance arrived." He sounded as though he did not believe what he was saying.

Claire grimaced. "No wonder Alfreda thought you needed some TLC."

There were murmurs from the others, and Wolf began speaking in the slow, deliberate way he had. "You know, it's a funny thing. You would think that if you had a wreck and weren't badly hurt, that all you'd have to do would be the practical things and it would be over. But every time I close my eyes I see it again: the bridge up ahead, the man on the railing, all ghostly in the fog, the man's silhouette hanging there with his neck in the rope, and then the man on my windshield. And then I swerved and hit a culvert and rolled the car. It's like a scene from a dark, old black-and-white film that someone plays over and over until you get it." Wolf, sober and bemused, reached for a handful of popcorn. "But I don't get it. Why me?"

Romy, who had up till now been easy on Wolf, said, "That's elevating your own importance. There isn't any 'why you' involved. It's pure chance."

Wolf was undismayed by her sharpness. "In one sense you're right," he said, "but I believe that we're supposed to learn from the things that happen to us, and this is a pretty major thing. I mean, from the dead guy's point of view, there isn't any reason why he fell on my car instead of somebody else's, but from *my* point of view, it's an event in my life to have killed a man, and I take that magnitude of events pretty seriously."

"It doesn't sound as though you killed him," Claire said. "I mean, if he had a rope around his neck."

"Right," said Wolf. "I can't tell. It didn't seem to me that he would have had time to die by hanging. The rope broke right away. It happened in just an instant. But maybe his neck was broken."

Romy said, "It doesn't make any difference. His intention was to kill himself, so you're not responsible."

Corky, who had been listening intently, spoke. "He's not talking responsibility. Or fact. When you're considering the way events in your life relate to you, it's the personal meaning that counts."

Wolf was nodding.

"The meaning of an event has to include not only the facts but the associations you bring to it, the responses of other people, the consequences, everything." Corky's power as a speaker was evident; all the group's attention was on him. His intelligent face, his deep resonant voice, even his thoughtful posture added weight to his words.

Claire watched and listened, thinking once again that she had married a man with an enormous range – and wishing that he would stay at this end of it. She said, "It may take awhile for you to assimilate everything this means."

Wolf nodded. He started to reach for the last handful of popcorn, then caught himself and passed the bowl to Claire instead.

"Oh, go on, take it," Romy burst out. "I can't stand it when someone wants the last bite but leaves it to be thrown in the trash for the sake of manners."

But Wolf had to convince himself that no one else wanted any before he cupped his broad hand and scooped out the last white puffs, mixed with the hard kernels and grains of salt left in the bottom of the bowl. "I keep thinking of a quotation to the effect that it takes killing a man to become a man," he said, not looking at anyone. "That sounds nuts, I know, but it keeps coming to mind." He cracked the hard corn kernels between his molars and glanced at Corky. "What do you think?"

Nancy took the empty popcorn bowl and disappeared.

Corky asked, "What's the quotation? It sounds like something out of The Compleat Drill Sergeant."

"I can't remember where it came from," answered Wolf. "Maybe I dreamed it."

"Always this interest in killing," exclaimed Claire. "Why can't men take more of an interest in nurturing?"

"Women benefit too," replied Wolf. "If men didn't do the killing, women would have to do it themselves."

"Don't be too sure of that," answered Claire. "That sounds like a good theory, but don't be too sure it would work out that way. Good-sounding theories have a way of taking unforeseen directions when they're put into practice."

"This guy I killed," said Wolf, "maybe he became a man then too. Not because I killed him, but because he killed himself."

"What a test of manhood!"

"The gentleman's way out," said Corky.

"The *easy* way out," said Claire, looking hard at him.

"Not so easy," said Corky. "Not so easy." He sat brooding for a moment, then said, "Being able to define ourselves as men is always a problem. We've had to assert that we're not gods, not animals, not machines, and not women."

"How about not children?" Romy interjected. She spoke so quickly she couldn't have given her words any thought, but having said them, she looked away from Corky.

"That too," he answered. "But we go too far." He turned to Wolf. "Which aspect of manhood does killing a man fall into?"

"Oh, strength, very likely," Wolf answered slowly. "Being not-woman."

Romy stood up deliberately, with an imposing anger. "It's just possible that if men could get over trying to prove that they are stronger than women, they could start pulling their share. Have you ever noticed who actually does most of what needs to be done? It certainly isn't the men. The men are too busy competing, which is another word for trying to kill each other off. And that leaves you-know-who to do the work." Romy's lips were white, her eyes fierce, her wide nostrils drawing oxygen, the better to combust what was left of her dead husband.

"And it doesn't matter whether we get one of the killers or one of the killed. We're going to end up lonely, we're going to end up with the work to do and the children to raise." The fury in her voice gave way to grief. "While they waste everything! While they waste everything beating each other out! Oh!" She hurried out of the room and up the stairs.

Wolf gazed after her.

It was easy to tell where Romy had gone, for almost immediately they heard Nancy cry out indignantly, "But tomorrow's Saturday!"

It was a few moments before anyone spoke, then Corky said, "You may have your answer right there. We may be working toward a new definition of manliness: not-extinct. Developing the cooperative side. Noticing the expensive social consequences of competition, as well as the ecological."

Wolf nodded, still looking bewildered.

"Romy's situation is a good example of what I mean. Her husband died last spring. He was a teacher, and from what I hear, a good one. But the competition for tenure had very little to do with that, and he lost the competition. It's quite likely that that's what led to his death. And some of the social consequences are a widow, an orphan, and one less good teacher doing his work." The room was quiet except for the ticking of the big keyhole-shaped wall clock, which had suddenly become noticeable.

Claire said to Wolf, "Romy's been in an awful fix. Her husband left a lot of debt when he died, and she's also been ill. But what she's saying is not just true of herself, it applies to everyone, to the general human condition. Her personal suffering puts her more in touch with it."

Wolf said, hesitantly, "I think I know what you mean. When everything's going well for me personally, I don't really notice what's wrong in the world. Oh, I may give a guy a buck on the street, but I don't really feel what its like not to be able to work."

Corky smiled a tight, wintry smile. "Yes. Like the goat that the Israelites turned out into the wilderness to atone for their sins. Used to be, my thoughts about that goat were pretty dispassionate."

Claire, noticing that the conversation was taking a turn that she wasn't ready for, abruptly ended it by stifling a yawn and stretching. "We're early-to-bed people, Wolf. Would you forgive us if we turned in? You're most welcome to help yourself to books or watch TV or raid the icebox if you like." She stood up decisively and folded her mohair lap robe.

Wolf said he was tired too and wouldn't mind turning in. "I'd like to make myself useful while I'm here," he told Corky as Claire turned out the lights and they all headed rather awkwardly for the stairs. "If there are any chores that need to be done, I wish you'd let me tackle them tomorrow. I get awfully restless if I don't have work to do."

"That's the best offer I've had in a long time," said Corky. "There's always work, and in ever-increasing amounts, since we don't keep pace with it."

Romy and Nancy's doors were closed; each had a crack of light at the bottom. Wolf hesitated at the guest room door. "Good night," he said. "Thanks very much for putting me up."

"Sleep well," said Claire. "Oh, and be sure to jiggle the toilet handle when you flush."

BREAKFAST WITH WOLF

Romy awakened first the next morning, moving cautiously. Her back did not hurt. Another restful night; another morning pain-free. She was gaining strength.

At the same time that she became conscious of her physical condition, she also became aware of Wolf's presence in the house, and for a moment she was glad. She had married so young and been married for so long that Frank's death had left her feeling orphaned as well as widowed, carrying with her everywhere a dark, unoccupied space that stood between her and the sun and demanded her constant attention without giving her anything in return. For just a moment it seemed that the space might be filled. Then she finished waking up and common sense took over.

But instead of going straight to the computer, she showered, and she took time to dry her hair and curl the ends. She chose corduroys and a red wool sweater with knots in the yarn, casual but pretty, and she opened her jewelry box for the first time in months to take out the thread-like necklace that caught and reflected the gold in her hair.

Out the kitchen window the sky was clear and blue. A ray of sunlight struck the beveled edge of a little mirror pinned to a cabinet door, producing a knife-blade of rainbow on the wall.

She poured herself a glass of grapefruit juice to drink as she stood at the window and waited for the coffee to drip.

The leaves were all down, even the Norway maple's, which had seemed to hang on the trees forever. A drift of leaves sloped up the fence.

Romy had never spent a winter in Portville. She had grown up in Indianapolis and had gone to college in Bloomington, where she stayed after graduation, having married Frank at the end of her sophomore year. It would be colder here, and windier.

She wondered about her house in Bloomington. Were the sycamore leaves raked? The storm windows in? She had rented it out last August, when she came to the parsonage, rented it fully furnished, right down to Frank's blue corn meal and extra virgin olive oil on the shelves and the down-filled comforters on the beds. The tenants, four senior women, seemed neat and intelligent enough, School of Business majors, but it was hard to tell how people would take care of a house.

The lease made it impossible to go back before May. If she and Nancy returned to Bloomington now, they would have to rent a place.

When she came here, there had been no serious danger of eviction from the parsonage. It was understood that Corky was really the minister, and the threat of being replaced was just that, a threat to keep him in line. But since his second arrest, with the roof over their heads dependent upon the congregation's good will, she and Nancy were situated more precariously. They could be asked to leave upon any notice the congregation cared to give. Claire had maintained all along that they were safe, that she had enough friends on the Board to assure them decent treatment. But after the furnace episode yesterday, this confidence was beginning to look misplaced. The threat of eviction was becoming a worry among worries.

The coffee stopped dripping. Romy poured a mug three quarters full and added milk. Time to get to work. She took her coffee into the living room.

There was a message from Henson, her boss at Omni, a few choice bits of office news, and instructions to send along whatever was running.

Her job, even at a distance, was a distinct plus in her list of minuses. In fact, here in Portville she was actually able to get more work done than was possible in the office with all the distractions. Here she could work any time without having to find someone to look after Nancy. Yes, she missed the office and her friends there, but missing the office was minor compared with losing her job. Most jobs would have been lost under similar circumstances.

She keyed in the symbols that took her to her work. In a few moments she was so absorbed that the last of her coffee cooled beside her.

By the time she was finished and had run the completed sections of the program one more time, she realized that she had been hearing sounds of activity in the kitchen. She sent her work off to Omni with a reply to Henson's message. This done, she had reached a stopping place. There was more to do, of course, a lot more, but she would have to begin a new section. The possibility of a day off came to mind. As she thought of it, she realized that she had been turning into a machine lately, a computer peripheral, attached to her terminal as though with a cable and pins like the ones that connected the printer and the modem. She darkened the screen and went back to the kitchen.

Corky, dressed for yard work, sat at the table opposite Wolf. Both acknowledged Romy with a nod, but the conversation continued.

"Environmental issues," Corky was saying. "Things like Amnesty International. And of course you have people engaged in social action as individuals. The ones who shelter unwelcome refugees, for instance. Even the people who picket abortion clinics are addressing themselves to a moral issue they feel strongly about. It's just that there is no great swell that gets media attention the way civil rights did or the Vietnam War."

Then Wolf, who had been leaning toward Corky with his forearms on the table, sat up and greeted Romy in a solicitous way, with his wide Arizona smile. "Good morning. I saw you working away in there. You didn't even know I was alive." Unlike Corky in his ancient war surplus pants, Wolf wore L.L. Bean "weekenders" and a red chamois flannel shirt. His hair was damp and his face clean-shaven.

"I knew you were alive, but I didn't know you were here," Romy answered. "The machine sucks you in almost to the point where you become part of it." The coffee pot was full of fresh coffee. She filled her cup and sat down with them, her blonde hair and red pullover mirroring Wolf's appearance. Together at the table they looked like two attractive models in an advertisement for "red, the color of fall."

"Weren't you talking last night about people needing to prove that they're not machines?"

Corky spoke more to Romy than to Wolf. "I was talking about men, not people. Women know they're not machines." He waited to see if Romy would take exception. "Both of you may be too young to remember the strong injunction for men to stifle their feelings. Men were rational above all else. The only feeling we were permitted to indulge without restraint was patriotism."

Wolf was already nodding. "Yes, patriotism. Nothing's changed.

There's lip service paid to men showing their feelings, but if you be-lieve it, and show, say, disappointment or hurt, you find out quickly that you've become a whiner."

"It's no different for women," said Romy. "Not long ago one of the women was fired from Omni, and she cried, and even some of the *women* said it was just as well they let her go if she couldn't handle the real world."

"The real world again," said Corky. All of a sudden he looked as though the thought itself had devalued him. "Isn't it amazing that nothing good ever happens in what's called the real world?"

"That's the world I'm supposed to settle down into," said Wolf. "My father's been telling me for years. But somehow it sounds so unat-tractive that I've been putting it off as long as possible."

"You make it sound as though there was some place you could be that was *not* the real world," said Romy impatiently. She wished she hadn't mentioned the term. "Even the people who do things with pills and powders and spend a lot of time in la-la land are in the real world. You're in it; you just aren't *settled*. You're on the highway of the real world."

"Not until I get another car, I'm not," answered Wolf. "In la-la land I can get to Arizona on a Persian rug, but not in the good old U.S. of A."

"Would you rather fly home?" asked Corky. "We could help you ship some of your things."

"Thanks," he answered. "But if I drive to Flagstaff, maybe by the time I get there, my head'll be in a place where I can deal with things. I should have money from the insurance company early next week, and I'll just buy a car here. There's no big hurry, actually. My dad's condition is stable."

Romy's hand stole up to the back of her neck. She reached under her luxurious hair and shook it out. "I pulled the plug on my life sup-port system for the day," she said. "A day off. If you'd like to, we could go around to the dealers this afternoon and take a preliminary look."

Wolf hitched forward on his chair, but he glanced at Corky as he answered. "That would be great, but I promised my services to Corky for the day."

"Doing what?" asked Romy.

"You're absolved," said Corky. "I can do the raking myself."

"We'll help," said Romy. "Surely there's some aspect of leaf raking that I can do without hurting myself." In response to Wolf's questioning glance, she said, "I've got a back that conveniently breaks down when things get rough, and then I get to lie around doing nothing for a while. I've been up and down for several months. My back's better, but I'm clumsy, and there are some things I still can't do: lift anything heavy, or make twisting movements."

"You can grace the yard and inspire us by your beauty," said Corky.

She gave him one of her looks. "I've been here inspiring you since last summer, and the work's not done." She stood up and went to the refrigerator. "How about some eggs and toast?"

"Help yourself. Claire fixed us French toast an hour ago."

"She did? I must have really been absorbed."

"You were. Nancy went to Heather's. The Merchants are going to the Dunes for the day and invited her to go with them."

"Yes, I knew about that." Romy put the eggs back and took out the milk instead. She poured herself a glass and opened the bread and peanut butter. "Where's Aunt Claire?"

"In the tub treating herself to a bubble bath."

"Is she all right?"

"Yes." Corky shook his head no. "She's as all right as you can expect."

Wolf looked out the window politely. Neither Corky nor Romy explained.

When Romy finished her breakfast, the three of them put on jackets and went out to find rakes. "What do we do with the leaves, once we've raked them?" asked Wolf.

"Bag 'em," Corky answered. He yanked on the garage door, which was stuck.

The parsonage lot was not especially large, but there were seven good-sized trees, three of them Norway maples that shed leaves like chip steaks, each one a tough little meal in itself. Romy stood at the garage door looking out at the work to be done, the leaves ankle deep over the stretches of lawn, deeper along the fences. An angry look came over her face. "Why should we rake them at all? Why not leave them for your good church people to find next spring? You won't be here. Let *them* worry about the raking!"

Corky brushed past her with a rake in each hand. "Claire may still be here," he said quietly. His manner did not invite discussion.

Romy stared at him. What on earth? Where did he think he would go without Claire? To prison? Was there any serious possibility that he would go to prison over this?

Corky handed Wolf the heaviest of the rakes and kept the gap-toothed bamboo for himself. Romy brought the box of heavy trash bags and the plastic rectangle to hold them open.

Under the top layer, the leaves were damp. They had been falling for weeks. The silver maple and hickory leaves were so curled and frag-ile that they hardly needed raking. The real work was the Norway maples.

Romy could not twist her body to rake, but she could bend if she did it carefully. She set herself to gathering leaves into the bag. After a few armloads she saw that she needed a scoop to work faster. A small cardboard box would do the job, and she had just such a box, one that had held computer paper. She went to get it.

Inside, she thought she might see Claire, but no, so she found the carton and hurried back out. A great many leaves had been raked in the short time she was gone. Already Corky had exchanged his inad-equate rake for a snow shovel and was shoveling into bags the leaves that Wolf sent across the lawn in great sweeps. Romy stood for a mo-ment admiring the ease with which the young man worked, then she joined Corky bagging.

CLAIRE'S INTERLUDE

Claire, upstairs, heard Romy come in and then go back outside. She looked out the bedroom window. There they were below. Wolf, powerful and efficient, was sending piles of leaves to the baggers so fast they couldn't keep up. Romy looked healthy. Corky looked happy.

But without Wolf, the work wouldn't be happening. Corky would be nodding in his chair, Romy frowning over her keyboard. And she herself would be tied to Corky's needs, automatically assessing the depth of every sigh, and just as automatically responding.

Claire had heard the shower running, and then Romy's hairdryer, early this morning, and then a little later the shower again, followed by the sound of Wolf's electric shaver. At the breakfast table she heard Corky and Wolf in the kind of discussion Corky loved. And so she too decided to take the day off and leave the others to their own devices. Corky was in his element. She could be spared for a while from her job of brightening the corner, of preventing the takeover of despair.

There was a certain amount of danger involved in removing herself, however. Neither Romy nor Corky could be trusted to keep from blurting out the sordid facts of Corky's situation. And if that happened, this little interlude would be over.

But Claire was tired. She had lain awake in self-review last night long enough to realize that the evening had been spent with her vocal cords tied in a knot, trying to keep everyone else from being indiscreet. But if they told, they told. She shouldn't – she couldn't – control their talk.

It was hard to stop trying. All her life Claire had heard other people divulge information without considering the effect it would have. Her own sister Claudine seemed completely unaware of the value of information held, withheld, or given out at an opportune time. Claudine, for instance, several years after her bitter divorce from Romy's father, had confronted him in a re-ignited fury over his infidelities. She triumphantly blurted out that she too had played around some, while he thought she was suffering meekly at home, but her revenge, sweet as it was, had cost the rest of Romy's child support, thousands of dollars that could not be collected. Claire firmly believed that receiving this piece of information just then had made it okay in the man's mind for him to evade his responsibility to Romy. She also firmly believed that Claudine should never have divulged her secret.

In the present situation discretion was the only thing that would keep their guest around. Once Wolf heard the words "child molester," those words would blot out everything he was drawn to in Corky. It had happened time and again, with friend after friend.

Claire sat on the edge of the bed beside the window. She wore a fuzzy, peach-colored bathrobe tied loosely under her warm, loose breasts. She was filing a fingernail, the problem one that was wider than the others, and flat, with a painful little sliver at the side. She had shaved her legs, clipped her toenails, washed and dried her hair; the personal care that used to be a matter of course was now a luxury. From time to time she looked at the yard below at the two yellow heads and the one in the moss-green cap. They were busy with the leaves, too busy to talk. Nothing had happened yet.

CARS

The back yard of the parsonage was planted for privacy, with a hedge inside the wooden fence. Both were high enough to discourage children and dogs, though the neighborhood cats could leap up easily and stretch out on the fence railing to sun themselves and bird-watch in peace, shielded from the yelling and barking that went on in their own yards.

The front, however, was open to the street. Wolf was raking there now, while Romy scooped up the leaves and Corky added a shovelful to the bag from time to time.

Corky's attention had been diverted to a homemade ramp in the street several houses down, where three stringy boys with a skateboard took turns riding up the ramp and jumping off as near the top as possible. Two girls of eleven or twelve in white athletic shoes bicycled past and called out insults to the boys. As Corky took it all in, two pre-school boys on plastic motorcycles vroomed past him.

Corky's eyes sparkled under the old green cap. His grin turned up at the ends. "I can't tell what they're trying to do," he said, "jump off at the highest point or go over and land on the board."

"They're trying to get out of school for a few days and go back with their leg in a cast," Romy answered. "Are you going to help bag or aren't you?"

On the other side of the street a small pile of leaves was burning in the gutter attended by a slight-figured old man in a gray jacket. The fire was small. Even so, its evocative, leaf-burning odor hung over the neighborhood.

"Don't you have a burn law here?" asked Wolf.

"Yes," said Corky. "It's not allowed, but he says he's burned his leaves that way all his life and he's not going to quit until they force him to."

"Shall I report him?" asked Romy. "He shouldn't be allowed to get away with poisoning everybody."

"Since when have you started asking my advice?" asked Corky. "Do as you like."

Wolf had stopped raking. Under his gaze Romy relaxed her bristles. "I don't live here," she said. "If his neighbors don't object, I probably shouldn't interfere." She scooped up a box of leaves and dumped them into the bag. "On the other hand, maybe the neighbors don't know they're being poisoned."

Corky was watching her. "Go on. I'd like to hear how you resolve this."

"As long as you put it that way, I'd have to put the community good against this individual's good. And I guess the community gains more by unpolluted air than he does by the convenience of burning his leaves."

Corky nodded. "But there's another factor. When the burn law was enacted, Portville was in violation of the federal pollution limits. We had three major polluters here. The burn law was enacted to keep those three from having to clean up their operations. The steel mill closed down two years ago, of course, but the other two are still spewing forth their poisons, while we're made to believe that air pollution is the fault of people like that little fellow over there burning a handful of leaves."

"But shouldn't little people do their part too?" asked Romy

"Of course," Corky answered. "But they're more likely to do their part when their part really makes a difference."

"So you're telling me it's not his fault, and I shouldn't report him."

"I'm telling you that one millionth of the problem is his fault while we're led to believe on hundredth of it is, and I still say do as you like."

"You're picking on me! How should I know what's the right thing to do?"

"I'm sorry. I didn't mean to pick on you." Corky's glance brought Wolf more deeply into the conversation. "You see how difficult it is to attend to the social issues. Going after the real problem is more costly than we can afford, so we attend to the fringes to make ourselves feel better."

Wolf turned the rake upside down and combed leaves from the tines with his fingers. "That's why I can't get very fired up about settling into the real world."

Romy struck instantly, her frustration having found a place to light. "Then save the real world, if that's what you think ought to happen. I'm sick to death of people who use any excuse to keep from going to work."

Wolf's answer came in a slow, deliberate way as he leaned on the rake handle as though it were a staff. "Would you like a run-down of the work I've done the last few years?"

"You said you'd been going around seeing the country."

"You can't get very far without money."

"Oh well, the picture I had was that some rich relation had subsidized this trip."

"I don't have any rich relations." He turned the rake tines down again and began sending piles of leaves onto the sidewalk.

Romy scooped up a box full and dumped it, then another and another. Corky had turned away to watch the children during the hostility, but now he faced Romy and Wolf again and glanced from one to the other and back, smiling expectantly at each in turn. They continued working in a silent rhythm, and Corky finally joined them.

It didn't take long, with the three of them working steadily, to finish disposing of the leaves. Then Wolf swept the sidewalk while Romy carried the rakes back to the garage. They lined the bags up at the curb and went inside.

The silence between them ended during lunch. Claire and Corky were planning to go to the beach to take, on a Saturday afternoon, what was usually their Sunday-after-sermon walk. Corky had been so cheerful that Claire invited him in married shorthand: "Walkie-talkie?" and he had answered: "On the beach."

Wolf asked Romy if her offer of a trip to the auto dealer was still good. It was.

"I'd like to go to the police lot too. There's still stuff in my car."

"Take the van," said Claire. "It'll hold everything."

A little later Romy and Wolf were on the high seat of Claire's van, heading downtown, with Wolf at the wheel. Romy held open a street map of Portville, necessary because she had not yet learned her way around town.

The day was still sunny and warm, in the high fifties, and people all along the route were outdoors to run the lawn mower one last time before winter, to wash the car, rake the last of the leaves. Joggers wore shorts again, albeit with leg warmers, and sweatbands. "I'll bet the beach is packed," said Romy, "even if it's too cold to sunbathe."

Claire and Corky had pulled away in Romy's little car just ahead of the van, and Romy watched with sucked-in breath as Corky maneuvered it in his haphazard way around the many obstacles that dotted Clover Street, gawking out the window all the while at kids on skateboards, kids on bicycles, kids with Frisbees, kids just hanging around.

Wolf too looked out the window, but he was well-coordinated enough to do so without inviting accident. "Look at that," he kept saying at a particularly large or comfortable-looking house or yard, at a corner playground that had imaginative equipment, at the red brick Chinese Community Church and the Russian Orthodox storefront with its triptych in the window and its brave little onion dome on top. "I can't believe this neighborhood. It's great. Who would ever have thought there was a place like this in Portville, Indiana? I certainly didn't know Indiana had an ethnic population."

"We don't, really. Not until you get closer to the Chicago area. Just a few little enclaves like this."

Romy sat on the high seat of the van enjoying Wolf's company. "I feel like a balloon with its string broken. I've been tied for months to either the computer or the bed. It's wonderful to be loose, just to be out of the house riding around."

"It must be."

"It wasn't that I absolutely never got out. I've gone to Meeting a couple of times with Claire to hear Corky preach, and I go to my widows' support group. In fact, I'm playing hooky from group right now. It meets on Saturday afternoons."

Wolf glanced at her. "It's hard to see you as a widow."

"I'm the only one in the group under fifty, the only widow, that is. But there are some divorcees too, and they're more my age, though I can't say that I identify with them either." Romy glanced at the map. "I think you turn left at the next corner." She watched for the Osborne Avenue street sign, and said, "Yes, here," then went on. "A death means that there's some finite limit to the hassle, but divorced people can go on making trouble for each other forever."

Wolf laughed. "When you said you went to a widows' support group, I pictured people sitting around weeping. I wasn't thinking 'hassle.'"

"Well 'hassle' is what it is," said Romy with the beginnings of heat in her voice. "There are two, just two, women in that group who have the luxury of feeling grief. The rest of us are so involved in hassle that it's going to take years before we ever get a chance to grieve."

"Paperwork?" he asked. "Moving to an apartment? I'm not sure what you mean."

"I mean money."

Wolf's lips compressed. "The nitty-gritty."

"There's one old woman whose husband had a management level pension without any survivor benefits. She didn't even know. She just assumed that he would provide for her. Can you believe there are still women that dumb?"

"My mother might be one of them," said Wolf. "Only I wouldn't call it dumb, really. I think my mother would know how things stood, but she might not stand up for herself if it meant she had to make a fuss about money."

"I can relate to that. I didn't dream that Frank was going to die so young, so there's some excuse for what I did, but I never put my foot down and insisted on living within our means."

"And now you're paying."

"I had two choices. Bankruptcy or go to a debt counselor and get help with a schedule that will make it possible for me to pay it all off some day. In the meantime I have to part with almost half of every paycheck for stuff I never cared about in the first place. That's hassle."

"Can't you let them repossess?"

"That goes on your credit rating."

"Would that be so terrible?"

"It would mean a strike against me any time I wanted credit."

"I mean, would it be so terrible not to have credit?"

She gave a half-laugh. "My car won't last forever."

He shrugged. "So?"

Romy made a click in her throat like a little cough and hugged her arms together. "Look, I promised myself I wasn't going to spoil a nice afternoon by getting mad."

He didn't answer immediately. Then, in his slow way he said, "You get mad a lot, don't you?"

Taken off balance by Wolf's sudden upping of the intimacy level, Romy hugged herself again. When Wolf asked if that was the police lot up ahead on the right, she made a show of peering out and agreed that it probably was. Wolf turned into the lot and parked the van.

Instead of going with him to find the lot attendant, Romy stayed on the high seat of the van and watched him walk through the aisles of Skylarks and Mustangs and Cougars to the squat little hut in the center of the lot.

It would be easy simply to get mad at the question itself, the implication that there was something wrong with her for feeling the way she felt. In the teeth of modern life, anger is, after all, an appropriate response: people who can feel content while being bashed have probably sedated themselves. But she did get mad a lot, and she knew it. A lot more than she used to, with no more reason. Being so vulnerable seemed to bare her to blows that would never have reached her when the roof over her head was tight and the man beside her strong, when there was enough energy between them to live graciously in spite of their problems. Everyone has problems. Thoughts of gracious living, however, ignited the anger all over again. Money. The pilot light of her anger: money. The fact that it was going to be a long time before she could call the money she earned her own.

But this wasn't Wolf's fault. And she didn't want to spend the day in a bad mood.

From her high seat Wolf's blond hair and red shirt were visible. He had found the attendant, a young woman in a security guard uniform, with bright red hair worn long in back. He had stood at the door with her and talked for several moments and was now following her along the side of the building. When they turned the corner and disappeared, Romy felt suddenly let down and apprehensive. What if he found that mass of coppery hair so attractive that he didn't come back – and didn't come back? The two of them had been standing in a way unmistakably male to female, Wolf tall and smiling, the young woman straight and sure but looking up at him nevertheless. In a most flirtatious way. What if he brought her with him when he did come back? Or didn't bring her along just at the moment, but went out with her this evening, while she herself sat at the computer tapping out the keystrokes that would pay Frank's bills?

Before she could erase this foolishness from her mind, a burning wash of fury bathed her. It felt as though it might consume her from the inside out, soft tissue first, then bone and gristle, nail and hair, with her bodily fluids boiling off into steam and nothing left on the seat of the van but melted vinyl, charred stuffing, and a pile of greasy ashes. She leaned her head back and took a deep, unsteady breath of air into her hot lungs. I do get mad a lot, she thought. Was this how spontaneous human combustion happened? It did happen, she knew it; she'd seen a newspaper story about an English lady where only her foot was left, still in a soft felt house slipper, and no evidence of fuel sufficient to burn a body. But this is ridiculous. This is dangerous. I can't stand it, feeling this crazy way over nothing, over the silliest thing in the world that I dreamed up myself. She opened the door.

She only meant to walk down the aisle of cars and let the fresh air cool her off, but that aisle led to a cross aisle, which led to the exit, and before she knew it, she was outside the police lot altogether, walking north on Osborne Avenue toward downtown.

Cooler now, she found herself in an area of two and three story brick buildings that held wholesale businesses and small manufacturers, places called "Elkhorn Supply" and "Portville Paper Products." The blocks were long and the sidewalks deserted. Away from the residential neighborhoods, traffic was light this time of the week.

She walked slowly, feeling tired and out of shape. That's what you get from bed rest, she thought. She stopped for a moment and leaned against the worn brick side of a building, letting her back and head press against the wall while her locked knees held her firmly in place. She closed her eyes to the deserted cityscape bathed in weekend sunlight. Behind her eyelids the view was a red and black swim of warmth, and she felt weightless, as though drifting off to sleep.

When she opened her eyes a moment later, the scene was the same, but intensified, like a painting by Harry Davis: that strange, impartial, final light, the perfectly preserved vacant buildings. She stared without moving. This was the way it might look after the bomb that destroys everything alive but leaves the artifacts: the traffic signals still turning red, then yellow, then green; the bank of TV screens in the appliance store still showing an endless loop of TV commercials to a long-since vaporized audience. She thought that if the earth were rediscovered soon enough, clocks would be found, but no clockmaker, computers but no programmer. Eons seemed to pass while she went on staring at the lifeless scene. Without anyone left to patch and tinker and muddle things through, the small, correctable, everyday errors would become strings of foolish data, which would multiply until they brought the system to a halt.

Romy's back was still to the wall, her knees locked tight. She could not tell how long this apocalyptic vision had lasted or whether she had been asleep on her feet and dreaming. She wrenched herself away from the wall that supported her, nearly tumbling to the sidewalk in her haste, and hurried back toward the police lot where there was something familiar in this strange city: the van, Wolf, even the red-haired lot attendant. When a jalopy appeared and its young, pimply passenger whistled at her, tears of relief came as she gave him the finger, grateful to be back in the real world, wasted and manhandled as it was.

The van was not where she had left it.

She walked across the parking lot, trying not to panic. Then, on the other side of the attendant's hut, she saw it. It was now parked crosswise in an aisle with all the doors open. Behind it was what must be Wolf's station wagon, with a cracked windshield, a flat right front tire, a stove-in right side and a dented roof. Dead grass was wedged like caulk in the window and door crevices. As she approached, Wolf climbed out the back of the van.

"Oh, there you are. Did you go for a walk?" His smile took a moment to progress to its widest point. "I thought you'd gone inside to the women's room, and I wondered if your back was hurting you."

"It doesn't hurt," she said, "but I'm so out of shape that the little bit of work I did this morning wore me out."

"Would you like to go home? It won't take me long to finish here."

"Thanks, but if I lie on the seat for a while, I'll be okay." She climbed up. The bench seat allowed enough room for her to lie comfortably, and then she was asleep. She did not wake up until the back doors of the van slammed shut.

THE DINNER HOUR

"Sure, it's fun to look at cars, but I can't really decide anything until the money comes from the insurance company and I know what I can afford."

Although Wolf's words were addressed to Claire and Corky in the dining room, Romy could hear him from the dimly lighted kitchen where she was warming one of the two pizzas they had brought for dinner. When they had arrived back at the parsonage, Claire and Corky were already home and were putting together the first few pieces of a jigsaw puzzle laid out on the dining room table. Wolf had joined them.

It was now almost dark, though not late, the bright afternoon having melted into evening. Romy stood for a moment, leaning on the counter, looking out the west window. In a streak of magenta sky, she could see tree limbs black against two horizontal strings of little popcorn clouds.

Wolf's words made ultimate good sense. He wasn't a Portville resident, didn't have a job at the moment, and had no credit rating at all. It was not likely that a local lender would finance his car. His words were not only sensible but true, and they irritated Romy beyond reason.

How did he think he could buy any kind of decent car for the money he would get from the insurance on a four year-old station wagon? But he evidently did think so. He had been looking around the dealers' lots with as much interest as if he could buy whatever he might like.

True, he wouldn't go inside a showroom. "If it's indoors, I can't even afford to look," he said. But he prowled the lots like a teenager planning to hotwire his favorite, and his favorites were not conservative.

Romy had sold Frank's car soon after his death, for less than she owed, of course. Even so, it was a relief to take the loss and get rid of it. She certainly didn't want to drive it. A car with a firm, upright seat close to the wheel was essential for the well being of her back. How Frank had been able to drive leaning back with his legs straight out and his butt dragging the pavement was more than she could understand. The car was only a few months old and still smelled new – but Frank never had a car that didn't smell new. He never shopped for it outdoors.

The oven timer buzzed. Romy put the second pizza in and carried the first one into the dining room. "Please!" she said, standing by the table where the other three sat absorbed in the puzzle. "I need some place to put this down."

Wolf stood up quickly and took the pizza and the two pot holders out of her hands, while Claire stood up quickly and grabbed from a nearby chair a small, imitation Oriental rug that was just the size of the table. Corky did not stand up. Instead, he sat with a bone-shaped piece in his hand poised over the puzzle. Claire waited. When he had fitted the piece in, she laid the carpet over the table top, puzzle pieces and all, and set a mat in the center for the pizza.

"A new wrinkle on sweeping your problems under the rug," said Romy. "You're making me wonder what's under the couch cushions."

"Probably more change than I have in my purse right now," said Claire.

Wolf said, "That reminds me." He unbuttoned his pocket and pulled out his wallet. "I'm going to chip in on the groceries while I'm here. Would you rather I gave you money or bought things myself?"

Corky shook his head, but Claire answered. "We'd rather refuse, but we're having – what is it you call it?" She glanced at Romy. "A cash flow problem?" Her dimples appeared as she said to Wolf, "Money would go farther. I know where the bargains are."

He selected some bills and handed them to her. "If I'm delayed, I can give you more" The wallet, thin and curved from wear, was buttoned carefully back into his pocket.

"I hope you're delayed!" said Corky. His wispy hair picked up light from the ceiling fixture over the table. "It's a pleasure having you here. Please stay as long as you can."

"I can feed you quite a while on this," said Claire, slipping the money in her pocket. "Let's have some wine with our pizza." The jug of burgundy was still out from the night before. She put it on the table and went to the sideboard for glasses. "Romy, honey, get us some extra napkins. We don't need plates and forks for pizza, do we? Corky, give us a grace. This is special."

Corky bowed his head. "We are thankful, still, for the ability to take time off, to find pleasure, to recover hope. Amen."

After serving everyone a slice, Claire tore into hers hungrily, spilling crumbs of sausage and black olive onto her napkin and quickly dabbing them up with a forefinger. "This tastes so good, and it's been such a long time since we had any," she said. Corky, too, ate quickly and made little noises of enjoyment. When the oven timer buzzed again, Romy brought the second pizza in. By this time everyone was eating more slowly, savoring each laden bite, disdaining the thin, bare rims of crust.

"One's not quite enough, but two's too much," said Romy. "We're going to have leftovers."

Claire's answer was a very wide smile held in place long enough to get the point across.

"It's too bad Nancy isn't here," said Corky. "She can have hers tomorrow."

"Don't worry about Nancy," said Romy, who wasn't as sorry about her absence as Corky was. "There are a lot of other things she likes better than pizza."

"I'm not worried. She'll enjoy herself with the Merchants. They'll go to Meeting in the morning, and she can be our contact."

Claire's hand flew into a shushing motion, which she immediately withdrew, and Romy rolled her eyes to heaven and said, "Just what we need!"

"You must be well-organized," said Wolf. "I thought a minister had to spend Saturday locked in his study preparing the Sunday sermon."

Everyone was quiet for a moment, even Romy, who held back a snort at the idea of Corky's being well-organized.

But Claire couldn't stand waiting in the charged silence while he pondered his answer. "Corky's not currently preaching," she said. "There's been contention among the members, and they're providing their own services until they come to some agreement."

Wolf glanced from Claire to Corky and back again, then at Romy.

"That's too bad. Let's hope they come to an agreement soon."

"You may be too young to have gone through a big church brawl," said Corky. "Our people are no worse than any others. It's just that without the support of a denomination, they haven't been able to resolve this question. It's like trying to override a veto. They can remove their minister by a two-thirds majority, but it takes a three-fourths majority to call a new one. And that's where they are, stuck in the slack. It takes more of whatever you're talking about to make something than it does to tear it down. Somehow or other, it costs extra to cooperate. Of course the benefits are greater too, but people don't seem to know that."

"I haven't gone to church since I left home," said Wolf. "So I don't have any experience as an adult, but in my parents' church people made a show of harmony in public and tore each other apart in private."

Corky leaned back in his chair, then bounced forward. The joints of the chair crackled. "My theory is this: that whenever you have an institution that asks for the best in people, it also brings out the worst. And when it comes to churches, people are not prepared to deal with the worst. They don't expect to find bad behavior there, especially their own. It's always some place else. It's in the other fellow's church. When we set up ways to deal with trouble, it's trouble from the outside we're anticipating, not self-generated trouble."

"What do they argue about?"

Romy snorted. "You name it."

"You're going to get me started talking," said Corky. "Without boring you with history, we have two opposing groups: the ones who basically believe that Meeting should help people contribute to the betterment of society and those who believe it should make them better individuals.

"I saw the need for some overarching principle to allow these people to work together. And it seemed to me that just as we had chosen to ignore our intimations of the divine and become agnostic, we could choose to pay attention to them again and allow God to re-enter our lives. But I was not able to put this idea across. I made a lot of atheists out of agnostics."

"Atheists? I'm surprised that people admit to being atheists in church."

"You'll notice that it's called a 'Meeting,' not a 'church.' Most of the members call themselves 'religious humanists.' They have religious feeling, but they cannot bring themselves to believe in God without a scientific proof. The same people who are willing to discuss the 'economy' as though it were something tangible get uncomfortable at the mention of God. But that's understandable. The 'economy' is a loose term to cover a certain kind of behavior, and so is 'God', but no one yet has personified the economy. It's still nebulous enough for anyone to have ideas about it. But God got codified, and it's very hard indeed to believe in a God created in somebody else's image." Corky stopped speaking and looked around the table. "I'm sorry. I've broken the dinner table rule again." He pushed back his chair to punctuate his speech.

Wolf had eaten the last of his pizza and was leaning on the table, part of his attention on listening to Corky and part of it on watching Romy, who had eaten very slowly and was just now finishing her second slice.

Clair had been tearing her napkin into small pieces, then rolling the pieces up into tight little scrolls. When Corky had been silent for a moment, she asked if anyone would care to join her watching the TV movie that was coming on soon. Her voice sounded pallid compared to Corky's enthusiasm for his subject.

"What's this sudden craze for TV?" asked Romy. "For months on end the TV screen is dark and all of a sudden you want to watch a movie."

"Come on, Romy, we're not that bad. You know we watch our favorites."

Wolf said, "On our way back here this afternoon, we passed a theater where they're showing 'The Pardon.' I thought of inviting Romy." He sounded shy. "Do you feel rested enough to go out?"

"I'd like to clean up if there's time."

Dinner was over then, and Wolf phoned the theater to inquire what time the next showing would be. "Not for another hour and a half." Romy did her part in tidying up by taking the leftover pizza to the kitchen where Claire met her.

"Are you really feeling well?" Claire asked. "I'd like to see you go out and have a good time, but you do look tired."

"I'll lie down. Time to clean up really meant time to rest. I just don't like to play the invalid."

"Of course you don't!" The two women stood in the kitchen, not busy, and not saying anything for a moment. Then they both began to speak at once. Claire yielded.

"I had an odd thing happen this afternoon. I guess it was because I was tired from this morning, or maybe it was because going to look at cars reminded me so much of Frank. But I had a fit of anger that was so intense I felt like I might burn up."

"Oh? Were you quarreling with Wolf?"

"No. I was alone in the van. I don't even remember there being any cause for it, but all of a sudden I felt this intense fury and I had to get out and take a walk, literally to cool off. And then I walked a few blocks and stopped to rest, and I had kind of a horrible vision of the end of the world. Oh, it was awful!"

She was speaking in a low tone, but even so, Claire edged over to the dining room door and quietly closed it.

"I'm not going to confess to an ax murder or anything."

"I have another reason to want privacy. But tell me the rest of your story."

"There isn't any story. When the vision or whatever was over, I went back to the van. I just wish I didn't feel so upset all the time. I'd like to feel happy once in a while."

"Have you talked about this at your group?"

"Yes and no. We all talk about it, but it isn't really personal."

"Your group leader ought to see that it is personal. Talking generalities doesn't help anyone."

"I wish, oh well, it doesn't do any good to wish, does it?" Romy's wish was a fleeting little selfish wish that she put aside immediately: that Claire was her therapist instead of her aunt, so that she could accept help without having to know that Claire's problems were as bad as her own.

Claire sighed. "It all depends. Sometimes a wish can lead to action that will move you toward what you're hoping for. It depends on how you frame the wish. And of course there are times when none of your choices are good. But I don't think you're in that bad a situation."

"You don't?"

"I don't. Look, Romy, you've taken a beating. You can't expect to feel happy until the bruises heal. But you're working on things. Your back is getting better. You're paying off your bills. These problems are finite. They'll be gone one of these days, and you'll have a different set." Claire moved close and gave Romy a hug, a gentle hug. "There, isn't that a comforting thought?"

Romy hugged back, then made a motion toward the door.

Claire said, "I have a request to make."

Romy waited.

Claire spoke in a near-whisper. "Wolf doesn't know about Corky's arrest, does he?"

Romy shook her head.

"Having him here is doing Corky so much good. I dread for him to find out. Please don't tell him, if you can possibly keep from it, would you please not?" Claire's words spilled out. "Corky has been so lonesome, now that nobody will have anything to do with him."

"Don't worry, I won't say anything. It's not the kind of subject that comes up in ordinary conversation."

Claire nodded. "Thank you, dear. Now go lie down for a little while, so you can enjoy the movie."

PUZZLE PIECES

After Romy had gone upstairs, Claire went to the dining room to sit with Corky and Wolf. The perimeter of the puzzle was fitted together, but the rest was going slowly, because the picture had a lot of gray pieces in it, sea water and sky, with no discernable horizon. It had come from a rummage sale in an oatmeal box, so no one knew exactly what the final picture would look like, though it wasn't hard to imagine, since there were faces and rigging, as well as gray background.

"I'm betting on the sinking of the Titanic," said Corky. "I keep finding these white pieces that must be the iceberg."

"No way," said Wolf. "The Titanic didn't have sails."

Corky struck his forehead with the heel of his hand. "How could I be so stupid? A perfect example of ignoring the obvious to make the picture fit one's interpretation." He studied the puzzle pieces spread around the table. "I still think this white is an iceberg, though."

"It's a double disaster, then. Look, this guy's got a weapon of some kind, so there's a sea battle going on."

Claire said, "Maybe the white pieces belong to some other puzzle. The note on the box only said there were no pieces missing. It didn't say whether there were extra pieces or not."

Corky smiled at her fondly. "Atta girl. It's nice to have somebody around who can move outside the puzzle and look at it from a distance."

"It would be even nicer if I could do that with the puzzle of my own life."

Wolf had stopped fingering the puzzle pieces. "Maybe I ought to clean up a bit myself. I could use the bathroom down here to wash, couldn't I?"

"Go right ahead," said Claire. "But you can go upstairs if you like. Romy said she was going to lie down, not shower."

Wolf left the table and went upstairs.

Claire had not cautioned Corky against being open about his situation. There had not been a good time to bring it up. But now she said again, as she had to Romy, "I have a favor to ask."

He folded his hands and gave her his attention.

"I'm afraid that if Wolf finds out about our troubles, it will change his attitude toward Romy. She's benefiting from his company right now. I know you don't like to hold things back, but I wish you wouldn't tell him about being arrested."

He nodded. "Of course. You'll notice that I haven't said anything. I've figured out for myself that this is not something I can tell people with impunity. But he'll find out if he stays here any length of time. You know that, don't you?" He stood up and came around the table behind Claire and held her shoulders. "Don't try to do the impossible. You wear yourself out taking care of everyone."

She stood up and buried her face in his shirt front. "I know." They stood together hugging each other, then she pulled back and said, "There really is a movie on TV. I forget the name of it, but it sounded like we might enjoy it." They walked awkwardly, not letting go, into the crowded living room, where they sat down close together on the couch. The movie wasn't due to come on yet, but it didn't matter.

AFTER SCHOOL

Eve and Duncan Flannery had been arguing for weeks about how to schedule the hours between the close of Josie's school day and the time one of them got home from work, those dangerous hours of free time when anything could happen to an unsupervised child.

Wednesdays were not a problem. Josie went right from school on Wednesdays to Janice Beam for her music lesson, which began with an hour of singing with three other girls and ended with a forty-five minute piano lesson alone. But that left Monday, Tuesday, Thursday and Friday to worry about.

Duncan was afraid Josie would run around the neighborhood and get in trouble. The dangers he foresaw included encounters with drunks from the tavern on Osborne Avenue, the bad influence of older kids, derelicts in the park, and, of course, Corky Pearlman, who, although he no longer was welcome at the Meetinghouse, was ensconced as an attractive nuisance at the parsonage. He also worried about her tangling with traffic when riding her bike and about her leaving the neighborhood altogether and riding off to places like the lakeshore where drugs were sold and so were bodies.

Eve was afraid she would come home and eat.

Duncan wanted Eve to quit her job and be a better mother. A better wife too, of course.

Eve knew that without her job she would be isolated, and without a paycheck she would be dependent. So, in spite of all the parental concern, Josie continued to be unsupervised for almost three hours a day, four days a week.

If anyone had been listening to Josie, they would have understood that the parsonage was not attractive, not with the nuisance Nancy also ensconced there. Nor was the Meetinghouse, without Corky. Nor was she interested in drunks, drugs, derelicts, or older kids who were usually bullies.

The place Josie liked best was the library. She could get there on her bike in good weather, and she knew how to ride the bus as well. Eve had taught how to get to her music lesson without assistance. If the trip on the bus to Janice Beam's for music was sanctioned, then Josie argued and won the point that a trip to the library ought to be sanctioned as well. Dunk frowned sourly on Eve for opening a can of worms, but the can was open now, and Josie was fishing.

At the library she could read undisturbed, read anything in the Children's Room, and even slip into the stacks or the periodicals and browse. Her size and appearance were deceptive. She could pass for pre-teen rather than pre-ten. And she'd been reading for so long and so well that she was no longer limited; she could read anything she wanted. If she needed to know what a word meant, she looked it up. She couldn't take adult books out on her children's card, but there was plenty to read right there in the building.

She of course took new books home frequently, to prove to her parents that she'd really been where she said she was, though the books did little to allay Dunk's suspicion or Eve's anxiety. A girl could meet unsavory characters at the public library as well as anywhere else, and was it really healthy for a child to spend so much time hunched over a book?

But people left her alone in the library. That in itself was a plus. She went there often.

Another place she went after school, though not so often, was Portvillage, the retirement center and nursing home that she'd first visited last year as a Brownie, then again with her Sunday School class. She had performed at the piano in the Entertainment Room, played "English Country Garden" and "Silver Faun" without mistakes. One not-so-old but badly handicapped woman had invited her to visit again.

The invitation was genuine and appealing. Josie responded. Here she was not left alone, but was petted and made much of. She wasn't used to it, and thus it wasn't exactly comfortable, but more and more often the undivided attention of a kindly woman who wasn't trying to correct and improve her was what she wanted most.

When Josie arrived on a Friday afternoon, Bess Kingman was

napping in her high-backed wheelchair, unintentionally asleep in a corner of the Games Room, her book closed on her thumb. It took awhile for Josie to find her. Other residents called out greetings as she checked in Bess's room and the Activities Center.

To Josie, Portvillage seemed a jolly place, with lots going on, and flowers, and people wearing bright-colored clothes and smiling at each other. When her mother suffered a memory lapse or a backache and talked in a doleful voice about "ending up at Portvillage," Josie did not understand what was so awful about that or why her mother always added, "I'd rather you'd take me out and shoot me." Eve's attitude certainly colored her own – she looked around curiously for what was wrong with the place – but did not gray it down completely.

She answered the "hi" from the nurses' station and went where she was directed, through the double pocket doors that slid into the wall at her approach, and there was Bess in the corner. She approached quietly and sat down nearby. Immediately her presence was sensed and Bess's eyes opened.

Whatever was wrong with Portvillage, it wasn't Bess Kingman. The eyes that gazed at Josie were warm and intelligent.

Bess Kingman wasn't interested in trying to improve anybody. Crippled by arthritis and other ailments she didn't even want to think about, she had plenty of time to reflect upon the futility of such endeavors. Despite the continual commercial touting of the notion that a person can make herself into whatever she wants, Bess knew a few important things: 1) You don't get to choose who you are. 2) You don't get to choose who your *parents* are. 3) Already packaged in genetic material, you're dumped into a culture not of your making. 4) Things happen to you, not of your choosing. 5) By the time you're old enough to make any improvements, a lot of things are already set. 6) Changes are made at great cost. 7) The choices you have are modest. 8) Being who you are is a lifetime task.

"Look who's here," she said. "Just the person I wanted to see. Glory be to God for speckled things."

Josie held out her arms. "Not as speckled as last summer."

"Let me see." With her thumb and forefinger Bess made an inch against Josie's arm and began counting. "Eight," she said. "But some of them look like two run together. Maybe there are really more than eight." She squeezed the girl's hand. "Let's call it ten per square inch, and you get the prize."

"What's the prize?"

"Come and see." Bess rolled her chair out of the corner. Josie followed her down the hall to the room where her bed and personal possessions were. "A box came yesterday. Nourishment."

Josie hung back.

"What is it, child?" exclaimed Bess. "What's happened? You look like bad news."

"I'm not supposed to eat," Josie replied miserably. "If I haven't lost some weight by tomorrow, my mom will make me quit LOVELY YOU, and then where will I be?"

"Oh-wo-wo," said Bess. "*That.*" She rolled her eyes. "But who said anything about eating?"

"You said a box came with nourishment."

"Right," Bess answered. "Food for the soul."

"But chitlins are soul food, and chitlins are fattening! The kids all call them 'greasy-guts.'"

"No, no, no. I'm not talking about *soul food*, I'm talking about *food* for the *soul*." She held up her hand against Josie's misinterpretation. "I'm talking about art supplies. A box of *art supplies* came in the mail yesterday. An order from Daniel Smith." She urged Josie over to the closet and had her open the door. "That box," she said. "The big one."

Josie dragged it out, a large carton indeed.

"I went hog wild," said Bess. "I went through that catalog and spent money like you wouldn't believe. But I needed food for the soul, and nothing does it like a few hundred dollars worth of art supplies. So dig in and let's find something to play with today."

"I'm not very good at art," said Josie.

"Oh, I'm so glad!" exclaimed Bess. She motioned for Josie to pull a crescent-shaped board out from under her bed. "I can't stand people who are good at art. They make me feel so inferior."

"Me too," Josie answered, warming. "What is this?"

"It's a doohickey," said Bess. "I don't know what they call it, but I can lay it over the arms of this chair and have me a table." She settled the doohickey across her wheelchair. "It hurts me, see, to write or draw at a table because it's too high, but this is just right."

"You're going to have a hard time if you need to hop out of that chair quick. I hope you don't have to make an escape."

"Honey, if I have to make an escape, I'll holler, and you wheel me out as fast as you can, okay?"

Josie giggled and accepted the invitation to dig into the box. Out came the treasures: packages and pads of paper, some of it colored; brushes and cute little paint rollers; fat tubes of paint; a box of oil crayons; a huge box of colored pencils; little jars of gold and silver powder. There were some boring things as well: jars of paste and acrylic medium, flat trays, masking tape.

"This'll get us started," said Bess. "You can use my table."

Josie tucked her knees under Bess's table and gazed hungrily at the oil crayons. Bess tore off the plastic cover. "Here," she said. "What color appeals to you today?" Josie chose red. "And what color does the red ask for?"

The idea of red asking for another color amused Josie. "Red is like the cheese in 'Farmer In The Dell,'" she said. "It stands alone." She leafed through the papers and chose cream, then hesitated. "I hate to spoil it," she said. "I don't know what to draw."

"Let's make a picture together. Would you like for me to make the first mark?"

Josie nodded.

"Shall I use the red, or would you rather I chose a different color?"

"I don't know."

Bess chose a warm brown and made several suggestive marks on the cream colored paper. "Now you," she said.

Josie colored in the space between two marks and drew some lines out from it.

Thus begun, the picture grew as each one added bits here and there. The green at the bottom of the paper suggested grass, Josie's red turned into a flower. "This is easy!" she exclaimed. "This isn't like art."

They continued until the paper was a veritable garden. "How about making a gold frame," said Bess. She reached for the little jar of gold powder. "Here, take my spoon and get a few drops of water."

When Josie returned, Bess mixed the glittering paste right in the spoon and handed the little girl a brush. "A frame keeps the picture from spilling out."

"Good idea," said Josie. "Can I come and visit you tomorrow?"

"You sure can," Bess answered. "Tomorrow's Saturday, and you can stay longer."

"I'm going to need soul food," said Josie. "I have to go to LOVELY YOU in the morning, and I always want to eat a whole candy store after that."

Bess contained her outrage until Josie had gone home, then gave her dinner companion a surprise lecture on the evils of foot-binding, corsets, the slave trade and dieting.

ELECTION DAY

Charlie, the night pharmacist at Rochester's, was sick again, his head cold having dropped to his ample throat and become quinsy. On the phone, apologizing, he had to whisper painfully, his throat inflamed beyond swallowing. And not only that, but his doctor insisted that even after the antibiotic took effect he must stay quiet throughout the course of treatment for the sake of his heart. This meant more time away from the store. It meant more work for Sara.

Sara was putting in twelve-hour days, running on nerves, missing sleep and meals. Fred was grumpy, not able to get away to the library, for Sara had to hand him the details she usually attended to herself: phone calls, deliveries, orders, displays, the weekly *Clarion* ad, customer complaints. Fred, who had all along closed his mind to the fine points of drugstore management, was now obliged to do these chores as best he could, for as long as he could, then go home, put on an apron, and make dinner for Mr. Rochester and Aunt Jenny.

But Sara wouldn't let him complain. He, at least, had been able to take time on Election Day to go to the polls and vote; Sara couldn't leave the pharmacy unattended. She had hoped to start out early that morning and stop to vote on the way, but when the time came, her father detained her.

It was a mix-up in his dry cleaning. He had sent out slacks, but instead of getting them back, he found someone else's clothing in the bag.

"I don't see how three pairs of slacks could have been replaced by a woman's dress and coat. Someone should have noticed an error like that." He was sure it had happened because there was a new driver on the route. "I've used Gabriel's for years and never had trouble before."

"Let Fred help you," Sara suggested. "He'll be out of the shower shortly." Fred wouldn't mind being a little later, while she herself had already skipped breakfast and drunk her coffee on the run to save time.

"I'll only hold you for a moment," the old man told her. "I've misplaced the cleaner's bag with the dress and coat in it. You can take time to find it for me. It has the slip pinned to it."

But eight thirty came and went, and then quarter of nine, with him still grumbling and her still searching. "I need the slip for when I call and I need to have the clothes handy for when the delivery man comes to pick them up."

"Are you sure the bag was hanging in the hall?" Any hope of getting to the polls was gone. Now it was just a matter of opening the store on time.

"Positive," he answered. "I put it there. I meant to have you or Fred carry it upstairs for me. The bag was slippery and I didn't want to lose hold of it."

No, Fred hadn't carried it upstairs. He was still in the shower, planning to come to the store a little late, after the trip to the polls. "I haven't seen anybody's dry cleaning," he called. "Not recently, anyway."

The last place Sara looked, after searching every other closet in the house, was Jenny's room. "Have you seen...," and there it was, the clear plastic cleaner's bag with the dress and coat, hanging on the hook on the closet door. She snatched it down.

Jenny followed her out into the hall. "Wait," she called. "Those aren't dirty. They just came back from the cleaners."

The ticket said, "Cavendish," not "Rochester." Sara thrust the bag back at Aunt Jenny. "Sorry," she said hurriedly. "I absolutely must leave the house this minute." She did not even take time to explain to her father; she was late, and if he was going to lecture her on promptness, then he would have to let her leave on time. When she reached the store, the phone was ringing.

"It was a mistake," she told him. "Don't call Gabriel's. It was Aunt Jenny's cleaning. Yours will probably come back this morning."

"I hope so. I've had a long wait for those pants. Gabriel's is fast enough for cleaning, but they take their time on tailoring."

Sara, fed up, said, "Please, Dad, I have a customer."

As soon as there was a lull, she took a spoonful of antacid, the first of the day, like the baker having an early morning Danish. I shouldn't drink so much coffee, she thought. When Ben arrived, she put him to work on the cleaning chores while she filled prescriptions for the nursing home.

Ben was an immensely valuable employee. Retired from one of the mills in Gary, he worked a flexible split shift. His huge body was only slightly softened by age, and he managed by his mere presence to keep trouble away from Rochester's. Since the school children knew he recognized each of them personally, only the trickiest dared to shoplift. And Sara attributed the fact that the store had never been held up to Ben's ferocious appearance and irregular hours. A would-be robber, looking the place over, would surely go somewhere else.

Fred arrived about eleven in fine fettle, whistling, "Hey, You Beautiful Doll," and wearing a sporty cap that said "Lamberghini" across the front.

"Where did you get the hat?" asked Sara. It was becoming to him, made him look rakish.

He took it off and hid it behind him. "I'm afraid to tell you." When she didn't beg, he told her anyway, "I found it." He clapped it back on, squinted into one of the mirrored pillars, and adjusted its angle.

"At the church? Oh, Fred, it belongs to somebody." The polling place was at the Lutheran church three blocks south on Osborne.

"Not at the church. I found it right on top of somebody's trashcan. I had to park down the block, and all the trash was out for the pickup, and there it was, a Lamberghini hat, for the taking." He waited for her attack, and when it came, he interrupted. "Don't talk about lice," he said. "I already had the conversation about lice. Your father told me the stuff I hafta use when I start to itch. But I ask you, where's a louse gonna find a hair to wrap its nits around on this head?"

Sara couldn't help laughing. "You did that in front of my father? Picked a hat out of the trash and put it on? Oh my God, that must have been a sight."

He rolled his eyes. "Yeah," he drawled with satisfaction. "I couldn't resist. Aunt Jenny was there too, and she didn't know whether to agree with him and bawl me out, or laugh."

But this reminded Sara that she hadn't gotten to vote. "I wondered, when you came in, what was happening at the polls to make you so happy. They can't know anything yet, can they?"

"Probably. They prob'ly got it all figured out. But whatever happens, I'll be happy. Either he loses and I'm happy he lost, or he wins and gets another four years to run the country into so much debt we'll get a real change next time. Listen, babe, you wanna go vote, I'll collar anybody comes in and chew the fat till you get back."

"It's not worth it." She didn't really care enough to bother. "I don't know who to vote for anyway."

"You haven't been listening to me all these years!"

"How can I help listening to you? Now for heaven's sake find something to do and let me get back to work."

GOOD DAUGHTER

Fred didn't tell Sara that Claire was on duty as a poll worker. No need to upset her, and any mention of a Pearlman would do it, he'd found that out. She'd had her betrayed look on the other night, when he returned from walking Claire home, her shoulders so straight her braid hung out away from her back, and her mouth set funny. She'd kept giving him looks during "Masterpiece Theater." But he had promised not to eat, sleep and breathe the Pearlman project, so he didn't tell her a thing.

A little knot of customers from the seniors' housing project came in, and Fred put on his "Rochester's voice," which wasn't much different from his usual voice except that the gravel sounded slightly oily, because he was only pretending to be interested in their symptoms.

Charlie's absence was bringing to the forefront the need to hire another pharmacist, not to replace Charlie, whose meticulous handling of details was irreplaceable, but to give Sara time to run the store. She stewed about the prospect of the task: the screening, the interviews, the anxiety of choosing. The brightest and best would already have been snapped up by Lilly in Indianapolis or by the chains or the hospitals; the only advantage Rochester's could offer was experience for someone hoping to be a corner druggist.

But how could she justify another employee to her father, even if she could find one? Mr. Rochester had never hired a third pharmacist, not in all the years he ran the store. He had managed in earlier years because drugstores had shorter hours and less merchandise. He used the family for unpaid labor whenever possible. Both Sara and her older brother, much earlier, had worked after school from the time they were ten or twelve years old; even Sara's mother had worked off and on, between illnesses. Later, when his wife and son were dead grown, the old man left the store only to eat and sleep. He had no so cial activities, no hobbies, no other interests, only the store.

But Sara's life was different. She needed more help.

The store could afford it. While it couldn't compete with the chains when it came to quantity savings on merchandise, Rochester's did have advantages. The building itself was owned, not leased, and had been paid off long ago. Another salary, however, even at the low end of the pay scale for someone right out of school, would eat up a chunk of the margin. And less profit would indicate that Sara was not doing well enough. So she kept putting off the first step, which was to clear it with her father. Instead she worked harder herself.

It was the same old pressure, her need to be a good daughter.

Fred had no patience with this need. "Sell the damn store," he had advised, as soon as he saw what a burden it was going to be. "You can get back in the hospital any day. Or go someplace else. You got no problem getting a job. Why bust your butt?"

This argument had taken place on a Sunday afternoon almost a year ago, while Fred was still working for Powkin. They had gone to the store, Sara to work on the books, Fred to lay out new merchandise. She had looked up, when the noise of his rustling packages ceased, and had seen him staring at something. Her gaze followed his to the end of the seasonal gondola where she had placed a rack of gloves, the kind with thick-ended fingers, so ill-shaped that it hardly mattered which hand wore which glove. Although she thought the gloves were ugly, "I have to carry them, like it or not," she said disconsolately.

It was the ad service she was talking about. A regional operation bought quantities of non-medical merchandise like gloves and distributed it to drugstores, then printed advertising flyers every month. Rochester's needed the ads. They usually sold the merchandise too, since the prices were low. "I know they're cheap. They're supposed to be cheap." She could feel her own failure thick in her throat. "We're just a corner drugstore in an old neighborhood where people run in, this time of year, and buy cheap gloves because they've forgotten to wear any. And we need the advertising that comes with them."

He answered, "I'm not criticizing you, Sara. I just wish you didn't have to be here, that's all. And you don't have to. You've given this place a try. You know it's not what you want to do. Your father's had his fun out of it. It's time to sell."

"I can't sell. I don't own it. You know that, Fred. Why do you keep after me to do something you know I can't do?"

He walked over to where she sat and stood in front of her belligerently. "So you can't sell. You leave, and he sells."

"I'm just trying to be a good daughter," she cried. "That's all there is to it. Wouldn't you do the same for your mother if she were alive?"

"I can't answer that, Sara, because she's not alive. But that's not the point. The point is that you're too *old* to still be trying to be a good daughter. The point is that some fathers don't *deserve* to have such good daughters." His voice rose. "The goodness of the daughter ought to bear some relationship to the goodness of the father. Think that one over."

They had worked in heavy silence, then, and had fought further versions of the fight in the intervening months.

He accused her of being in competition with her brother.

"What a cliché'!" she had answered. "You've really come to a deep understanding of things, haven't you? I can't even remember having a brother, and here you tell me I'm in competition with him."

"That's not what you said before."

"So what did I say before?"

"You said you missed him when he left, and that you wrote him letters."

"A five year old? Sure. I wrote him long letters full of news."

"Have it your way, Sara. I'm wrong. You didn't write him letters."

But Sara changed her mind. "I did write him letters. Scribbly little letters. He never answered. I wrote to ask him to come home for my birthday, or for Christmas."

Fred's voice lost it combative edge. "Did he come?"

"No. Not very often. And when he did, he wasn't nice to me. I can remember following him around, and what he'd say to me was, 'Lay off, Sara.' I remember, 'Lay off, Sara,' just the way he sounded. And when I'd want him to hold me on his lap, he'd say, 'Forget about it.' Those are the things I remember him by: 'Lay off, Sara,' and 'Forget about it.'"

"So you became an only child. That's a good way to get even."

"Honestly, Fred. Why are you picking a fight about my brother, for God's sake? Somebody who's nothing more than a name to me."

But the fight was about the store, about getting away from the store, which Sara wanted as much as Fred did.

She had always wished that she could settle in a place far from Portville, far from the store, from her father. To that end, when she was young and unmarried, she used her vacations to scout around for beautiful places: Colorado Springs, Santa Fe, Seattle. Cultural centers like Boston and Washington. She could choose her place, the place that made sense to her, where she could take her best stand on life. With pharmacy as her profession, she could support herself almost anywhere.

But after the vacation and the two or three weeks of hotel living and sightseeing were over, she always returned. Portville, much as she hated it, had a hold on her. The store had a hold on her. Was minding the store going to be the meaning of her life? What a depressing thought!

And she did hate Portville, with its Hoosier identity crisis and its anxious pretensions to urbanity and culture. The whole idea of starting from scratch to develop yet another port on Lake Michigan, where no port was needed, which was how the town had originated, had given it a bad start from which it had never recovered. Portville had not come into being through natural features that people settled around. Rather, an Indiana port had been deemed commercially desirable back in the early boom, so the natural features (a shoreline with swamps and sand dunes) had been drained, leveled and covered over. There was no concern about ecological impact, only economic impact. Ads were taken out about business opportunity; streets and squares were plotted and given optimistic names such as Freighter Square and Harbor Street; sums were spent on dredging and construction. Businesses and residents came and settled. Like Indianapolis to the south, the city grew. But the port itself did not survive the crash, and now the words "Port of Portville" caused a moment of silence followed by a gush of anxious enthusiasm about the renovations going on in the old part of downtown, the wonderful indoor mall with dozens of specialty shops and covered connecting walks between the old Port buildings.

The "Port of Portville" had come to be nothing more than a marina for pleasure craft.

Sara should have escaped when she had the chance. She felt ill at ease here, disconnected, as though in all her life she had never found the soul of the place and made contact with it. Maybe it didn't have a soul, she thought. Maybe it was like those people who try so hard to become what the world wants, those people who drain their psychic swamps and level their personal sand dunes and mold themselves in the image of success. People like that sometimes manage finally to kill off their souls, or at least make them unavailable; perhaps Portville had done the same thing.

Perhaps also it was her own loss that Sara was feeling. She had *not* realized her hopes, had *not* gone far away. To be met on the street by a high school classmate embarrassed her. "Yes, I'm still here," she always had to say, "and no, I don't have any children." When she heard herself saying this, confronted with these facts, she suffered. Being childless in Portville meant that she had failed herself.

And being back at Rochester's this past year had heightened her sense of failure. Managing Rochester's was entirely different to Sara than it might seem to someone who didn't know her hopes. To most of the customers it appeared to be a natural, desirable thing for her to do. The son, Tom Jr., Sara's older brother, who would have stepped into his father's business, had been killed in the war, and how fortunate old man Rochester was to have a smart, modern daughter who had interested herself in pharmacy!

After her externship, Sara had taken a job at Portville General. She worked hard there, but when quitting time came, she could go home. And a job in the hospital had good benefits, not to mention such a luxury as a lunch hour, albeit short, when she could eat in the hospital cafeteria with friends. Only when her father's hands had begun shaking so hard that pills went rolling around the floor had she left the hospital for the family business. Customers assumed it to be the act of a kind and mature daughter to relieve the old man of the work he could no longer do.

But Sara felt it otherwise. She was still under the thumb of her father. On his payroll. Wearing his starched "Rochester's" smocks, typing labels on his old Royal.

And in spite of all her efforts, she was not a good daughter. A good daughter would not be so repelled by her father that she couldn't bring herself to tie his tie for him, or unbutton his buttons. So thought Sara. Some daughters even kiss and hug their fathers; but whenever Sara saw such a display of affection, she felt herself bereft of the right feelings. The girl in the pinafore, hair in long finger-curls, saying, "I love you, dear Papa," like Elsie Dinsmore, and kissing him somewhere on the face, surely not the mouth, but not just a peck on the cheek either. They always said, in books, "She planted a kiss…" Was this like planting a bomb, or a clue, or was it more like planting a seed? And what grew or exploded, or was solved when a kiss was planted? Sara always turned her gaze away when she saw it about to happen.

Sometimes the woman in the book wanted to tell her father how much she loved him. She herself would have to lie to say such a thing.

It had never seemed false for her to tell Fred she loved him, but that was because he was her husband, though sometimes women, in books again, of course, crossed their fingers when they said it to their husbands, right after pretending to have orgasms. Not Sara. She did love Fred, and she didn't mind telling him when the feeling hit. It would happen suddenly, his face would crease up with fun and a smile come over it that made his mouth look roomy inside, as though he had a secret too big to keep, or maybe he would lean forward in his chair to listen, and put his forearms on his knees; Sara would feel this flush of emotion, and she would tell him. It always pleased him. His head turned pink under tan and his hazel eyes glistened, and he'd get up and put his arms around her.

But it hadn't happened for a long time. They were so seldom alone, and, "Fred, you're so neat. I love you a lot," would not go over well at the dinner table where her father did the talking.

She couldn't remember even wanting to tell her father, "I like you," let alone, "I love you." Which was too bad, really. Other people liked him. Why couldn't she? Customers would tell her what a fine man her father was, what a good druggist, how he had brought the medicine himself in the middle of the night, and the baby got well. Clean as a pin, they would say, honest and fair in his pricing, prompt as prayers at the convent. You could set your watch, they said. Sara heard constantly from the old-timers what an exemplary person she had for a father.

She wished she could love him. It would make life easier. When you love somebody, you don't have to be a good wife or a good daughter, she thought. It's enough that you love him. You plant the kiss and that takes care of everything.

But not everyone is demonstrative, she argued. Maybe I'm just not the kind to hug and kiss. The answer? A good daughter could at least listen to her father give the benefit of his experience without feeling picked on and put down. Especially when he knew so much about her own field.

Maybe this was a lot to expect from herself? Fred thought it was; maybe he was right. She had given up a good job to take over the store. That was something, after all. There had to be points for that.

But no, she couldn't claim points for that, really, because owning your own drugstore is a desirable thing; it's one of those dreams pharmacy students talk about a lot. Being able to run it the way you want to, and the idea that you aren't limited the way you are when you work for someone else. With your own store, it's up to you how much money you make. You don't get points for being lucky enough to have a family business to move into.

Of course she didn't own Rochester's, her father did, which was why she couldn't satisfy Fred by selling it. But she would inherit it. There was no one else for him to leave it to.

And that was the rub. Because she knew that he still grieved for her dead brother.

Here Sara would give up trying to straighten out her thoughts. It was impossible; she didn't know what was the matter with her. Nobody ever knows the nature of his own wound, she thought. And what good would it do to know? All you can do anyway is work.

The work never ended. The time after Fred left for the day, the evening hours, lasted as long as the whole rest of the day put together. She'd gotten spoiled, and getting unspoiled is so hard on a person. She'd had those years of evenings with Fred, when they had fun, and then to give them up... Not that they did sophisticated things, went to cocktail parties or the theater; most of Portville went to bed early. But they would play, and it was fun, like being young kids together. They'd play dominoes, or Scrabble, and they'd watch awful TV programs and laugh themselves weak. They'd take their shower together and then run out of the steam down the cold hall and jump in the big bed, where Fred would roll her around in the covers and growl like an animal, and then it would change and he'd quiet down and say, "Sexy Sara," and they'd make love in slow motion, climbing up and up and up, and around and around; and hanging there; up some more and around and up, nudging each other closer, inching toward the edge, and hanging there; and hanging, with nothing at all underneath; until the slightest motion set off the trigger, and the uncontrollable rush of convulsions brought them down breathless and sweaty to where the room with the big bed was.

Oh, how she missed it!

Customers came in the store all evening: school kids, singles, couples, seniors from the housing project. Insulin, Tagamet, Naprosyn, Inderal, Valium, all the antibiotics... Sara counted and measured and typed. "Be sure to take them all," she would say, or, "Come back when you need a refill."

FREETHINKERS

In the midst of Sara's turmoil, Fred found himself longing for his job. Powkin would be a refuge from the drugstore right now. He had never considered it so when he worked there, but in those days he hadn't spent enough time in the drugstore to need a refuge. But thinking about Powkin was painful, and he remembered the story Sara had read to him about the wildlife refuge that had become so toxic that birds were fired upon to keep them from landing.

That's the kind of refuge Powkin would be now, toxic. The takeover had polluted it beyond recognition. Fred drove out of his way to avoid the sight of the building so he wouldn't have to endure the squeezing in his chest that came on when he remembered too vividly what had happened there.

Hardly anyone over forty had survived the early rounds of the purge except a few members of top management, and after that, after the old Powkin managers, who had once been each others' friends, had fought for the jobs that were left, after they had done the dirty work of firing everyone else, then they too had been purged. "Purge" was the word Fred used to describe what the Amalgamated annual report had called the "restructuring" of its new acquisition. Like the political purges in communist China, the capitalistic Powkin purge had devalued Fred's contribution and that of his co-workers, labeled the persons who were making this now-worthless contribution "dead wood," and proceeded to "prune."

The heart of Fred's job, as a translator between the manufacturers of equipment and the users, had been seeing to it that the instruction manuals that passed across his desk would be comprehensible to Joe Blow. His job description did not stress comprehensibility; he had taken it upon himself and was proud of what he did. But on the day he was told that his job no longer existed, he realized that lucid instructions did not contribute to the only thing that mattered to management: profits. Because so many products originated overseas, and so many instruction books were written by people not fluent in English, the standards throughout industry were low. The public did not demand comprehensibility – perhaps didn't even recognize it; therefore management did not value Fred.

And so he had no refuge. No sacrosanct job that required his presence no matter what was happening at the drugstore. Sara was the one who had responsibilities that took precedence. Fred was the one who helped out.

At home he spent most of his time in the kitchen. Tuna-noodles with green olives and beer. Bean soup with smoked hocks and cayenne pepper. Iceberg lettuce with Hellman's. Chili with the works: beans, meat, hot chili gravy, tomatoes, onions, and spaghetti. Fred had his choice of menus night after night, but he didn't enjoy it without Sara.

He would, however, enjoy going to Meeting on Sunday. He felt guilty letting Sara go to the store alone, but not guilty enough to accompany her. He had done nothing thus far to keep his Pearlman story on the hook. It would get away if he didn't start pulling it in.

Jenny went along. She made remarks during the service, which she considered inferior, and complained about Corky's absence.

Fred liked the talk better than Jenny did. The speaker, a Freethinker from the human potential faction, spoke on "Self Esteem Management," and the part Fred liked went like this: When people compare themselves invidiously with others, two different viewpoints are used. Other persons are seen as they present themselves, dressed to the nines, with their faces composed, their houses in order, and their accomplishments on display, while one's own self is not even *seen* at all, but is *felt* from the inside, shivering, with every uncertainty and inadequacy a sharp little stone in the shoe.

Yes, thought Fred. So obvious when you think of it. But how do you use this insight to change anything? During the Coffee Hour after the service, he met the speaker, Velma Winters, a handsome woman of about forty, large in all dimensions, wearing a brown tunic decorated with a fake fur leopard whose head was appliquéd over her left shoulder and whose tail draped over her right, while its feet dug into her shoulder blades. Fred took advantage of the opportunity to bring up the question.

"It can be done, she answered. "It can be done. We tailor the packaging to fit the individual." Her voice boomed enthusiasm. Her gestures swept so widely that Fred was careful to stay out of the way of her coffee cup. "The most important thing I do in my job is help restore self-esteem." She explained that her work was with crime victims.

Another Freethinker, at the fringe of the conversation, moved closer and spoke. "Be careful, waving that coffee around, Velma." He held her arm still. "You're a battlefield medic. Tending the casualties. If we didn't have the war going on, your work would be superfluous." The man nodded down to Fred from an imposing height. "I don't believe we've met. I'm John Kidder." His luxurious eyebrows were set like eaves over the deep, bony caves that housed his eyes.

Fred introduced himself, shook John Kidder's hand and went back to the conversation. "And what war is it you're talking about?"

Velma Winters answered. "Crime," but John interrupted. "Crime's only one of the many battles. The war itself is built into the structure of our society. I'm talking about the continual competition between thee and me and everyone else. It's a miracle that the idea of self-esteem is still around, after the beating it takes."

Velma said, "All we can do is tend the casualties, John. The system is ever with us. And if it wasn't, we'd have an even worse one."

Fred plunged in joyfully. "People are in love with competition. They think it increases productivity," he said. "Actually, competition, for a lot of folks, increases productivity like blood-letting restores health."

Both Velma and John laughed, and Fred went on. "Self-esteem, who's got it? Who do you know that can really count on his self-esteem being there when he needs it? Most of us got enough of it to know what it is and want more, but with everybody out to make a loser outta everybody else, nobody can keep it safe."

Velma was looking more and more skeptical as Fred talked. "Do you really think people try to make losers out of everyone else?"

"No, ma'am," he answered. "I overstated my point. I think a lot of people do try to bolster each other up. But every tennis player is trying to make a loser out of the guy on the other side of the net, and whichever one goes home without the prize, there's not much his wife can do to bolster him up."

"There's a lot his wife can do," said Velma. "She can remind him that there's always a next time. He hasn't lost forever."

"Some help that is!" broke in John Kidder. "Another chance to lose."

The three of them now had an audience. "Is this a private fight," asked one woman, "or can anyone join?"

She wasn't given a chance, however, because someone else said, "We can all be winners," in the syrupy tone people use when they say things like that.

Velma nodded vigorously. "Exactly," she said. "That's another thing the tennis player's wife – or husband, may I remind you – can point out. That improving one's performance is as worthy a goal as making a loser out of the other player."

Fred shook his head just as vigorously. "You're confusing the issue, using the word 'winner' two different ways. Winner A is the competitor in the tennis match. Winner B is the kid out in the alley knocking tennis balls up against the back of the garage. Don't switch players in the middle of the match."

"But improving your skill is just as worthy a goal as winning," she said again.

John Kidder spoke up vehemently. "The statement that everyone can be a winner is as dumb as anything I've ever heard. There is no such thing as a winner without a competition, and when there's a competition, there's at least one loser."

"People can compete against themselves," said Velma. "Against their past performance."

"That's not competition. My daughter tries to play her Chopin without hitting the same wrong notes she hit yesterday. That's called *practice*, not competition. But when she represents her school in the piano competition, and eleven kids sit there and wait while the judges decide who played the best, you can bet that all eleven of those kids are going to go home losers, ten because they didn't win, and the eleventh because what the winner gets as a prize, in addition to the hatred of the others, is the chance to go through the whole damned agony again at the next higher level. And that doesn't even begin to address the problems that come when he gets *hooked* on winning."

Velma patted John's sleeve. "Susan's going to be just fine," she said.

"She's one of the lucky ones: loving family, good education, blessed with health, intelligence, talent."

But John refused to be comforted. "If the lucky ones feel as little self-esteem as Susan does, what about the unlucky?"

"You wouldn't believe how bad off the people I work with are," said Velma. "Being the victim of a crime does more than make you angry or afraid. It lights up all the old fears that you thought were over and done with. Your everyday fear of normal competition is nothing by comparison."

"I'm not going to say it," said John. "I can see that I'm getting nowhere with Velma."

"You're getting somewhere with me," said Fred. "Go ahead, say it."

"Well, my point is that everyday normal competition *weakens* people instead of making them stronger. It *weakens* their self-esteem, which then is susceptible to the next blow, and on and on. It weakens the *losers* by telling them that society doesn't value their efforts. It weakens the *winners* by getting them addicted to winning and then demanding more and more soul-selling to feed their habit. There's no *self* esteem here, only the esteem of others. Maybe Velma's crime victims wouldn't have so many old fears to be lit up if they hadn't been subjected to competition all their lives."

Velma was looking around as though ready to find someone else to talk to. "Well, John, we're on different sides of the fence, but if that's the way you feel, I'm surprised that you compete in union politics."

"I wouldn't, if I didn't have to win the political race to do the work I want to do, which is a whole nother issue I'll be glad to expound upon any time."

Velma moved backward a step and waved at someone across the room, then excused herself, but as she was leaving, she explained to Fred, only half-jokingly, that John Kidder managed to get out of doing chores for the Meeting by always being busy with union work.

Fred saw his chance and grabbed it. "I'd be glad to volunteer for chores. I'm new here and don't want to be a buttinski, but someone was saying they needed people to help paint or something."

John Kidder, too, was withdrawing, since no one had taken him up on his offer to expound. "You're in the right ballpark." He nodded in the direction of one of the women who had been listening. "Here's a live one for you, Helly."

"You're willing to paint? Wonderful!"

With a firm agreement made to participate in the inner workings of the group, Fred had accomplished his purpose and could have gone home, but he was enjoying himself so much he kept Jenny waiting for him in the library for another half an hour.

In the next few days, thinking it over, he connected this talk to his ideas about blame. The connection seemed obvious to him. "Blame is to Competition what Responsibility is to Cooperation," he said into the tape recorder, then added soberly, "and we're rapidly reaching the point where we can't afford it any longer."

"Responsibility is what you take upon yourself when you Cooperate. Blame is what you put on somebody else when you Compete."

"Blame is what Competition busies itself with when something goes wrong. Who did it? Not what do we do next, but who's to blame? Only part of Competition is winning; the other part is placing and avoiding Blame.

His eyes would squint as the car held its place in the line of traffic along Portville's avenues and streets. "And instead of using its own vocabulary fair and square, Competition cheats. It's actually creating a society of losers, but it covers this up by calling the innocent and worthwhile improvement of skills 'competing against yourself.' And it steals the word 'responsibility' from Cooperation when it oughtta use its own word 'blame.' It oughtta come right out and say, 'So-and-so's to *blame* for this mess' instead of 'So-and-so-s *responsible.*' With that load put on Responsibility, nobody wants any. Taking on Responsibility no longer implies seeing that something gets done; it implies taking the Blame for its *not* getting done."

Sometimes his own rhetoric made him mad. "How the hell can they call our system a meritocracy? The only thing of merit when push comes to shove is the ability to compete. How can we expect a president to have any sense when his main job is self-promotion, self-packaging, self-presentation? When's he gonna read Plutarch, for Christ's sake? How can he possibly do what's right when he's always having to avoid blame and worry about his goddam *image?*"

Since Sara called his arguments "foaming at the mouth" and wouldn't talk when he really got hot, he could hardly wait for his next encounter with the Freethinkers.

It came soon but turned out not to be what he'd expected. For one thing, it involved kids. To Fred, kids were kids and adults were better company.

Thus the best mood he could muster was teeth-gritting endurance when he found himself the next Saturday in an unfamiliar part of the Meetinghouse with an unfamiliar group of Freethinkers that included several children.

"It's bad luck to crawl under a stepladder," he said to one of those children. His ankles were pressed for balance against the sides of the ladder, between the fourth step, where he stood, and the fifth, which was slowly denting a bruise across each shin. With his right hand he lowered the roller into the tray of red paint, while leaning with his left on the concrete block wall of the fifth grade classroom in the Religious Education wing. Even though the stepladder was sturdy, putting the roller down was awkward and hanging on was precarious.

The girl he was talking to crawled the rest of the way through the legs of his ladder and retrieved a paintbrush, then backed out and bumped into the ladder as she stood up. "Why is it bad luck?" The provocative tone matched the tilt of her head full of pink plastic curlers. She looked up at him through greenish-brown eyes set far apart in her slim, freckle-dusted face. With her bony little hip thrust out, she looked like the child that was mother to the flirt she would be in a very few years.

Fred continued to hang on in case she came back. "Because you'll get red paint in your pretty yellow curls." Accidents happen, he thought hopefully. He shifted his weight. The paint climbed the right side of the roller tray that was hooked to the ladder. He shifted his weight again. The paint moved thickly to the left, but none splashed out.

He picked up the roller and considered dropping it on her, but she was out of the line of accidental fire.

"They're not just yellow. They're Princess Golden Comb-In with Lustre."

"All the more reason to be careful. You wouldn't want polka dots in your Princess Lustre, now would you?" A deliberate drawing down of his arm painted another swath of fire-engine red in front of him. Around the room two other men and a woman also pushed rollers up and down the classroom walls.

"Probably not. I have a session this afternoon. Every Saturday afternoon." She heaved an existential sigh. "I'm a model. I have to go to the studio and get photographed in a swimsuit so people will know what to buy next summer. Polka dots were big last summer, so you can be sure they'll definitely be o-u-t this year. I mean next year." She bumped against the leg of the ladder again. "Oops, here, I'll steady it for you."

"Just get out from under it, will you please?" He clutched the top of the ladder. "If I fall offa here, you got worse troubles than polka dots."

"Come here, Tina," called the man in blue coveralls, who was her father, Doug. "Here's a brush you can use on the orchid corner."

"I already have a brush." The little girl joined two other children who were slathering Easter orchid over the moss-green that covered the concrete block rectangles of the lower half of a corner. The opposite corner, already finished, was painted daffodil yellow.

With Tina gone, Fred breathed easier. He continued to paint. "Could somebody tell me who dreamed up this color scheme? Not to be nosy or anything."

Laughter came from the people behind him. "Good question."

"This is democracy at work." It was the woman speaking, Helly. "The fifth grade uses a color scheme as an issue to study and vote on. They bring paint samples and campaign for their favorite colors. The colors evolve into parties, red being the House Majority this time, so to speak, because it got the most votes." Helly's voice was earnestly enthusiastic, the voice of righteous causes. "The kids figured out how much area would correspond to the number of votes red got. The orchid and yellow corners tied for a poor second." She seemed to be the person in charge of the work party. She had brought the paint cans from her car and found the rollers and trays in the basement, and when Fred had wound up with the only roller without a long handle, she was the one who apologized and told him where the ladder was.

"What woulda happened if each kid voted on a different color?" Fred craned his neck to look at her, but quickly had to right himself to keep his balance.

"That happened a few years ago when we first started the project. We painted the room in stripes, floor to ceiling, each one equal. The kids liked it so much they voted to keep it that way when it was time to decide on their compromise scheme."

"You mean this room gets painted every year?"

"Twice a year." Doug's voice. He did not sound delighted. "The first time it's each kid holding out for what he wants. Then, after they've had a good chance to see how the colors clash, they have another election and compromise."

The other man added, "And then the Maintenance Committee comes in and helps the kids put the compromise on the wall."

"I thought the walls looked pretty good the way they were before we started," said Fred. "Do the kids ever just let well enough alone?"

"No," said one of the children in the orchid corner. "We're not supposed to."

"Freethinker children? No way." Helly again. "But you'd be surprised how much they learn about individuality and compromise. The costs are right there in front of their eyes every Sunday morning. The clash when each person does his own thing without regard for the others. The regret at having to give up a beautiful vision because nobody else will buy it."

Fred descended and moved his ladder. Now he was next to the door that led to the hallway. Just outside, a red-haired girl in jeans and a denim jacket stood looking in. He motioned for her to come in, but when she didn't move, he climbed the ladder again and dipped his roller in the paint. "Sunday School's come a long way since I was a kid. Back in the Stone Age we used to sing 'Jesus Wants Me for a Sunbeam' and learn the Ten Commandments." A generous swath of red followed his roller down the wall.

"Sure," said Helly. "Bronze Age too. That's one of the reasons we're Freethinkers." There was a rustle of drop cloth as she changed position. "Oh," she said, her voice taking on extra enthusiasm. "Come on in and help, Josie." The tone alerted Fred. It held a lot more welcome than the situation warranted.

The girl at the door came inside and hesitated. Fred's thought divided between the child and the conversation. "But what's democratic paint got to do with religion?" Josie was the name Mrs. Claire had told him. Josie. This girl might be his reason for being here.

Two voices at once: Helly saying, "Get a smock and help with the orchid corner. The yellow's all finished." and the other saying, "This church is a democratic institution. The members run it. We try to teach the children how the process works."

Fred's section next to the door was finished. He stepped down to watch Josie as she dumped her jacket out on the hall floor and put on a smock covered with paint daubs. Then he rearranged his ladder so that he could paint the section above the door.

Maybe the girl's parents would show up too. After all, the father was supposed to be the boss of jobs like this. Maybe they would invite him to their house for dinner, take him into their confidence and tell him their side of what had happened.

Sure, he thought bitterly. Piece of cake. Suddenly the smell of paint was almost more than he could bear.

"If you're interested, you could sit in on some of the classes," said Helly. "There's a segment running now in Junior High on democratic psychology. It treats the person as a system of sub-systems, each needing to be recognized so that the whole can find direction instead of floundering in anarchy."

Fred realized she was talking to him. "I'm sorry, ma'am. I missed what you were saying."

The other man spoke up. "Come on, Helly, nobody in his right mind would want to sit in on Junior High. Give the guy a break."

Fred sent him a grateful look.

Helly's plump shoulders shrugged. "You men."

"Corky's a man and he goes to Junior High," called out Tina from the orchid corner, where she was using a brush at the floor line. "He goes to all the classes." Her reedy voice bounced off the classroom walls.

"Used to," corrected Helly. She paused. "We have to give Corky credit where credit is due. He made this church school what it is today."

"Yeah," said Tina, "a meat market."

Fred couldn't believe his ears.

"Enough," said her father.

"You're the one that said it!"

"Enough," he repeated. This time a threat was embedded in the tone.

Fred climbed his ladder and painted above the door, eyes straight ahead.

It was Helly who finally broke the silence. "We believe in openly discussing the issues." Her voice faltered, but picked up determination. "Or at least that's what we say we believe in."

Fred felt the ladder under him bumped. He pressed the roller against the wall over the door to keep his balance. A glob of paint squeezed out and fell. He looked down.

Creeping under the ladder out the door was Josie. She had taken off her smock. The glob of red paint had smacked into a flattened pool at the crown of her head, where it lay in her coppery hair like a crimson cow plop. She picked up her jacket from the hall floor and headed away from the classroom.

Fred teetered, then backed down the ladder and followed her, leaving the people in the classroom to think whatever they wanted.

He caught up with her at the heavy glass door that separated the Religious Education wing from the Meetinghouse proper. He pushed it open and held it for her as he had done for every female who had gone through a door with him since he was a small boy.

"Thank you," she said. Her voice surprised him. It was clear and ringing and mature beyond her years. But she was at an awkward stage, her teeth too large for her mouth and her middle too large for the waist of her jeans. She struggled with her jacket, trying to get it right side up. The red dropping quivered in her hair.

"May I hold your coat?" asked Fred formally.

"Thank you," she answered again in that plangent tone.

"Be careful. There's paint in your hair." She reached to feel, and he said quickly, "No, don't touch it. It's wet."

The large entrance hall was quiet and empty. To the left in the alcove, empty hangars were arranged neatly on the long coat racks. To the right, wood was stacked in front of the fireplace. From the sanctuary came the sound of a vacuum cleaner.

"Are your parents here?" Fred asked.

"No." Josie headed for the front door.

Fred kept up with her. "Where are you going?"

"Home."

Fred held the door again and followed her out. He was in his shirt-sleeves, but he knew she would not wait for him to go after his jacket.

"How far away is home?"

"Over there." She pointed vaguely.

He had no idea where she meant. They passed his Pinto, parked on the street, its rust spots more noticeable in this unfamiliar setting. He looked at it longingly but did not suggest driving.

"Where are *you* going?" she asked.

Fred ignored the possibility that he was intruding and cultivated his shepherd instinct. "I'm taking you home, wherever that is," he answered. "I want to make sure you get there okay."

She gave him a quick glance but said nothing.

He wondered what she was thinking and walked carefully apart from her to let her know he wasn't dangerous. He also wondered just how far away she lived.

But after only three blocks, they turned off Plainfield. Ahead an old woman in a big flowered scarf was sweeping her sidewalk. When Fred and Josie caught up with her, she glanced at Josie's head. The red paint was crusted over like an untended wound. "Lordy, look at that!" she exclaimed.

"It's paint," said Fred quickly.

"Well that's a mercy." Her gaze turned to him. "You'll catch your death, out with no wraps."

"Yes'm," he answered. "I can feel it coming on."

Just before they reached the corner, Josie turned and climbed three concrete steps into her front yard.

Fred felt like a trespasser, an interloper, a stalker of children, but he doggedly climbed the steps behind her and continued up the walk. "You wanna eat, you gotta hustle," he muttered under his breath, excusing himself for his rudeness. "Think like a writer. The story is everything." He would see her to the front door. Then, if nobody was around to talk to him, he would go back to the church. Maybe they would be finished painting. He could always hope.

The house, like many in the area, had no porch, only a small stoop with the roof jutting out to shelter it. It was a nineteen-twenties house, stained brown, with an ugly green roof. The door did not open when

Josie turned the knob. She rang the bell. They waited for a moment, then a man appeared behind the curtained glass, looked out and opened the door a crack.

"Good God," he said to Josie, opening the door wider. "What happened this time?"

"Nothing." Making herself as small as possible, Josie slipped past him and disappeared.

"She's not hurt. It's just paint."

The man was unquestionably Josie's father, Duncan Flannery, with red hair and the same skin, aged of course, but still so fair it probably didn't take on color, even in sunlight. His hilly accent came from the south, but not far enough south to give it grace.

Fred introduced himself and said, "I'm new at the Freethinkers." He went on. "Your daughter had just started to help with the painting when one of the other children made a crude remark to her and she left."

"Damn!" Dunk came out on the stoop. "I warned Evie to keep her home."

Fred's instinct told him that he would not be confided in by a man who looked as if he shot squirrels for meat and strangers for the hell of it. Even so, he had nothing to lose. "Look," he said. "I'm thinking about joining the Meeting, but I want some idea what I'm getting into. I wonder if you know anything about the trouble the reverend up there is in."

"If you ask me, there's not enough trouble on earth for that son of a bitch." He glanced past Fred out to the street where a Subaru was being parked at the curb.

"It sounds like I could have chosen a better time to get interested."

Duncan scowled. "Well, coming in now, you won't have any illusions." He edged past Fred. "Excuse me. My wife needs help with the groceries."

At the curb a short, pretty woman in pink jeans and high-heeled shoes struggled to lift a bag of groceries from the trunk of the car. Fred followed Duncan down to help.

"I told you not to let Josie go over there," said Duncan to his wife.

"Over where?""

"Over to the Meetinghouse."

"I didn't let her go. I didn't know anything about it." The woman was looking at Fred, and Duncan adopted a friendlier stance.

"This is my wife, Eve. Evie, say hello to – what was it you said your name was again?"

"Fred. Fred Bekin. I'm pleased to meet you, ma'am. Let me carry that bag inside for you." He took the grocery sack she couldn't quite reach and a carton of Coke, while Duncan carried the rest.

The vestibule, a little square room, had a green and white tiled floor that looked freshly washed, while just ahead a dark, varnished staircase turned the corner at a landing several steps up. Eve led the way across a long living room with lace curtains and fat furniture and pleated lamp shades into a crowded dining room and on around into the kitchen. "Just set everything on the table," she said. "I thank you very much."

When Eve removed her jacket, Fred saw that she was wearing a cuddly pink sweater with a darker collar that matched her tight jeans. Her brown hair was long and fluffy, like a magazine cover girl. Even for a trip to the grocery store she had made herself attractive with eye shadow and blusher.

Fred had now gained the house, but he hadn't yet figured out how to hold it. The strategy for getting along with women that because of his upbringing came naturally – finding out what kind of help they needed and providing it – had petered out. He couldn't very well open her cupboards and help with the groceries. He stood there awkwardly for a moment while Duncan took the Cokes into a pantry and Eve opened the refrigerator to put the milk away. Then, since both of them were busy, he began to feel so much in the way that he started to leave. He could endure being an interloper only so long.

Before he could reach the door, however, Josie reappeared. The paint was gone, her fiery hair wet and plastered to her head. Her shirt was wet too, as though she had plunged her head in a wash basin. The girl had a stooped posture, and Fred noticed that she was trying to close her lips around the teeth that were too big for their housing.

"What on earth!" Evie exclaimed. "Josie, stand up straight. Pull your shoulders back."

"Go dry your hair," said Duncan shortly. "It's not summer."

Josie turned tail and disappeared again.

"I'm glad the paint came out," said Fred. "I was afraid it might take more than soap and water." At Evie's incredulous look, he explained to her why he was here in her house.

"Sit down." Eve pulled a chair out from the table. "Let me get you a Coke."

The phone rang in the living room. Duncan went to answer it. Fred sat down at the table.

"There wasn't any need for you to walk Josie home. She's used to running around the neighborhood. But it's thoughtful of you." Eve poured Coke into two glasses and added ice. There was an ashtray and cigarettes on the table. She offered them to Fred, then sat down and shook out one for herself. Fred lit it for her.

"Well, I was looking after my own interests too. Being new and all, it wouldn't be too smart to spill paint all over a kid and not even apologize to her folks." He squirmed with impatience to blurt out questions, but he held back while Eve smoked, talking instead about the democratic paint and the pleasure of conversation with Freethinkers at the coffee hour. Finally, after a decent interval, he asked her what kind of trouble the reverend was in.

"You mean you haven't heard?" She stubbed out the last of the cigarette. "I would have thought everybody in Portville knew by now. He's a child molester." Her little face hardened as she sized Fred up. "That fine way he has, so 'good with children,' is not what he and the exalted Claire make it out to be. It's just his way of getting them to trust him so he can do his dirty things."

Fred had to pretend surprise. "That's terrible. I never would have guessed it. I thought it had something to do with his preaching."

"That too."

Fred watched her eyes, which darted around, seeming to search for something in the air. She talked, distracted, about how Corky's leadership had gone downhill. Less and less attention to the necessary details of his job, more and more quirkiness. "I knew all along there was something funny about him, but unfortunately I didn't know in time what it was. That's not something that leaps to mind." She fumbled with the cigarette pack. Fred lit her another.

After a little more neutral questioning, Fred asked casually, "How on earth did they find out what was going on?"

Here Eve had to stop talking to size him up again, but this time he must have passed the test, because she took a long, meaningful drag of smoke and said, "Look. This was *my* daughter he molested. Her and another girl that we know of, and who knows how many more."

"Oh no. I'm sorry."

"It's okay. You'll hear about it. Everybody else knows. You might as well too." She poured them both more Coke.

"I supported Corky last spring when he molested the other girl. I didn't believe he did it. It's hard to believe *that* about somebody you know." She gazed earnestly at Fred. "And we wouldn't ever have found out about Josie if Celia Merchant hadn't heard through her daughter and told us that Josie was making up lies about Corky. Duncan even disciplined her for lying. We still didn't believe what Corky was doing. I mean, I've had to face up to the fact that Josie isn't the kind of girl that men are going to fall all over."

Fred knew what she meant. It did seem odd, he had to admit it, that Corky had chosen this ungainly girl to molest.

"But Josie insisted that she wasn't lying, and the more we thought about it, the more things seemed to fall into place, how peculiar the man is, hanging on there where he isn't wanted, and we thought maybe it was really true. There's a woman at Meeting that works for the prosecutor and I called her up and asked her if she thought I ought to make a fuss about it."

Eve stopped talking then, and Fred took it to mean that the woman at the prosecutor's had encouraged the fuss. He sipped his Coke and wondered if people would have felt differently about Pearlman if he'd molested some cuter girl, the precociously little glamour girl who'd tried to jostle him off his ladder, perhaps. "And so you had him arrested."

Eve nodded. "They sent a policewoman out to talk to us, and later we went downtown to the prosecutor's office. Then Josie had to go and be filmed telling what happened, but that wasn't as bad as having to appear in court. They may be able just to show the videotape at the trial, you see, and that way, she won't have to go through it again."

All this was news to Fred, whose ideas about criminal prosecutions came from movies, TV, and one stint of jury duty. He had a quick vision of Pearlman sitting at a big shiny table in the courtroom, watching that videotape. He felt that it would be crude to ask the particulars, but – you wanna eat, you gotta hustle, he decided. He looked for a way to finesse the question. "What'd he do?" was how it came out.

"Oh, he denied everything," Eve answered. "Or at least his lawyer did. I hear he's going to plead not guilty."

"Not guilty of what?" Fred pressed.

"Of child molesting. Class C." Eve's voice picked up assurance. "Fondling a child under twelve with intent to arouse or gratify sexual desires. That carries a sentence of two to eight and a possible fine of up to ten thousand."

"Two to eight?"

"Years. In prison. And we're working toward eight. Since it was a second offence, we've got a good chance, even if they won't let us count the first offense. That one was dismissed, but there are ways you can use it anyway."

"That sounds like hardball. Eight years in the cooler isn't a slap on the wrist."

"It's not near enough. Not when you consider the damage he's done. And could do again, if he's let go free. One molester can ruin the lives of lots of children." She sounded almost glib, as if she were putting out a canned speech that she didn't understand.

"I guess that's true." Fred didn't really understand what damage she was talking about. After all, fondling somebody didn't exactly break bones.

"And even the full eight years would only mean four, when you take in good behavior."

"Yeah." Since prison sentences with fine points like good behavior were far from Fred's consciousness, he had to cast about for something to say, and he didn't find anything. The whole thing was making him a lot more nervous that he'd anticipated. He couldn't bring himself to ask for any more details. "Look, I really gotta get back and help paint. I could sit here and accept your hospitality all afternoon if you'd let me, but I only meant to make sure I didn't cause your daughter any grief spilling paint on her." This sounded thin. He added some padding. "She's had all the grief she needs. And you too."

Eve walked him to the door. Duncan was nowhere to be seen. The Subaru had disappeared too. "Well, we surely do welcome you to the fellowship. I apologize for Dunk running out, but he had to go in to the shop. He's supposed to take Saturday off, but it never works out."

When Fred arrived at the Meetinghouse, no one was there. The main door was locked. A little offended, he walked around the side of the building. What if the bereaved and the bereft had wanted to go inside and pray, he wondered. A house of worship oughtta be open. The side door was locked too. The parking lot behind him was empty. Helly's car was gone, and so were the others.

"Oh shit." So much for hoping they'd be finished painting. You get your wish, there's a catch to it.

His jacket was locked in the building, his car keys in the pocket. It wasn't freezing out, but it wasn't warm either. He started walking. At least the twelve blocks home would give him some exercise, like it or not, and that would win him points with Sara.

NIGHT CHORES

During this period of long hours and hard work, Sara was not sleeping well. She resolutely turned in before midnight to give herself at least six hours, but then she would waken suddenly, with a rush of guilt and grief, recalling something she was supposed to do. She would remember, for instance, that she had promised to stock a new life-giving diet supplement for a customer who was wasting away before her eyes. She had forgotten it again. The customer was an emaciated young woman who came into the store almost every day with three little girls, apparently walking them around the neighborhood while she did errands. It was absolutely essential that Sara not forget again tomorrow. This woman was counting on her. She would reach for the paper and pencil on her nightstand to make a note. Then, as her mind cleared, she would realize that she'd been dreaming again. There was no such diet supplement, no such customer. She hadn't forgotten anything. She hadn't neglected anyone. She was only dreaming.

But the realization brought no relief. The grief and guilt stayed with her. Such a dream, repeated with variations again and again, had to mean that her work was slipping. She was losing control in the one place she felt most confident: the pharmacy.

It was always hard to get back to sleep after being roused in this way. The blanket would be too warm or not warm enough. Fred would be too close or not close enough. His solid body was a fiery furnace to be kept at just the right distance.

This time it was moonlight streaming in. Sara had forgotten to close the curtains. At first she thought it was morning, but the clock plainly said 3:30, not 6:15. She was too hot. Fred's chest was stuck to her back with sweat. She was wide awake and still tired.

She unglued her skin from Fred's embrace and eased her hair out from under him. She would go have a cup of Sleepytime.

Sleepytime it would have to be. There were no sleeping pills in the house. Mr. Rochester's rule was to keep drugs at the store, not at home. Thus the medicine cabinet, a small one behind a lavatory mirror, had empty spaces between the few bottles that were on the shelves.

With a cornucopia of drugs available and the knowledge of how to fine-tune their effects, temptation had to be kept under lock and key. Sara agreed with her father, but she had trouble with the rule simply because it was *his* rule, not hers, and she envied the seeming ease with which he followed it and avoided temptation. Many a time when she filled a prescription, she wished there were someone to serve as her guardian or control the way she as pharmacist served her customers. Then she could comfort herself temporarily with drugs and rest easy in the knowledge that unavailability was built into the prescription. As it was, Charlie's presence helped just as her co-workers' had at the hospital because of the potential shame of being found out, but in the end it was only by being a stickler like her father that she could keep herself from slipping into the abyss of addiction.

Sleepytime it would have to be.

As she crossed the room to get her robe and slippers from the closet a cloud slid over the moon and left her in sudden darkness. She moved quietly so as not to waken Fred. He would get up if she woke him. He would talk and get in the way and be friendly when what she wanted was some time to herself. And a cup of tea. And some more sleep.

Just inside the closet on the floor she could feel her dirty clothes basket, full. Might as well take it down and put a load in the washer. There were things in there she would need for work.

Soft slippers kept her steps quiet as she carried the clothes basket past the bathroom and the doors to Aunt Jenny's and her father's rooms, past the door that closed off the unused bedrooms, past the attic steps. She took the back stairs down and pushed open the swinging kitchen door with her basket.

This big house made no sense for a childless couple. Originally she and Fred had been looking for something sensible, something neat and attractive that they could keep up without spending all their free time working on it. They had seen one place that would have done beautifully. It was in a quiet neighborhood of some graciousness with amenities that this house didn't have. Carpet on the floors, for instance. Two full bathrooms. A coat closet. Aluminum storm windows with attached screens that stayed in all year round. With panes that popped out for washing – and you could have clean windows without much trouble – instead of the heavy wood-framed storms that took a weekend to do. Their first offer for that house had been turned down and they were about to make a second when they saw this place, twice the house for the money even if a little rundown, and all their careful reasoning lost its power.

Out in the glassed-in room that had once been a summer kitchen Sara loaded the dirty clothes into the washer and started it running. This room had been one of the reasons for taking the house, with its view down the back yard to Sweetwater Creek at the bottom. It was sunny, painted yellow and white, with plants in red clay pots on the shelf that ran under the windows on two sides. The seller had left the plants behind: the tall ones had grown taller and the vines crept around and between and over and down, so that now Sara could hardly find the pots to water them.

She had been in her early thirties then. The house had brought with it the feeling that there were possibilities. Something good would come of it. All those rooms. People accommodate to their houses. The way to accommodate to a big house was to fill it up. There was even a rope swing in the oak tree, the rope too rotten to swing on, but the seat was still good, a sanded slab that would outlast another rope and a great many children.

But look what the possibilities had led to. An old folks' home. How could she want something so badly, something that seemed well within her capabilities, yet get something quite different instead? Sara always answered that mute question with the pop psych answer that didn't help a bit: "If you *really* wanted it, you'd get it."

With her load of clothes sloshing around in the washing machine she heated water in the microwave and added her teabag. Marigold, who had wakened when she came downstairs, heaved herself slowly to her feet, gave a brittle stretch and a yawn, and headed for the door, looking apologetic and wagging feebly.

"You can wait till I get my tea." Sara tried to ignore the dog, hoping she would give up and go back to sleep. "What do you do nights when nobody's up?"

But when the tea was brewed and sweetened and Sara was seated at the white-topped table to drink it, Marigold came over and nosed her knee.

"I ought to wake Fred and make him take you out. You're his dog, not mine." She had never liked this dog, but she couldn't be mean to an animal just because it didn't appeal to her. She got up and opened the kitchen door. "But I'm not going to stand out there and wait for you to sniff all over the yard. You can bark at the door when you want back in."

It was windy outside. The moon was still covered with clouds. She closed the door quickly.

Sara had not turned any lights on when she came down. The fluorescent light across the back of the range was bright enough to see what she needed to see, even in the summer kitchen. The laundry sloshed and gurgled as she sat with her tea while the clock on the wall continued its never-ceasing electric cricket noise. That clock would have to be replaced, and soon. Fred had discovered that the noise could be hushed if the clock were rotated so that the five was at the six o'clock place, but Sara couldn't stand having it that way. The scratching noise was less distressing than the sight of the catawampus clock. Every time she saw it hung out of line, she would start over to straighten it, then remember and flush with anger at having to live the haphazard way she did in a place impossible to maintain, never getting anything done right, never having time to keep things under control.

If Fred would learn to notice what needed to be done and do it, she wouldn't have to. But no. He would pitch in and help if she asked him to but she had to spell out what he was supposed to do. He couldn't take the trouble to see it for himself. He was too busy talking to people. At the store. At the library. Wherever he went. What he saw in some of the people he talked to she couldn't imagine, but he evidently found them worthy. He had told her a story once that he thought was funny, about the guard at the library sleuthing around to find out which one of the derelicts that hung around there was pissing in the men's room wastebasket instead of the urinal. It had made her so mad she couldn't even fight about it: Fred, with his bizarre sense of humor, talking to the library guard and other weirdoes as though it were the most important thing in the world while she beat her brains out at the store. He didn't have any discipline.

She stirred the tea and sipped it. Going down it burned, threatening to rev up the heartburn that was always waiting for the slightest provocation.

But how could Fred have possibly learned any discipline brought up the way he'd been by two women who doted on him and spoiled him? No, not spoiled him. That wasn't the right word. A spoiled man would expect to be pampered by his wife and Fred wasn't like that. It was more that he had been protected from the harshness of life. An only child. No brother or sister to die or leave. Mother healthy and alive until he was grown. Father never there to begin with, so no loss when he left.

But no discipline either. If Fred's mother had been anything like Aunt Jenny, it was no wonder he was as disorderly as he was. That was one thing Sara had in her favor: discipline. She was able to see what needed to be done and do it without a lot of agonizing. Her problem was that there was more to do than all the discipline in the world could get done.

The washer stopped sloshing and began to drain.

The ceilings in the house were high. In the kitchen, to break the awkwardness of one of the walls, a plate rack had been installed about eighteen inches down. On it stood a row of painted plates that Sara had at one time enjoyed collecting. Delicate flowers or swollen, blowsy ones. Commemorative plates from the Columbian Exposition and souvenirs such as the one from New Orleans with a picture of a window with a wrought-iron grill. Those bars on the window always made her think there were family secrets hidden inside. Suddenly Sara noticed that these plates in the shadowy kitchen were laden with shrouds of dust.

It was not compulsive housekeeping that drove her to the broom closet to fetch a stepladder. She hated housekeeping. She would just as soon never touch a vacuum cleaner or a mop again.

She turned on the kitchen light.

And it wasn't nasty-niceness that sent her up the ladder holding her robe out of the way to take down the first two plates and descend with them. No.

It was the realization that if she didn't do it, no one else would. That the dust would continue to settle until the plates became invisible. That she was the only person in the house who gave a damn and that if anything was going to get done, she would have to do it.

There was a time when her father would have noticed and cared. He would have seen to it that something was done. Not that she hadn't hated it when she was a teen-ager and came across "Sara!" written on a dusty table or across a spattered mirror, but by God, somebody had to set standards. She was glad now that someone had taught her instead of letting her slop around. He deserved a lot of credit. He could have farmed her out when her mother died, put her in foster care, sent her away to school. He could have brought in a stepmother.

Sara's mother had died after years of illness, bouts of depression and cancer, when Sara was only eleven. She remembered her mother in bed with the windows covered. Daylight made her head ache, she said, but there was always a small lamp burning near the bed. The housekeeper, Molly, would fix her the same lunch she fixed Sara and would coax her to come out and eat with Sara in the kitchen. Looking so pale and blonde as to be almost colorless, with the blue eyes and the soft, vulnerable mouth that Sara now saw every time she looked in the mirror, she made a show of asking what was going on at school or around the neighborhood. But Sara knew she was supposed to be selective about what she told her mother. The sick woman could be made sicker by bad news. If something bad happened, Sara knew to keep it to herself.

Early in her marriage, before the illnesses that invaded so many of her years, Sara's mother had worked at the store. From the time she could remember Sara had heard her father speak of the days when his wife Gladys and his son Tom Junior were with him at the store. She could tell by the brightening of his voice and increased color in his face that those were indeed the good old days. The days she had interrupted by being born – an accident – ten years after her brother, when Gladys was in her forties. In his account her father never failed to mention with a shake of the head and a chuckle, "how that boy loved the soda fountain." Once she interrupted, "I loved it too, especially the pineapple," and his faced dropped. "Yes," he said, his voice back to its usual subdued monotone. "I suppose something like that would attract children."

The washing machine spun to a stop. Sara transferred the load to the dryer and added a softener sheet. Noticing that her hands felt dry from handling the dirty plates she washed them in warm water and rubbed in some cream from the jar by the sink. How could she have let dirt like that get the upper hand?

Her father would still care enough to have standards if he were not so depressed about the store, she thought. That was one of the reasons she hung on to it, to show him that it hadn't really failed, as well as to show him that she could manage. He may have lost his son and heir, but a daughter could do at least as much as a son, if not more. She saved up little tidbits of news to bring home, things that made the business seem to be doing better than it actually was.

Not that it was doing so badly. There wasn't the volume that Walgreen maintained, of course, but there wasn't the debt either. She kept reminding herself of that.

With one load of wash done, Sara thought it might be just as well to get a second load started. She took her empty basket and went to collect all the dirty towels. There weren't many, only the ones from this week, she discovered, collecting from the upstairs bathroom and the downstairs powder room – and the rim of the tub where Aunt Jenny had draped her towel last night. But it certainly wouldn't hurt to get the jump on laundry. It would save time later if she went ahead and washed them.

So the washer began its sloshing and gurgling all over again while Sara moved the ladder and went up it for another two plates. She had also decided to dust the rack as she went along using soft, dampened paper towels that she could throw away: dirt, dust and all. She dusted gently, mindful of the possibility that she might leave a clean streak that would necessitate a much more thorough washing. As the plates came down she stacked them in the sink with hot sudsy water.

She was on the ladder reaching for the last two plates when she heard the stairs creak and there was Fred in the doorway, shading his eyes, looking at the clock. "Don't tell me, let me guess," he said. "Your guru told you to meditate on top of a mountain to the sound of a waterfall. At four thirty in the morning."

He had on red and white striped flannel pajamas. "You told the guru your flatlander circumstance and he said a stepladder and a wash machine would do."

"I came down for a cup of tea," she said.

He looked at her teacup half full on the white-enameled table. "I see that," he said. "Sure." He went to the sink and began to wash the plates.

She brought the last two down and put them on the counter beside him. Putting her arm around his back as he stood there with his hands in the suds, she said, "I hate it when we're in a fight."

He nodded and turned on the water to rinse. "Do you want these dried or will the drain rack do?"

"Of course the drain rack will do. Don't be silly." She took the first few and arranged them. "Am I that bad, Fred, seriously. So bad I would dry these instead of letting them drain?"

"Yes. You're that bad."

She knew he was right. She was so bad that if he'd put the plates in the drain rack when they were supposed to be dried, she'd have been irritated with him. "I hate that," she said, suddenly aware of how it must look, her on a ladder routing dirt in the middle of the night when she needed rest as badly as she did. "It's just that when I see things falling apart, I have to do something about it. I can't just let it happen. I care too much." Her hands found the towel that hung over the counter. She picked one of the plates out of the rack and dried it.

He went on with the washing.

"Can't you see?" She dried another plate.

He sighed deeply. "If I saw things falling apart, I suppose I would have to do something about it too, but when I look up at the plates, all I see is that they're getting dusty."

"It's the same thing," she said, almost pleading. Surely there was some way to communicate with him, to get him to understand. "Don't you care how we live?" The stack of dried plates grew.

"Of course I care how we live," he answered vehemently. "I want us to live comfortable and be able to sit down and take a deep breath once in a while. Which is what we can't seem to do anymore." With all the plates washed now, he rinsed out the sink with the sprayer and hung the dish rag over the now-empty drain rack to dry.

Outside it had begun to rain. Drops pelted sharply on the dark window over the sink. Fred spooned coffee into a white filter cone and turned on the coffeemaker. He sat down at the table and patted the back of the chair around the corner from him, beckoning for Sara to join him.

She started to sit down, then heard the dryer shut off. "Just a minute. My clothes will wrinkle if I don't get them out of there."

Fred withdrew his arm and sat hunched forward with his head in his hands, elbows propped on the table. Sara laid out and hand-pressed the creases in her uniforms, her slacks and skirts, her blouses. The odor of coffee filled the kitchen. When Sara had finished folding her clothes, she sat down at the table with Fred.

"What's wrong with us?" she asked. "Us" didn't mean them individually, but rather them together, their relationship. She reached for his hand for reassurance.

He squeezed her fingers but didn't answer. He stood up to pour the coffee. "Want some?"

She nodded.

"Nothing's wrong with *us* that some deaths and maybe a fire wouldn't help," he said. "What's wrong with *you* may take a shrink, and what's wrong with *me* is going to take a miracle. Next question?"

"So you think I'm sicko."

He put a cup of coffee down at her place. "Look, Sara, the way you drive yourself isn't right. I'm not saying you're sicko, just that something isn't right. It's not your fault. You had troubles growing up."

But she was already interrupting. "I did not have troubles growing up. There wasn't time for me to have troubles. I didn't have a chance to put on a big rebellion or go through phases. And who are you to tell me something isn't right, anyway?"

"I'm your husband, who loves you," he answered.

"Who picks on me."

He leaned over and rubbed her shoulders. "I'm not picking on you. I want you to be happy, to have a delightful life, and when you die, choose me to live with in heaven."

The towels rumbled in the dryer and the clock on the wall continued its syncopated chirp.

She put her head down onto her folded arms and let him rub her back. His hand felt good on the tight muscles. "Like when we bought the house and were so close, working on it together and all," she mumbled into her forearms.

He stood up to rub with both hands.

"Another joint project is what we need. Something to work on together." She leaned away and looked around at him. "It could be like that if you'd learn to manage the store. Then I could concentrate on the pharmacy."

"That's what I've *been* doing, isn't it?

"Not really. Your heart's not in it. I still have to tell you everything."

"Sara. I hate drugstores. They ruined drugstores when they took out the soda fountains and started selling paint. A drugstore now is nothing but a K-Mart that fills prescriptions."

Stonily she mustered her strength, straightened her backbone and stood up. The store was her responsibility, not his. It was her job to get to work on time, not his. "It's almost morning." The crickety clock said five twenty. Rain still made little noises against the window. "Is it going to be cold?" She kept her voice formal.

"I didn't hear the weather last night." Fred went to the door and opened it. "My God!"

"What is it?"

"Marigold's out here." He turned the spotlight on and went out.

Sara went to the door and peered through the rain.

The dog was lying on her side at the foot of the four steps up to the door. She lifted her head and looked up at Fred.

"Come on, girl," he said. "Let's go inside."

She struggled to heave herself up and made it part way, then fell back on the sidewalk.

Sara's eyes burned. I've killed her, she thought.

Fred squatted and loaded the dog in his arms. Sara held the door wide for him.

"She's wet," he said. "Where do you want me…"

"Just put her down," Sara burst out. "Do you think I'm going to complain about the floor?" She opened the drawer where she kept tablecloths. "Here, wrap her up in this." She laid a large terrycloth square on the floor. It was cotton; it would bleach. "I'm sorry. She wanted out. I should have watched her, I know, but I thought she'd bark at the door when she was ready to come in. Maybe she did and I didn't hear her." She knew she was babbling but she couldn't stop. "Oh, Fred, I'm sorry."

Fred didn't appear to have heard, or to notice that he himself was wet. He eased his burden down onto the cloth. The dog immediately floundered around, trying to stand up, but she couldn't and soon lay back on her side and looked at them with an air of resigned dignity. Fred got down on his knees and wrapped the tablecloth around her, gently rubbing her filthy coat with the white terrycloth. The smell of dirty wet dog rose as he rubbed.

Sara stood back from the odor. Her soft lips trembled. "I'll bathe her," she offered. "If you want to run some water in the tub, I'll get some shampoo and give her a bath."

"What for?" he asked. "I can just dry her off with this."

"I feel so sorry for her," said Sara, trying to control her voice, which was vanishing into a thin stream of words even as she spoke, "having to die this dirty and all."

"She doesn't care about being dirty," he answered. "And she's not ready to die yet anyway. The rain gave her enough of a bath for now."

"Well, okay." So Sara, feeling useless, watched Fred pat and stroke and rub the dog dry.

After a few moments she went back to the task she had started. She dragged the ladder along the wall and climbed it, dragged it and climbed it, stopping here, and then here, and then here – and she put the washed-and-dried plates back up on the dusted rack: the painted flowers, the Columbian Exposition, and the family secrets behind wrought iron bars. When she was finished, it was time to get ready for work.

GROWLS AND GRUMBLES,
RUMBLES AND GROANS

The afternoon he came back to the pharmacy Charlie was greeted with solicitude and relief. Christabel was already there, and Ben came in a little later, after the school children had gone home. Fred went to the liquor store two doors down for a bottle of champagne to celebrate, and everyone found a moment to slip into the stock room to fill a paper cup and toast Charlie.

Charlie didn't show the effects of his illness the way a thinner person would, but his attitude had changed. "It gives you respect, quinsy does," he said. "It makes you grateful for antibiotics."

"People used to die of quinsy," said Fred. "Didn't somebody's mother die of it? Whistler's mother, or Abe Lincoln's or somebody?"

"Everybody's mother dies of something," said Sara. Fred would be leaving now that Charlie was here. She always felt cross this time of day.

But Fred ignored her cranky tone. "Thank God you're back, fella." He clapped Charlie on the back. "Take care of your health." And as soon as the celebration was over, he put his hands on Sara's shoulders and kissed each cheek and the tip of her nose. "Dinner at seven sharp." When he was out the door, he remembered and stuck his head back in. "Romaine."

"Go on," she said and shook her head, but she was pleased.

There wasn't enough afternoon left for Fred to get anything done at the library. Instead he shopped, in good humor, not only for romaine, but also for fresh catfish to broil and a nice bottle of gray Riesling. He planned to put candles on the table. It had been quite a while since Sara had been home to eat dinner with him. He also picked up a paper carton of minestrone from the Jewel deli for Aunt Jenny, who occasionally considered it a treat to have an early meal away from Mr. Rochester.

When he opened the front door, Fred sniffed the air, but for once he smelled nothing from Marigold. In the kitchen he found Jenny, enveloped in an apron, crouched on the floor in front of the open refrigerator. Beside her was a pan of water. She was scrubbing with a toothbrush along one of the seams that always gathered crumbs or mold, or both.

Fred went to get out of his drugstore clothes while she finished. Mr. Rochester had spread the evening paper on the dining room table where it wouldn't shake the way it did when he tried to hold it. Fred started to go in and tell him that Charlie was back and Sara would be home for dinner, but thought better of it and continued up to his room to change clothes.

Back in the kitchen he emptied Jenny's pan of water. The clean refrigerator reminded him that he'd forgotten to buy milk, but he decided to wait and go out later. "How about letting me have the apron?" he asked.

Jenny sat at the kitchen table to talk while he scrubbed potatoes and put them in to bake. Marigold was in a heap underfoot, waiting for him to drop something good. He asked Jenny whether she would rather have soup now or dinner later, knowing what her answer would be.

Her eyelids lowered and her pointed little tongue ran quickly across her upper lip as she tasted for what she wanted. "Some soup and toast now. I never learned delayed gratification."

"But you taught it to your pupils."

"Oh yes, I had to teach it to them, but my heart was never in it. It's always seemed to me that 'later' is an iffy proposition."

Fred set the minestrone in the microwave to warm and put out the butter for Jenny's toast. In a short time the little meal was ready. He opened a beer for himself and sat down with her.

"Sara's worn out," he said. Jenny answered, "I'll bet she is." They talked about the store and then about the election. Jenny, who prided herself on being an Independent, didn't think Reagan could handle the job.

"That old man's almost as old as I am." She stirred her soup and sipped a taste off the edge of her spoon. "He's not capable. That debate he had with Mondale, that was downright embarrassing. He was pathetic. It made me feel as though Mondale ought to be gentler with him, and you don't like to feel that way about your President."

When she had finished her soup and toast, Jenny went upstairs to read. She needed a large magnifying glass now to decipher the print. "I can see far away," she claimed, "but up close is a different story." She told Fred once again how much her taste had deteriorated because of it. "I used to like literary books," she said. "But now the glass goes darkly over metaphor." She was reading one of Simenon's Maigret mysteries at present, one of a stack of large print books from her last trip to the library with Fred.

The potatoes done, Fred took them from the oven to scoop out and mash for twice-baking. He added cheese and seasonings and pounded the contents of the bowl vigorously with an old wooden pestle. After he had refilled the potato skins, he gave the bowl to Marigold and washed his hands at the sink.

"It's no wonder that dog lacks dignity." Mr. Rochester stood tall in the doorway, his height and bearing making him look commanding.

Fred involuntarily straightened his shoulders and sucked in his gut, then caught himself and slumped back into his preferred posture. "Yes, well, a dog's a dog." He placed the potatoes back on their pan.

Mr. Rochester wore gray slacks with fresh creases, tailored to fit like another skin, a white oxford cloth shirt and a dark blue and red tie tucked into a gray cardigan with all the buttons fastened. His thin white hair was parted low on the left with a few meager strands combed high over the dome of his speckled head. His hands shook. It must have taken him half the day to button those buttons and comb that hair, Fred thought. Fred fought the urge to take off Sara's apron and stuff it in a drawer.

"Even an animal is happier when its behavior is under control," said the old man.

"Yes sir, you're probably right," Fred answered. "Marigold's had a pretty miserable life."

Hangdog Marigold looked the part, miserable, with the bowl licked clean and nothing else forthcoming.

Mr. Rochester stepped carefully into the kitchen and lowered himself into the chair at the head of the white-enameled table. "I've thought of something Sara should do."

Fred bristled and started to say that Sara already had more than enough to do, but his father-in-law kept on talking. "She could get the city to mark off a 'Customers Only' area on Brewster Street along the side of the store. That would allow space for half a dozen cars. It wouldn't be in front, of course," and here he fell silent for a moment. Then he said, "Two things ruined the store. Bill Fletcher turning Osborne Street into a racetrack and Grogan selling out to Walgreen. If it hadn't been for those two things, we'd still be a real business."

There was nothing for Fred to say. His father-in-law had begun his litany of grievance. He would sing it to the end.

"I thought I could count on Grogan. All those years I looked after that family, sent things over special when Mabel couldn't get out." His cold monotone grumbled on. "I must have given them thousands of dollars worth of service that they never got billed for. And then to turn around and stab me in the back."

Fred had argued with Mr. Rochester at first. Sociological forces were at work, he said. Fate, even. Traffic to the suburbs. People in cars instead of on foot. Chains buying cheaper, selling cheaper. "You can't stop it," he said. "It's change. It's always change."

But the argument made no difference to the old man. Grogan was to blame. Formerly a nearby merchant and friend, Grogan had sold his property to Walgreen and moved to Florida: punch number one of the old one-two. Walgreen was a well-forged chain with plenty of pull, and if that wasn't bad enough, add to it a good location and a new store with new fixtures, new lighting, new everything. And a parking lot.

The lot was the bitterest blow. Rochester's had no parking lot and no place to put one, not with the people in the house behind the store adamant about staying. Mr. Rochester had tried at first to deal with Walgreen's lot derisively. "They can't even decide where to paint the lines," he sneered when the first set of lines was erased and another set painted. Then, "Got it wrong again," when the angle turned out to contribute to nasty little property damage accidents. But people continued to park at Walgreen and to shop there.

Then came punch number two. Osborne Street had been made one way, and parking along it was prohibited. Rochester's fronted on Osborne Street.

"Ruined," he had said. "I'm ruined."

At first he had blamed himself. He should have gotten out when the neighborhood began to change. He should have seen the writing on the wall, should have been more foresighted.

"But I was too busy to lick my finger and stick it out in the wind every day. I had a business to run. People depending on me

"No," he said. "I wasn't to blame. I was an excellent druggist. There's blame to be placed, but not on me.

"Grogan's the one. He didn't have to sell. He had plenty of money. Notice he didn't come around to say goodbye. He knew what he'd done to me."

Mr. Rochester's right arm was shaking badly. He looked at it with hatred, as though it were not a part of himself but some uncontrolled animal. He held it down with his left hand.

"I blame this on them too," he said. "I had no sign of tremor before. Oh I know it has physical causes, but something has to bring on the physical causes."

The growling monotone went on. Fred's eyes glazed.

"Fletcher's move finished me off." Bill Fletcher had been the mayor at the time Osborne and other arteries to the suburbs were made one-way. He too had been part of Mr. Rochester's network of friends and associates. "Ever since they gave cars the right to vote, the politicians have been kissing their exhaust pipes.

"Fletcher had to get re-elected. He couldn't be satisfied with a decent law practice, a respectable living. No. He had to be a mover and a shaker. Friendship counted for nothing. Probably figured as old as I was, I wouldn't be around to mind for long."

Fred was tidying up the cooking mess, rattling things in hopes of drowning out the old man, when suddenly the back door opened. He was startled.

It was Sara, home earlier than Fred expected. She glanced at her father sitting at the table, caught Fred's eye and gave a tight, artificial little smile. She turned away quickly without falling into the old man's gaze. "I left it with Charlie," she said. "I'm so tired I can't trust myself not to make mistakes."

"Oh there you are, my dear," Mr. Rochester said, without missing a beat. "I'm glad you're home. I was just telling Fred that you ought to insist that the city…"

Fred deliberately dropped Aunt Jenny's soup pan on the floor. In a manner as different from the old man's as he could possibly make it, he hugged Sara out of the kitchen and into the hall, where he took her raincoat to the row of hooks. He went to the dining room cupboard for the wineglass she liked best, a thin bell. "A little wine before dinner?"

She nodded. He opened the bottle and poured her a glass. "Come sit down." His voice dropped. "It won't last long," he whispered. "He's already past Grogan into Fletcher."

Her face relaxed for an instant and she held up her glass in salute.

Back in the kitchen the old man started over. "If I could have one moment of your time, please, Sara, I have a suggestion to make."

Sara froze at the door, then took a deep breath and went to the table.

Her father did not look at her. "A merchant still has a few rights in this town," he said. "You can insist that the city designate the section of Brewster nearest the store for customers only. I think you ought to look into it right away."

She answered immediately, but in a voice without interest. "That might help." She took a medicinal swallow of her wine.

Mr. Rochester leaned back, closed his eyes and suddenly looked as though he were made of thin porcelain. "I haven't felt too well today."

No one urged him to describe his ailment.

"Catfish sound good?" asked Fred. He hastened the meal, now that Sara was home.

"It does," she answered. "Mrs. Worrell came in again today. You know, the lady who's been trying every few days to get me to refill her pain medication?" As she talked Sara distributed the plates and flatware that Fred had already stacked on the table. "How about Aunt Jenny? There are only three plates here."

"She's already eaten," said Fred. "If Mrs. Worrell still hurts, maybe her doctor ought to give her another prescription."

At this Mr. Rochester opened his eyes and gave Fred a pitying look.

Fred saw it and thought: the Vigilant Pharmacist, ever-careful not to relieve too much pain.

"I don't think she still hurts, not from the surgery anyway. There was probably a time when the medication kept her usual aches from bothering her and now they've come back."

The meal was on the table now, the romaine, topped with carrot shreds and chopped olives, in wooden salad bowls beside each plate. Mr. Rochester tucked an extra napkin in the neck of his shirt. Sara sat down looking dazed with fatigue.

Fred forked the broiled catfish neatly off the bones and served some to each of them. He poured wine, then remembered the candles and went to the dining room buffet to get them. "A celebration," he said, setting a candlestick on either side of the table. Seated again he raised his glass of gray Riesling. "To Charlie's health."

"Charlie's health?" asked Mr. Rochester.

"He's had quinsy," said Sara. "He came back today." Her voice was flat. "We were glad to see him. To say the least."

"I've felt a little off today myself. A little uncertain in the gut. You'll forgive me if I don't eat much." He went on. "That's one you don't often hear of anymore, quinsy." And he told them how it used to be with quinsy, so terrible, while they ate their salad and their catfish and their potatoes. He would take bites as he talked, but small ones, in the middle of sentences, so as to hold the floor for himself.

Sara did a creditable job of keeping her eyes open and nodding occasionally, but Fred was intentionally noisy with dishes and silverware.

When the topic was finally exhausted, Sara, earning good-daughter points, said, "Oh, and here's something that will interest you, Dad. A man came in and said he used to stop at the store after school – that was back in 1950 – and have a pineapple sundae at the soda fountain. He knew right where the soda fountain used to be, too, under where the windows used to be, where the paint and stuff is now."

"He may have known Tom Junior then."

"No, this was in 1950."

"Tom Junior would have been at Cranbrook then," said Mr. Rochester. "His junior year. He was killed in '53. He could have stayed out of the Army if he'd tried." This was presumably for Fred's benefit, though of course Fred had already heard Sara's family history many times. "Tom Junior worked at the store after school from the time he was ten until he was sent away to school," said Mr. Rochester. "No doubt you've heard about this before." Although his voice had not changed from its chilly monotone, some feeling did show in the bleakness around his eyes. "Is that a cheesecake? If so, I'll save room for some." Mr. Rochester ate sparingly. His food never covered his plate, and when he was finished, some of it was always left.

Some of it was always left on the napkin he kept tucked in his collar too. His hand often trembled between table and mouth, and he would not lean over his plate.

Now he ate three bites of the cheesecake, left the rest on his plate and excused himself. "There's a show on TV I want to see." He started toward his room off the summer kitchen where he usually watched TV, then changed his mind. "I think I'll sit in the living room tonight," he said. "Closer to the bathroom, just in case."

When he was gone, Sara said, "That's odd. I didn't think he ever had the runs. He's had to use laxatives ever since I can remember."

"Don't knock it, enjoy it." Fred set about to tempt Sara into comforts. "The kitchen's ours. I'll clean up the dishes if you'd like to have a nice hot bath." The room was much more pleasant with Sara in it.

"A shower, maybe."

"We could both enjoy it if you soaked in the tub. I'll wash your back."

"Oh well, I don't know why not. It's as private as it's going to get." Sara left the table to gather up her bath oil and lotions and set them on a chair beside the tub.

A few minutes later steam scented with Jasmine Nights floated over the kitchen and bled in sudden little trickles down the dark November windows. Sara tested the water and ran some cold before undressing and settling her bottom into the bubbles, then turned the hot on again in a small stream.

Fred poured some more wine in her glass. "Will milady have a *glahss* of wine in the *bahth*?" In the tub of bubbles her small breasts floated high and round under her wide shoulders. Her pale silvery blonde braid was pinned securely to the top of her head with a large brown barrette. He put the wine down on the chair beside the tub and fished for a breast. "My God," exclaimed. "You're gonna cook in water that hot."

"It's not really all that hot," she said. "It just feels hot."

"Something feels hot *is* hot!"

"Something looks good *is* good!" she said. The old quarrel again.

"Okay, okay. We have differences. You want your wing scratched?"

"I always want my wing scratched." She hunched her left shoulder blade out of the water. He raked it as she shivered with pleasure.

He kissed the spot. It was hot and wet and it smelled like Jasmine Nights. "The subterranean itch machine."

"Enough. You'll wear out the feathers."

While Fred washed the dishes and wiped up the kitchen, Sara soaked and rested, almost napping, then washed, shaved her legs and stepped out of the tub with bubble-fuzz scattered in patches over her body. The water ran out quickly with a long, retching gasp. She dried herself thoroughly, seesawing the towel across her back, flossing between her toes, between her legs, and patting up moisture from every crease. When she was finished, her face was pink and shiny with no trace left of makeup, and her braid hung down once more over her fleecy blue robe.

Fred gazed at her, feeling tender. That frail body. Her appealing, old-fashioned mouth with its full, soft lips and slightly overlapped teeth. It made him feel protective. "You gonna stay awake a while?" He still had his errand to run.

"Maybe. The bath rested me."

"I gotta go get milk for breakfast. I won't be gone long." He struggled into his jacket.

"I'll read the paper." On the dining room table Sara found the newspaper open to the comics. Her father always read his favorites, but she had never seen him crack a smile over them. She gathered up the paper and left the lovely aloneness of the dining room to go and sit in the living room with him. More good-daughter points.

But he was no longer there. The TV was still turned on, so Sara sat down in the wing chair, assuming he would be back in a moment. She read "Dear Abby" and Mike Royko's column out of Chicago.

Then she heard her father's voice. "Sara," he called. "Sara."

She sat stock still and listened.

"Sara, I need help. Quick, help."

She stood up and tiptoed quietly into the hall. Through the closed door of the powder room under the stairs she heard him again. He sounded panicky. "Sara!" Her face burned as though struck.

She turned and hurried away, still tiptoeing. "Oh no," she heard him say. Through the living room she went, and up the stairs, down the hall and into the bathroom, where she locked the door, flung off her robe and stepped into the shower. She turned the water on. She could no longer hear the old man calling: she could hear nothing but the water. It was cold at first, and she huddled in the corner, but she did not step out. There was not much hot water left after her bath. She adjusted the flow and unfastened her braid. With tepid water running down her stinging face, she reached for the shampoo.

Fred came home a few minutes later. Not seeing Sara, he called out for her. He was answered by Mr. Rochester, still in the half bath under the stairs. "Is that you, Fred?"

"Yes, sir," he answered. "Me and nobody else."

"I'm afraid I'm going to need a little help. Could you come here, please?"

Fred pushed the door open and the smell hit him, worse by far than Marigold. Mr. Rochester was standing by the toilet holding onto a towel rack. "My zipper's broken," he said. "I'm afraid I've had an accident."

"Oh my God," said Fred. "Let me get my jacket off." He put the milk away, too, and came back, dreading what he would have to do.

The old man kept his face turned away while Fred worked on the zipper. The slacks were skin tight; the zipper had to give somehow, or they wouldn't come off. "It's broken," said Fred, trying not to breathe too much. "I'm gonna have to cut it open."

The old man nodded. "Do whatever you have to."

Fred found shears in the kitchen and used them to cut around the part that was causing the trouble. He peeled the slacks down a little. "Wait, let me get a newspaper." With the evening paper on the floor underneath, he helped the old man lower the foul-smelling pants and step out of them. Mr. Rochester tried to wipe himself off, but couldn't. Fred wiped his meager bottom for him and wrapped the newspaper around the soiled pants. "You maybe better take a shower," he said. "Here, I'll get something to wrap around you to go upstairs." The terry tablecloth he'd dried Marigold with had been laundered but not yet put away. "Here. Like a sarong." He draped it gently around the old man and tied the corners. "Remember Dorothy Lamour and her sarong?" he said, trying to soothe the old man with memories of the movie star. He helped him up the stairs.

Sara had gone from the upstairs bathroom by now, but the rug was wet. "I'll get you some pajamas to put on when you finish washing," said Fred.

"My tie." Mr. Rochester still wore his white shirt, tie and neatly buttoned cardigan under the tablecloth sarong. "I need help with my tie."

Fred unfastened all the buttons and removed the tie while his father-in-law stood meekly. When he had brought pajamas and robe to the bathroom, he asked, "How about I help you with the shower this time?"

"I think I can manage. Leave the door open and I'll call out if I need help."

In the bedroom behind a closed door Fred found Sara shuddering on the bed, in the state after heavy crying. He sat on the edge of the bed and took her hand, wondering what else he might be called upon to do tonight.

Finally she got breath enough to speak. "Is he all right?"

"No, not really. He's humiliated. He shat his pants. He's not gonna die of it, but I can't really call him all right." Fred stroked Sara's hand.

"He was calling me, and I couldn't go."

"I thought maybe something like that."

"I couldn't go. I couldn't make myself go in there."

Fred waited.

"It was like the time in the bathroom."

He waited some more. "What time in the bathroom?"

"The time I told you about. The time he hit me."

She had never told him about being hit. Fred felt like he ought to be a psychiatrist or something, but since he wasn't, all he could do was squeeze her hand. "I don't remember. Tell me."

"I didn't remember either. But I do now." Her words were coming out unevenly, in gasps. "It was in the bathroom. I was little, early school age, maybe. The bathroom rug, I remember it. A green border and faded purple roses." She breathed raggedly.

There was another long wait. "Why were you in the bathroom with him?"

"Because that's where I was. He had me by the hair, and he slapped me in the face." Sara began crying again in great sobs. "He said I was trash in the early stages."

Fred felt punched in the belly. The son of a bitch. I knew it, he thought. He said nothing, but he reached around and under Sara and held her.

Sara was screaming now behind her hands. The sounds she made were muffled and alarming. Her back arched, and her screams were those of a person tortured. Fred could do nothing to help her, so he simply made a shelter of his body and held her.

When the terrible spasm had passed, she whispered, still partly from behind her hand. "He was naked."

"My God," said Fred. "You poor kid."

Sara's head made nods he could feel in his arms. "I'd completely forgotten," she said. "One of the worst moments in my life and I completely forgot it."

"I'm not surprised you would."

Now she cried quietly as though these tears were more healing than the just-ended explosion, like a quiet rain on the embers of a fire. Fred shifted her weight off his arm that had gone to sleep, but he continued to hold her.

He was way out of his depth, trying to be a psychiatrist and a mother and an old folks home attendant all in one evening. But the evening wasn't over yet. He couldn't quit. "I wanna tell you that I don't think you're trash in the early stages or in any stages. You're a beautiful princess." He held her and made little noises while she cried. When he sensed that she was all cried out, he said, "You wanna dry your hair or do we sleep in a wet sack tonight?" She started to roll over. "I'll get it, stay here. I'll bring it and you can dry your hair like royalty right here in bed."

Mr. Rochester was out of the bathroom. His door was closed. He must have decided against much of a shower. Fred didn't trust himself to look in on him. He brought Sara's hairdryer to the bedroom and turned on the lamp.

"Is he all right?" She looked battered from all that crying.

"He's all right. He had a shower and I think he's gone to bed now."

As he watched, her face went through several contorted expressions. "Fred," she said. "I used every drop of the hot water."

Then they both laughed, and kept on laughing. They laughed until they were weak, laughed until tears rolled down Fred's cheeks as well as Sara's.

"I only wish he knew he had it coming," said Fred. "Maybe I'll go tell him."

"No!" cried Sara. "Please don't ever say a word about this. Promise, Fred, you have to promise!"

"Of course I promise," he answered. "But I don't promise to salvage his pants."

Sara sat up and dried her long hair. When she had finished brushing and drying, she seemed to have found new energy. For the first time in quite a while she turned to Fred with an embrace that warmed and invited him. He let himself respond to the tickle of her hair against his skin, the sweet freshness of her breath, her soft mouth against his, the length of her body against his, let himself respond to her responses.

OLD FOLKS TANGLING

Selling her four year old Mustang had been hard for Jenny Cavendish to do, and she did it with ill grace. A young man had promptly answered her ad in *Buffalo Wheel Deals*, but when she saw his partially shaved punk hair, her own reaction surprised her. She usually enjoyed the disguises of the young. "Sorry," she told him, picturing that raw, pathetic scalp in the window of her neat blue car with its clean white stripe. "It's already promised."

What a lie! But it gave her a few days to think some more about what she was doing.

Was it really time for her to cut back? So soon? With the sun barely over the yardarm? It had taken most of her life to raise the sun that high, and here it was threatening to dive into the ocean to the west without giving her a decent afternoon.

Jenny had taught fifth grade in Buffalo for a forty-five year morning, one of the many unmarried career teachers of the era. By the time she retired, she had taught two generations and had accumulated a priceless collection of pictures, patterns and strategies. For her teaching was a calling, not just a job, and in the classroom she was as good as they came. But the classroom had shielded her from the rest of the world. Retirement then presented such an array of choices that for a while she was paralyzed.

Reading helped some. Sitting in front of the balcony window in her apartment with her library bag at her feet, she indulged herself in the books there had never been time to read before. She also traveled. But after both of the friends she traveled with died, the travel became solitary, something different entirely. She had persisted, however, wanting to see places for herself, to hear languages even if she didn't understand them, wanting the messy, unedited version: the sweat of hot places, the chill of cold, the tiredness of muscles walking uphill and of different muscles walking down.

Reading and travel satisfied her hunger for education, but she needed also to provide community service. To that end she volunteered two nights a week on the crisis hotline. Working there she found that many of the skills she had used to serve children worked just as well for adults. Wasn't a good teacher a children's advocate? And wasn't an advocate what adults in crisis needed? But often someone to listen was their most immediate need, so she listened. As soon as she had made sure the caller was safe, she would say, "Now take some deep breaths and tell me what's happening." After a moment she would question further, "And how do you feel about it?"

Then suddenly she was in her seventies slowing down. She was alone. One of these days she would need help. She had no children who could make decisions for her if she put them off too long. No, she wasn't ready to sit down and listen to her brain cells die, but she started reading ads for those graduated retirement communities where help becomes available as you need it.

And then Fred's offer had arrived. He had invited her, let her know that she would be a welcome presence in his home. With a touching mixture of reluctance and honesty, he told her, "Look, Mr. Rochester's falling apart, and we gotta take him in. It sure would be nice if you came too. That way he'd only be one fourth of the population here instead of one third. Couldn't you start having fainting spells or something? Just enough to make you need your nephew?"

Well. She'd like to help Fred out, of course. But there certainly had to be satisfaction in it for her, too, or it wouldn't work.

"We got plenty of space, you know that," he assured her. Not only could she have the back corner bedroom that looked out over Sweetwater Creek where birds were plentiful and the little woods filled up with wildflowers in the spring, but she could have another room as well to furnish as she pleased and use as a private sitting room. Not that she'd be restricted from the rest of the house. Far from it. "The place is yours," he said. "Kitchen too. You can do your own cooking or not, whichever you want. Best of all, you could cook for all of us." Fred assured her that he would enjoy Cavendish food again after years of other arrangements.

The house turned out to be as comfortable and pleasant as she remembered it from visits. With such a large bedroom, she decided against a separate sitting room. Her desk went under one of the four windows, and the time she spent there was rewarding.

And at first she enjoyed cooking. Well-prepared, nourishing food had always been a Cavendish tradition, one worth preserving. The satisfying ritual of cooking helped to structure her time: the planning, the grocery list, the setting out of ingredients, the chopping and mixing, the laying of the table.

Her mistake had been in being cordial to Mr. Rochester. If she hadn't given him the time of day in the first place, perhaps he wouldn't have felt free to interfere. With Jenny imprisoned in the kitchen where he could easily join her, he would stand leaning against the door jamb and talk. About his own concerns, of course, not anyone else's. His monologue. Any comment that she might make would only fuel the stream of opinions that were aimed in her direction but did not include her. His personal monologue alternated with his instructions on food preparation.

First he told her that food shouldn't taste too good.

She said nothing. She recognized the comment as a put-down of her work, and she refused to dignify it with an answer. She poured the aromatic broth and white wine over the browned veal, onions and garlic, then ceremoniously dripped a little of the gravy from the large spoon into a small one and tasted it.

Standing in the doorway with an air of courtly condescension, he looked down at her and said, "A cook can do a great deal of harm spicing up the food so that people eat more than they need."

"I wonder why the good Lord gave us taste buds if we're not supposed to use them." Without looking up at him, she selected a bay leaf and measured the tarragon to add to the simmering stew, whose fragrance rose from the pan and suffused the kitchen.

"It's possible to train ourselves to ignore taste," he said. "It takes effort, but it can be done."

She was surprised at how angry this denial of life-sustaining pleasure was making her. "People need nourishment," she answered firmly. "That's why food is supposed to taste good. People die when they lose their appetite."

"They die indulging it too, in droves."

Jenny could not cook and gather points for argument at the same time. He had obviously thought his position through before bringing it up. Although she knew it was dangerously distorted, she was not able to spell out quite how. He was correct about the effects of gluttony, but the severity of his remedy seemed likely only to make the problem of nourishment even worse. She enclosed herself in a protective cocoon of non-attention while she continued with the preparation of the meal.

During her teaching career Jenny had struggled with certain children who refused (or were unable) to accept the nurturing she offered, whose hooks in the brain for nourishment had been damaged somehow so that good things slid right off them. Mr. Rochester, and Sara too, reminded her of these children. Maybe the social workers or the psychologists knew what to do with them, but she didn't. She found such people so unappealing that she didn't even want to learn. Fred, she supposed, had fallen in love with Sara's quiet beauty and hoped that he could in time win her over, but Fred had more patience than she did.

Mr. Rochester continued to come to the kitchen and talk while she cooked. Her lack of response did not put him off at all. He seemed not even to notice that she wasn't participating in his conversations. Most people require a listener to make little clucks of acknowledgement once in a while. Most people feel uncomfortable when their listener doesn't look at them. But not Mr. Rochester. It was almost as if he didn't know the difference. Jenny wondered sometimes if anyone, ever, had actually participated in his stream of speech.

But it was when he told her how to cook that she found him most objectionable. "You could chop faster if you'd use a big knife and swing your forearm this way," he said every time he saw her cutting up onions with a paring knife. The first time he said it she directed his attention to the smallness of her hand and arm, and the fact that the counters had been built for someone several inches taller. The second and third times, then, she ignored him. But when he brought it up again for a fourth time in so many weeks, she was ready.

"Mr. Rochester," she said, pulling a voice from her schoolmarm repertoire, "does the ape tell the gazelle to travel through the treetops?

You may prefer to chop with a French cook's knife. I prefer a paring knife. If you'd like the job of chopping, the please be my guest." And she offered him the countertop with a sweeping gesture.

Although his arm didn't happen to be trembling at the moment, he held it down and said in a hurt tone, "My days of handling a knife are over."

"Mine are not." She knew that reminding him of his disability was hitting below the belt, but that's what it was going to take to get him to leave her alone.

But he was more persistent than she imagined. One evening just before Fred and Sara were expected home for dinner, he was standing at his place in the doorway, leaning against the jamb. Grease was heating in a pan. The shoestring potatoes had soaked and were now drying in a towel. Jenny was hungry, and she decided to fry a few bites of potato to hold her until dinner.

"Your grease isn't hot enough," he said.

She started to drop the potatoes in anyway, but he was right, so she turned up the burner and waited.

In a moment Marigold, who was outside, woofed at the door. Jenny went to bring her in. When she looked back at the stove, a column of flame was rising from the pan.

Mr. Rochester was looking around the room, agitated. He groped in a cupboard. "Isn't there a fire extinguisher? We need a fire extinguisher, quick."

Jenny scurried to the stove. The lid. The pan lid. But this particular pan did not have its own lid, so she grabbed a cookie sheet and clapped it over the flaming grease. She yanked the pan from the burner and turned it off. In a moment the fire was out. Trembling, she left the smoky kitchen, where the odor hung in the air, and went to her room. Fred found her there five minutes later, still trembling.

After that, Jenny went to great lengths to wait until Mr. Rochester was asleep or occupied with television to prepare her own breakfast and lunch, and she did not cook the evening meal again. She stayed in her own room and read or dozed. She felt herself become more and more lethargic, but she did not have the energy to pull herself out of it.

What else, really, was there for her to do? A little dusting, sweeping up the dog hair, occasionally washing the dog snot off the windows where Marigold enjoyed panting after squirrels. No one actually kept house here. When the grime got intolerable, Sara would start washing walls after dinner, whereupon Fred would either take on the job of cleaning a room or two himself or would call in The Maids. Jenny kept the refrigerator washed out and the newspapers picked up and whatever else could be done without fuss, but mostly she read and napped in her room.

She did not approve of the television that Mr. Rochester spent so much time watching. Although she liked the evening news and had a few favorite programs, she drew the line at daytime television, no matter how entertaining it might be. Reading and puttering weren't much better, but they were less seductive. She was still *available* to work, she thought. You could stop reading and the book would still be there when you came back, but once you were sucked into a TV show, you had, to all intents, become unavailable.

Mr. Rochester's TV was distasteful to her on other grounds, too. Easy Christianity, she thought. Accepting a manipulated, rehearsed Christian image. An image that neither challenged nor was challenged by real people in a real congregation helping and pressuring each other to grow spiritually. The whole notion of TV churches offended her. Religion, actually, was a private matter. The only excuse for organized religion that she could see was its use as support. The Sunday morning support group. And for a support group, a person needed real people around him.

But who was she to sneer, she concluded reluctantly. She didn't go to church either, unless Fred took her to Meeting. Although he was doing so now, she understood that this would cease when his investigation was finished. She had no way to get there without him. She could walk, but not that far, especially now that she had let herself get weak and out of shape.

The move to Fred's had been a mistake. She had given it sober thought and had finally grown to believe that she was needed, that there was still something she was meant to do in life. But she had been here for more than a year, and instead of being useful, she had begun to dodder.

The worst of it all was losing her car. She had sold it, finally, telling herself that it was time, that she simply couldn't trust her eyes to read new street signs and seek new destinations in the traffic of an unfamiliar city. And now she was housebound, dependent on Fred for trips to the library, the beauty shop, church, everywhere.

It was in this frame of mind that she phoned Corky Pearlman to request a ministerial visit.

Meeting was not turning out the way she'd hoped, that first night. Mr. Pearlman was no longer in evidence, and the speakers no longer provided sermons. It was none of her business, of course, but she thought they should have waited for the poor man's trial before they found him guilty. They shouldn't have ostracized him without giving him a chance to prove his innocence. She herself was certainly not going to allow her thoughts to dwell on the possibility that he was involved in such a nasty business.

Someone else answered the phone at the parsonage, and when Mr. Pearlman came, he sounded groggy, as though he had been sleeping. He perked right up, however, when Jenny said she'd like very much to have a visit from him if he could spare the time.

The prospect of a guest of her own made Jenny feel alive and capable again. Before Corky arrived the next afternoon, she took advantage of Mr. Rochester's nap to bake a batch of cookies. When they were cool enough, she piled them on a fluted plate from the dining room buffet. She also dusted the lamps and vases and picture frames with a raveled piece of undershirt. As she dusted, she noticed through a visitor's eyes the roll of toilet paper Fred kept on the coffee table, and because she was afraid it would lead Mr. Pearlman into thoughts about incontinent old women instead of vengeful old dogs, she put it back in the bathroom. When she saw the car in the driveway, she lit the fire Fred had laid for her and closed the hallway door so that the sound of voices would not lure Mr. Rochester from his room at the back of the house.

"Of course I remember you," said Corky, shaking Jenny's hand warmly. "You and Fred were the last visitors I had a chance to preach for. It does me good to see you again. I always have such hopes for new people."

Jenny was relieved. She did not want to be visited merely as a duty. "Call on Jenny Cavendish, the poor old soul." She wanted to give as good as she got, somehow, though in her present condition, she didn't know how she would do it. "Yes," she said, "and it does me good already that you have hopes for me. That's exactly what I need, hopes."

He nodded, and then he nodded some more, thoughtfully, and laid his coat over the back of the wing chair. Marigold, resting there, flopped her tail.

Jenny had dressed carefully for this visit. Her suit was from her teaching days, classic, a mauve color that had always been becoming to her fair skin and blue eyes. She had heated up Sara's curling iron to refresh the flattened pieces in her white hair. As always, she was concerned to add some substance to her body, so instead of a blouse with the suit, she had put on a sweater. As small as she was, she had to take care not to look disposable.

Fred's fire had consumed the twisted newspapers and was crackling away at the kindling. Jenny led Corky to the couch in front of the fireplace and put the plate of cookies down between them. "There," she said, taking a cookie. "Please help yourself." In no time Marigold had joined them, her long nose quivering toward the plate. Jenny rapped the nose with her finger. "No," she said sharply. Marigold backed away a few steps and sank to the floor with a sigh.

Since she had asked for Corky's visit, Jenny felt it necessary to explain what had led her to do so. "I've been fretting about being housebound," she said, "but it occurred to me that perhaps it's time to stop troubling myself about what I can't have and attend to what I can. I thought perhaps you could suggest a course of spiritual development." She looked at Corky munching away at his cookie and continued, trying to adopt a tone that was lighter and less mournful than her real feelings. "Strengthen my inner muscles, you might say. I've been lax in that area, and now when I need them, they're flabby."

Corky did not hasten to offer a cure. Instead, he drew her out to talk about her life, her career, about what had brought her here. "And what have you been doing recently," he asked.

"Nothing. Absolutely nothing." As they talked, she had been hearing sounds in the hall, Mr. Rochester's afflicted footsteps shuffling into the powder room under the stairs. Her calmness began to ravel out. "Oh," she said, "it's so difficult being under the same roof with that man." She indicated the footsteps with a tilt of her head. "And I've gotten so small-minded. My whole attention is focused on him and how to avoid him, and I hate thinking about him almost as much as I hate being near him."

The powder room door opened with its characteristic squeak. Jenny listened while Mr. Rochester's slow steps approached the living room door. Marigold gave a short woof at the unfamiliar sound of this little-used door being opened, but when the old man entered and she saw what the noise was, she saved herself the trouble of getting up.

He looked immaculate, as usual, with his tie tucked into his tan cardigan and his posture erect. His pants were new and a bit bulky: tan corduroy, with an elasticized waistband like pajamas that had just enough give to pull off in an emergency without unfastening the fly.

Jenny stood up. "Pardon me, but I have a guest," she said, her meaning clear.

"How do you do?" he said, ignoring Jenny and approaching Corky's end of the couch with his hand out.

Corky too stood up. "Corky Pearlman," he said. "I used to be a customer of yours. I didn't expect to see you here."

"I didn't expect to end up here, but it comes to that eventually. You're the minister, aren't you? The Freethinker?"

Jenny's voice was stern as she stood her ground against this invasion. "Mr. Rochester, we're discussing some personal matters."

"Don't let me interrupt." He gave no indication of embarrassment. "I noticed as I came through the kitchen that the oven was on. I thought you'd want to know."

She couldn't tell whether he was accusing her of wastefulness or forgetfulness, but this was no school boy that she could dismiss at will. "Excuse me a moment." She went to the kitchen to turn the oven off. Marigold followed, her toenails clicking on the bare wood floor.

When she returned, the two men were seated on the couch, Mr. Rochester in the place she had vacated. Corky had helped himself to another cookie. She saw how things were going to go, and she stood in the doorway, unable to move, but shaking with anger. Marigold, still with her, nosed her skirt and wagged, then abandoned her for another try at the cookie plate.

Then, miraculously, Corky stood up. "I've overstayed my time," he said, consulting his watch. He went to the wing chair for his coat. "It's been a pleasure seeing you," he said to Mr. Rochester. "I look forward to continuing this discussion." He leaned over the couch and shook the druggist's hand. "And I'll phone you this evening," he said to Jenny. "My niece Nancy has been talking about a wonderful place to go for ice cream. I thought you might join me there some time. Some time very soon." The mischievous look on his face told Jenny that he understood about Mr. Rochester.

Smiling broadly, she saw him to the door.

"Thank you," he said, just as she was about to say the same thing. Unable to speak, then, she patted his sleeve and closed the door after him.

Ignoring Mr. Rochester, she crossed the living room to the staircase and went up. He wouldn't follow her, she thought. He liked help coming up the steps. When she had reached her bedroom and closed the door firmly, she heard him call her.

"Jenny," he called, raising his voice on the second syllable. "Oh Jenny."

On the third call she opened her door and answered, "Yes?"

"Did you want this plate of cookies left here on the couch?"

She closed the door again without answering. Marigold would eat the cookies and throw up on the floor, she thought, but it was not the first time, and it wouldn't be the last.

JOSIE, CARRYING

On Saturday, Jenny was not the only one who spent the morning getting ready to go to the ice cream parlor. Josie Flannery also had her hair trimmed and curled at the beauty shop. Josie Flannery also chose carefully what to wear, albeit with Eve's anxious help at Sears rather than in her own closet at home. She too, again with her mother's practiced help, put on makeup: a little blusher to hint at cheekbones and some eye shadow that drew attention away from the problem area of her mouth. She had been allowed to skip LOVELY YOU to get ready for the occasion, which was the tenth birthday of a classmate, who had included Josie in the party, not through special friendship, but because she had invited all the girls. The whole feminine half of the class would be there, including Nancy and Heather.

It was Eve who persuaded Josie to attend. "It's your social life," she said, when Josie tried to beg off because it wouldn't be any fun, to put it mildly. "You have to take advantage of opportunities like this. You go, and take your gift, and be nice and do what the other girls do, and you'll have a good time." Eve didn't know, because Josie no longer talked about anything important, just how bad the situation actually was.

After enduring school five days a week with these girls, Josie knew what to expect. She prepared for the ordeal without her mother's help. She borrowed from Eve's key chain a short, leather-covered stick that looked merely decorative but was weighted to feel like a billy club when it struck. Duncan had supplied Eve with this weapon and, in Josie's presence, had taught her how to use it. Portville had its share of street criminals, and Duncan knew he could not protect his womenfolk personally twenty-four hours a day.

Thus Josie, in her new blue velveteen dress, a little too long and too tight around the waist, was going to the party armed. Even without practice, she knew how to swing the little club, gouge with it, even apply its tip to a pressure point or its length to a windpipe. She was tired of being a victim.

JENNY, DRIVING

Frosty's was located in Portville's newest shopping mall, Osborne At The Toll Gate, southeast of town near the Indiana Toll Road interchange. Although its clientele was mostly adult, attracted by Italian ices and gourmet coffee, one corner could be reserved, on Saturday afternoons only, for birthday celebrations. A parent who couldn't face the prospect of a dozen kids at a party at home could take them all to Frosty's for refreshments and leave the mess to someone else. A movie might precede the refreshments, or, in nice weather, games at a park. Saturday afternoons at the birthday corner were booked solid for months.

Corky did not drive directly to Frosty's after picking Jenny up. "We have time for a side trip, haven't we?" He turned off Osborne and went to the empty parking lot at the high school gym, where there were no obstructions, drove around it for a moment as though unable to cope with such a large selection of parking places, and finally stopped crosswise in one of the aisles.

Jenny, who had been paying more attention to the conversation than the view, looked out the window at the expanse of concrete, then over at Corky.

He was beaming, his eyes a-twinkle and his big, doggy smile permitting a generous view of his pebbly teeth. He took the keys from the ignition and handed them to Jenny. "You drive the rest of the way," he said. "We've got to get you back on wheels."

For a moment she stared up at him, her head cocked. She looked at the car keys in her hand. "I've given up driving."

He shook his head. "The spiritual muscles work better in conjunction with the physical. Come on, give it a try."

"I'll drive around the parking lot. I can't do any damage here."

They got out of the car to trade places. Corky took off his overcoat, folded it into a pillow for her to sit on. He adjusted the outside mirrors and showed her where everything was. And off they went, slowly at first while she got used to the feel of a car again, then faster as her confidence returned. She drove from one end of the lot to the other and round the perimeter twice. Then she pulled up close to the gym and stopped. "I thank you for that," she said. "My spiritual muscles feel tighter already."

"We're not there yet. This is the high school, not the shopping center. We're only about half way. Surely you're not going to stop now."

"I don't think I can do it. I just can't see the street signs well enough when I have to pay attention to traffic."

"No problem. I'll tell you when to change lanes and when to turn." He reached across and pulled a knob on the steering column. "This turns the flashers on," he said. "If you get a case of overload, just yank on it and slow down until you see a place to stop. Here, pull it a time or two and get used to the feel. No problem at all."

It took Jenny a long mental struggle to lift herself from her swamp of resignation into the hopeful anticipation that would allow her to act. Corky waited, and at just the right moment, he said, "Picture yourself hot-rodding down the street, going wherever you feel like, while some *other* little old lady sits home and dries up."

"Rots," she answered instantly. "It may look like drying up, but it feels like rotting." She started the car. "You'll have to tell me if I do anything wrong."

"The blind leading the blind."

She paused at the exit. Nothing was coming. She waited for his instructions.

"Oh," said Corky. "Turn right. You go two blocks and then turn left. That'll be Osborne Avenue."

When they were back on the main street heading southeast, Jenny relaxed enough to joke. "What we need is a sign for the top of the car, all lighted up, that says, 'Hazardous Vehicle.' Let them know they're in danger if they get too close." Her tone was no longer sadly resigned but happily pugnacious.

"If fifteen minutes at the wheel does this to you, I'll bet you like football."

"Oh I do!" She speeded up a little, then slowed down when she found herself tailgating a police car. "I do indeed. I have a healthy appetite for vicarious mayhem. I've been a fan of the Buffalo Bills for years."

With Corky navigating, Jenny managed not only to drive to Osborne At The Toll Gate but also to survive the parking lot. She found a place in the Central/East section.

Outside in the wind, Corky put his overcoat back on and Jenny turned her collar up. "Just a minute," said Corky. "I'm going to keep my wits about me this time." He took out a pen and picked up a scrap of pink cash register tape that had blown near his foot, then copied "Central/East" from the sign on a nearby light post. He counted rows and wrote "7". "There," he said. He tucked the paper in his pocket and held his arm in a crook for Jenny.

Jenny had decided against wearing her rainbow-hued tam. Corky, too, was bare-headed. They both held their collars up against the cold wind in their faces as they walked together, more or less in step, past the assorted vehicles that filled Central/East.

Jenny had cars on her mind. She noticed the preponderance of expensive makes and recent models. "Look at that." She pointed to three BMW's in a row. She could tell he didn't understand what she was showing him, but because it was cold, she didn't stop to explain. She also noticed that the structure they were approaching was varied and interesting instead of the customary concrete-block monolith of a shopping mall.

When they had braved the crossing from Central/East to Inner/East, Corky fumbled in his pocket and pulled out a heavy, sheepskin-lined glove. "I've got a finger that turns blue if it gets too cold." Neither he nor Jenny noticed the pink scrap of paper as the wind caught it and blew it high over several cars.

Then suddenly they were shielded from the wind by the building. Thick glass doors opened into the warmth of an enclosure furnished with a beige trash can, two phone carrels, and several urns of white sand. The floor was carpeted with thick fiber matting that could absorb great quantities of water or snow.

Inside a second row of doors Jenny stopped and said, "Oh my," admiringly. An avenue paved with brick greeted them, with shops on either side, each one a miniature building, architecturally distinct from its neighbors. Slender evergreens set in circles of brick pointed toward skylights in the roof. Shrubs and vines on trellises basked in the mixed warm and cool fluorescent light of shielded lamps. After passing half a dozen stores, they reached a side street from which the next avenue could be seen, with more shops, like a miniature town.

As they strolled along, Jenny noticed that each shop had a holly wreath pinned near the door. "It's way too early to start on Christmas, but I have to say that they've done it unobtrusively." There were no Christmas trees, no lights, no Santa Clauses, no bell ringers for the Salvation Army, no "Joy to the World" from loudspeakers – no loudspeakers at all. "I've never seen anything like this before."

"It's the latest thing in shopping centers. The only places to eat here are real restaurants, not popcorn stands. No grape drink or orange slush."

"They don't want garbage on their brick streets." Jenny slowed down and stopped at a kitchenware shop window. As was the case with all the stores, no merchandise was on view there. The small square panes made the window look like one in a private home.

Inside, a larger-than-life model kitchen was furnished with every piece of equipment a cook could want. All the cupboard doors were glass, their contents easily viewed. Long-handled utensils stood on end in decorative containers. Counter-to-ceiling poles all over the store held funnels, strainers, mugs, pans – anything that would hang on a peg. To buy something, a customer copied its number on an order form, then went to a sales booth to await delivery from stock.

"This is quite a place!" Jenny strolled on, leaning on Corky's arm. "Garbage is not the only thing they've eliminated." She noticed the other strollers dressed in wool, not polyester, with accessories of silk and leather. "There's not a bench in sight. They don't like loafers."

"Come to think of it, you're right. There's no central plaza with benches, just more corners and more streets."

"No kiddies in strollers either. They stay home with the maid."

Corky continued the list. "No store called 'discount' or 'outlet'."

"No 'Colossal Sale' signs."

"No video game arcade."

"No place to rent a tux."

Corky laughed at that one. "Right. If you don't own your own tux, you don't shop here. And there's no place to get your hair straightened either."

"Or buy a girdle. I'll swear there's not a fat woman anywhere to be seen."

Corky stopped. "Here's the place to find one if she's here." They had come at last to Frosty's.

But the patrons here looked much like the ones outside: slim and rich. When Jenny and Corky had been seated and given menus, Jenny glanced over hers and said, "If it's called a glacé, that means they don't serve much of it, no more than you can work off at the spa. You don't come here for a triple banana split."

"We could special-order one, if you'd like." Corky's voice was vague, his attention drawn to a nearby table where two young women sat with three little girls.

"I'm too exhilarated to fall back on a banana split. This is my day to try something different." Jenny consulted her menu while at the same time watching expressions flicker over Corky's face as he responded to the sight of the children. Their mothers seemed very much in control, even while talking to each other. The girls traded bites of their ice cream; one mother offered a napkin without losing her train of speech. Corky sat watching, with a look that was by turn benevolent and wistful, as though he'd been transported back to childhood himself.

Jenny wondered just what his attitude toward children really was. Interested, certainly. It struck her as something quite out of her usual experience to be at an ice cream parlor with a suspected child molester, though she didn't for a minute believe he'd actually done anything wrong. It was a misunderstanding of some kind, it had to be. The face before her was fascinated, but in no way malevolent.

Not that Jenny thought the girl was lying. Children lied, of course, she knew from much experience, but in cases like this one they'd be much more apt to lie in the other direction. They lie to keep themselves out of trouble. They say they're not hurt at all when they've broken a collar bone, or they say they understand the math problem when they don't, anything to keep themselves clear of unfavorable consequences. They also lie to glorify themselves. This was much more likely to be the case here, an embroidery, perhaps, but not a lie, simply a girl telling someone, her parents, perhaps, that she needed more affection. "The minister loves me, even if you don't." Jenny had heard such ploys many times, only this time someone had misunderstood and called the police.

Having thought the problem through and solved it to her own satisfaction, Jenny had no doubt as to Corky's innocence. And the next time she peeked over her menu at him, he had turned away from the children and was reading his own menu.

"Have something extravagant," he said.

"I shall," she answered. She dismissed both sherbet and frozen yogurt and decided on a double fudge parfait layered with crème de menthe, and a cup of cappuccino. Corky ordered the same.

Several more groups came in before they were served. With the birthday corner still vacant, people tried to sit there but were placed elsewhere by the hostess.

Corky and Jenny had eaten down into the middle layers of their parfaits, melting cold bites of ice cream with sips of cappuccino, when the birthday party arrived from the cinema, carrying their coats and chattering. Corky's back was to the door, but his head turned when the noise level changed.

Having taught as many children as Jenny had, each new one she met reminded her of one she'd known before. Thus the parade she saw across the room seemed made up of familiar faces collected in a new grouping.

But even the grouping was not unknown. It contained a Beauty Queen and her little court of admirers who already knew whom to stay close to for high social position. A Rival Queen, less beautiful but more personable, chattered vivaciously to two hangers-on. A Little Woman was attached to one of the chaperones. Two Inseparables, arm-in-arm, giggled over their private joke. Two Ugly Ducklings came in last, neither one welcome to associate with anyone else.

The other Ugly Duckling was Leslie, the sorry little Bo Peep of Halloween night. Jenny had met her, but did not recognize her now. Nor did she recognize Heather or Nancy, the Inseparables.

Corky, of course, smiled at Nancy immediately.

She smiled back. Then her eyes widened as she sized up the situation.

Josie was straggling at the end of the party, still close to the exit. Her makeup looked garish and her shape made her seem out of place among the self-controlled and slim. But it was not her appearance that caused Nancy to leave Heather and push through the group.

"You can't come in here," she said in a low tone when she reached Josie. She spread her elbows to block the way and advanced, giving the bigger girl a determined shove back toward the door. "Get out." Her voice was quiet but furious. "My uncle's not allowed to see you. Get out."

As Nancy pushed a second time, Josie dropped her coat and stepped suddenly backward to give herself room to swing. Nancy, off-balance, stumbled over the coat and took the blow high on the side of her forehead, where it hit with a hard, leathered thwack.

Then Josie turned and ran. Before anyone could intervene, the blue dress and the flaming hair had disappeared down the brick-paved, tree-lined indoor street.

Nancy did not cry out, but Corky was on his feet immediately. "Pardon me," he said, drawing himself thin between two tables of people. "Excuse me, please." He reached Nancy ahead of either of the chaperones, who had already gone to the birthday corner to seat the guests. The little girl's head was down, and Corky took her by the shoulders and shook her gently, as though to wake her up. "What happened?"

"She hit me." Nancy cupped her hand over the wound.

The chaperones arrived at the scene to take over. "What happened?" asked one. "Are you hurt?" asked the other.

A woman from a nearby table said, "I saw the whole thing. The girl with the red hair hit this child on the head with something and then ran."

Nancy was given a chair on the spot. The adults examined her forehead. Since the skin was not broken and not much damage had been done, the chaperones expressed relief. After a few moments Corky left Nancy to her party and went outside the door to stand, visibly distressed, looking up and down the street. "Did anyone see where she went?"

No one answered.

He picked up Josie's coat still lying at the doorway and took it to the nearest chaperone, who was beginning to fuss over how to locate the missing child. Several girls at once identified the coat as Josie's.

The chaperone sighed with relief. "That means she'll have to come back for it." She thanked Corky.

Nancy was being well cared for. A waiter had brought a napkin filled with ice to apply to her forehead. The chaperones were herding the girls to the birthday corner.

There was nothing further that Corky could do, so he went back to the table where Jenny had been watching. He no longer looked gleeful, like someone allowed to relive a satisfying childhood event, but like a worried old man in poor health. His face had lost its color and his posture its life. He himself might have been the one struck by Josie's blow. He slumped into his chair, looked at Jenny, and sighed deeply.

Jenny had been wondering who these girls were that Corky felt entitled to take part in their affair. In fact, her opinion of him had been undergoing a rapid revision. After all, there were adults in the party to take care of the children. He was the only person in the store who had felt it necessary to intrude. Just what degree of liberties was he accustomed to taking? He was, of course, a minister, and ministers, like doctors, were public servants of a kind, expected to take charge in emergencies, but was a minister really needed at a little girls' cat fight?

"This is all my doing," he murmured. "All my doing."

"Don't worry about it," she said, thinking he was apologizing for bringing her here. Was he going to cry? She edged backwards in her chair.

Corky made a visible effort to pull himself together, straightened his shoulders and took a deep breath. "That's Nancy," he said. "My niece."

"Oh, I see." Jenny was relieved. "No wonder you're upset."

Looking at her empty dishes, he said, "You've finished, haven't you? I don't want to hurry you, but would you mind leaving now? I have to see to it that Josie gets home all right."

Jenny was in the dark. Hadn't he just said his niece's name was Nancy? "Don't you want the rest of your ice cream?"

"I'm afraid it's past its prime." He caught the waiter's eye and asked for the check.

There was a little argument then. Jenny had decided she would not accept his treating her, since he was out of work and poor, but he paid the bill anyway. "You can treat next time."

"Somewhere else," she said, starting for the door. Then, feeling ungracious, she added, "Oh, this is a lovely place, and I've enjoyed it so much."

Outside the ice cream parlor Jenny was quiet and watchful, waiting to find out what Corky had in mind next. He had started out purposefully, but now he stopped and said, "I haven't a clue as to where she went."

"Are we looking for the girl who ran off?"

"I'm sorry," he said, startled. "I'm not making sense."

Jenny kept her thoughts to herself.

"I feel responsible for what happened. It seems only right that I make sure she gets home safely. But how on earth can we find her?"

Jenny, lacking crucial information, couldn't know what had really happened. Perhaps it was his duty as a minister, she thought. Maybe he was carrying Christian charity to some absurd but personally necessary extreme. "She'll go back to the party," she assured him. Seeing his hesitation, she added, "She'll realize that she's missing out."

"Do you really think so?"

"Of course. She's embarrassed, but she'll get over it."

"I hope you're right."

Jenny, holding his arm for support, then said something she would remember later, to her chagrin. "You're not the One who's supposed to notice every sparrow's fall."

"But when I shoot one down, shouldn't I nurse it back to health?"

"That isn't always possible."

He sighed deeply.

After a few minutes of aimless walking, Corky got himself under control. He dug in his pocket, then in the other one. "Hairballs," he said. "I've lost the place we parked."

"Central/East," said Jenny. "Seventh row."

"No flies on you, are there?"

"I've been senile long enough to have learned to take measures."

Jenny did not drive home. Corky was moody and did not offer her the wheel. Before leaving her off, however, he promised to take her out again soon. "We'll get you so familiar with the routes that you'll be able to drive with your eyes closed. And then I'll help you shop for a car."

She took his promise with a grain of salt, hoping, but also knowing how some people are when it comes to intentions.

JOSIE, PUNISHED

It was almost seven that evening when Josie appeared at home to face her whipping.

She had not gone back to the party, but had hidden out for a while at Software Solutions, where she thought no one would look, then had left the shopping center, running to keep warm without her coat.

At the Osborne Avenue entrance, her heels already blistered by the dress-up shoes, she hitched a ride with a woman and two children. She was scolded by the woman for hitchhiking, but taken safely to her own doorstep.

At the party, however, people had been awaiting her return for a long time. The refreshments had been served and consumed. "Happy Birthday" had been sung by the chorus of waiters, and still no one could go home. Finally one of the grownups called the Flannerys' house, and Eve agreed to come and wait for Josie, so that the party could end.

Neither Eve, having sat for half an hour at Frosty's before Duncan phoned to say that Josie had come home, nor Duncan, having paced the floor worried as hell, was amused. Eve, projecting this misbehavior into the ruined future, along with everything else that was wrong, lectured the silent Josie along the lines of, "I don't know what we're going to do with you."

Duncan, on the other hand, knew very well what to do with her and he did it, vigorously, with the belt. Josie did what she had always done when she was being whipped: melted into the wall until the time when tears would make him stop instead of making him madder.

BUDDING ROMANCE

The parsonage on Clover Street, in its sixties, near retirement, was getting the workout of its life these days. When built in 1922 to house a working-class family, its nine rooms had felt spacious, because such a family did not have many possessions. Nor was it likely to be burdened with constant presences, since everyone was gone during the day, the parents to work and the children to school. The house could creak and breathe, undisturbed. Lately, however, it had been crammed like a goose for pâté. Its dry old joists were weighted down with the burgeoning necessities of modern life plus thousands of Corky's books – books stacked everywhere – history, biography, philosophy, religion: the hideouts of a man on the run. Since much of the floor was inaccessible, and many of the walls and windows too, the house had not been treated to paint or paper or even a scrub since Corky and Claire moved in. And lately it had been stressed to the seams with people, stuffed with their heavy sighs, for Romy's work and the Pearlmans' lack of it kept them there all day.

What affected the house took a toll on its dwellers as well. From morning till night there were movements and sounds. Everyone felt the strain. Thus Corky's afternoons out with Jenny made a difference. One person gone left extra oxygen for those who stayed behind.

His absence ought to have made a difference in Claire's emotional well-being too, for she always exerted herself in corner-brightening when he was around. With him gone, she had a few hours to spend as she liked. But Claire's work life had kept her too busy to learn to use personal time to her own advantage, and now that she had some, she spent it worrying.

The fact that her previous clients still needed her was a worry, minor by comparison to her worry over Corky, but a worry nevertheless.

The children were still being beaten by fathers out of work and screamed at by mothers out of patience, both parents out of control. Pimps and pushers were still waiting with open arms for the children to run away. The difference: it was no longer Claire's job to get them cared for and counseled and schooled. It was no one's job. The Center was closed. The kids were on their own. Claire worried, but it did no good. It was as useless as worrying about Corky.

When Corky left for Jenny's in the afternoon, she found herself rocking in her own chair only minutes after being relieved that he was no longer dozing in his. She found herself staring out the window at the gray day or, for a break from worry, bringing home library books chosen, not for interest or merit but for thickness and absorbability, like diapers. Some of them were good as well as thick, but Claire was willing to read lesser works if they promised relief from the present.

The present was bad indeed. The word from Neil was bad. "Your chances if this goes to trial are not good."

"I'm a dead man," Corky mumbled.

"Not necessarily," said Neil. "We can almost certainly see to it that you're not put in with the really dangerous ones. There's a good case here for a treatment facility."

Corky had looked at Neil strangely. Claire now worried over something nameless.

She sat in her rocker by the bay window, feet on a stool, pillow on her lap to hold her heavy library book. She would look up and be surprised to find herself still here at the parsonage, Romy still clicking away at the other end of the room, the house still offering protection of a sort. The chair would slide a few inches back and bump a table. She would hitch it forward into place, then drop her gaze to her absorbing book and not know where she'd left off.

Corky's escapade at Frosty's added to her worry. "So stupid!" she hissed, when he arrived home woebegone and full of apologies. "How could you take a chance like that?"

His doggy smile tried feebly to wag its tail. "I didn't know I was taking a chance," he murmured. "I didn't know who was going to be there." To make amends, he hung his coat in the closet instead of draping it over a chair.

"You could have asked! At a party for Nancy's class it would have been damned strange if she hadn't been there." Claire was having to make an effort to suspend disbelief.

"I'm sorry." His dejection deepened. "You're right. It was a stupid thing to do. And I'll probably hear from somebody about it."

Romy, contemptuous as always, clasped her hands together out in front of her. "You'd better walk around like this," she said, exaggerating the hand clasp, "so your right hand will know what your left hand is doing." Then she swung her arms behind her. "Or you'll be walking around like this again." She held her wrists tight together.

This was enough to send Claire back into her role as Corky's protector. "Well, it was an innocent mistake," she said heatedly. "The idea that a person can't even go to an ice cream parlor is ridiculous. He could have run into her anywhere. The supermarket, the drugstore, anywhere." Indignation was a palatable attitude. Claire fanned it a little and in the process fanned away the aroma of suspicion. It didn't make sense to think that Corky would have taken such a chance deliberately. "No one can fault you for taking a housebound old lady out for a parfait!"

But the more Claire insisted that Corky had acted innocently, the more depressed she became. All her energy was going to maintain her belief in Corky's goodness.

Nancy had arrived home from the birthday party quite a bit later than Corky, her face pale below the bruise. She couldn't lie this time. Corky had been there and seen what happened. Even though he hadn't actually heard what she said to Josie, Nancy didn't know this, so her account had to be fairly accurate.

"I just told her Uncle Corky was there and she'd better wait outside, and she hit me and ran."

"Did she ever come back?"

"No. I hope she gets picked up and taken to juvenile."

Corky let his fist fall on the table. "That could very well happen."

"Her mother had to come and wait for her so we could all go home. Heather says she'll get a whipping even if she doesn't go to juvenile."

Claire and Romy glanced at the other. In their family, children were not whipped.

Wolf came downstairs then, fresh from the shower and wearing a sport coat. "Sorry I took so long." His smile was for Romy. "I think we still have time to make it." He didn't even notice Nancy's wound.

Romy fetched her brown suede coat, a gift from Frank that she was still paying for. When Wolf held it for her, she gave a bitter little laugh and slipped it on, then posed and turned like a model. She kissed Nancy. "Go to bed when Aunt Claire tells you. See you in the morning."

For Claire, keeping Wolf in the dark about Corky had become difficult in a way that she had not envisioned. A simple secret would have been easy to keep just by not talking about it. But to have an event unfolding in front of him without filling him in was not so easy. Having the thing most on her mind unspeakable was a severe test of resolve.

Romy was having no such trouble. Outspoken as she was, she would have taken back her promise and blurted out the story if she'd been thinking about it. But she had problems of her own. And in her eyes the charge against Corky was too ridiculous for anyone with a brain to believe. It would be found out for what it was, a dirty-tricks attempt at a church coup, and Corky would be cleared. Yes, he might have to pull himself together and act like a responsible adult, but that certainly wouldn't hurt him. Therefore there was nothing to worry about, and it irritated her that Claire and Corky were so depressed.

As far as Wolf himself was concerned, the deception was a snap. Wolf surely knew that something was awry: even a casual visitor can tell when there's an elephant in the kitchen, if only by the droppings. But he would have had to be told flat out just what the trouble was. The magazines that were full of the newest outrage, child sexual abuse, didn't reach Wolf. He hardly ever read a magazine. That a minister would molest a little girl was not an idea that was currently credible to the great majority of people. It would leap readily to mind only later, after public consciousness had been raised high enough to pull private consciousness along with it.

It was on Claire's mind all the time: Wolf didn't know and would have to be told. It looked now as though he was going to be around for a while. The longer he stayed, the more imminent the revelation became. He was making himself part of the household, and he never took his eyes off Romy.

Wolf had replaced his car immediately. The insurance money

came, and with the actual decision to make, he stopped looking at performance cars and settled on a two year-old station wagon.

Romy took a keen interest in this transaction. Buying a used car was new to her, and buying a car with cash was unheard of.

"It's the only thing I *can* do," said Wolf. "No one's going to loan money to someone who doesn't have a job."

But within another couple of days, he did have a job. While Romy was busy working for Omni, Wolf was out exploring Portville. One evening he brought a black lunch box and a thermos to the kitchen. "Looks like I'm going to need these tomorrow." His Arizona smile widened. He had noticed, a few streets away, a man digging the foundation for a new addition to his house. Wolf stopped to talk, and a few minutes later he had a job. "He's glad for the help," he explained. "He's anxious to get inside before bad weather."

"Construction work usually stops around here by mid-November," said Corky.

"That's what he told me," Wolf answered cheerfully. "But he wants to get it done."

The next morning Wolf arose in the dark and busied himself in the kitchen. He packed sandwiches and soup. Dressed in layers of wool, he went to work. In the evening he came home hungry with a face scoured by the wind.

"Domestic as all hell," said Romy, but the flesh was soft around her eyes and mouth when she said it.

Wolf was a man like no one Romy had ever known, an exotic in her high-tech life, a man to whom tiredness was physical.

"I like working," he said, in response to her question. "It's what I'm used to doing."

Wolf was third in a family of five. For his parents it had been a struggle to see that each child had the right opportunities: sports, Scouts, various lessons that the Rausch parents felt were worth what they had to give up to pay for them. When the time came, his four brothers and sisters had been placed in appropriate colleges, but Wolf had gone into his uncle's construction business instead. He wanted to work, he'd said, not sit on his butt. He wanted to learn how to do something useful.

That he had succeeded was evident to everyone at the parsonage.

In the short time he'd been here, he had taken an hour here and two hours there to glaze a broken window, to put new innards in the toilet to make it flush right. While nothing but major renewal was going to solve the house's problems, he was able to find small improvements that he could make. Even Nancy's bicycle tire was repaired and ready to roll.

Romy responded to Wolf's continuing presence in her own way. She washed and tended her heavy blonde hair every day, then scrunched it down severely as though punishing it for being beautiful. She scheduled her work and took evenings off, then shut herself in her room to read. He would leave before long. She didn't want to care too much when he did. It was only a matter of time: if they didn't walk out, they died, and if they didn't die, they walked out. The more attracted she became to him, the more she hid, for lovemaking was becoming inevitable, and lovemaking makes love. And love makes the desertion all the more painful.

Thus when Omni asked if her back was well enough for her to come to Bloomington for a meeting, she was relieved at the prospect of doing the leaving herself, if only temporarily.

In the meantime Nancy coaxed her to come downstairs one evening. The little girl openly liked having Wolf around. He played board games and cards, a welcome change from Corky's favorites, which were original and fanciful, but seemed to be getting more demanding as Corky got more desperate. Wolf pushed the coffee table full of books out of the way and stretched out full length on the floor, while Nancy and Romy sat cross-legged, to play Monopoly.

"You could play on the table," said Claire. "We could move some of this stuff somewhere else." She picked up the toaster. Crumbs rained down. No one cleaned them up.

"You don't play Monopoly at a table," said Nancy. "That would spoil it."

Monopoly was not a game that appealed to Corky. He tried to lure Nancy away by filling water glasses part way full and playing "Let's Go Out to the Ball Game" on their rims.

She looked to Wolf for support. "I'm tired of being creative," she said. "I'm interested in owning Boardwalk."

Corky wisely withdrew from this scene of unbridled materialism.

He bundled up in his overcoat and coaxed Claire to go with him on a long walk around the chilly neighborhood.

The next morning, a Thursday, Romy was getting ready to drive the two hundred miles to Bloomington for her Friday meeting. "Too bad you have to work," she told Wolf as he was packing his lunch. She could say it, secure in the knowledge that he was too dependable just to take off, but perversely she wished that he would. "There's more to Indiana than Portville, isn't there, Aunt Claire?" Romy too had the family dimples, and for once they were visible.

"I'll come to Bloomington with you another time." He said it in that slow, sure way he had, and Romy's color heightened.

Corky started to search for *The Three Indianas*, a history book from the library, but Claire followed and stopped him. "They're not talking about Indiana. Leave them alone."

Romy's meeting would last until noon Saturday, and she had some other things to take care of in Bloomington, but she would be back by Sunday evening at the latest.

Wolf was on her mind as she drove south from Portville. She had chosen the old road, not the freeway. Traffic was light. A bleak, flat landscape surrounded her under a gray sky. The car was her cocoon, and she inside it, and in her mind Wolf's words began their ferment.

"I'll come to Bloomington with you another time." The voice so calm, "time," the words so plain, "with you," that they rang with meaning.

"Verily," she thought.

She half-thought, "Thou shall be with me in paradise."

Romy was not religious, but her Methodist upbringing had given her the vocabulary, and words like those did come to her once in a while, always in inappropriate contexts. They fell into her mind like chunks of ember too hot to brush away. When it happened, she didn't know what to be angry at herself for – knuckling to the opiate of religion, or committing a sacrilege. "I don't know how to love him," she hummed, from *Superstar*, not really aware of what she was doing, feeling only a potent erotic awe.

Then she brushed it away and was Romy again, driving to her meeting in Bloomington. She rolled the window down. She rolled it back up. She pushed buttons to adjust the outside mirrors. AM radio had nothing to offer but hog prices and commercials and the wrong music. She switched to FM. That was a little better. Golden oldies. Blood, Sweat & Tears.

Ahead was a dark blue Harvester silo. It looked new and expensive. So did the barn. How much had they cost? A hundred thousand? Beside the nearby house a farm wife in jeans and parka hung bedclothes on the line. Her little girl handed her the clothespins. How much did they still owe? "You make me so, so very happy, baby," sang Blood, Sweat & Tears. Domestic as all hell, thought Romy, passing the barn, the house and the mother and child, now waving. She remembered the smell of line-dried sheets. The tidy farm gave way to stubbly fields. She hoped there wouldn't be a foreclosure. "I'm so glad you came into my life."

Should she stop in Indianapolis to visit her mother? Yes she should, but she decided not to. A visit with her mother wouldn't make so much difference if she were already miserable, but today she wanted to hold onto the mood she was in. She was beginning to believe that Aunt Claire might be right, that she wasn't so bad off after all. Her back was healing. The bills would be paid some day. She felt less like the widow cast screaming on her husband's pyre. She was looking forward to seeing her friends at Omni, and she realized that it took a certain feeling about herself and her possibilities to enjoy friends again.

In the fencerows brown flower stalks stood high over flattened grasses. Farther away small streams harbored shrubs with red canes. A flock of birds swooped around a field of stubble, lit, and in the same movement, rose in unison and flew away. Romy hummed with the radio.

Her evenings out with Wolf had been movie dates followed by food for talk at the brightly-lighted, cheerfully impersonal Waffle House, where amid clatter and voices they spoke of personal matters.

Wolf was still concerned about the man who had died on the hood of his car and brought up the subject by way of the movie. "That scene they kept flashing back to," he said. "You know, the scene of the rope hanging there." This film had been the first one they'd seen together, *The Pardon.* "It was really spooky, how much it reminded me of the man who fell on my car."

Romy had hardly noticed the rope, though she remembered after Wolf drew her attention to it.

"It was kind of a motif, the way the movie opened, you know, without any sound at all, and just that gray fog swirling and the frayed rope hanging there, sort of stirring as the fog moved. Stirring as if it had something alive in it." A look of revulsion passed over his face. "And then there were the other ropes. The kids' swing, with the tire on it, and the rope with knots that the guy climbed to get in the window, and the hangman's noose that he kept visualizing during the trial."

He went on. "And there was the theme too of having to kill a man to become a man yourself."

Romy held her temper.

"It doesn't have to be violent. Violence is not the point. The point is space to be who you are. Like, killing a man makes room for you. It's metaphorical."

Romy would never understand this. But instead of jumping on him, she asked him questions. "Have you thought any more what to make of the suicide happening on *your* car?"

"I can't make any sense at all of it, except that it has the aura of stumbling into someone else's life. You know, those warps where the person opens a door and all of a sudden he's in some other story instead of his own?"

She nodded. That's how it had seemed to her, too. Wolf was just an extra in the suicide's movie. Was he also an extra in hers?

"Only once you're there, you've got a part. There's your car in the ditch totaled and you have to replace it. That can be a major derailment. And in my case, it put me in Corky's house with you all, which I couldn't have imagined in my wildest dreams. It's almost like falling into another dimension."

"So, do you like it?"

He thought for a moment. "Yes and no. Some aspects of it I like very much." He gave her a quick glance. "I like some aspects very much indeed." Then his look changed. "But I can't get over the sight of that rope, like some implacable evil that just hangs there over us all. It just hangs there from the bridge. Inescapable."

Laughter and the clatter of dishes hovered around their booth, then entered. "Enough gloom and doom," said Wolf. "Would you like more syrup?"

The next time they went to a movie, it had already become habit to go to the Waffle House, and this time Romy took her turn unveiling herself a little in response to what they'd seen at the theater.

Wolf started by asking, "If a marriage is that bad, why do people keep it going?"

"Spoken like a bachelor!"

"I'm serious. Don't you wonder too?"

"No I don't. They keep it going either because they don't know it's bad or because they're afraid ending it would be worse."

"How can they not know it's bad?"

Romy's shoulders held their shrug while she tried to formulate an answer. "I draw a blank on that," she said finally, "but I know it happens because it happened to me. I didn't realize until after Frank was dead that our marriage had been a disaster." She followed up quickly. "Not that his death wasn't a disaster too."

Wolf was watching her. "What kind of disaster?" he asked. He pulled back. "Don't talk unless you want to."

"A disaster of absence. Not fights or anything, just the absence of what would make it good. A cold disaster." She half-laughed. "Maybe that's why the aftermath has been so hot. My problem is that I can't control the thermostat."

"You see," she said, "my husband was charming, a charming intellectual. Everyone thought he was terrific, his students, our friends, the garbage man, you name it. Even my mother liked him, and my momma don't like nobody. He was like the chocolates they wrap in gold foil. Expensive. High-status. A super high-calorie treat. I was nineteen years old, and he was my Shakespeare instructor. When he deigned to discuss Coriolanus with me privately, in his office, and tell me what a pretty smile I had, I just about wet the floor."

"What smile?" Wolf asked.

She couldn't help laughing.

"Not bad," he said, cocking his head to look. "A little rusty, maybe."

She nodded. "I wore it out, being married to Frank. My face ached all the time from having to smile, and I didn't even notice until after he was dead. I didn't understand that there's something wrong with eating nothing but gold-wrapped chocolates morning, noon and night. I was the luckiest woman alive, wasn't I? Underneath, I was malnourished and overfed, but when I noticed how sick I felt, I thought there was something wrong with me. How could I be such a sourpuss not to appreciate living with Frank? And in case I didn't appreciate it, there were plenty of other women who would."

Romy drew back her lips into the caricature of a smile. "Displeasure was a moral flaw to Frank. He was a meet-life-with-gusto person. The kind who calls labor pains "contractions" and thinks you're having an *exalted* experience when you've been there for twenty-seven hours and what you want most is an *out of body* experience. Everything had to be positive. It absolutely wore me out."

"That's amazing," said Wolf. "You see people put on that act in public, but you figure they go home and snarl a lot to make up for it."

"Not Frank. Not until he was denied tenure. And then you have never heard such rage. I came home from work that evening, and he was in the kitchen, walking around, almost breathless. It looked for a minute like he was making dinner and doing aerobics at the same time, and then he started breaking eggs, squeezing them in his hands one after the other, killing them, and gasping when he talked. The anger, the hatred he felt for everyone in the department, for the whole university, and egg dripping from his hands all over the floor. He carried on like that all evening, not with eggs, of course, because we ran out, maybe all night, I don't know, but the next morning it was over and he was absolutely quiet for about three days. And then he was just like his old self. You'd never know anything had happened, and he never told me what he planned to do about his career. It was my business, too, to know what he had in mind, but he didn't tell me. He treated the whole subject like Christmas morning. What wonderful gift was he going to unwrap next? That may be a good positive attitude to have, but I had career plans to make too. How was I to know but maybe he'd decide to leave Bloomington?"

"And then he died?"

"And then he died. And here I am. They tell us in the grief group to let go, and I want to let go, but I have to pay the damn bills."

Wolf reached across the table for her hand. "Let me buy you a waffle."

"Do I have to smile?"

"No," he answered. "You never have to smile."

She wrinkled her brow. "Never?"

"You don't have to smile the smile," he said. "It smiles you when it's ready."

"Hey," she answered, after a moment. "I can live with that."

Later she had noticed the smile smiling her a couple of times and she noticed it now, as she saw from the car window a small field of unpicked corn. The wind had been at it. The stalks all leaned in the same direction like rows of wintry monks in tattered tan leaves, the low-slung, bursting ears thrust out in a calisthenic hard-on. This sight struck her so funny that she laughed out loud. A pickup truck passed. When it pulled back into the lane ahead, both blinkers flashed on and off crazily before it sped away.

TIME TO CRY

Romy's absence from the parsonage gave Claire some breathing room. When Corky too left that afternoon to go to the nursing home, Claire was actually alone in the house for a while.

She used the time for the one thing she couldn't do when anyone was there. She cried. The door had no more than closed behind Corky when the tears began to well out and stream down her face.

What on earth was she going to do?

Everything rested on her, and she rested on nothing.

Always before, in the face of threat, she had been able to extrude something from herself to fashion a temporary support. She had always been able to act provisionally, to act *as if* a support were there, and this act of faith would give her a footing firm enough to stand on.

But now she seemed to have nothing to extrude. She had been squeezing and squeezing, but nothing came out her pores the way it used to. This time, things were different. There was nothing she could do. Others would make the decisions. A judge would decide what happened to Corky. The Meeting would decide whether or when she joined the homeless in the library doorway. Maybe a job would open up for her, maybe not. Almost certainly not for Corky, not with his reputation gone. So what was she asking? What was going to happen to *them*, or what was going to happen to *her*? Only the judge could say.

At this point it seemed easier to think about the possibility of being alone. Corky was contributing nothing to her well-being. He was completely dependent. His usual contribution, the one that made all the care she gave him worth it, had been his wit and playfulness, something she lacked in her own makeup and needed from him for balance. But now the only play he seemed able to manage was what he put forth for Nancy. He was so used to children's games that he could play them to his last breath under the worst of circumstances, but the sophistication or wit to appeal to an adult was beyond him now.

And without his levity, things were intolerably grim. Claire was worn out. She said it aloud. "I'm worn out." Anger seized her and she screamed, "See what happened to me? See what I get for trying so hard?" Her gaze through the tears fell on the top book in a stack before her, one of Corky's, *Jesus As Healer*. She made an ugly face unto the Lord, who had closed up the healer's shop just as she knocked on its door. He opens and closes the store, she thought, and he closes it just when you need something.

There had been times in the past when more was required of her than she had to give. She had met these challenges by telling herself that the situation was temporary and that she could borrow the strength from her reserves to last out the hard times.

Claire was proud of her ability to use herself this way. It was a trait that seemed inbuilt, something she depended on, something that had always been there, clear back to early childhood, when she had been needed to care for her sister Claudine.

Claudine had been the problem child in the family, the screamer, the one in trouble. Three years old when Claire was born, she had been Claire's responsibility instead of the other way around. Because she was always bringing trouble upon herself, excuses had to be made for her and care taken, often by Claire, in spite of Claire's being the baby. One particularly vivid instance was the time Claudine had picked a neighbor's tulips and brought them home. Since Claire was the little one, the cute one with the dimples, she was the one sent over to apologize, because "poor Claudine" wouldn't have been forgiven. Even at age four she knew how to assume this responsibility, and she was rewarded by the neighbor with cuddling and a chocolate rabbit.

This childhood prepared and strengthened Claire for her role in life. After putting Neil through law school and taking care of his mother until she died, Claire fell naturally into social work. She began working as menial help in a home for retarded children when her daughter Elizabeth started to school. From there she got her degree and progressively better jobs. The sixties and seventies were good times for social workers. The society needed what Claire had to offer and was willing to pay for it.

She knew, intellectually, that she was still needed even now, but the rejection implied by joblessness was undermining her faith in herself at the emotional level. This, coupled with her absolute inability to help Corky, was making her feel that she ought not to eat too much food or breathe too much air, since she was contributing nothing. To Claire, failing to contribute was the worst thing that could happen to her.

She cried still in great gasps. "What am I going to do?"

There was no answer, nor did she expect one.

And then, on this afternoon, much to Claire's dismay, Corky came home earlier than usual. She saw the car nose uncertainly into its space at the curb. "Can't he even park his own car?" she whispered through her teeth. When she heard the vicious tone of her own voice, she hurried upstairs to hide in the bathroom.

It didn't take Corky long to find her. "Claire," she heard him call from the stairs. Then he knocked on the bathroom door. "Claire, good news."

"I'll be out in a minute," she called. Good news, good schmooz. I can hear it later. I don't believe it, anyway. What good news could there be?

She rinsed her face and touched on a little tinted lotion. Her eyes were still red: she put the bad kind of drops in them, just this once. It wouldn't help at all for Corky to know she'd been on a crying jag.

But he knew. Downstairs she saw that the floor around her chair was littered with soggy tissues.

"I'm sorry," he said. His blue cheeks sagged. "You deserve better."

She couldn't answer. It would make him feel terrible for her to agree. "What's the good news?" she asked, automatically moving close for a hug.

"They want me to preach Sunday." He bent his knees a little and she stretched up on her toes. The hug felt false.

"Who, the nursing home?"

"Uh-huh."

"That *is* good news." She wished it made her feel better. "How'd it happen?"

"Somebody cancelled, the Baptist, I think, so the super asked if I could fill in. I'll be on the list, then. I'll be preaching every few weeks."

"Do they know?"

"About me? I suppose so. Who doesn't? But what harm can I do in a nursing home?" Corky gave her a wicked gleeful smile, like she hadn't seen for weeks. From it she gathered in as much sustenance as she could.

SPOILED FOOD

On Saturday evening Claire was washing dishes in the kitchen while Nancy dried and Wolf put the food away in the refrigerator. Corky was upstairs writing his sermon.

Claire heard a clatter and a soft "Damn!" from Wolf. "What is it?" she asked, keeping her soapy hands suspended over the sink as she looked around.

"I've spilled the milk."

She dried her hands and took a closer look. "I'll wipe it up when I finish the dishes."

The milk had splashed on the taller items on the top refrigerator shelf and run through to the second, where it puddled on the cover of a leftover casserole. The refrigerator was stuffed with little plastic tubs and packets, one thing stacked on top of another. In removing the casserole then, Wolf managed to spill more milk down through the rest of the shelves.

He began taking things out. "I'll just clean it," he said. "I've gotten milk on everything." Something in his eagerness made Claire suspect that the accident was not entirely accidental.

"I should have done that weeks ago. I'm ashamed."

"A refrigerator gets filled up before you know it." He opened a bacon package that seemed thin. It was empty. "Shall I throw this out?"

"I can't believe I put that there." She reached past him and pulled out a vegetable drawer. Under it was a bare slice of yellow cheese, hard and rimed with mold. "This is terrible."

"Gross," said Nancy, peering in.

"I've seen worse," said Wolf. "Why don't you let me clean it out while you go watch TV?"

The phone rang. Nancy went to answer it. In a moment she was back. "It's Heather," she said. "May I spend the night with her?"

Claire thought about it. "I don't see why not." Nancy would get to Sunday School in the morning if she stayed over at Heather's. She might even bring home tidbits of news.

Claire dried the rest of the dishes herself, and soon Nancy had finished her phone conversation and was in the kitchen again with a flight bag. "Could someone give me a ride? Or will it be okay if I walk?"

"I'll drive you," said Wolf. All the food from the refrigerator had been set out now, mostly on the floor nearby, the only place for it, since the table and countertops were already cluttered with papers, books, utensils, and whatever else anyone from time immemorial had put there to sprout and multiply. "Please wait and let me help with this. I made the mess, and I should at least help clean it up."

Claire laughed. "Sure," she said. "You made the mess with your own little patty paws. Don't worry. It'll still be here when you get back."

Alone then, Claire sorted through it to find what was salvageable. The mozzarella could be scraped and pared; the rat cheese had white mold in the crevices. The inner stalks of celery were still clean and firm, but the lettuce was slimy all the way through. There were half cans of tomato paste and mushroom soup, a spoonful of chopped green chilies, three green olives in a pint of cloudy brown juice, a hardened glob of macaroni, and on and on. What on earth had she been doing while all this food spoiled? She had never been a person obsessive about cleaning the refrigerator, but always before, she had kept an eye on things. She separated out the containers of still usable food and carried the empties to the sink for washing.

The task depressed her. It gave her a picture of herself as helpless. She scrubbed a crusted-over lid and read the words, "To open, press down and rotate." This somehow sent her even lower. She was depressed about being depressed.

Wolf hadn't been gone long enough to be back already when she heard a knock at the front door and then the door opening. "Anybody home?"

Almost without knowing it, Claire felt the voice as a blow. She automatically steeled herself and retreated behind the steel. It was her sister Claudine. "Come in," she called. "I'm in the kitchen."

Claudine appeared in the doorway, thinner and sharper-faced than ever. She had certainly taken genes from some other eddy of the pool. Only the fact that she had produced Romy proved her to be a member of Claire's family. She was much taller than Claire, with wide shoulders, and lean as a model in her crisp, belted raincoat. She wore stiletto-heeled boots and a stylish fedora with a fan-shaped feather in the band.

"What brings you up north?" asked Claire. Claudine certainly didn't look as though she were paying a casual visit, but then Claudine never looked casual, so Claire couldn't tell. It was possible that she had dropped in on her way home from a buying trip to Chicago for her boutique.

"How else can I get a look at my grandchild?"

Claire was silent, while all the mean, sarcastic things she thought of saying ran through her mind: You could hang around the school yard. You could invite her for a visit. Try treating her mother better. If you weren't so abrasive, your grandchild would be living with *you* now instead of with *me*.

"You missed her by about five minutes. She's gone to spend the night with a girlfriend."

Claudine made a gesture of annoyance and piled her heavy purse on the nearest chair atop a defunct toaster-oven awaiting Wolf's hands. Her attention shifted to the scene in the kitchen. "Is this a gourmet meal you're preparing?"

Claire kept her voice steady and calm. "Left Ovaire Supreme. Take off your coat and stay a while."

"Where should I hang it?" Claudine asked, her voice pointing out a lack.

Seeing what Claudine saw, it became obvious to Claire that indeed there was no place in the house suitable for her sister's coat. It belonged where everything was new, in Claudine's boutique perhaps, where nothing would soil it. Wearing it out in the rain would offend it, and so would hanging it to rub against of any of her own clothes. Claire happened to have on an old gray sweater of Corky's at the moment, a sweater riddled with holes, but warm, so warm that it held close the flush of anger she felt rising. "There's no place to hang it. You can stand there wearing it if you want to, or if you'd like to take it off, you can fold it inside out and put it over a chair." Having said this much, she pulled off the sweater to cool herself and donned her usual, more comfortable attitude of sympathy toward Claudine, who must feel badly to be so shut out of her family's life. "We can go get Nancy. I'm sure she would hate to miss a visit from Grandma."

Claudine stopped unbelting her coat and turned with narrowed eyes. "Does she call me Grandma?"

"Sorry," said Claire. "Actually, I don't know what she calls you." She had never heard Nancy mention her grandmother. She thought about telling Claudine so.

But Claudine had lost interest in Nancy. She was focused on the unlovely food on the floor. "I suppose you've buried Romy in the back yard."

Claire knocked the side of her head with the heel of her hand. "Come again?"

"Well, she's not here. I see all this poisonous-looking garbage, and I come to the obvious conclusion. How about Corky? Is he in the back yard too?" As she spoke, the front door opened and closed. Her reaction when Wolf came through the dining room door was instantaneous: here was a handsome young man. Her lips parted, a middle-aged Marilyn Monroe, and her voice became breathy. "You've done away with Corky and taken a young lover." She looked Wolf over. "I approve, Claire. I approve heartily, but you really ought to fix yourself up."

Wolf looked uncomfortable.

Without leaving a moment for Claire to speak, she went on, talking rapidly. "Are you going to introduce me? Maybe you don't dare. Well, I'll introduce myself." She held out her hand, and when Wolf shook it, she didn't let go. "Hello there. I'm Claudine, and I'm not an alcoholic, I'm Claire's sister. She may not have told you that she *has* a sister. I doubt she tells anyone. I'm the black sheep of the family and she's the little white lamb, and she'd like to disown me but she can't." Still holding Wolf's hand, she interrupted herself with a laugh, then went on talking without a pause. "I used to feel bad about being the black sheep. Claire had the breaks and it pissed me all to hell. But we've come full circle. I may be the black sheep, but at least I'm not married to a child molester." And here she let go of Wolf and looked around triumphantly, like a five year-old proud of herself for having smashed the china.

Wolf seemed bewildered by this barrage but did not react specifically to the news. "Pleased to meet you," he said hesitantly.

Claire felt as though her face were covered with a mask of stone. She played dead and acted polite through force of long habit. "Claudine, this is Wolf Rausch. He's from Arizona, and he's a guest here as a result of an accident he had passing through town. Wolf, this is my sister Claudine. Romy's mother."

"Oh." Wolf's smile was tentative through the fog of his bewilderment. "How do you do?"

"Speaking of Romy," said Claudine. "Where is she? Unless she really *is* buried in the back yard." She addressed Wolf again. "My sister tells me that my granddaughter is spending the night with a friend, but I'm not going to believe her until we've dug up the back yard. My daughter's missing and so is my brother-in-law, and from the looks of the menu, I'm surprised anyone survived." She talked with zany animation, without leaving any openings for an answer, taking quick breaths in the middle of her sentences, punctuating herself with little laughs and gestures that held the floor. "Unless they've already put Corky in prison?" She turned to Claire. "Is that it? I thought the wheels of justice took longer. Don't the lawyers usually string it out as long as possible so they'll get a bigger fee?"

Still without stopping for an answer she asked Wolf, "What do you think of all this?"

He looked from Claudine to Claire and back again, speechless, as though hypnotized, then at the refrigerator door standing open.

"You asked why I came to Portville." This was to Claire, and it left Wolf free to move unobtrusively to the sink where he turned on a small, quiet stream of water and took up the job Claire had been doing. "Well I came to take Nancy home with me. News does travel through the grapevine. I can't in good conscience let my granddaughter stay under the same roof with a known molester, and if I have to fight to get her out of here, then so be it, I'll fight, and it won't be the first time I've had to take drastic measures to do the right thing."

At last she stopped. Claire, behind her defense, stayed still. She wouldn't have to fight with Claudine over Nancy. All she had to do was leave Nancy at Heather's. As for the insults to Corky, she had been protecting herself against these onslaughts for a long time. She could hear Claudine's machine gun, but the bullets did not penetrate.

And as for Wolf, well, that was one problem out of her hands. The secret was no longer a secret. She even felt a bit relieved. After Claudine left she would have a long talk with Wolf and tell him all about what had happened. He knew Corky by now. He would see that the accusation could not be true.

"Excuse me, Claudine," she said, bending to pick up another load of condiment bottles. "I'd better get on with the job here before anything spoils." She corrected herself. "Spoils any further." Pushing a chair out from the table with her toe, she said, "Sit down. Make yourself comfortable." After all, this was her sister, badly behaved as she was. She had to offer hospitality.

Claudine seemed soothed by her outburst. It was a pattern that Claire knew well. Claudine even joked about it herself on occasion. "I come in with guns a-blazing, and that lets the folks know I don't take no shit off nobody." After the initial blast was over, she would calm down until something set her off again. Claire knew not to add fuel and prolong the attack with a response of any kind. She was also adept at modifying the atmosphere to keep new aggravations to a minimum.

"Romy's in Bloomington," she said. "She'll be home tomorrow."

"I'm glad to hear she's well enough to travel. Last time I called, she couldn't get out of bed to speak to me on the phone."

This had not actually been the case. The truth was that Romy had begged Claire to lie for her. She hadn't been in bed at the time, but talking to her mother would *put* her in bed.

"You got a cup of coffee?" Claudine pushed aside the newspaper and cleared a space at the table to lean on.

"If you don't mind instant." The hospitality Claire was willing to offer was limited. It did not extend to grinding coffee. She gave Claudine a clean cup and spoon and set the hot teakettle on a trivet. "Help yourself. There's milk if you don't want powdered whitener."

Wolf had continued to work on the refrigerator. A good many things were ready to put back in, but he was going to have to bump past Claudine at the table to put them there. Claire saw his plight and sent him away. "You've done all you can, dear. I want to arrange things the way I want them." As nearly as a big man can do so, he melted out of the kitchen, and in a moment, the sound of the TV came from the living room.

"My daughter must have rocks in her head to leave a hunk like that with nothing better to do on a Saturday night than clean out the ice-box and watch TV."

Claire had thought much the same thing, but she found herself defending Romy. "She hasn't been to Bloomington since summer. She had a meeting with Omni and a whole list of other things to do including, I think, some social things."

Claudine's face took on a look as though a new idea had struck her. She stared into space for a moment before speaking. "Maybe she'll move back to Bloomington and I won't have to take Nancy," she said slowly.

"What a horrible attitude!" Claire's restraint vanished. "To think that you'd try to take a child you don't want away from people who do want her!"

"I'm not going to lie and say I really want a child in the house again." Truth-telling was a habit Claudine considered one of her virtues. Though it was often carried to abusive extremes when talking about others, it did also extend to being open about herself. "I'm used to my freedom. And the shop takes a lot of my time. But I'd never forgive myself – or you or Romy either – if she ended up the victim of a pedophile."

"I can't stop you from believing the worst about Corky. You believe the worst about everybody. But even if it were true, Nancy's better off with us than she would be with someone as hateful as you. Touching a child's genitals isn't the only destructive thing you can do."

"I hear you saying that even if Corky does touch children's genitals, it isn't so bad. To me, that means you believe he did it." Claudine leaned toward Claire as though accusing and persuading at the same time. "You know very well that Corky has all the earmarks of a pedophile. Anyone who acts the way he does with kids has got to have a screw loose."

"Claudine, you're no expert in abnormal psychology, and you'd better watch out how you throw accusations around."

"I didn't make the accusation. I didn't have to. A couple of little girls made the accusation, on two separate occasions. You're the expert in child development. You tell me, have you suddenly become convinced that it's *good* for little girls to be fondled by dirty old men?"

"Of course it's not *good*. I'm only saying that it's not the *only* bad thing that can happen to a child. I'm also saying that the way the event is handled has a lot to do with whether it's harmful or not. I happen to believe that what happened in Corky's case is not only a disaster for us but is harmful to the girls as well. Whatever *did* happen was magnified by the parents and used for purposes having nothing to do with the children's well-being. And that's exactly what I think you're trying to do, too. Your sudden 'grandmotherly' interest in Nancy isn't grand-motherly at all – you can't even stand to be called 'Grandma.' It's not for Nancy's benefit, it's to be spiteful to me and to Corky, and even to Romy. Nancy's just a pawn. And *that's* real child abuse. Whether a dirty old man fondles a child as though she were nothing more than an object to him or a grandmother seizes the child in a self-righteous at-tempt to one-up somebody, it's all the same. It's treating the child as not really human. As a thing. As a means to your own ends."

As the words rushed out of her, Claire listened to herself saying them. She heard the momentum. The more she said, the more she felt, and it was the most she had felt, except depression, in quite a while. "I'm serious about this. Romy left Nancy in my care, and she stays here until Romy gets back. What happens then is for her to decide. If I have to break off with you over this, I will. I've stood up for you all my life, and that's worth something, but I'll break off if I have to."

The room was very still for a moment. Then Claudine answered. "You need me. You can't break off with me."

"I need *you*? That's backward. Recall, please, who it is that comes through for whom. And now that I'm down, instead of helping me, you're enjoying it."

"Wait just one goddam minute." Claudine's face was sharp as a lance and pointed at Claire. "I did too come through for you. I cut open Mom's featherbed the time you almost suffocated."

"What's that got to do with anything? That happened a hundred years ago. And you didn't cut it open to save me, not on your life. You cut it open to make a mess."

"That's the whole point! I *did* cut it open to save you. Would you do the same for me? No sir. You wouldn't make a mess to save anybody or anything, not even yourself. You're too damned goody-goody to make a mess. That's why you need me. To cut open the featherbeds you wrap around yourself."

"That's a novel way of explaining yourself. Why is it that when you get done ripping things apart, I see feathers strewn from here to hell and back, but I don't feel saved?"

"I can't help that. You're too busy cleaning up feathers to feel saved." Claudine tasted her coffee and made a face. "Mind if I pour this out and start fresh? It got cold."

"I don't know why I don't just throw you out of here." Claire's anger was turning to exasperation. "But go ahead, have some more. Better still, let's make a pot of real coffee."

"I knew you were holding out on me!" Claudine poured out the cold coffee. "You're too kind, clean and reverent to throw me out. You know it's a long drive to Indianapolis and I don't see all that well at night." She chuckled her throaty laugh.

"Oh God. You mean I'm stuck with you as a houseguest?"

"You're blessed with my presence for the night. Now bring out the real coffee."

Claire had already opened the freezer. "You'll have to make it. I absolutely must get this stuff put back in the refrigerator." She was half-talking to herself. "I *must* put the milk away. The eggs. The cheese. Here, here's the coffee, and the grinder is under that stack of potholders on the counter, right over there." She stopped suddenly. "You do realize, don't you, that this is Corky's house too? You're his guest too."

"Where in the hell *is* Corky, anyway?

"He's working on his sermon for tomorrow." The thought of having Claudine and Corky together under the same roof for that long knotted Claire's stomach all over again. Claudine would never stay on her good behavior, and Corky didn't need any more hassle. "Claudine, promise me you'll go easy on him. He's having a terrible time."

"He *should* have a terrible time! He's done a terrible thing." Claudine cranked the grinder vigorously.

"Can't you see the good in anybody?" Maybe she really would have to throw her sister out.

"Can't you ever see the bad?"

"What good does it do to focus on the bad? Of course I see bad things in people, but I…"

Claudine interrupted. "You can't see things you won't focus on. It's not humanly possible. Eyes don't work that way. If you don't focus on the bad in people and really see what's there, how the hell can you protect yourself from it?"

"Maybe that's another of our differences. I've had good people around me most of my life. I've never felt the need to protect myself."

"That's a crock. You protect yourself indiscriminately from everybody. This obsessive belief in everyone's goodness is a featherbed you wrap around yourself. It protects you, and it also suffocates you."

"Maybe you're right, Claudine. I don't know. What I do know, though, is that I do not want to witness an attack on Corky. I am at the absolute bottom as far as feeling bad is concerned. One more attack is one more than I can stand."

"You ought to be bound and gagged when people are having words with Corky. Then you wouldn't have to rush in and protect him and you could pay attention to what's being said."

"Well, it's not going to happen. I'm not going to get the benefit of that little scenario. So just promise me you'll keep your mouth shut." As Claire said this, she became aware of somebody talking in the living room. It was Wolf. She listened. Since no one was answering him, she concluded that he was talking on the phone, and her curiosity was aroused. It was okay, it just surprised her, that's all. She didn't know he was well enough acquainted around Portville to have someone to call on the phone. She went back to talking to Claudine. "Okay?"

"You're not paying attention to me," said Claudine. "You didn't hear what I said, did you?"

"Of course I heard what you said. What did you say? I'm trying to get you to promise me something, and you're trying to distract me. That's what you always do." Claire made fly-shooing motions. "Run a conversation around some crazy way so that no point can be made."

"I give up. You're hopeless. Now sit down and drink some coffee with me."

Claire sat down, profoundly uneasy.

LEAVE-TAKING

The next morning, instead of Wolf, it was Claudine whom Claire found already in the kitchen. The coffeepot was giving forth its agitated slurps of culmination. "Oh, good morning," she said. "When I smelled coffee, I thought Wolf was up."

"He is," answered Claudine. "He made the coffee and went back upstairs to pack." She wore a crisp, red wool robe with a cape collar and a large patch pocket. "That young man is a real jewel. Too bad he has to leave so soon. We had the best chat. He told me his life history."

From long habit Claire was able to cover her dismay. She wouldn't give her sister the satisfaction of knowing she was hurt. Of course Claudine was exaggerating as usual; there couldn't have been time for more than a few minutes' talk. But why was he leaving so abruptly? Oh, she knew, she knew! But why would he talk to Claudine about it instead of to her? Wasn't it just like Claudine to come into her house and accept her hospitality and then appropriate her friend!

Claire busied herself with cups and spoons, with napkins, with milk from the refrigerator. She yawned, in a display of greater sleepiness than she really felt. "It's going to take a cup of coffee to get me going. I'm pretty groggy in the morning." She did not want to find out from her sister anything more about Wolf.

Claudine had been put in Romy's room for the night, after an evening of talk at the table during which Claire steered the conversation away from Corky into Claudine's personal passion, her boutique. She thus heard more about fashion than she ever wanted to know, and about people to whom fashion is important. Being bored was better than being attacked. Fortunately Corky had stayed upstairs with his sermon until bedtime, giving Claudine little room to jab at him.

There had been a few times during the evening when Claire did enjoy being together with her sister. The kitchen radio had been on, quietly, as it often was, and once a familiar tune came on, Al Hirt and "Java." As if ignited by a common spark they got up from their chairs and joined hands to dance the turkey trot as best they could in the crowded room, clumping with outstretched legs and arms like fold-and-cut paper dolls, laughing like thirteen again as they stumbled into things. Claire was surprised and touched at how frail Claudine's body felt under the sharpness, the little bird-bones in her hands protected by red talons so perfect they were surely artificial. "Inside out," Claudine had cried, through the giggles, "let's do inside outs." They turned back to back. But inside out they lost it. Their hands were upside down, their arms twisted, and their bodies at the wrong angle, and although the turkey trot is supposed to be an awkward dance, the dancers themselves can't be awkward. After a moment of crashing around the kitchen, they collapsed back into their chairs.

"I sure do miss Mom, don't you?" And the conversation took another direction, into the family scrapbook. This track was safe. It prevented talk in which crime, prison and Corky were brought together in the same sentences, and it was certainly more interesting to Claire than clothes and skinny women. This time she offered anecdotes as well as questions. "Can you still do the Charleston?" Their mother had been a member of the flapper generation and had taught both daughters how to dance.

But even though the talk was of Mom and home, and even though the hurtful things in some of the anecdotes no longer hurt, there was the layer of protection that Claire had to wear, just in case. Her pleasure was muffled thereby. She was glad when bedtime came at last.

Now she asked Claudine what she'd like to eat.

"What have you got?" Claudine sounded ready for a farmhand's breakfast.

"Eggs," Claire answered. "Cereal. No bacon. I could make pancakes, I guess." She felt energy drain away at the thought of providing service, as though the calcium were leaching out of her bones, making her skeleton too weak to hold her up.

"Sounds great. Let me help."

Claire was not used to help in the kitchen, at least with the cooking itself. She didn't know how to allocate the work. "No, just sit still," she said. "The place is too small for both of us to move around."

But she found the task of putting pancake batter together almost more than she could handle. Where was the mixer? Under something, no doubt, but what? To get Claudine out of the room so she wouldn't be there watching her clumsiness she said, "You can set the table. Here," she said, handing out the plates, "and here." She put napkins and utensils on top.

Claudine was back all to quickly. "Claire," she said seriously. "This place is a disaster."

Here was the attack she'd been protecting herself against. "Isn't it just!" She made her voice light. "I absolutely must get busy and do some cleaning. I'll be going back to work before long, and I'd like to have everything spotless by then."

"You've got a job?"

"Well no, not yet, but something'll come along pretty soon."

Claudine tilted her head skeptically. "What makes you so sure? Everything I hear says programs are being phased out and people riffed right and left."

"I have to believe I'll find something."

Her voice must have given some indication of her imperiled condition, for Claudine, instead of carrying her thrust further, came close and put her arms around Claire.

Claire's thin breath fluttered.

"I just want you to know that you can count on me."

"Thank you." Count on you for what, she wondered. "Thank you."

"Now let me help you get breakfast. I'm not as incompetent as you think I am. I do, after all, manage to put food in my mouth every day."

Claire's smile was thin. "I'm incompetent right now, not you. I can't even remember where I left the mixer."

Claudine went to the long counter under the windows. "If I were a mixer, where would I be?" Confronted with a space so tightly packed that even if she found the mixer, there would be no place to set it up, she said, "How about let's use a spoon?"

Claire nodded. She read down the list of ingredients. "Yes. The griddle is in the oven. If you'll make the pancakes, I'll do the rest."

The two women busied themselves. Presently Corky joined them in the kitchen, followed almost immediately by Wolf. Both were clean-shaven and dressed. Corky, disheveled in his preaching suit, looked animated.

Wolf, though well put together, looked preoccupied. "Would you excuse me for a little while?" he asked. "I have to run an errand. Don't wait breakfast. I'll just grab a bite when I come back." He was carrying his jacket and now shrugged into it.

Claudine said, "That coat is perfect for you." Her practiced eye sized Wolf up. "You must have someone who goes shopping with you."

"No," he answered. "But since I don't have the money or the space for a lot of clothes, I'm careful not to buy things that aren't right." He backed away as he spoke, avoiding Claire's gaze.

When Wolf had gone, Corky asked Claire to run the power duster over his shoulders. Again she felt her energy drain away. The duster could be anywhere, under any pile of stuff, in any drawer. Finding it was a task too big for her. Still, something had to be done about Corky's suit. She didn't even need to see it through Claudine's eyes to notice how scruffy it was. Without knowing where to look, she went to the very cabinet where the duster was, right where it belonged, with cleaning rags and furniture polish. Miraculously, the battery had not worn down.

Corky sat well back from the table while Claire tended him. His shoulders were scarecrow thin under the pads in his coat. Just below the surface of his scraped cheeks and chin was the hint of blue that would become pronounced by this afternoon, when his sermon would be delivered. His fine sand-colored hair, though combed, still looked as though it had been mowed like hay, then tossed helter-skelter back on his head. His appearance moved Claire almost to tears, the way he had been made of spare parts that went together funny. No wonder he'd been trying to find God. He needed to be recalled and made right. She ran the duster with one hand while grooming with the other, patting, picking, brushing, tugging lapels into place. "Let me see your socks," she said. He lifted his pant legs.

"Good." The socks matched. It was amazing how black socks could be so many different colors, and there were times when Corky didn't even manage to put on two black ones.

"You're dressed awfully early," she said.

"Why not? Are you coming with me?"

"Not today." If she did, Claudine might come along, invited or not. Having her sister witness Corky preaching at the nursing home was something Claire could not endure, his cathedral the innocuous chapel, his pipe organ the mirror-covered cocktail lounge piano in the corner, his congregation tied into their push chairs so they wouldn't fall out. Corky, in his innocence or his humility or both, would accept this ministry, and she loved him for it, but Claudine did not love him. Claudine would jeer at him and thus at her, how the mighty had fallen to this lowly place in life. Oh, pride was such a pain! Claire ran the duster quickly through his hair, and when he winced and she turned it off, the hair looked none the worse.

"Where's the syrup?" called Claudine from the kitchen. "The first batch is ready." The syrup was on a high shelf with things not often used. On its surface was a scum of mold. Claire dropped it in the trash to join what was already there from last night. "We'll eat jelly on them," she said defiantly. "Raspberry jelly. It'll melt. We won't know the difference."

The first batch was Corky's. Claire sat at the table with him, and soon Claudine brought a plate of pancakes for her too and one for herself. They were still eating when Wolf returned. Claudine jumped up and went back to the griddle.

"I brought you a Sunday paper," he said. He handed it to Claire as though delivering a peace offering. He smelled cold from the air he brought in with him. "I went over to talk to Ralph. I hate to do this to him." Ralph was the man he'd been working for, building the new room on his house. "He wasn't very happy about it, just wrote me a check and didn't say much."

"Do what to him?" Claire knew, but she wanted to hear it from Wolf.

He exhaled a deep sign and pulled another chair to the table where a place had been set for him. "I got it in my head to call home last night," he said. "Oh, and I left some money by the phone." He shook his head at Claire's gesture of annoyance. "I hadn't talked to the folks in quite a while. Things are not very good with them. My dad's health is going down, and Mom wants me to come home."

Corky put his forkful of pancake back on the plate. "Oh dear," he said. "We're sorry to hear that. Sorry that your father is ill and sorry to see you go."

"Well, yes." Wolf glanced toward the kitchen at Claudine dishing up a stack of pancakes, then back at Corky, who was watching him. His gaze sank instantly and swam underwater to Claire's place, where it came back up but not quite all the way. "It's been quite an experience, being here. I said once that it was like a warp where you fall into someone else's movie. The way you people took me in and all."

"It's been a pleasure." Claire was not going to get the chance to talk him out of leaving. If he had already quit his job, the decision was made. She knew from the way he looked why he was going home. Claudine's blurting out all that stuff about Corky had started him thinking. Oh, she knew what he must be thinking! His family didn't sound any worse off than they were when he first arrived. But now he was going.

He was still trying awkwardly to explain himself. "It's time I moved back into my own movie. And there's my dad in Arizona. It's just time for me to go home, that's all."

Claudine brought another plate of pancakes in and set it before Wolf. "Best eat a good breakfast," she said. "Or would it make you sleepy on the road? I never know who eats and who doesn't." She laughed. "What I mean is that if you don't want these, don't eat them."

"You're leaving right away?" Wasn't he even going to wait till this evening when Romy came home? "This is terrible!" Claire felt grief welling up, first for Romy, but then for herself. "I'm going to miss you. You certainly did fit right in." Then she put her chin higher. "Your parents did a good job raising you, and they deserve to have you come home."

"Well, I certainly have to thank you both."

Claire said, "You know, Wolf, some people belong in one kind of story and some in another. You fell into a family here, and that's the kind of story that's natural to you. If you'd been an adventure-seeker or a loner or a warrior-type, you wouldn't have stayed past that first night."

He smiled his Arizona smile for the first time that morning. "You're right. I had to get the travel bug out of my system, but lately I've thought it might be time to settle down." Then his gaze dropped again. The jelly on his pancakes had not melted but lay there clumped in glistening black tears.

When his car pulled away, another pang of grief hit Claire for Romy's sake. He really shouldn't do this. He and Romy ought to have a chance to get better acquainted, at the least.

It didn't help things at all when Claudine sat her down and gave her a talking to about the future. She was going to have to think, Claudine told her, about what she would do. Even if Corky didn't go to prison, she ought to leave him. As long as she stayed by his side, stood up for him, took care of him like a mother, she was depleting herself, feeding him off her own flesh. "What do you want?" Claudine asked sternly. "Are you trying to wreck yourself completely so that someone else will have to take care of you?"

And that started the argument about Elizabeth. She should call Elizabeth and tell her what was going on. Elizabeth should come home and help.

"No!" Claire burst out. "I can't ask Elizabeth to interrupt her career to come solve my problems." But as she said it, she thought of Wolf's mother, who let her son know she needed him. But such was not for her. She believed that parents had to give their children up to the world when they were grown, not cling to them for support.

"I may have to do it for you," said Claudine ominously.

"Claudine, you wouldn't." But even that was said without much force. Claire simply did not have the strength right now to tell Claudine to go back to hell where she came from.

ROMY RETURNS

When Romy arrived home on Sunday afternoon, she thought nothing of Wolf's car being gone. His job was informal. He might very well be working at Ralph's. But her mother's shiny Buick was conspicuous at the curb behind Claire's battered van. Oh God, thought Romy. She wasn't in the mood for this. All the spaces nearby were taken, and when she reached the first one available down the block, she drove on past instead of parking. This was like an enemy attack on a holiday. Your defenses are down.

If there had been anywhere else to go, she would have gone there. But she wasn't a barfly. Nor did she have an office to hide out in. That's the trouble. When home is where you always are, home's the only place to be, and you have to face whatever's going on there. She drove around the block. When she came to the parking spot again, she stopped.

What was going on was her mother beating up on Aunt Claire. The house was cold. Aunt Claire was huddled in her rocking chair wrapped up in that little plaid lap robe she always used. And her mother was striding up and down the living room, jabbing the air with one of those ghastly fingernails like a woodpecker on wormy wood.

When she saw Romy, she stopped, with her finger in mid-air, and turned, then continued jabbing, only this time in Romy's direction. "I was just telling Claire and I'll tell you too, this can't go on."

"Of course it can't, and it won't. I won't let it." Romy was used to fighting with her mother. She didn't want to play that game, but she certainly knew how. "What can't go on?"

"This state of affairs. This cancer. It's like having a cancer and refusing to have it treated."

"And I suppose you're the doctor. You know everything, and

you're going to do the cutting and the ordering of chemo." This idea sparked anger. "You like that role, don't you? You like to decide what's cancer and what's not, don't you? You like to get in there and cut where it hurts and call it treatment." She'd had much experience with Claudine as surgical shaper. Now she stood her ground.

Claudine brushed Romy's accusation aside with a display of motherly interest. "Let me look at you," she said, grasping Romy's shoulders in the suede coat and turning her around. "Good," she said. "The coat is good, but you need a hair cut."

"Mother! My hair is my own business." Romy had indeed tried to make connection with her hair stylist in Bloomington and failed.

"I'm glad you're back on your feet." Claudine kissed her lightly on the cheek. "Come sit down and help me talk to Claire."

When she took off her coat, Romy noticed again that it was cold in the room. Claire was still wearing her fuzzy bathrobe and her mother had on a high style sweater that enveloped her from chin to knees, worn over slim gray wool pants.

"When have you ever needed help talking to Aunt Claire?" She pulled Corky's chair over and sat near Claire. "Where is everybody?"

A glance passed between Claire and Claudine. Claire answered, "Corky's preaching this afternoon. He'll be home before long. And Nancy slept over at Heather's."

Romy knew something was being withheld but didn't know what.

"That's what I came here about," said Claudine. "Nancy. I'm serious when I say Nancy ought not to be under the same roof with Corky. I know, I know, you both insist he hasn't done anything. But even the suspicion! How can you take that chance?"

"Mother, I simply don't feel like I'm taking a chance. Aunt Claire and Uncle Corky were good enough to come get me when I needed help, and they've taken care of Nancy while I was sick. Besides, she's never alone with him. I'm here all the time, and so is Aunt Claire. What could possibly happen?"

"A lot can happen right under your eyes if you don't keep them open." Claudine, still frowning, finally sat down. "Tell me about Bloomington. When do you get possession of your house again? I'll feel a lot better when you're back home."

"You and my boss agree on that. But the house is leased through the end of May."

"Maybe you could find a place to rent until then. I'd even be willing to help with the expense."

"Mother, I can pay my own rent! I'm paying rent here, to Aunt Claire. You don't think I'd just move in and live off Claire and Corky, do you?"

"Hardly. It would be Neil you'd be living off of, not Claire and Corky." Here Claudine's face twisted and her expression turned malicious. "I have to give you credit, Claire. You're the only woman I know whose ex-husband is still her lawyer and financial advisor and sometimes even her financial backer fifteen years after the divorce."

Romy felt her internal boiler light with a poom! and her internal temperature start to rise. Her mother's ex-husband, her own father, hadn't even paid child support. Claire *did* deserve credit. But even though she was heating up inside, outwardly she was shivering. She attended to the outward feeling. "It's cold in here," she said. "Is the furnace on the fritz again?"

Claire stood up, clutching the mohair around her. The chair behind her rocked to a stop. "I was beginning to feel a little chilly too." She went to the thermostat. "You're right. It's only sixty-two. Oh I hope we're not going to have furnace problems again." She moved the dial. "I'll set it up and see what happens."

"I'll go see if the furnace came on." Romy left the room and made her way to the basement. The light was dim. She didn't want to get pissed off. She didn't want to have a fight with her mother. The furnace was quiet and cold. She didn't want to spend Sunday in a cold house either.

Back upstairs she said, "It's not working. Why don't I drive over and get Wolf? He could at least tell us whether he can fix it or whether we have to call the service man." She picked up her coat from the couch where she'd left it.

"Wolf's gone," said Claire. "He went home." She approached Romy as though to touch her.

Romy stepped backwards.

"It was his family. His father's health is getting worse. He talked to his mother last night and she asked him to come home."

Romy felt stillness inside where a cold breeze stirred, as during the onset of a storm.

Claudine said brightly, "If I'd been you, I wouldn't have gone off to Bloomington without taking him along. A hunk like that."

Romy stared.

"If you don't make the most of your opportunities, you'll be a widow the rest of your life."

"You met Wolf?"

"Of course I met Wolf. He was busy cleaning the icebox when I arrived. On a Saturday night, cleaning the icebox. I thought right then, what kind of a daughter have I got, that she would walk out on a man that gorgeous."

Romy began to take steps, careful steps, like a cat with ears laid back getting just the right distance between herself and the intruder cat. "What did you say to him? What did you do?" Her breath came in short sniffs.

Claudine looked hurt. "What do you think I did? I chatted with him, that's all. You have no right to be jealous."

"Are you crazy?" Romy stalked Claudine, who was sitting still. "I just want to know how you acted. What did you say to him?"

"Why, I acted the way I always act."

"That's what I was afraid of."

"Oh, and I told him that if he ever got back this way to stop in and visit me in Indianapolis."

"And you're crazy enough to think he would! Well he won't. Not any more than my father did after you drove him away!"

Claudine rose, angry herself now. "Your father, if you'll recall, ran around on me the whole time we were married, and even so, I didn't drive him away."

"You did! The way you act would drive anybody away. You're a horrible person. You pick and tear at people. You never have a good word, never a bit of encouragement. No wonder he ran around. Around and around, and finally out the door for good. It's your fault I didn't have a father. And I hate you for it. And now you swoop down here like some ugly bird with claws and drive away somebody I was just getting to know." Rage washed over Romy. Afraid of her own violence, she went to the door, still carrying her coat. "I'm going to Heather's to get Nancy," she told Claire. "And then we're going to a movie." She turned again to her mother. "And when I get back here, you'd better be gone." She slammed the door behind her.

Matricide was a crime. She didn't want to end up in prison for the rest of her life as a result of a moment's action, no matter how sweet the moment.

JOSIE'S TESTIMONY

The colors and objects in Velma Winters' Friend of the Victim waiting room had been selected to lift the spirits and calm the souls of her clients. Headlight glare from the evening traffic outside was screened from view by pale yellow Venetian blinds that matched the woodwork. A luxurious spider plant hung in front of each window, and a red and white amaryllis on the magazine table was popping its second bloom. Soft incandescent light streamed from corner floor lamps. Comfortable furniture in pastel colors made two friendly groupings, each under a cheery poster. Everything tried to say: "You have a friend here."

But Josie and the adult Flannerys were neither friendly nor cheery as they sat in one of these groupings waiting for their appointment with Velma. Eve, dressed in high heels and a full skirt, and Josie, fidgeting in her parka, were pressed together on a small sofa, while Duncan, in a chair to one side, read the evening paper. His black shoes were shined and his vivid hair disciplined for propriety's sake, but his face was hardened against the message of Velma's decor.

On the wall across the room where they could not fail to see it hung a picture of the rising sun above the words: "Today is the First Day of the Rest of my Life." A disparaging "Pah!" from Duncan had accompanied his impatient gesture as he turned his gaze away from the poster.

Scrunched against Eve, Josie made herself as blank as possible, breathing her mother's complicated odor of cigarettes, Tabu and hair spray, and trying to protect herself from the stormy feeling she always got when she was with both parents at the same time. At home they rarely occupied the same room. There, if Duncan was reading the paper in the living room, Eve would work in the kitchen or go upstairs to watch TV. If Eve had the downstairs TV on, Duncan went to his wood shop in the basement. But here they had to present a unified front on Josie's behalf, and their presence together was overpowering, an inescapable discord, as though Duncan played his part in the key of F-sharp minor while Eve played hers in C major. Josie hummed to drown them out and secretly tapped her middle toes inside her shoes.

None of them wanted to be here. But even Dunk Flannery was susceptible to guilt. Prosecutor Bayer had urged them so strongly to do the right thing and give their daughter the benefit of Velma's services that the elder Flannerys had been bringing her here twice a month since September. Both Eve and Duncan wondered how much longer the obligation would last, neither believing that the sessions were doing Josie any good.

Their first session with Velma had been in early September soon after Eve had called the police and talked to the prosecutor. It was here in Velma's office that Josie had told her story for the record while she was still more or less willing to talk about some of it anyway, when telling was the only way she had to protect herself against the accusation that she was lying.

She was taped reluctantly answering Velma's questions. Her parents looked on and Kathy Greer, a neatly-tailored deputy prosecutor, took notes in the background. Everyone was seated on small chairs in the children's room, where there were paper and crayons, blocks and puppets. Velma's three office cats, two marmalade females and a massive gray-striped tom, played bit parts in this drama, kitty-rumbling and moving from person to person to be petted. Although Kathy Greer was present with notebook and a second pair of sharp eyes to evaluate the story, it was Velma who conducted the questioning. She too was part of the prosecutor's team, the Friend of the Victim.

"No, it wasn't at Meeting, it was after school. I stopped by the Meetinghouse on my way home from school." Although Josie's voice trembled, it was a strong voice, ringing out unexpectedly clear and expressive.

"Where were you in the Meetinghouse?" asked Velma.

"In Corky's room with the books. His office."

"Was the secretary there, Marge? Was Marge there?" Velma, being a Freethinker herself, had the advantage of knowing the people and how to phrase the questions, as well as knowing the story that Eve had already told the prosecutor.

"Hmmm. She sits at that desk outside. That's where she usually was."

"Usually?"

Josie nodded. "I think she was there. She works in the office." Her frightened blue eyes looked pale and pink-rimmed. Although she was trying to shrink into nothing, her flaming hair was so conspicuous that there was no way she could become unnoticed. And, of course, she was fat. Not roly-poly, like some children whose nature it is to be round and cherubic, but awkwardly so, as if the fat were an invasion, an occupation, taking so many resources that she didn't have enough left for much else.

Velma gathered up several puppets and some blocks of various sizes and spread them on the table. "So Marge is outside at her desk like this." She put a lady puppet in a dress on a block-chair, with more blocks suggesting a desk and a partition wall. "And you and Corky are inside his office." She added a man puppet and a little girl in braids. "Was the door closed?"

"Maybe. I don't remember. I think it was open." Josie sat frozen, her determined attention on the gray-striped tomcat rather than on the questioner, as though she could ward off questions by not looking.

"So did you visit Corky more than once?"

"Yes. I went lots of times, especially after Nancy moved here and Heather started liking her better than me."

Velma cast a questioning glance at Eve.

Eve spoke up anxiously. "She calls me at work the minute she gets home from school. They don't like for us to take personal calls, but they know I'd quit if they said anything." Her speech was rapid and breathy. "I want her to have a social life, so I have to let her do things after school. How was I to know it was dangerous for her to stop in at the Meetinghouse? Marge is there. The kids go there all the time and help her put the Bulletin together. How was I to know?" Eve paused. "We should have believed Liz Skinner about Beth last spring, but no one did. Even when they fired Corky, it wasn't because anyone thought he did it. It was other things, plus the bad press. It's just not something people think is true."

Duncan blew his nose loudly.

"You couldn't have known, dear. None of us knew. It's a hard thing to believe about a minister, especially about our own minister." Velma turned again to Josie. "Tell me who Nancy and Heather are."

"Heather used to be my best friend. We walked home from school together and were partners when you have to choose partners. But when Nancy came to live at Corky's, Heather started running around with her."

"There's a little girl living at Corky's?" Velma's voice raised.

"She's a niece of Claire's, I think," Eve answered. "A relative of some kind." Velma's apparent alarm prompted Eve to continue. "Oh, her mother's living there too. She's not alone in the house with them. Though I'd think that Claire's presence would be enough to inhibit any hanky-panky that Corky might try."

Velma shook her head, then turned back to Josie. "So you started going to the Meetinghouse instead of going home. Why did you choose the Meetinghouse? Instead of some place else, the library, maybe?"

"I do go to the library. Lots of times. But Corky said I should come by and visit and help out with things. He said I was really needed."

"You said he read you stories. Where did you sit when he was reading? Here, make the puppets sit the way you and Corky did."

"On the couch." Josie did not touch the puppets."

"Did he sit on the couch too?

"Yes, unless he was walking around. He did that a lot when we acted out the part while he read."

"Um, and were you sitting on his lap?

"Some of the time." The tomcat batted Josie's shoestring. She wiggled the string to entice it further. Her voice was a whisper.

"Show me with the puppets, dear. Here, here's the couch, now show me how you were on Corky's lap." Velma pushed a long block into place with another behind it to make a couch.

Josie flushed in blotches. She glanced at her mother, but Duncan spoke up. "Do what she tells you." So Josie put the man puppet on the couch with the little girl on his lap. Her hands were clumsy as she arranged the skirt and legs and leaned the girl against the man's chest. Duncan pushed forward, anger blooming on his face. He was shushed by little motions from Velma. Then Josie sneaked a look at her father and fixed the man's arms so they encircled the little girl, with the hands together as though holding a book.

"And what happened then?"

"He read a story."

"What story did he read?"

"Which time? I don't remember what particular story. He had a whole book of fairy tales that he read."

"Yes, I know that book." Velma leaned toward Josie in a friendly way. "What fairy tale do you like best?"

"I don't like fairy tales. I like Nancy Drew."

"Oh yes, I did too when I was your age. But Corky likes fairy tales, so you listen, is that it?"

Josie smiled uncertainly, then tried to close her mouth around the teeth that her face had not quite grown into. Her mother flinched at the sight and looked away.

The questioning got more serious. "Tell me what was going on when Corky kissed you."

After a long, painful silence, Josie said, "We were probably acting out 'The Sleeping Beauty.'"

"Show me with the puppets."

Josie placed the little girl puppet on the couch with the man kneeling beside it. "Beauty pricked her finger with a spindle and went to sleep for a hundred years," she said in a singsong voice, as though reading. She glanced down shyly and frowned. "I was embarrassed to be Beauty, but Corky said it was all right, that I was beautiful in the way that Beauty was. He said the story's not about being a prom queen." She was quiet for a moment, her face turned away, her hair so bright it appeared to glow from within. "And when the hundred years are up, the prince finds her."

"And then he kissed you?"

The man puppet bent over the little girl and pressed his face against hers. Kathy Greer wrote furiously in her notebook. Josie's own face was again blotchy as she mashed the one puppet's face down on the other's.

"That's a pretty long kiss," said Velma.

Josie nodded miserably. "It takes a long kiss to wake Beauty. She's awfully sound asleep."

"How did you feel about it?"

The girl swallowed convulsively. Then she said, almost inaudibly. "It scared me." She gulped again and put her face in her hands.

Velma spoke in a comforting tone. "It scared you then, dear, but you're safe now."

"He's too old to be the prince." Josie murmured behind her palms. "He smells old."

As though for the benefit of the imagined audience listening to the tape, Velma said indignantly, "People may think a kiss doesn't mean much, but when it's the awakening, it stays with a girl forever, smell and all."

Josie was crying awkwardly and trying to stop. It took several minutes of hugging and reassurance from Eve before the questioning could resume.

"Was it when he kissed you that he breathed funny?"

Josie nodded.

"How did he breathe? Can you do it the way he did?"

She wrinkled her nose. "Kind of like snores," she said. She took a long, noisy inhalation and let it out like an out-of-shape jogger.

"And then what happened?"

"Beauty woke up and married the prince." A ruined look passed over her face before she hid behind her hands again.

Everyone was quiet.

Velma spoke gently. "I mean what happened between you and Corky."

"Nothing else happened," she said urgently. "I told you, that's all that happened. That was the end of the story. I said I'd better go home and do my homework and he said he'd better get some work done or he'd get fired again."

"Did he touch you?"

Josie shrugged that she didn't know. "I guess so."

"I'm sorry, dear, but you do understand, don't you, that I have to keep asking you questions?" Velma took from the shelf a booklet, which she opened to a picture of two children, a boy and a girl, in swimsuits. "You're safe here, so don't hold anything back. We need to know everything that happened. Did he touch you on any places that a swimsuit would cover?"

"Well, I sat on his lap, so I was touching him where a swimsuit would cover."

"With his hands, Josie. I'm sorry. Did he touch you with his hands?"

"Maybe a little. He moved me around on his lap, like to get comfortable."

A significant look passed between the adults. "How long did it take him to get comfortable?"

"I don't know. A while."

"Did he ever ask you to touch him?"

"No!" The girl looked terrified at the question. She spoke quickly to cover her fear. "Except that he always asked if I wanted to sit on his lap while he read."

"And did you want to?"

"No!" Josie hesitated. "I'm too big to sit on people's laps."

"How about the breathing? Did he breathe funny when you were on his lap?"

Josie nodded yes and made a face.

"What did you do?"

"I pretended like I didn't notice. You're not supposed to notice when people make funny noises."

"That's a good, polite girl, but sometimes people won't stop doing things that bother you unless you let them know you *do* notice and don't like it."

Josie nodded miserably. "Corky's my friend."

"Did Corky ever ask you to take off your clothes?"

The girl shook her head.

"You have to answer in words, dear, for the tape."

She murmured, "No."

"And did he ever take off any of his?"

She shook her head again, but less certainly. "No."

"You don't seem quite so sure of that. There's nothing to be afraid of now. Tell us what clothes he took off."

After a long hesitation she answered. "He showed me his scar once, but he didn't really take anything off."

This bit of testimony was obviously news to Duncan. "What scar was that?" he asked harshly.

"His appendicitis scar."

"What?" he exclaimed.

Velma fended him off and reached for the man puppet, which was still kneeling over Sleeping Beauty, the long wake-up kiss now askew. "Show us on the puppet what he showed you."

Josie unbuttoned the puppet's pants to show its abdomen.

"Did you see his penis too?" She gave a swift, stern glance to Duncan, whose chair was scraping the floor noisily.

"I think so," the child whispered.

"It's all right, dear," said Velma, still holding Eve at bay. "You didn't do anything wrong."

Josie's expression indicated otherwise.

But Velma reassured her. "Corky is a grown-up and you're still a little girl. Whatever wrong was done was his fault, not yours." Josie did not seem comforted. Velma went on, as though to get this finished before Eve went to pieces or Duncan started breaking furniture. "Did he touch his penis? Or ask you to touch it?"

"No!" She squinched her eyes. "He was making a big effort to keep it covered and still show me the scar. So I pretended I didn't notice that it was there. I didn't want to embarrass him."

"That's typical molester behavior," Velma burst out. "Getting the child to worry about *his* feelings and ignore her own." She opened another booklet. This time the picture she found was of two penises, one standing out erect, the other small and limp. "Which one of these penises did it look the most like?

"I didn't see much. He was trying to keep it covered up."

"He was trying to make you *think* he wanted it covered up, but you can be sure he intended for you to see it."

"I didn't see much."

"I know, dear. Of the part you did see, could you tell us which it was most like? It's important."

"What I saw was mostly hair." But the open book was still there, so Josie closed her eyes and started to point. Duncan pounded his fist into the palm of his hand. But her finger never reached the picture. She opened her eyes and said, "I don't remember." She looked as though she might vomit.

"It's all right, Josie. You have done absolutely nothing wrong. You're a brave girl, and telling us this may keep some other little girl from having to go through an experience like that. Now try to remember. It could be important."

"I didn't see much. I was looking away."

Velma yielded. "Maybe you'll remember more later. Tell me, did anything else happen then?"

"No!" said Josie urgently. "Nothing else happened. I keep telling you."

There were a few more questions, but the interview gleaned nothing more of substance. It finally came to an end. In subsequent sessions Josie would quit talking as soon as the questioning began. It looked as though a Class C felony would be the most that Corky could be charged with, if that, though Prosecutor Bayer instructed Velma to keep trying for more information, which she did.

Now Velma's inner office door opened and a woman exited, a gray woman in a gray coat. Only the red feather on her lapel matched the cheeriness of the room.

Velma, healthy and large by comparison, came out right behind her, warm in maroon and rose. "Welcome, welcome, dear people," she boomed to the Flannerys. "Josie, come in and let's get started." To the parents she said, "I'll be with you shortly."

The children's room furniture was similar in tone to that of the waiting room, only scaled down small, too small, actually, for Josie. The cats were curled up asleep, the two orange ones together in one of the soft chairs, the tom alone in a corner. "What would you like to play with this evening?"

Josie did not hasten to any of the toys or even the cats but stood silently by the door. She was dressed in jeans and big padded shoes, and although she still wore her parka with the hood tied around her face, she seemed cold.

When Velma asked, "How have things been going for you?" Josie turned away without answering. Thinking it was possible that the child hadn't heard the question, Velma repeated it. There was no response.

After a moment she said, "So that's how it is." She went to the table and opened a box of crayons. "These are brand new," she said. "Nice sharp points. Maybe you could draw what your feelings would look like."

Josie, lumpish and intent on the vinyl under her feet, was the very picture of a young victim, designed to attract blows. Velma took note of her own impulse to shake her.

"I'm going to talk with your parents for a while. You're welcome to play with anything you see here. I'll be back soon." She closed the door behind her.

Josie might well be mistrustful, given the ambiguity of Velma's position. Being a "Friend of the Victim" meant providing support and counseling as well as direction to any needed legal advice. But because she was on the prosecutor's payroll, she was a psychological double agent, so to speak, even though her sentiments were with her clients. It was a hard fence to straddle. She had to give herself continual pep talks to convince herself that her clients were really better off when their attackers went to court, that there really was such a thing as Justice, under which wrongs were actually redressed.

To complicate matters further in Josie's case, Velma's association with the Freethinkers gave her a personal ax to grind. She was not only acquainted with both victim and perpetrator but had allied herself with the pro-Corky faction in the days before the child molesting scandal had broken. She cared not a whit that he was scatterbrained; she wished there were more like him. Being ineffective kept a person from making more than his share of trouble, she thought. But messing around with little girls was something else, and Velma felt all the more offended by it because she had always liked and trusted Corky.

Thus she had her own confused feelings to cope with.

She escorted Eve and Duncan into the adults' consulting room.

This room was filled with floor pillows and mats instead of chairs. Eve took off her high heels to sit in a bean bag, but Duncan simply crossed his legs and folded himself to the floor, still dapper.

Both were wordless. Eve was trying heed Duncan's admonition to avoid "running off at the mouth". Duncan himself would be damned if he was going to get involved in this bullshit. Velma, after waiting for several long moments, asked them, too, how things had been going since last time.

"You told us to make sure Josie talks about what happened," said Eve, "but it's getting so she'll hardly talk at all, let alone about that."

Velma nodded. "It's the last thing she's going to want to talk about."

"I can't help being worried about her. She's so quiet. Not like herself at all. You know, when she was a baby, she had a wonderful personality, but now she's downright sullen."

Velma turned to Duncan. "Does she talk to you?"

"She never did talk to me. Her mother's got her all sewed up."

Eve's gesture negated his words.

"Never?" Velma asked. "Tell me how that happened."

Duncan ran long fingers through his bright, thick hair. "I'd just opened the shop when Jo was born." he said. "Evie glommed onto her and I never saw her again."

"We hadn't been in Portville very long. I didn't know a soul. And there was Dunk at the shop day and night and me with a new baby. What was I supposed to do, stick her under the hood of a car so he'd notice her? He didn't have time for her but I did. She was all I had."

"And that hasn't changed?" Velma asked Duncan.

"They're like Siamese twins."

"If you'd wanted a relationship with her, you had every opportunity."

He shrugged.

"Is she getting along in other respects? Is she sleeping well?"

"Too well," said Eve. "She never wants to get up when I wake her in the morning. She says she's sick. She says her throat hurts and can she stay home today. And then I have to worry about her throat because of her singing."

"Singing?"

"She takes singing lessons." A proud smile wiped the worry off Eve's face for a moment. "And piano. Her teacher says she's gifted." Then gloom settled in again. "She has to take care of her throat. If she's going to be fat, she'll have to make the most of everything else she's got."

Velma held her tongue. "Could she stay in bed later? Maybe she needs more rest."

"I let her sleep till the last minute, but I have to go to work and she has to go to school."

Velma nodded.

"She used to like school, and she always did well, she's a smart girl, but now she's constantly harping on how bad it is, how she doesn't feel well in school, her stomach is upset, she has to go to the nurse."

"That's not unusual. It wouldn't hurt to let her stay home occasionally. She could make up her lessons."

"I'd have to lay off work."

"Oh yes. Well, I'm trying to think of ways for her to have some satisfying experiences. That's as important as working on the problem itself."

"One thing she likes is going over to the nursing home. Of all places. There's a woman there who's nice to her, so she goes over after school pretty often."

"Make the most of it."

"I'm just thankful we found out soon enough to keep anything really bad from happening."

"It's hard to tell what's really bad to a child. For one thing, they rarely tell the whole story. They're frightened and ashamed, and their greatest desire is to forget about it."

Duncan spoke up. "That's my greatest desire too. Isn't coming here supposed to give her some perspective? I don't mean that what the son-of-a-bitch did was okay, but the way she's acting, you'd think it was the end of the world. It seems to be getting worse, not better."

"Sometimes it takes years to heal a wound like this."

"I'm sure it does, especially when you keep picking away at it. Doesn't there ever come a time to put it behind you and forget about it?"

"Josie's not going to forget about this, not in her bones. And if she forgets consciously, it'll be the worse for her. That's what usually happens, you know. The child is told to forget about it, and she does. Then it works its poison underneath."

Duncan snorted. "No one would forget something as noticeable as this. That's ridiculous."

"Remember how Josie said she knew she wasn't supposed to notice? And how she was already starting to forget? It happens, Duncan, it happens. Very often. The experience is so traumatic that the victim forgets about it. That's what we're up against."

He shrugged in disbelief. "Well, you said we're supposed to be honest in here about what we think, and what I think is that we're stuck in a routine that's not doing any good. Back when you shot the son of a bitch that fondled your daughter, people got over their troubles."

"It's your and Eve's decision how to handle this. I can't guarantee anything."

"What can I say?"

Eve interrupted nervously. "The molesting isn't the only thing that worries me. I'm worried about all this weight she's put on the last year. She's way too big for her age. I've got her on a diet, but she eats on the sly."

Velma winced and answered in a neutral tone. "You want the best for her, I'm sure. She's probably worried, herself, about the changes in her body. If you worry too, it could get exaggerated from being a difficulty she has to deal with into a lifetime calamity."

"Yes," exclaimed Eve. "That's exactly what I'm worried about. That if we don't catch it early and get her weight down, she's going to saddled with it all her life. She goes to LOVELY YOU with me, and I've seriously considered something more than just the diet, but Dunk won't hear of it. Once those fat cells take hold, there's only one way to get them off permanently, and I say why wait?"

Duncan's face was a storm. "That's the dumbest thing I ever heard of, these women getting hunks of themselves sliced off and other hunks added on. And her wanting to do it to a nine year-old child!"

"She does seem a little young."

"Well, I say take care of it while there's still a chance for her. It's perfectly safe. There's no reason to let it go."

"It's one more asshole thing you're thinking up," said Duncan. "Trying to make a floozy out of her!" He turned to Velma. "Do you know what Evie did? She took Jo to dentists all over town trying to get someone to pull out some of her teeth. Fortunately they laughed her out of the office, but she'd have done it if she could."

"Getting a second opinion isn't going to dentists all over town! He's living in the Dark Ages. He doesn't understand what modern technology can do to improve people's lot in life. People don't have to live with deformities any longer."

"Jo doesn't have deformities! She has *teeth*, for God's sake."

"He just doesn't understand what it means to be a girl."

Velma inserted a question. "What does it mean?"

"It means you have to take care of yourself. The standards are higher for a girl. She has to look her best. You and I know that you can't just sell your product, you have to sell *yourself* to get ahead, and packaging is important. What good will her singing do her if she can't get the roles? We may not approve of it or like it, but that's the way it is, folks. And I don't want my daughter to grow up with three strikes against her."

But Duncan had something to say too. "I hold Evie responsible for what happened. If she hadn't filled Jo's head with ideas about boys and romance and how she has to look, I think Jo would have had the good sense not to let Corky slobber all over her."

"Whoa," said Velma. "There are always things we can think of, that if they hadn't been that way, it wouldn't have happened. You know Eve didn't want Josie to go through what she went through any more than you did."

"I'm not at all sure of that. If a mother really cares about what happens to her kids, she stays home and takes care of them."

"How can you say that? This isn't 1954."

"We're supposed to be honest about our feelings here, right? Well, that's what I'm doing, being honest. It's not like you *have* to work. The shop brings in enough we could get by just fine. You go to work and leave her to run the streets, and you try to dress her up for the boys, and it's not boys her own age you're trying to dress her for, because boys that age don't care. And now you want to put her through surgery to take fat off of her. Next thing you'll want to add fat and give her boobs when she's ten. Well, you put all that together, and you're asking for trouble. She's fair game for dirty old men."

Velma spoke firmly. "No one is fair game for dirty old men. Dirty old men have to learn to keep their hands to themselves and their pants zipped up. I hear what you're saying, both of you, that you're worried about your daughter. The blame has to go somewhere, doesn't it? When we're stressed out, we often lay it on the person nearest and dearest."

"Yes, it's all my fault, isn't it?" said Eve. "He never gives a thought to his own part in this. All he can think of is to threaten *me*."

"Oh?"

But Eve quieted down. "He just doesn't like for me to work. I stayed home with Josie until she started school, and Dunk got spoiled, having dinner on the table when he got home and never having to help out."

"I help out, but I draw the line at cooking."

Velma, eager to leave the bickering and attend to Josie, brought the session to a close. "Think this week about what Josie's being fat means to you, Eve. Your own feelings about it. We'll talk some more next time." Duncan, she noted, looked less than enthusiastic about another appointment. It was time, she thought, to refer them to a family therapist.

They all struggled up from the floor. The Flannerys sat down again in the waiting room while Velma went to the children's room.

Josie had taken her parka off and used some of the blocks to build a pretend cage for one of the orange cats. The other two were stretched out nearby, watching the caged one intently, with their ears forward and their tails twitching. The girl stiffened when Velma entered the room. The cat leaped out of the cage and hissed at the other two.

Josie picked it up and held it close. "They're mean, aren't they?" she murmured into the cat's fur. "Two against one." The cat struggled free and settled into a vigorous washing of its paws and ears.

Velma lowered herself onto the floor among the blocks left over from the cage.

Josie watched.

Velma waited, counting on the rapport built up in previous sessions.

Finally Josie spoke. "I don't want to talk about Corky."

"What *would* you like to talk about?"

Josie thought about it while the cat rubbed the side of its face vigorously. "Everybody talks about Corky. It's all about how terrible Corky is. Nobody cares about *me* and how I feel."

"How *do* you feel?"

"I feel picked on, that's how. Everybody picks on me. At school it's Heather and Nancy and at home it's either Mother or Daddy."

"What do they pick on you about?"

"Heather and Nancy make fun of me and say mean things."

"What kind of mean things?"

"Oh I don't know. They call me things and they sing mean songs."

"That hurts, doesn't it? Especially when it's someone who used to be your friend."

With her head down and her attention on the cat, Josie nodded miserably. The front of her hair had been cut into bangs since last time, and they straggled above her sad face.

"Does your mother know?"

Josie nodded again. "It's my own fault."

"Oh?"

"She says I don't have to be this fat."

"What do you think?"

"I don't know." She shrugged. "I guess I don't. I try to stay on my diet, but I just can't. Nobody else in fourth grade has to go on a diet. It's not fair." Her hand clapped over her mouth. She giggled behind it. "I almost said that Corky told me nothing's fair, that life's never fair."

"But we're not going to talk about Corky tonight, are we?"

"He's wrong about that. Life's fair for some people."

"What people?"

"Well, Nancy for one. Her looks are perfect. She's got pretty clothes. Everybody likes her. Except me, and I hate her."

"Do you have pretty clothes?"

"No! How can I have pretty clothes when I'm this fat?"

Velma exaggerated a questioning look. "What's being fat got to do with having pretty clothes?"

Josie gave her a pitying glance. "They don't make pretty things in my size. And even if they did, no matter how pretty it was, it would be ugly in a big size. Mother says she'll buy me two new skirts if I lose ten pounds, but she hates to waste clothes on me when I'm still this fat."

Velma twisted her hands as though she had Eve by the neck.

"I'd better lose the ten pounds." Josie said.

"I'm wondering if we couldn't find someone to help you make some clothes of your own. You're probably old enough to learn to sew simple things. Would you like that?"

"I may not be allowed to do that."

"Why not?"

"I don't know. But I have to stay out of trouble."

"How could learning to sew get you in trouble?"

"I don't know. But I didn't have any idea that going to the Meeting-house was going to get me into this much trouble either."

"Josie, learning to sew is perfectly safe."

Josie nodded. "But you never know, do you? Trouble can be any-where."

"I see," she said. "You have to stay out of trouble."

Josie nodded.

"And you aren't sure how when even your minister can bring trouble upon you?"

She nodded again.

"But you didn't do anything to get in trouble over Corky. He was the one, not you."

Here Josie disagreed. "I told. That's what made all the trouble. I told Heather and she went and ratted on me. So part of it's her fault too, only she didn't get in any trouble."

"Why did you tell Heather instead of your parents?"

"I didn't want my parents to know!"

"So you don't tell your parents when you need help?"

She shook her head.

"Who helps you then, if you can't tell your mama or your daddy?"

"I try not to need anybody to help me. If I stay out of trouble, I won't need anybody to help me. Then I don't have to worry."

"Sounds rough," said Velma. She grabbed a chair and used it to pull herself up from the floor. "May I try to arrange sewing lessons for you? I'll make it okay with your parents."

Josie nodded uncertainly.

"Good. And if you ever want to talk to me extra, even if you don't have an appointment, you can call or come in. Do you understand?" She felt in her pocket for a business card.

Josie nodded.

"This has both of my phone numbers on it. Hang onto it, and if you feel like you'd like someone to talk to, you can call me. If nobody answers here, call me at home. Okay?"

"Okay. Thanks." Josie tucked the card in her pocket.

Velma followed her outside to where her next client was waiting. Eve and Duncan were sitting on opposite sides of the room, each reading a magazine. Velma told them what she had proposed to do and got their permission to talk with the seamstress she had in mind. "Same time next week?" She wrote the appointment in her book.

But Duncan Flannery won on the issue of letting things drop. Eve, believing that Velma had gone completely wacky asking her to concentrate on her feelings about having a fat daughter instead of on how to cure the fatness, began to see his point. These sessions weren't really helping. The Flannerys cancelled the next one and did not bring Josie back.

SANTA'S LETTER

It was now late afternoon. Josie was at home in her living room struggling to write the perfect letter to Santa that would say just what she wanted it to. Not that she believed in Santa. It was too bad but Santa Claus was just a myth. Writing the letter, however, was the way to tell her parents what she wanted for Christmas without sounding greedy.

She had to get the letter just right or it wouldn't come true.

She was sitting in an outgrown little rocking chair that she had retrieved from the basement just a few minutes ago. Her father had glued it back together again the last time she popped the joints, and she'd left it down there with the Goodwill stuff until now. She'd been afraid its days were over. But writing to Santa was a task that felt all wrong sitting at the dining room table. So she had fetched up her chair, and if she slid in from the front instead of down from above, she could still squeeze herself between the little wooden arms. Scrunched in that way so close to the floor, her denim-covered knees stuck up high.

Toys were out, she decided. There was no point wasting a wish on toys. Her mother would buy her another doll whether she asked for it or not, and stuff for Barbie. Her father would give her quarters, some of them wrapped in foil like a Hershey Kiss and strung together with the cranberries and popcorn that her parents put on the Christmas tree for old times' sake. He saved his quarters all year for this gift. She had checked the jug every so often to see how it was coming along. It was getting pretty full. With this money she could pick out what she wanted after Christmas.

Last year she had waited to see what toys Heather got before she chose her own. Eve took the two of them to the toy store and she had Heather's help spending all those quarters.

This year there was no point thinking what would appeal to Heather or what the other kids would want to come to her house to play with. Nobody but Leslie came over to play any more. Nothing was fun to play with Leslie.

She had to think about what she wanted just for herself.

Now she rocked, being careful with the little chair. Her letter paper was fastened to a clipboard. She had drawn a Santa at the top like a logo. To further invoke Christmas she was wearing a silk poinsettia in her hair.

The TV was turned on. She rocked the chair in time to the lead-in to *Vampire Love*. But even though she liked this program she was not paying much attention to it today.

What would she like to have, just for herself?

Her mental video screen went blank. The only thing that was really fun to do alone was read. But even that was soured by the social failure it implied. "Books," she wrote. Books were at least better than TV. You could stop and think without missing anything and you could go back over the good parts. But then she erased "books" and put the clipboard down to rock the chair, nose to knee, and back. She didn't really want to waste a wish on books either. Library books were better. Library books took you away for a while, but you didn't have to read them over and over like you did your own.

The knees of her jeans smelled like school. Like kneeling on the floor in the girls' bathroom where she had to throw up this morning. The floor had smelled antiseptic from the cleaning stuff they use. Now the knees of her jeans still carried that faint odor. This morning she had thought maybe she was getting hard core sick, but it had made her feel better to kneel there touching the cold porcelain and throw up.

On TV the vampire was already working toward today's meal. You could tell when they put Lady Helena in danger that it was really going to be the maid that died. They could always get another maid. She would be the one the vampire bit and sucked dry.

Josie thought about a dog. A dog would really be good to have, but only if it was the right kind. The thought of letting either of her parents choose a dog for her was pretty chilling. Her mother would want a Pomeranian or a toy poodle, something horrid and fluffy and little, and her father would want something mean that showed its gums a lot. She didn't mind seeing a dog's *teeth* Their *teeth* showed when they smiled. But if you saw their gums too, it meant they were snarling. What she wanted was a friendly dog that smiled a lot.

A dog would be good, but it was still just a substitute for the real thing. It was probably the best she could do though. What was important in the letter was to make the dog was the easiest thing on the list. The objection her parents always raised on the dog issue was how much trouble a dog would be to take care of, but if she asked for a horse, the dog wouldn't seem so bad.

Actually, she didn't even want a horse. People who had horses had to keep them out in the country. They had to go visit their horse. Wasn't that amazing? What good was a horse you had to make an appointment with? There was no way either of her parents was going to have time to take her to visit a horse out in the country, and brush it and all the things you had to do.

Anyway, what she really wanted was someone to play with, not something to take care of. A brother. A twin brother.

Yep, she was right about the vampire. Lady Helena's neck was being shown close up to mislead the audience. They always mislead the audience about who the victim will to be. Showing Lady Helena's neck meant the maid was about to get it. They mislead about who the vampire is too. You never really find out. It could even be Lady Helena herself.

Somebody on her side, in her own house. Like an ally. That's what she needed, an ally! There was nothing in the world as good as that. That's what a brother would be.

There would be the two of them together and they would do things that were just fun-fun, like build a tree house, not the everlasting things that are supposed to improve you disguised as fun, like singing lessons to cultivate your voice and swimming lessons to slim you down. Like camp, especially fat camp, where she was going to have to go next summer if she didn't get the weight off before then. She was still too young for Miss Adeline's Dancing School, thank goodness, where you got vastly improved if you lived through it. But her mother had already started to talk it up, how much fun it would be and all. Boys had to learn how to do things and it was probably hard for them too, but at least some of the things they learned were *useful*, not just things to improve them and make them pretty. And girls who had brothers got to learn some of the useful things that boys knew how to do like build a tree house.

Girls who had brothers with them for protection also got to go places outside the neighborhood to play, like to Angels' Park where the rides were or to the dunes near the beach, instead of having to stay close to home like a baby.

If you have a brother and your parents are in a fight, you can go out in the tree house and get away from all their noise and dirty looks. And if the kids treat you mean, the brother helps you beat the shit out of them! He might get bawled out for fighting, but everybody knows that the bawling out is just a formality, that boys are *supposed* to fight when somebody picks on them. They're also supposed to fight when someone picks on their sister! And they don't get bawled out both for fighting and for being unladylike.

But kids aren't mean to girls who have brothers. They don't dare be. And other girls like to come to your house to play because the brother is there too. He's somebody who shows off while they all pretend to ignore him. Somebody for your girlfriends to think about for when they get older.

And if something terrible happened to you, you could tell your brother about it and he would stand up for you. "Nobody's going to do that to my sister!" In the first place, he would *believe* you. He wouldn't sing, "Liar, Liar," at you. And he wouldn't tell you it was your own fault. He wouldn't tattle and bring down the whole world on you. He would be on *your* side. He would be your *ally*, somebody on your side right here in your own house!

Like Hansel and Gretel. When Gretel's wicked stepmother didn't want to feed her any longer, she had a brother who was right there with her. And when her parents put her out in the woods to starve to death, if it hadn't been for Hansel, Gretel would have just laid down and died. Hansel was the one who knew the path through the woods. If Gretel had been alone at the witch's house, she'd have been the one in the cage being fattened up to eat and wouldn't have been able to push the witch in the oven.

Josie retrieved the clipboard from the floor. "Dear Santa," she wrote. "I hope you have not gained any more weight this year. Tell

Mrs. Santa to take the skin off the chicken and buy you sugar-free soda pop."

That ought to put her mother in a good mood.

Her father was tougher. "Keep the sleigh oiled and the runners waxed," she tried. "And be careful in shopping malls. You're asking for trouble holding all those kids on your lap."

The glimpse of Santa Claus that came unbidden to her eyes, Santa with his pants unzipped, was so ugly and gross – like the pit full of rattlesnakes and the heroine hanging over it by the thumbs – that she dropped the clipboard again and rocked the little chair all the way back onto the ends of its rockers. And the smell! Oh-oh. The loud crack she heard told her that the chair had popped its joints again. It always broke when she went ass over teakettle in it. She never learned, did she?

Carefully she righted the chair. It would be okay if she didn't rock. And rocking made her feel funny. She was feeling a little funny anyway. Like she might throw up again. She had eaten potato chips from the drugstore on the way home from school. Maybe she would feel better if she threw up. Food gets gross after you chew and swallow it. It's better to get rid of it.

Uncertainly, with rubbery knees, she went into the bathroom and raised the seat on the toilet. Maybe she *was* coming down with something. Maybe she wouldn't have to go to school tomorrow. She twisted her hair and tucked it into her collar, then felt the poinsettia fall to the floor. She knelt and bowed her head.

The toilet was cold. *Think about something gross. Look down there in the water and see a big mouthful of something totally disgusting. Chewed food or something full of little white garbage worms. Then act like you're gagging.*

It took no time at all. When it was over and the toilet flushed, she felt clean. It was a good feeling, a washed-clean feeling, a triumph.

In the mirror her face looked pale. She pulled her hair out of her collar and pinched her cheeks to bring back the color, then returned to the living room.

Holding that clean feeling close she continued her letter. "You may think I'm too old to write you a letter, but I'm not as old as I look. I'm only nine and I don't want you to bring me grown up woman things! Ha Ha!"

But this was edging over into a magical belief in a *real* Santa Claus who was like he was supposed to be. She must remember who would actually be reading this letter.

She put on a sugary face to go with what she was writing. "Bring my mother a pink parka with real fur that will show off how pretty she is. And a Jaguar for Daddy with its own special bay at Import Service for when it has to be worked on all the time."

Santa Claus would be interested in the state of the world. "Take plenty of candy to the terrorists to sweeten their disposition. And some bags of bread crusts for the ducks to get them through the winter." Feeding the ducks on Fingerling Pond was a duty she attended to religiously. She took stale bread to them every afternoon first thing when she got home. They couldn't survive Portville winters without help from people like her.

With all the polite parts written, she started on the nitty-gritty. "I only want three things this Christmas. One, a brother. Not a baby brother, one my own age. If you brought me a brother and left him under the Christmas tree, my parents couldn't very well send him back. They'd have to adopt him. That's my first wish."

"My second wish is a horse. Brown with a little white is best, but I would take any color except gray. And some bales of hay to feed it."

"My third wish is a dog. I'd rather have a puppy, but a grown dog is okay if there aren't any puppies available."

She signed the letter, "Jo Flannery," deciding to go by that name now. She was sick and tired of being Josie. "Jo" at least *sounded* tough. She kind of liked it when the weird old guy at the school crossing called her "Jo." Sometimes she ran even when she didn't have to, just to make him yell at her.

Leaving *Vampire Love* to play on without her, she carried the little chair back to the basement and put it where she found it, where her mother was collecting things for the Goodwill. Its days were over for sure. It was pretty sad, but she knew better than to ask her father to fix it again.

WRITER'S BLOCK

Fred's freelance writing had become stuck, mired in a shallow, stagnant pond. His difficulties did not lie in the drugstore this time or in Sara's problems. They lay in himself and his own problems. He was able to get away from the store every day at noon, but even the library he loved felt more and more inhospitable as the days went by and the swamped work smelled worse and worse. He no longer bothered to keep dibs on his typing cubicle by removing and taking with him to the men's room one of the essential metal rods from the typewriter. He stayed out of the cubicle much of the time and let the teenagers have it for their homework, while he went from table to table in the different rooms trying to align himself to the voice of his Muse, to position himself at the spot where she could come in loud and clear.

But she wasn't coming in loud and clear. She wasn't coming in at all. The Muse waves were jammed with wet noises and even an occasional evil-voiced threat, such as "If you don't get cracking, you'll have to give the writing up," followed by, "and then who will you be?"

Indeed, who *would* he be if he gave the writing up? The all-too-visible answers to this terrifying question slouched and dozed all around him. Becalmed and drifting aimlessly, these men without jobs or goals filled the library, reading the paper, walking disconsolately from Business to Periodicals and back again, as though somewhere in this repository of words they might find and reclaim their lives.

What separated Fred from the pathetic men around him was the paper on which he wrote and his degree of separation depended upon putting words on that paper. If the words were not there, he was no better than they were.

During all the years he'd had a job he had been able to walk past such men and say to himself, "There but for the grace of God," and believe that he somehow merited being one of the favored. Or he could say, "God helps those who help themselves," and believe that he had indeed been the power behind his success.

But now he saw that he had been successful only in fitting himself into the system, which then carried him. He also saw that the energy that had allowed him to help himself was a gift from some source outside his conscious control. He didn't – he couldn't – will it into existence. And now he was more dependent than ever on something other than his own willpower. He was no longer carried by the system. Working alone this way, he was instead "employed" moment by moment, the next moment up for grabs. When words came, he was a writer writing. When they didn't he was just like the rest of these poor souls.

"Unemployed." That's what he had to call himself when the words were withheld. He was too young to call himself retired. His pension check did not justify sitting in the rocking chair. He still had too much in him. And besides, the rocking chair was *boring*.

"Unemployed." That word, like "homeless," defined a person as an undesirable. "One of the unemployed" sounded even worse than "one of the homeless." Both the homeless and the unemployed were part of that larger category, "the worthless." The homeless were at least viewed with a little sympathy, while the unemployed, especially the college-educated unemployed, were thought to have brought their circumstances on themselves and viewed with the special antipathy directed at failures.

The word "failure" was certainly a part of this picture. A few months ago Fred had been able to thumb his nose at being considered a failure by others just because he didn't have a job. "So I'm a failure," he had said to himself, albeit defensively. "Now I can do what I wanna do." But now that he *couldn't* do what he wanted to do, he was faced with being a *true* failure, a failure in his own eyes, and this was a different matter entirely.

Fred's piece, *How to Structure Your Time When Unemployed*, had come back. The magazine editors had decided not to use it after all. To a pro this would have been no more than an irritation – all in a day's work. But Fred was not a pro. He was marginal, a "would-be," and getting ever closer to a "won't-be."

Reading the manuscript again before starting over with the query process Fred saw how useless it was. Selling it would not make it less so. It was fodder to keep the publishing industry and its jobs and reputations intact, not worth cutting a single branch from a single tree for the paper to print it on. There were hundreds of magazines filled with thousands of such articles: thinner thighs for the women's fantasies, thicker ones for the men's, neither one adding or subtracting a single ounce of actual fat or muscle. *How to Structure* would add nothing to the life of its readers. The only thing that would help one of "the unemployed" was a job. A job that met his needs and used his abilities. The only thing that would help was the personal spark of grace that inspired a person to compete for one of the existing jobs or the societal spark that brought more jobs into existence.

Oh, there *were* jobs, as Sara kept pointing out, but Fred wondered who wanted them. In a valued and nurturing society people get satisfaction even from menial work, because the society itself is perceived as worth it. But the present society, as far as the eye could see, was soulless, overgrown, addicted to self-indulgence, out of balance with its environment and poisoning itself in countless ways. It was no longer enough to be a team player. The team was losing too heavily. In such a milieu one had to find work that was *personally* satisfying, *personally* worth it. Feelings had been stirring in Fred that it was no longer enough to be a cog in a wheel of the great chariot of commerce, not enough to flip hamburgers, sell soap, write claptrap for a mighty Mammon vehicle on a suicide course.

Somewhere in him he knew that it was not enough, though he didn't really realize it yet. He had stopped sending out résumés and had admitted to himself that he'd known all along that sending résumés was not really the way to find a new job. He hadn't really *wanted* any of those jobs, or he'd have gotten one. He knew how to do it. He'd been doing it all his life. Now he wanted something different.

Still he rewrote and readdressed his query letter and dropped it in the mail slot. "You wanna eat, you gotta hustle." It was habit. He had always hustled. Now, although his pension would keep his body fed, his ego still needed feeding. If the only food it could get was the poor thin gruel of selling one more trivial magazine piece for a few bucks, then that was what it had to have. He hoped to do better with the Pearlman story if only his Muse would speak up.

But the Pearlman story was not going well either. Fleeting thoughts about the value of what he was doing had been attacking him here too. What could this story accomplish? The magazines were full of titillation posing as information, greasing the wheel. It was almost as though the chariot of commerce had a canny but one-sided brain seeking to satisfy its insatiable, inhuman appetite, never mind what was used up or crushed beyond use in the process. Sure, the public was aroused against child molesters but what good did it do? Next week the public would be aroused in a different direction and the abuse would go on the same as ever, privately, secretly. The children were not going to benefit from his story. And neither would the reverend, even if he was innocent. So his story got told, who would believe it? And who would care? Any potential benefit would go to the almighty self-absorbed vehicle and to the people who drove it. Even if the present drivers were thunder-bolted from behind the wheel, there was an inexhaustible supply of would-be Apollos high on sniffs of power and waiting for their chance. Thoughts like these sabotaged Fred's efforts but he couldn't keep them at bay.

And if that weren't enough misery, he was even having painful second and third thoughts about the job at Powkin that he had enjoyed for so long. He too had been serving the machine, albeit in his own way, by keeping it running with service manuals and instruction books, enjoying his skill without noticing the vehicle's course.

Take *How to Fix the Air Conditioner*, for instance, one of the many service manuals he had written. Fred had always liked air conditioners. He was old enough to remember summer nights spent on the living room floor because the bedroom was too hot and his bed too sticky to sleep in. He liked physical comfort, which hot muggy air made impossible. So keeping air conditioners fixed had seemed worthwhile to him. But fixing them often meant discharging the Freon and replacing it. Discharging it out into the air. And Freon was bad stuff. It zipped straight up into the atmosphere and gobbled the ozone layer that protected the earth from too much sunlight. Even when the air conditioners worked well enough not to need fixing, they still leaked Freon, especially from cars. And now so many people were out there using so many air conditioners that the ozone layer was being gobbled at an alarming rate. It was becoming thin and holey. Everybody's suntan was catching cancer. The world was getting worse because of the air conditioners that made it better. The thought boggled and depressed Fred.

Looking back on those years at Powkin, maybe they hadn't been so good after all. Maybe he'd been kidding himself, thinking he enjoyed the teamwork. What had he done that was really his? Even the writing projects he'd done outside of Powkin, the how-to articles he'd done for *Popular Mechanics*, drawn on information gleaned from the books he'd worked on for Powkin - these had not really been his. They were all grease for the wheels.

Fred had again abandoned his cubicle and was sitting in his present misery at a table in the alcove of the large second floor room that housed 100-499, Philosophy, Religion, Social Sciences and Languages. He doodled on a tablet to look busy. He shifted his weight to keep from taking root to the chair. His Muse was silent.

Nearby a steam radiator clanked and hissed. He became aware of an odor not usually associated with libraries. The long gray coat draped over the radiator to dry was beginning to smell so bad that Fred wondered if there was some dog hair woven into the wool. He was acquainted with the coat's owner, C.T. John, a lanky and mournful poet. C.T. always worked in this room, writing on yellow tablets, staring from *Lives of the Saints* up to the ceiling, where his gaze would hang for a while among the cobwebs and then fall back to the saints again. Even less successful than Fred, C.T. lived with his aged mother and subsisted on her Social Security plus occasional small contest prizes and arts grants, a part-time teaching job at the psychiatric hospital and fees from readings attended by the few poetry-lovers there were in Portville.

There had been a bright spot in his career, financially speaking, a year ago, when C.T. had obtained a position as Poet in the Schools but it hadn't lasted long. He was unable to cope with the suburban PTA and the school administrators, so he lost the job and moved down the hog again from shanks to knuckles. He could not afford a daily quarter to put his coat in a locker, but he didn't really need to. Not even the destitute would steal C.T. John's smelly coat.

Last summer Fred, in a fit of generosity, had brought an extra sandwich and invited the poet to sit outside on the steps in the sun and eat.

This was soon after he had been replaced as Poet in the Schools for the coming semester.

C.T. had spoken gloomily about his predicament. "I can teach," he said. "I taught the children to write poetry. I teach the crazy people to write poetry. But I can't seem to relate to ordinary adults at all, and they're the ones who do the hiring. Crazy people and children are more like poets than ordinary adults are," he said, swallowing a bite of braunschweiger sandwich. "Their heads are full. Very full. Getting some of the images out onto the paper gives them relief." As he spoke he scratched his head. Flakes of dandruff flew from his thick black hair and settled like images on the shoulders of his tan tee shirt. "But ordinary people have heads full of adding machine tape, you see. The problem is to get rid of the adding machine tape and stock their heads with images like a pantry and then have them open up the cans in the pantry and mix everything around. You'd be surprised how unwilling they are."

"I'm not at all surprised," said Fred. "I hate it when a can in my pantry loses its label and I don't know what I'm going to have for dinner until I open it."

"I don't want to know," said C.T. "I peel the labels off and throw them away."

Fred was no longer sure what they were talking about. "Have you considered trying the greeting card market?" He had still been thinking uncritically in terms of products and markets.

"Of course. I'm not proud." C.T. had stretched his long, matchstick legs down the steps. "I'm willing to try anything. I mow lawns and rake leaves and shovel snow. I work in the fields during the season. I'd be happy to write greeting cards if I could. But when I sit down and think 'greeting card' or 'market', everything in my head disappears and it's as though there are no cans in my pantry. I don't have anything to put on the paper."

Fred remembered the condescension he had felt. He himself had been keeping a portfolio of snappy ideas precisely so that he would never have to face a blank page. "They say greeting cards pay well," he said. "Here, take another half a sandwich."

C.T. shook his head. "You know, Ezra Pound didn't have it so bad, being locked up in St. Elizabeth's writing poetry all those years. Nowadays they shoot them full of thorazine and walk them right back out into the real world. A pity," he said dolefully. He unfolded himself and stood up, looking extremely long and thin, like a walking stick with joints. "Thanks for the lunch."

"My pleasure."

Fred had not brought C.T. a sandwich again. He wouldn't have begrudged him the food, but he had found the conversation disturbing and saw no sense in carrying it any further. You gotta protect your own interests, he thought.

Now he gingerly rearranged the poet's coat on the radiator to dry the other side. Ugh! he thought. Smells like a damn dogsuit. He moved to a different table.

The poet was working on something of his own, no question. Fred knew only vaguely what it was: his magnum opus, a series of formal poems based on the lives of saints. But there was no market for it whatsoever. He'd probably have to publish it himself and would be lucky if he could give away copies even after adding elaborate flattering autographs. That's the way it was when a person did his own thing without respecting the marketplace. Fred shivered.

Still. If the poor slob's mind went blank at the thought of the marketplace, what could he do? If his real life took place in the realm of the saints between the dust-shrouded ceiling and his yellow lined tablet, then that's where he had to live.

Restlessly Fred moved again. This room was one of the somber, dreary ones He rarely used it. Now he went to Periodicals, which was much more lively. More colorful. Not such a high ceiling, not so much dust. Recent issues of the popular magazines were displayed in cutaway boxes on shelves around the wall. He sat down at an empty table.

This was the room he used when he was having fun. Here was where he gathered instances of blame for his *Anatomy*. Here he also collected statistics for a different project, one that tickled his funny bone. He'd had an idea that if he collected enough statistics about illnesses, hazards, disasters and death, he could prove that everyone now alive had already died. Everyone would have already suffered a fatal wound or illness and furthermore, everyone would have to die at least twice and often three or more times to make the statistics add up. The last time Fred sat in this room he had found statistics about radon gas seeping into people's basements. Basements full of radon gas would probably add a good half a death to everybody's life. He had also found a Heritage report declaring that Democrats, not Republicans were actually responsible for the poor getting poorer. This would be a good item for *Anatomy*. He hoped that he could find diversion from his troubles again today.

The previous occupant of the table had left behind several crumpled sheets of paper and some magazines. Fred's lackluster gaze fell on a title, "Is the Corporation Responsible?" He reached for the magazine, feeling his eyes brighten. Sure enough, it wasn't about being responsible at all but about being to blame. Just as he'd suspected. Grist for *Anatomy*. Another polluter. The government spending millions trying to punish someone, the polluter spending more millions trying to avoid punishment, the lawyers fattening their wallets, no one being responsible for *what now*. He read eagerly, scribbling notes on the three-by-five cards he was supposed to fill with information about Corky Pearlman.

How could it be that all the good and noble uses of the word "responsible" were lost? Why was it that the only use currently in favor was the one that meant "to blame?" Whatever happened to the notion that being "responsible" might mean being able to respond to a need? How about the *neutral* connotation of "being responsible for" as "being the *cause* of?" There was little neutrality about it these days. Being the *cause* of something didn't mean being *generative*, it meant being *to blame*.

Fred had been known as a "responsible" boy. He had responded to his mother's need for him to be the man of the house and had done the best he could. When he didn't do very well, he was shown how to do better. He had not been subjected to paternal harshness and criticism, and thus had learned late, in school, rather than early, at home, how to cover his ass. The need to do so was a conscious irritation to Fred, not an unexamined and overriding necessity, as it was with people immobilized by deeply ingrained fear of criticism. He could look with amazement at people's inability to move out from the morass of blame into *what now*.

But the present activity was not furthering the Pearlman project. When Fred caught himself foaming at the mouth over The Way Things

Are, he put his three-by-five cards back in his pocket and did not look for any more magazine articles to feed his interest. Besides, an hour had slipped by while he'd been fooling around, and it was time to prepare for his appointment.

LIBRARY BOOKS AND
COTTON PANTIES

Face it, Fred, he said to himself on the way home that evening.

Face what?

You know what.

Yeah, I guess so.

He drove in the rain, wipers scraping the windshield, not even listening to *All Things Considered*.

It's damned hard to give up on something unless you have something else to replace it, he argued.

But you know it's not gonna work.

I keep hoping.

Shit, man, there comes a time when you gotta cut bait. That interview you did was a fiasco. If nothing else would convince you to hang it up, that ought to.

I been trying not to think about that.

Well, think about it.

Yeah, well.

The interview in question was with Corky Pearlman. It had taken place in the reverend's car in the library parking lot. That morning Fred had prepared for the interview by writing a list of diplomatically worded questions that he hoped would elicit Corky's feelings about such things as little cotton panties. In Corky's actual presence, however, he turned out to be unable either to find or to remember the questions. His failure to get anything worthwhile accomplished was so humiliating that he broke off the talk prematurely, pleading another appointment.

He had invited Corky to meet him at the library, since that was the closest thing he had to an office. He expected to take Corky to his typing cubicle, pull in a second chair and do the interview. He had the metal rod from the typewriter in his pocket to assure himself possession. But

Corky had asked him to wait for him outdoors in the parking lot instead.

The typing cubicle office, like the locker he had learned to jiggle open and closed without paying the quarter, was one of the few perks Fred's life as a freelancer afforded him. He felt no guilt about claiming these perks. The library wouldn't be in business without people like him. The library owed him something.

Sara had overheard him once telling a prospect to come to his office, the typing cubicle. "How can you stand to make such a fool of yourself?" she had asked. "Nobody's going to take you seriously if you act like that. The reality is that you don't have an office any longer. The reality is…"

"That's one of the realities, Sara," he answered. "But why should I dwell on that one? The one that keeps me from getting anything done? Why not expand the definition of an office? An office is a space that you can close off and work in. That's what I do in my office, work. Sometimes I write, sometimes I bring somebody in and close the door and let him talk. If I can oozle a little good humor into my situation, why shouldn't I?"

"Don't you think there's some value in recognizing reality?"
"Dammit, Sara, I *do* recognize reality. I recognize that the only reality anybody knows anything about is the one inside his head. The one he sees or hears. Or hears about. Or feels. Or dreams up. There isn't just a single reality. It's like camera angles. You can move the camera around, can't you? You can higgle with the lens opening, can't you? Control the shutter speed. Why on earth shouldn't I choose the angle of looking at things that's going to help me out? I need all the help I can get. If I keep telling myself I'm a poor schnook without an office to go to, how will I be able to work? As it is, I say I got a nice little office, and then I give a little wink because I know it's funny, and then I go there and work."

"But it's not true!"

"So what? Who knows what's true anyway? All we know is what's in our heads. Who can figure out 'true'? I try to see things from as many angles as I can, and then I choose the one that's gonna help me out the most and I act as if it were gospel. You tell me what's wrong with that."

"You don't care what people think of you at all, do you?"

"Surely to God other people got a sense of humor."

"Not like yours."

Fred was unable to convince her. The argument would come to rest for a while, but it was always there on the back burner ready to heat up again. Sara continued to be dogged about reality.

It had stopped raining, but only momentarily. Fred waited for Corky's arrival in the car, with the engine running for the sake of the heater. The lot was almost empty except for the Bookmobile in its slot and the employees' cars in theirs.

Then Corky's old Chevrolet pulled into the lot. It lumbered uncertainly up the empty aisle as though on every side there were vehicles that had to be dodged. It narrowly missed the only car nearby and came to a stop taking up two spaces on Fred's left. Fred cringed. If anybody could have a wreck in an empty parking lot, he thought, this guy could.

He switched off the ignition and got out to meet Corky.

"Sorry," said Corky, opening his car door. He looked awful, thin and blue-cheeked, under an unbelievable green cap that might have come out of a missionary barrel. "We'll have to stay out here to talk. Come sit in the car where it's warm."

That threw Fred off track immediately. "Okay," he said. Settled inside Corky's Chevrolet he asked, "But why don't you want to go indoors?"

"Oh, I'd love to go indoors," Corky answered, "but they won't let me in."

A picture of Corky chasing schoolgirls around the Children's Room went through Fred's mind. In the mad chase librarians shrieked, books were scattered, their loose pages falling out, and little wooden chairs were overturned. Children ducked under tables. "But you haven't had a trial yet," Fred protested.

"No, no," Corky answered, his doggy smile appearing in spite of it all. "That's not the problem."

"Well, what is the problem?"

"I owe $387 in fines. I'm not allowed inside the library until I bring the books back and pay up."

"Jesus Jumping Jennifer," exclaimed Fred. "How can anybody owe $387 in library fines?"

"By having taken books out and then losing track of them. I know they're around somewhere, either at home or at the Meetinghouse, but I can't lay hands on them, especially the ones at the Meetinghouse, since I'm not allowed there either." He looked anxious, like a child who didn't really understand why he was being punished for something that was beyond his control.

More for the sake of the library, so woefully short of books, than for Corky-the-suspect's sake, Fred offered to take a list of the overdue books to the Meetinghouse next time he went and find whatever ones were there. Enlisted, then as Corky's helper, he found himself unable to move into the role as Corky's inquisitor. His list of questions was nowhere to be found, neither in his briefcase nor in any of his pockets, nor had he any idea where it might be in the library. To fill the awkward moment when he had no question to ask, he inquired after Claire.

"She's trying to find work and not getting very far. She's so talented, it's a shame there's no place for her."

"That's too bad. We got the opposite problem at our house. Sara's got more work than she can handle. She's real heavy into the good daughter routine, and no amount of work she can do is ever gonna satisfy that. And she's got a real mean son of a bitch to be a good daughter to."

"I've noticed that Mr. Rochester can be a bit overbearing. Your aunt has trouble with him too."

"Overbearing's not the half of it. I try to tell Sara she should sell the store. That way she could at least go to work in the morning and get away from him for a few hours. I mean, I realize that she's not gonna put him out on the ice to die, which is what really oughtta happen, but she could at least get rid of the damn store."

"It's not as easy as that," said Corky. "We may think we're rational creatures acting in our own best interests, but that's the biggest delusion of all. When we think that, we're ignoring what's really going on."

"So what's really going on?" asked Fred, hoping to kill enough time to remember his questions.

"I am not at all sure," Corky answered, "but I'm working on trying to find out. There's nothing like a period of trouble to inspire you to delve into these questions." His gaunt face seemed to have moldered since Fred saw him last. "I've been doing a great deal of writing lately," he said, "on the trail of what's really going on."

"Well, let me know if you find out." Fred felt himself being facetious but was unable to engage seriously in a discussion of this topic, even with Corky. Especially with Corky.

The interview had deteriorated even further then, and Fred, thinking it over later, realized that the Pearlman project was dead.

It was dead because he didn't have it in him to ask the necessary questions. It was dead because he didn't want to know their answers.

At home he felt so grouchy he didn't even go into the kitchen. Instead he snapped on the TV in the living room and sat down with Marigold to watch the local news, which made him even grouchier. The news was bad enough, all the hocus-pocus about attracting business to the Port, but the commercials were worse. He wasn't quick enough zapping them with the remote, and the intrusion of even an instant of commercial into his house made him feel insane, over the edge. He switched off the TV, and instantly he had the morbid feeling that if the end of the world were coming, he wouldn't know about it with the TV turned off.

Shit, let it come, he thought. I don't hafta know about it. Besides, if the end of the world comes, I'll know anyway. I don't need a goddam anchorman to tell me.

Aunt Jenny came in, looking anxious to see him sitting in the living room. "Can I help with anything?" she asked. "Do you want me to turn the oven on?"

"Umh," he grunted. "I guess you're right. We gotta eat."

"You wanna eat, you gotta cook," she came back at him. "No two ways about it. Unless you'd rather I did it tonight."

He looked at her funny. "That sounds like something I'd say, not you."

"Actually," she answered, "it's something your father used to say, only he said, 'You want to eat, you got to hustle.'"

"My father said that? Come on, my father never even existed."

"He did too exist. I only met him a couple of times, but I remember that he struck me as a go-getter, and it was a real shame whatever happened that made him leave your mother. I never knew what it was, and I don't think she did either."

Fred stood up. "I'll cook," he said. "You wanna eat, you gotta cook. Come on, Marigold." He left the couch to Aunt Jenny, who wanted to watch the news and didn't mind the commercials as much as he did.

So the old man existed, did he. It gave Fred a very peculiar sensation to be connected with his vanished father by such a personal thread as a common mantra. Maybe his mother had used the phrase when he was small and he had picked it up all unbeknownst. You can remember stuff like that without knowing you're remembering.

As a youngster Fred had thought quite a bit about his father. He'd had a little game he played with himself when he was out on the street and there'd be people around. If that man coming toward me were my father, what would I say to him? It always ended with Fred telling the man some exploit or accomplishment and the man clapping him on the shoulder and saying, "Good!" Because he never knew when someone looking out a window might be his father watching him, he developed a military posture and a purposeful stride.

Then later, when he was older, he sneered at that old game. Jeeesus, he thought, who's he to judge? Why should I roll over and play dead for him? He thought that if his father ever showed up at the house, he'd let him know that he was too late, that he'd ditched his mother when she needed him most, but she didn't need him any longer. Fred was the man of the house now, and his father could go to hell.

Sara had asked him once if he didn't want to appeal to the organization that reunites lost parents with their children. But he had already decided by then that Mr. Rochester was all the father they could stand. What if he found his own, and he moved in? Things could be worse. Let sleeping dogs lie.

He also had the feeling that he'd used the mantra for the last time. If it was shopworn by the time he'd picked it up, it had to be threadbare by now.

Who knows, maybe the poor s-o-b is still around somewhere, pushing himself to rustle up a little activity. The thought wore Fred out.

Maybe it's time for me to quit hustling and consider the lilies of the field.

But what in the world was he going to tell Claire if he bugged out on her? And why in the hell did it matter?

He wasn't in the mood to cook this evening, but it was part of the deal, so he opened a couple cans of hominy to throw together with green chilies and Monterey jack. It was easy, and he liked it.

He was tearing lettuce for the salad when Sara phoned. "I'll be late," she said. "Don't wait. Charlie was in a car wreck on the way to work. He may make it in later, but he may not too, so don't expect me till you see me."

Fred thought about offering to go in to keep Sara company, but he decided that in his present mood, he wasn't even fit company for himself. He served the meal and tried to be civil to Aunt Jenny, but he exchanged very few words with his father-in-law.

A TURNING POINT

Business at the drugstore was slow this evening. Sara had time to fill the nursing home order for the next day. This would give her a pretty good break, come morning, since a large part of her prescription business came from the nursing home. She counted, and typed, and stapled. The pile of neat packages grew.

Christabel had time to gossip with the regulars. These were mostly older people, some from the housing project, others part of the cadre of homeowners holding out against progress. They stopped in for a little something during their evening constitutional around the neighborhood.

Tonight Sara could hear Christabel talking to "the sisters." She and Christabel always called them "the sisters" even though they weren't related because they always shopped together. The two of them in their down-stuffed winter coats took up the whole space by the cash register, making it difficult for Christabel to ring up anybody else's sale. But no one else was here at the moment, so she took her time with them.

The more striking of "the sisters," Mary Louise, had to dump out her elbow-deep purse on the counter to find change to pay for a box of extra-strength pine tar cough drops. Mary Louise was large and bunchy, with coarse black hair repeated in fierce eyebrows and a tufted mole near the corner of her mouth.

"Look at that," said Kay, the sharper, more angular one. "She's got enough stuff to open a variety store. That bag must weigh a ton. I wouldn't carry a bag like that if you paid me."

"Nobody's paying you," retorted Mary Louise, pulling out a purple plastic change purse folded to look like a flower.

"You take care of that cough, now, hear?" Christabel told Mary Louise. "You don't want to be sick for Christmas."

Kay said, "She doesn't have a cough. She likes pine tar. Takes all kinds, doesn't it?"

Mary Louise piled everything back in her bag and said, "If they hadn't cut the pine woods down, I wouldn't have to spend seventy nine cents for a whiff of something I used to get just by breathing."

"You think a hundred years from now they'll make auto exhaust cough drops to remind us of the good old days when we still had gasoline?"

"I won't be around to find out, thank goodness, and neither will you." Mary Louise popped two cough drops in her mouth and herded Kay toward the door.

This was no zanier than most of what Sara half-heard out the corner of her ear, working in the cage, counting out the Desyrel for all the depressed people in the nursing home. She could stand some Desyrel herself. Her mood wasn't the highest. Not when a break, come morning, was the best she could hope for. Hope wasn't really in the picture. Her father's agenda would go on forever. He would feed on her until there was nothing left. He would outlive her. What was there to look forward to but a few hours with a little less work?

She had given up on Charlie's arrival by now; he wouldn't come in this late. She was worried about him. He had told her that he wasn't hurt in the car wreck, but she worried anyway. She just hoped to God he didn't have injuries that he hadn't known about when he called. It would be just her luck - and his - if it turned out that he had to spend a month in traction.

Christabel's boyfriend came in a little after eight. He was a vibrant, laughing, red-cheeked man with dark brown eyes and a generous beard. Vivid as he was, however, Sara disapproved when he came for Christabel and hung around for an hour before quitting time. She also disapproved of her own attitude and tried her best to be more relaxed about it. After all, Christabel continued to do her work perfectly well. But the old man within her coughed and scowled, and she felt mean-spirited.

"Go on home," she said, to counteract her ugly feelings. "Everything's caught up." Her face felt tight and envious of the life flowing through this couple, but she gritted her teeth against the tightness and smiled. She was the one running this show, not her father, and she was going to be easygoing if it killed her.

"Thanks a mil," said Christabel. "I appreciate it, I really do. Tell Fred I already cleaned the freezer. He won't have to in the morning." She wasted no time leaving, arm-in-arm with her other half.

Sara was tempted to close the store and go home a little early herself, but the old man won this round. It would be unpardonable to disappoint the customer who counted on you to keep regular hours. In Sara's imagination, that last-minute customer had a high fever and needed an antibiotic. In actuality, of course, it would be another Mary Louise wanting extra-strength pine tar.

She wondered whether she would do anything different if her father were dead. Unlikely. After all, most of what he insisted on was good policy. How can you fight good policy? It was just that she couldn't tell where his good policy left off and hers began. He lived in her inner house as well as at her address. Only with great effort could she take an individual stand long enough to let an employee go home a few minutes early.

It was a little later when the three men came in. They were dressed a little wrong, bundled up a little too much. She knew they were not customers. She knew she was in for trouble. Her heart knocked in her throat as she stepped down out of the cage.

"May I help you?" She held herself erect, a mannequin of poise and fearlessness, as she walked toward the register where the alarm button was. Just in case. Just in case she was right about being in trouble.

The one who answered her was young, high-school age, probably. He wore a dark green parka with the hood on, and sunglasses, but his face still had an unformed look. Some mother's boy-child. "Duck tape," he said. He sounded nervous, new at this business.

The second man, several years older, looked fully formed and insolent. He moved between Sara and the counter with the register. His parka was khaki-colored, and instead of the hood, he wore a ski cap pulled down over his hair and ears. His hands in his pockets made him look threatening.

"I'm sorry," she answered, wondering if she should try to make a run for the door. "We don't carry duct tape. You'll have to go to Walgreens or the hardware store."

The third man said, "Adhesive tape, then." He moved toward her. His sunglasses were the silvered kind that took away a person's ordinary humanity.

"Right over there." Sara's mouth was dry. She pointed to the aisle where the first aid supplies were displayed.

"Show us where."

There was nothing she could do. There were three of them.

The boy and the one with his hands in his pockets went with her. In the mirrored pillars she could see repeated reflections of her slender, green-coated self with the two of them standing uncomfortably close, one on each side. She smelled beer and something else, that other odor that went with the smell of beer on a man's breath, an uncontrollable roughness. Panic licked around the edge of her consciousness.

She had felt that way once before. When she was a pharmacy student, she'd been accosted in a parking garage by a man who tried to drag her into his pickup truck. She had fought him and screamed, but that wouldn't have been enough if another car hadn't passed. Its headlights scared the man off and she'd run to her car and locked herself in.

"Keep quiet," said the boy.

Nobody would hear her scream here. Nobody would hear them shoot her either. Best give them whatever they asked for. She hoped they would demand money from the register. The alarm button was well-placed, hidden but accessible. She could set it off without their knowing.

But they didn't. The third man had already found the door to the back room. "Bring her in here," he called.

She went like an automaton, without a struggle, praying to her guardian angel not to let them hurt her.

The boy's hands were clumsy getting the tape out of its plastic bubble. Once out it fell on the floor and slid into a pile of empty corrugated boxes. He cursed, going after it.

This was where stock items were stored still in their cartons, where the rest rooms were and the door to the basement. The floor was linoleum, not tile. There were no windows.

When he put the tape over her mouth, Sara realized with detachment that the green-coated mannequin was being tied up. She noticed that the mannequin's lips stiffened and her teeth were bared, hoping to bite through the tape later. If there was a later. A strand of hair caught and came out by the roots as the boy wound the tape around and around the mannequin's head. Sara felt it, but it didn't hurt.

When the men left her, she could see herself lying with her cheek on the chilly floor of the back room. Her hands were taped together behind her and her feet, also taped together, were drawn up from her bent knees and fastened to the tape around her wrists. Was she going to watch herself die? In this extreme position she could not move, but she could hear, hear the men out in the store, hear the cash register clang open and the stool in the pharmacy cage bump against a shelf. Everything in the cage was clearly marked. They would know what to take.

She could hear them talking, but not what they said. Then the bell jingled on the front door. "Merry Christmas," one of them called. Some joke. The door closed.

What couldn't have been more than a few minutes while the men were present had lasted a long, long time. Now the only sounds were the discordant buzzings of the furnace and the freezers, seeming much louder than usual because her ear was to the floor. She realized that she was not going to be killed. She lay quietly, becoming calmer, slowing down.

Then something strange took place inside her. It seemed as though a heavy door swung open and a flood went through it, picked her up and carried her along. Now's my chance, she thought, feeling herself yield to a force almost like gravity, only it sucked her forward instead of dragging her down. Things are going to be different now, she thought.

She had never felt this way before, so free. Whatever happened, happened. She was not running things any longer. The world was running itself, including her bailiwick, including her molecules. The whole thing was out of her hands. It was like being dead, only still there.

She floated. After a while she tried to move. Being free was wonderful, but there were better places to enjoy it than the floor of the back room. She could lift her head and could rock slightly from side to side, but it got her nowhere. The noise she was able to make screaming was no more than a loud hum. How long was it going to take before Fred came looking for her? Her arms and legs had gone numb. They felt like dead lumps. There was nothing she could do but wait.

She could not judge time. She had been waiting for what seemed hours, drifting, when the bell on the front door jingled again. For a moment joy flooded her, but the steps she heard weren't Fred's steps, and the bell went on jingling. The noise meant that more than one person was coming through that door. They had come back to kill her. She closed her eyes. How ironic! Free at last, but only free to die. Behind her eyelids the sight of her mother's raw, open grave appeared and the pile of brown earth, an ash tree nearby with a robin on the ground underneath it, busy between bursts of song, listening to the grass for worms, and overhead the blue and white summer sky like a piece of moiré: the unforgettable view of the end that she remembered from the funeral so many years before. Her breath caught. She waited.

"Hel-lo-oo." It was a man's deep, friendly voice.

She screamed behind her bared teeth. The hum filled her head and hurt her throat.

There were people walking through the store. "Is anyone here?" This time it was a woman calling. Customers.

Sara rocked sideways as hard as she could and managed to bump the pile of boxes. One of them fell, making a little thump.

Then the customers were in the back room with her.

"Good heavens, what happened?" came the woman's anxious voice. There was a short silence. Then Sara heard, "Just a minute. We'll get this tape off. Honey, that little knife is in the zipper part of my purse."

"Umhumm."

With help finally at her side, Sara felt herself collapse even further inward. As she floated away, the tape was cut, her feet lowered, her arms released. She was rolled over gently by the man and something was stuffed under her head to prop it up. "This is going to pull." Hands worked on the tape that wound several times over her mouth and around the back of her head. "Better go call 911," he told the woman. "I'll be as easy as I can," he said to Sara.

Sara still could not move. Everything was numb. Through a screen of unreality she crossed her eyes and watched down the edge of her face to where the hands stretched the skin tight to ease off the sticky tape. He slowly worked it off her hair. It pulled, and some of her hair went with it, but she had plenty to spare.

When the woman came back from telephoning, the man left the room. Sara watched the woman take off her quilted khaki coat and bundle it around the mass of numbness that she recognized as her own body. She knew these people, but she couldn't make the connection of who they were.

After a few moments, the man returned. He leaned over her and said, slowly, as though reaching for her consciousness. "I called Fred. He'll be here right away."

She looked at him. She didn't question his knowing to call Fred. What was to question? These two people seemed like a mother and father and she a baby. They made arrangements for her, they comforted her body. They knew just what to do, whereas she could do nothing. It wouldn't have seemed at all strange if they had given her a bottle of warm milk. "Thank you," she murmured. That was how she found out her voice worked.

The next thing she knew, a little more time had rolled by and the police were there, two of them, and she was able to answer their questions, but still from a distance. "They were after drugs," she said. "I could hear what they were doing." She was not able to go to the pharmacy cage and list what was missing. She didn't care what was missing. She was what was missing. The police called for an ambulance. Some more time rolled by and then Fred arrived at the same time as the medics.

"Sara." Fred's hands were cold, his hazel eyes stricken.

"I'm all right," she said from far away, to comfort him. This was untrue, but only in a sense.

The two medics did things that confirmed enough all-rightness that she need not go to the hospital. She was not injured. But she was going to be one sore lady when the numbness wore off. In fact, even now, if she touched base with her body, she could feel a stabbing that let her know it was still there.

She was not ready to participate, however. And no one seemed to expect her to do so. This was an unaccustomed luxury in a way, and Sara lay under the down-filled coat and let things happen around here. I might never come back, she thought.

But Fred pulled on her. He sat down on the floor of the stock room and gathered her into his arms and talked into her hair. "It's over," he whispered. "It's going to be all right."

He seemed to be talking about something more than the events of the evening. He seemed to know what had happened, to understand her amazing lightness. She had someone on her side who saw something more than the facts. She nodded yes.

The policemen finished whatever they were doing and left. The man and woman who had rescued her reappeared in the doorway.

"Can I help you walk to the car?" said the man, and suddenly Sara recognized that gaunt blue face.

"I know who you are," she said.

"But you didn't before, did you?" His doggy smile relieved the wretchedness of his appearance.

She fumbled under the coat and tried to stand up.

"Wait, let me help you." Fred steadied one side and Corky braced her other elbow, while Claire retrieved her coat. In this way Sara managed to get on her feet where she could lean on the two men. Fred switched off the stock room light and closed the door behind them. "Do you want to look around?" he asked, glancing at the pharmacy cage.

She shook her head. "They took what they took."

Fred locked the cage and the cash register and turned out the lights while Corky and Claire steadied her. She was in no hurry to give up the sensation of having let go, no hurry to put herself in gear again and resume control.

Claire and Corky had been taking a walk when they dropped in the drugstore. Now Fred offered them a ride home. They accepted. "Better still," he said, "you drive Sara's car home for us and then I'll take you over to your place."

From the passenger seat in Fred's car Sara watched her own car in front of them, proceeding down the street without her in it, almost like the way her body had been proceeding without her in it. Claire was driving. The left tail light was out. Sara noticed herself noticing it and also noticed that she didn't care. "I've come unhinged," she said. "I'm not really here."

"Yeah you are," he answered, turning a sudden smile on her. He squeezed her knee. "If it feels real, it is real."

Colored lights decorated almost every house along the way, some of them outdoors on roof lines and porches, others on window wreaths and Christmas trees. When Fred pulled into their own drive-way, Sara noticed something different about the house, the red Christ-mas star shining from the single attic window high over everything but the tallest trees. "Did you put that up today?" she asked. "I didn't no-tice it before."

"Yeah," he answered. "I just now did it, in fact. I felt so grouchy about you not coming home for dinner that I figured I was in the right mood to play Merry Ho Ho, so I went up in the attic to bring down the decorations, and while I was there I decided to hang something in the window. Looks pretty good, doesn't it?"

"It looks beautiful."

"Just don't go up there and look at the way I hadda plug it in."

She knew how he must have plugged it in - with an extension cord dangling from the ceiling fixture - but she didn't care. When he came around and opened her car door, she made no move to get out.

EGGNOG

Fred needed Corky's help to half-carry Sara from the car, though she felt to him like live-weight, not dead-weight. She did help propel herself by putting one limp foot after another over the bumpy ground between the driveway and the front porch. "Take it slow," he told her. "We got all night if we need it." Claire walked ahead, lending support by her sturdy presence.

Mr. Rochester had already turned on the outside light and was standing anxiously with Marigold at the open door when they reached the porch. He had been in the room when Fred took Corky's call informing him that the store had been held up, and now he appeared concerned to the point of dishevelment: the hairs that he always arranged carefully over his high speckled dome were mussed, and his tie had been pulled loose under his collar.

"You must have been worried sick," said Claire. "The ambulance crew checked her out and gave her a clean bill of health. Shaken up and sore, but not shot or stabbed, thanks be for small favors."

"How bad was it?" asked Mr. Rochester. "We're covered, of course, but was there any damage?"

"To the store? No, I don't think so."

Sara said nothing. Fred helped her off with her coat and sat her down in the wing chair, then turned to Claire and Corky. "Make yourselves at home for a minute and let me bring you a glass of eggnog."

"Sure," said Claire. "Thanks."

Fred left the others to tell Mr. Rochester the details of the robbery while he went to the kitchen to find glasses and a tray. Marigold went with him. He could hear Claire's voice doing most of the talking, interspersed with questions from the old man and additions from Corky. As he listened, he noticed that Sara did not speak at all. Worn out, he thought. The old man wanted to know what drugs had been taken and how much money. He was upset when no one could tell him. But he expressed no concern over the effect on Sara of being forced by three men into the back room, tied up and left helpless. No concern, and no sympathy. I can't believe this, Fred thought. Only I can believe it.

He loaded a tray with the glasses and the jug of home-recipe eggnog that Aunt Jenny had helped him make in the blender the other night, getting ready for Christmas. Egg yolks, cream, brandy, Jamaica rum, Kentucky bourbon: all the heart-attack stuff. If he'd known then that he'd be serving it to celebrate that Sara was still alive, he'd have made twice as much.

In the living room Claire pushed aside the magazines and the toilet paper so that he could set the tray on the coffee table. Marigold sat down by the table and grinned. "No, girl," he said. "Nothing for you this time." He poured everyone a glass and handed them around, then squatted on his heel beside Sara's chair. "To the living," he said, raising his glass to her.

"To the living," echoed Corky.

Sara smiled dreamily at Fred and raised her glass. She was leaning back in the chair in a posture Fred had never seen her use before, head relaxed in the corner against one of the wings. She tasted the eggnog, licked her lips, then took another sip. She smiled at him again but said nothing. He covered the hand that was resting on the chair arm with his own and squeezed.

"This is wonderful eggnog," said Claire, "and I'm a connoisseur." To Mr. Rochester she said, "Aren't you going to drink yours? Oh do!" she exclaimed. Her dazzling smile appeared, followed by the dimples near her mouth, then the one in front of her ear. "What you drink at a celebration won't hurt you."

To Fred's surprise, the old man's face softened a little as he yielded to Claire's charm and lifted his glass. "It seems strange to celebrate a robbery," he said, "but it could have been worse. I don't suppose you feel up to going back tonight to check over the pharmacy, do you, Sara? That way you could get an order in first thing tomorrow to replace whatever was stolen." He looked at her hopefully.

She shook her head, still dreamy, and took another sip of eggnog.

"She's not going to the store tomorrow," said Fred. His voice claimed authority.

"But the insurance company has to be notified, and that's going to take a list of what was stolen," said the old man, aggrieved. "The police will want to know that too, won't they?"

"Why don't you go in tomorrow yourself?" asked Claire. "Let her rest. After all the years you put in there, you'll surely be able to tell what's missing. I'll come with you and be your right hand if you like. Between the two of us we can manage."

The old man scowled. "I haven't worked for more than a year."

Claire said nothing but looked at him in a challenging way, almost as though she were asking underneath, "Are you still a real man or aren't you?"

Fred watched this little scene with admiration. Claire had done in a moment what he himself had been trying to do for months: get the monkey off Sara's back and put it where it belonged, on the old man's.

"You can't handle pharmaceuticals."

"Charlie can," said Fred.

The old man looked at Sara.

She shrugged and smiled.

"What's the matter with you? They said you weren't hurt."

"Leave her alone." Fred started to stand up.

"Well, if you're going to act like you've been knocked in the head, I guess someone has to take over. Do we have Charlie's phone number?"

"I'll call Charlie," Fred offered. "He oughtta be damn glad he wasn't there tonight."

"Isn't it pretty late?" asked Claire.

"Charlie's on a late schedule. I'm sure he'd rather I called tonight than waited till morning." He gave Sara's hand a squeeze and stood up.

On the phone he had to go through the whole story all over again for Charlie's benefit. Charlie agreed to work extra tomorrow, come in at nine and meet Mr. Rochester to go over the pharmacy. "Tell Sara not to worry," he said.

"Thanks, old buddy." Fred hung up.

"What about his car?" Sara's voice was rusty.

"I didn't ask him about his car. That's his problem, not ours."

"So you've got it all worked out," said Claire. "You won't be needing me, then." She sounded disappointed.

"Yes ma'am, we will," said Fred. He didn't know what they needed her for, but the thought of her being in the drugstore tomorrow lightened his feelings about having to go there himself and spend time with his father-in-law. "I'll pick you up at quarter till nine."

"Good," she said. "I was looking forward to a change of scene."

Fred glanced at Corky, who was picking at a whisker on his neck, looking bemused.

"Corky's upstairs writing all day," said Claire. "I'm no use to anybody at home. I'd be glad to help out any way I can for a while until Sara feels steady again." She addressed Sara. "I think you ought to see Velma," she said. "The prosecutor probably won't send you, since they didn't do you any violence, but you've been through a lot." She explained who Velma was. "I'll call her for you tomorrow if you like."

Sara pulled back deeper into the corner of the wing chair.

"You don't have to decide right now," said Fred. He pictured Velma, hearty and leopard-draped, as she'd been at the Meetinghouse, ready with pop-psych slogans and large gestures. He didn't like seeing Sara cast in stone as a Victim with Velma as her Friend.

But Claire knew things Fred didn't. "You really should see someone about this right away, if not Velma, then someone else. All kinds of old wounds get broken open when things like this happen. If everything's really okay, you'll know it before long, and if it's not, then you're in a position to get help."

Sara nodded.

Mr. Rochester was still talking with Corky about the robbery. He had just found out that it had taken place before closing time and that Christabel had already gone home. "What good's an alarm system if nobody stays at the register to use it?" He turned to his daughter. "I wonder at you, Sara. You keep talking about hiring more help, and then you let the help you have leave the store unattended." Then he seemed to notice how removed she was, how far beyond the reach of his lecture. His fingers went to his sweater front and fumbled with a button. "Of course, it didn't amount to much this time."

Fred thought Sara had never looked so beautiful. The worry lines between her eyebrows were relaxed. Her soft lips were parted slightly, as though she could afford to let go of a little breath.

Corky stood up. "Well, Claire, we certainly didn't expect our evening walk to bring us here, did we?"

Sara said, "I'm glad it did." Her tone and glistening eyes pointed up the understatement.

Fred noted the irony, remembering how Sara hadn't even wanted to hear the Pearlman name mentioned.

And that jolted him into remembering what had completely vanished from his mind under the stress of the last couple of hours. The Pearlman project was dead. He would have to tell Claire.

Corky was shaking hands with Mr. Rochester.

"I'm certainly indebted to you," said the old man. "You could have turned around and walked out again without investigating."

Claire took her leave of Sara, stooping beside Sara's chair and offering to help in any way she could for as long as necessary. Sara reached for her hand and kissed it.

I don't hafta say anything tonight, Fred thought. "Don't you move till I get back," he told Sara. He drove Claire and Corky home as though there were nothing more on his mind than the robbery.

CHANGES

"Aunt Claire, I need to talk to you."

That's the way bad news begins, and that was the way Romy had opened the conversation, shortly before Christmas, to tell Claire that she was planning to move back to Bloomington. "At the end of the month," she said, "during the semester break, because of Nancy's school."

Claire was obliged to listen, like it or not. Romy had a life to live, and a job, which happened to be in Bloomington. "Of course," she said. "We'll help you move."

She thought about the house without Nancy's presence. How could she and Corky face each other at the dinner table every night without something to focus on besides the problems they were having? Without Nancy, Corky would sleep his life away.

And wouldn't Claudine crow, winning this one? It felt like losing a custody battle. Claire had been lucky when she and Neil split. There had been no custody battle over Elizabeth. It had worked out well, the way she and Neil had shared Elizabeth. But now Elizabeth was grown and gone, really gone, living so far away that she couldn't even be readily reached in case of emergency. Nancy was all she and Corky had.

Claire put out a few feelers. "Have you thought of who's going to look after Nancy when you're working late?"

"Of course. That's a big worry for me. But Nancy's almost ten now, and I think she can manage to take care of herself for a few hours. Lots of kids have to."

Claire did not reply in words, but she gave Romy a searching glance, as if to ask whether she really wanted her own daughter to be one of those kids who have to.

Another time she asked, "If you can't move back into your house until June, will Nancy be able to go to her old school?"

No, she wouldn't. The apartment was on the other side of town.

"That's a consideration, isn't it? Mightn't it be better to let her maintain her continuity here until she can go back to where her old friends are?"

In the meantime, Nancy herself argued her case. "Oh please, Mama. I don't want to go to another new school." Her anxiety was evident. "I don't want to have to come home and stay in an apartment every afternoon. I don't know anybody there. I won't have any friends. Please, Mama."

Romy's own needs lent weight to Nancy's plea. She needed to get on with her career, to progress, to earn more money. And having a few months without any other responsibilities might make all the difference. Just a few months.

The taboo subject was not mentioned: would Claire and Corky's tenure in the parsonage last that long? And what would happen if it didn't?

The other taboo subject was not even to be thought about except for the subterranean decision not to think about it.

Nancy would remain in Portville.

Christmas was over now. It was the end of December and tomorrow was moving day.

Corky had dragged the Christmas tree outdoors already so that the living room could be used as a staging area. The needles that dropped off between the bay window and the door had scattered into the rug. The tree's path was now obliterated by the packed and the to-be-packed. The living room furniture – couch, coffee table, rocking chairs – now filled the dining room, while Claire's cherry drop-leaf table was folded small by the front door, ready to go. Since Romy's house had been leased out furnished, she was borrowing furniture: bed and chest, table, chairs, dishes. The cartons were stacked high.

Claire tucked a rolled-up towel into the last empty corner of a box of linens and folded down the cardboard flaps ready to apply tape. "I don't know how you get this monster to work," she said. The tape roller made a jerky, ripping noise as she ran it along the seam. "It's supposed to be a help, but how do you keep it straight?" Under her hand the seam was still partly open and the tape bunched up and stuck together alongside it. She yanked it off and started over.

"Practice," Romy answered.

Omni wanted Romy back in Bloomington badly enough to be sending a truck and helpers, but the moving crew couldn't pack, not knowing what to box up and what to leave.

Claire had unacknowledged reasons to fill these boxes and seal them, and then fill some more. Her Noritaki. The linens, including her best tablecloth, embroidered in Venice. She had actually bought the cherry table especially to fit that cloth. It had been Neil's mother's but had ended up hers by virtue of a trade during the divorce. Neil took the garden tiller, which Claire didn't want. She was sure he had never used it.

The word "jettison" kept coming to mind, the thing you do to lighten the load in a sinking ship. All the books that the bookcases would hold, and the bookcases too, as many as Romy's apartment would hold. Even so, Claire did not allow herself to dwell on why she felt the urgency to jettison her possessions.

It wasn't that she'd never thought of what they would do if they were evicted from the parsonage. In her worst moments she still pictured them huddled in doorways like the homeless, but this was just her way of viewing the worst possible scenario to make other possibilities seem better by comparison. They could get help if they asked for it, and she was working on her pride issues so that if she had to ask, she could. There were people. She still had friends.

But help is more readily given the less it's needed. She didn't want to have to ask for help with all her possessions as well as for simple shelter. "All the pictures," she said. "I don't want anything left hanging on the walls."

Romy had gone out of the room and didn't answer.

Claire took down the biggest picture, her favorite because of its rich colors that seemed to have not only hue but substance. It was an abstract painting that she thought was animals and Corky thought was dream territory. She wiped the cobwebs off the back and stood it against the table.

"We don't have a box for that," said Romy, coming back in the room.

"Oh no," Claire mourned. "I knew I was forgetting something. Well, I can bring a load in the van later. You'll want some pictures." She hung the painting back up to cover the lighter place on the wallpaper and closed her eyes to the cobwebs that festooned even the clean spot.

Claire was still helping out at Rochester's during the day, but of course it was nothing permanent. She hadn't even had a nibble in her own field. A real job would do a lot to add to her feeling of security.

In the meantime it had been a welcome distraction to go to the drugstore every day and put her own life out of her mind. She remembered Merlin's advice to Arthur in *The Once and Future King*: to use the darkest times to learn something new. The ins and outs of merchandising were new to her. And she liked the people. Even the old man. *Especially* the old man. There was something to be said for a person who never gave a thought to anyone else's welfare, a person who was never nice. She got a kick out of his growling and grumbling, his jerks and glares and apoplectic flushes. Her role there, as she saw it, was to keep him entertained teaching her all about the drugstore. That way he stayed off the employees' backs and let them do their jobs.

The work took her mind off her troubles without adding any stress. The stress was Mr. Rochester's, and he was feeling it, because Sara had not yet returned to work. Someone had to run the place. If Sara didn't do it, he was the only one left. Nobody else had the good of the business at heart.

The entire back room of the store had been rearranged to suit the old man and give him some office space. Fred and Ben had moved storage shelves and brought in a desk and Mr. Rochester's Supreme Court Justice chair. Claire too had a place there, a typing table and chair beside the old man's desk, with a stack of packing crates for storage of papers.

Claire found out from Fred that Sara was feeling pretty well. From Corky (who saw it when he went to pick up Jenny for their afternoon excursions) she found out that Sara was spending her days reading paperback romances and watching the soaps. This amazed Claire. Wasn't Sara a dedicated pharmacist like her father?

"She's turning out just like her mother," said the old man. "Her mother piled up in bed and never got up again. Read a lot of trash."

Almost as an afterthought he added, "Of course, she did have cancer."

Wow, thought Claire.

Mr. Rochester also told her about his son. "We sent him over to Detroit to a private school when he was fourteen." In talking about the school itself, he sounded proud. "But I've never forgiven my wife for insisting on him going. It was the ruination of the store. He never lived at home again."

"I don't follow you," said Claire. "How was that the ruination of the store? If he was only fourteen?"

"It was the ruination because he never came back! He was young blood. He would have come into the business with the energy to relocate when the time came, to keep up." The old man's hand trembled and flew around as he spoke. He clutched it with the other to hold it down. "My son would have saved the store. I saw the writing on the wall, but I was too old to do what needed to be done."

Claire didn't see the store as ruined, so she didn't feel much sympathy for Mr. Rochester. "Well, from the neighborhood's point of view, it's a good thing you didn't move." The store provided service for the area. Furthermore, several people made a living here. She didn't call that ruination. "And Sara did a wonderful job."

"She doesn't have any gumption," he said. "She came home every night and whined about this and whined about that. I had to tell her every little thing to do."

Mr. Rochester was providing a new and a different light on the story of the corner drugstore, and Claire was glad to get caught up in it for a while. Each day she could look forward to some further outrageous remark from the old man. Even the thickest novel comes to an end in a few days, while the Rochester saga had already helped her through what might have been a wretched Christmas season.

THAT CHRISTMAS SEASON

The store had been closed, of course, on Christmas day itself. If it hadn't been for Romy and Nancy, especially Nancy, Claire and Corky would have tried to pretend that the twenty-fifth was just another day. But with a child in the house, they should celebrate: tree, gift exchange and holiday dinner.

Claire sounded Nancy out about Santa Claus early in December. She discovered that Santa Claus was kid stuff, and that clothes were already more welcome than toys. An appeal to Muriel at the thrift shop where she bought her own clothes brought word of a red cashmere skirt and sweater outfit that had just come in. The gift was a hit. Immediately on unwrapping it, Nancy put it on and admired herself in the mirror from time to time all day long.

It was Claire's intent to make the holiday festive in a traditional way, which included one last use of the dining room before everything was packed up to send to Bloomington. She wasn't the world's best cook, but she could make turkey and trimmings as well as anyone. "Too bad Wolf isn't here to help us eat all this," she said. Then she saw Romy's face and was sorry she'd said it. She had the wild hope that he might call Romy, might realize what he'd left behind in his haste, might contact her again. Christmas was a good time for things like that to happen.

She had also been hoping all day that Elizabeth would call. Since Elizabeth had no phone of her own where she was living, Claire could not call her. But as the day wore on, she supposed that the village where Elizabeth lived was involved in a celebration that her daughter couldn't leave. The phone did not ring. She put aside the wishes and devoted herself to making it Christmas for Nancy.

FM radio played "*Rudolph, the Red-Nosed Reindeer*" and music by the

Mormon Tabernacle Choir while Claire and Romy cooked. Claire apologized for the plainness of the meal.

"I like it," said Romy, stone-faced.

Claire and Corky had eaten one of Frank's fabulous meals in Bloomington last year. She couldn't remember the names of the dishes, but everything had been rich and wonderful. Claire had taken it all at face value at the time. She hadn't known then that the gourmet groceries, like everything else, were on the charge cards, to be paid later, much later.

Corky carved and served. After the mince pie was gone, he asked everyone's indulgence, saying that instead of the Christmas story he'd like to read something different this year.

Nancy had made plans to sleep over at Heather's that night. She wanted to go right away without hearing the story.

"No," said Corky. "This story is especially for you."

Claire was surprised. "What story is it?"

"Saki's 'The Storyteller.'"

Claire wasn't familiar with it.

"Go ahead," said Romy, who was taking plates to the kitchen. "I can hear you."

"Oh, all right," said Nancy.

"Thank you, doll," said Corky, bestowing his sunniest, doggiest smile upon her.

Under his warmth, Nancy melted, and wrapped her foot around the chair leg to listen. She started out only listening to do him a favor, sitting restlessly while he read the part about the children on the train, who were also listening restlessly – to nicey-nice little stories told to them by their aunt. Safe stories where good children do all the right things. Stories with a moral about being rewarded for being good. But then the story caught Nancy's attention, just as it did for the children on the train, when the stranger across the compartment took over the storytelling. This story was different. It had more zing to it. In this story the good little girl in her white pinafore with her three large good-behavior medals pinned on it was permitted, because of her goodness, to walk in the prince's park. There a hungry wolf was looking for something to eat for dinner. Here was an element of danger. What would happen next?

What happened next was a real shocker. The excellent little girl in her white pinafore hid behind a bush. The wolf came close. The girl trembled with fear. Her trembling caused her three large good-behavior medals to clatter and clink together. The wolf heard them, located her, and ate her up.

The children on the train liked that story very much. So did Nancy. She clapped. "That's better than the one where the angel of the lord comes upon the shepherds and they get sore afraid. Now can I go call Heather?"

"Wait," said Corky. "Don't go yet. I read you that story for a reason."

"I promised Heather I'd call her as soon as I finished eating."

Dishes clattered in the kitchen sink where Romy was working, now that the story was over.

"This is more important," said Corky. "What do you think that story is all about?"

Nancy rocked her chair back and forth. "It was a good story, but my brain isn't working right now. Why don't you just tell me what it's all about and let me go call Heather?"

Corky's head bowed. "All right. I'll tell you. It doesn't mean anything to you now, but remember that I told you. On Christmas day at the dinner table I told you. There is evil in the world, Nancy. Wolves get hungry and eat whatever they can find, and people do too, only they get hungry for more than just food. And when they want something really badly, when they get really hungry, they eat. Whether it hurts someone or not. Being a good girl doesn't protect you. That's what the story's about, Nancy. When there's a hungry wolf in the neighborhood, it's like evil in the world. Being good doesn't protect you."

Claire sat chilled. Was he really saying what it sounded like he was saying? The idea was too terrible to entertain. "Saki's quite a story-teller himself, isn't he?" she said bravely.

"Now may I go?" asked Nancy.

"Of course."

Afterwards, Claire cornered Corky on his way back upstairs. "Why in the world did you read a story like that on Christmas?"

"Telling the truth has to start somewhere," he answered, and his expression was so forbidding that Claire was afraid to ask him anything more.

MORE CHANGES

Some days before Christmas Corky had stopped sleeping in his chair. Instead, he been spending many hours upstairs at the desk in their bedroom. While Claire went to Rochester's every morning, Corky went upstairs to the desk in their bedroom. What he was writing, she didn't know.

"Nothing, really. Just thinking. If I don't write it down, I cycle through the same thoughts over and over. But if it's on paper, I only have to think it through once and I've got it."

"Maybe it'll turn into a book." she said hopefully. She had often encouraged him to write a book. Sermons, she thought, the un-preached even better than the preached. The ideas he had that people weren't ready to hear.

"No," he answered with a painful smile. "I'm writing to myself, not preaching."

She wondered what he would be writing to himself. Corky's thoughts were a mystery to her. All she knew was that their relationship had broken down. Could he be thinking about that?

It hadn't been an immediate thing, a sudden dropping of the vessel that had contained them. Nothing had smashed. Not even the police at the door had smashed it. But there were cracks. Leaks. Small realizations.

She was becoming aware of their sex as a reflection of what was going on. One day something made her think about sex and it suddenly came to her mind that she and Corky had not made love for a long time, weeks, maybe months. She couldn't really remember.

There hadn't actually been a cutoff point. No one had said, "This is the last time we're going to do this." Now that she noticed it, she was surprised that it had come to mean so little that the lack could go on and on without impinging.

They seemed to be aging at different rates. Corky was fourteen years older than she. Men slowed down. And as he grayed and wrinkled and became thinner and more frail, he seemed at the same time more and more needy, more and more a child. She had to be careful with him. She had to take care of him.

When had she started mothering Corky? Not right away, she knew. There had been plenty of good times early on. That's always the case, isn't it? But being in bed together now was a matter of comfort, not excitement. They held each other, sheltered each other, and she held and sheltered him a lot more than he did her.

That's what she was now, Corky's mother. Being mother to such an old man made an extremely old woman of her. She had no sexual feeling at all, which was just as well. What would she do with it if she had it?

Was this the way things were for women? First being young and curious, then a flaming moment of glory that all too quickly ended in being old and used as a pillow? What had happened to her? There had been a time when she had sung along with, "I feel the earth move under my feet," and the earth had moved, but no longer.

This feeling had come to her late. It wasn't with Neil that the earth had moved. That had been a genre marriage. An example of the institution. The time had come to be part of a couple, and Neil was the best available partner. She had believed herself to be in love, but she didn't know then how messy and extreme love really was. No, the earth didn't move for her until she was much older and got involved with Corky at the end of the sixties, when Elizabeth was half grown.

She had left Elizabeth to finish grade school at home with Neil, thinking it was no place for a child to be watching her mother go through what she was going through. She was in graduate school then, commuting from her loft over the paint store to the University of Chicago, where she studied and taught during the week, and back to the loft in Portville on weekends to.

Corky had been a Unitarian minister then. All the women were half in love with him. He wasn't handsome. Corky had always been put together wrong somehow, but he had a deep, passionate voice. He could have looked like a toad. They'd have loved him anyway. And she was the one he had chosen. He fell in love with the same dimples, the same smile that Neil had told her were manipulative.

The backdrop of a church had made their affair seem holy instead of sordid. It matters a lot where you do it, she thought.

Everything had changed when she and Corky decided to get married. Elizabeth came to live with them, and Claire went back to motherhood. She had finished her course work in Chicago, then wrote her doctoral dissertation across the table from Elizabeth doing her high school homework. She landed the job with the Children's Center on the day Elizabeth brought home brochures about the Peace Corps.

"That's for me," the girl had said. "That's what I want to do. I can't wait." She still had most of high school and all of college to get through before she could do it, but the idea had come then, and she had taken extra courses and gone to summer school to cram four years of high school into two and a half years.

With Elizabeth in the house, Claire's relationship with Corky changed. Being a mother came first, and Corky seemed to fall right in with it. He treated Elizabeth the same way he did Nancy, like a little princess, making up to her, playing with her, and generally siding with her against Claire's parental discipline. Because Neil still took an active role, Corky said he felt no need to be Elizabeth's father. Claire was still a mother, however, and the way Corky was, it sometimes seemed as though there were two children in the house.

By then they were a long way from Claire's loft and the Unitarian church. Claire had left the loft and Corky the church. They lived in a house, with a child. The Freethinkers had come into existence, had organized themselves around a nucleus of disgruntled Unitarians and Episcopalians. They were busy and it was a heady world they were living in, a time of new freedom, new exhilaration.

And where were they now? Claire looked around. The house was a pit of despair. The walls and windows were grimy, the floor littered, the furniture on its way to the moving van.

She hadn't been able to bring herself to clean house for months. Maybe years. With so much stuff there and people always in the way, she couldn't even get at anything to clean it.

This was not the backdrop for love.

She didn't blame Romy for leaving. Of course Bloomington

pulled; but Portville pushed too. Why would a young woman with prospects want to stay in such a place? She wouldn't stay herself if she didn't have to.

But there was no place for them to go, and Corky couldn't leave anyway, because of his trial. Until that ordeal was over, they were in limbo. A limbo that did not feel like a way station for heaven.

CLAIRE VISITS SARA

When Romy was gone, Corky moved his desk and made himself a den in her room. He began sleeping there too, so that he wouldn't wake Claire coming to bed late after his hours at the desk.

Claire asked again if he wanted to talk about what he was working on.

He shook his head. "It's nothing I can talk about."

"Can't you tell me anything?"

Another head shake. "It's a wrestling match. I've got ahold of the devil, and he won't let go."

Claire frowned quizzically and started to say that if Corky was the one who had ahold, then he was the one to let go. But Corky had already turned away to go upstairs again.

Claire and Corky went their separate ways during the day, Claire to the drugstore and Corky upstairs to his desk or away on visits to Portvillage and outings with Jenny Cavendish. Claire left work mid-afternoon to be there when Nancy got home from school, so she still cooked, but they usually ate quickie suppers in the kitchen. Sometimes Nancy was there, but not always. Corky went alone for the evening walks around the neighborhood. Claire had a job to recuperate from now. She stayed home.

One evening, however, she decided to get better acquainted with Sara. Here she was, working at Sara's store, more or less on Sara's behalf, and she hardly knew the woman. Corky had brought home mums from the nursing home that day, the excess from a funeral. Claire arranged them in a vase and went to call upon the sick.

Driving into the Bekins' driveway, she saw that the living room was dark, so she went to the kitchen door where the lights were. Through the window she could see Fred and Jenny at the table playing Scrabble.

She felt a surge of resentment at the sight, the same childish dismay she felt mornings at the store, seeing Fred stocking shelves and ringing up sales as though he had nothing better to do, when he ought to be working on his Corky article. There hadn't been a good moment to ask him how the work was coming along, and the longer she waited, the less possible it became to bring it up. He was doing them a favor. She couldn't nag. But the thought was always there, and when she saw him doing other things, she felt like importuning him. Better still, telling him to forget the whole idea. Continuing to hope for this favor was too painful.

Marigold woofed when she knocked. Fred answered the door. "Shhh," he said to the dog. "Yes, ma'am, come in." His face flushed.

She remembered the first time she had come to talk to him. How things had changed since then. They had been strangers then, but close; now they were associates, but distant, the unkept promise a barrier. She wished she hadn't come here.

"Oh my, look at those flowers," exclaimed Jenny.

"I thought Sara might enjoy them," said Claire. The mums were impressive, blossoms that started pale in the center and shaded into ruffles of deep peach. "I don't know whose funeral they came from, but whoever it was got good flowers." She rattled on explaining how they had come into her possession.

"I'll go get Sara," said Fred. In a moment he was back in the doorway. "She says to come in where it's comfortable." He took Claire's coat.

She followed him into a den with desk, bookcases, and a brown leather couch where Sara sat curled at one end. Sara wore a smoky blue velour housecoat with the sleeves rolled up. Long slender toes peeked out between the blue hem of her skirt and the brown leather of the couch. Her hair hung loose, and the light from her reading lamp picked up individual strands and made them glow.

"What wonderful hair you have," exclaimed Claire. "I've never seen you without a braid." She set the flower vase on the desk.

"Or a green coat," said Sara. "Sit down." She gestured toward the other end of the couch. "Those flowers are beautiful."

Fred went back to the kitchen, and Claire felt less a silent supplicant and more a minister's wife visiting the sick. She told Sara the story of the flowers' origin. She noticed the title of Sara's book laid open on the floor, *Rachel's Flame*. So Corky's report was accurate. Paperback romances.

Sara saw what Claire was looking at. "My secret vice," she said. "My father thinks I'm degenerate." But she smiled slightly as she said it. "I've decided that if that's what he thinks of me, I'll go ahead and give him good reason."

"Your father thinks *everyone's* degenerate," Claire answered. "Isn't he wonderful? A prototype grouch. I wait every day to hear what he's going to say next."

"It gets to be predictable," said Sara.

"I'll bet it does," said Claire. Being this man's daughter could not be easy. Of course it wasn't! As she settled into Sara's feelings, the last of her own discomfort went away.

Sara made some polite inquiries about how Claire was getting along at the store. Claire filled her in. Then, "I haven't had a chance yet to thank you for rescuing me," said Sara.

"Well, it wasn't much of a rescue, but I'm glad you didn't have to lie there any longer than you did. How are you doing? You must have been shaken up."

Sara glanced at the doorway. "Yes." She nodded. "Actually, I feel like I'm not here." Her fingers waggled. "It's weird. And the strange part is that I could be here if I wanted to, but I don't want to. Fred says to hang in with it as long as I can."

"Atta girl," said Claire. "Take your vacations where you can get them."

"That's where you *really* rescued me. Getting my father to go back to the store. That's what he should have done a long time ago, hired pharmacists but managed the place himself."

"I'm surprised he does so well," said Claire. "The way he stumbles and shakes, you think he's going to be confused, but he's not, not a bit."

"If I can stay on my space trip long enough, he'll have to hire another pharmacist. He can't make Charlie work twelve hours a day forever. My problem is holding out. I get to feeling sorry for Charlie."

"Don't do it," Claire answered instantly. "Charlie's okay. And you're absolutely right. You *do* need another pharmacist. Your father couldn't do the managing and handle the pharmacy too, the way you've been doing, and you shouldn't have to either. I'll bring what pressure I can to bear." She gave Sara a conspiratorial wink. "Maybe we can get the place going so well you'll *want* to come back."

But Sara looked forlorn. "Maybe," she said wanly.

"You're tired," said Claire. She stood up. "I won't keep you talking anymore now, but let's get together some time. Maybe go to lunch. I'd enjoy making your acquaintance. I feel as though I've moved into your life, and it seems impertinent to do that without knowing you a little better." She felt the power of her own charm radiate toward Sara.

Sara nodded and held up a hand. Claire squeezed it. "I *am* tired," Sara said. "Thanks so much for coming, and thanks for the flowers." When Claire had almost reached the door Sara added, "And for everything else too."

The hall ended at the kitchen, where the game at the table was almost over. Jenny was ahead. They were playing on a turntable board, confirming their words with a battered three-volume Webster's that took up much of the table.

"House rules you can fish in the dictionary," said Jenny, "but Fred has the advantage because I can hardly lift it."

Claire walked around the table and peeked at both their letters. The visit with Sara had put her back into a comfortable role, and her feet felt good, as though they had trodden these boards before. She was back in her gracious self.

Fred had the q and the z, but he'd placed them at the far right of his letter rack as though he didn't really have any hope of using them. Jenny had a clear victory in sight with the seven-letter word "reverse" on her rack.

"Go ahead and play," Claire said, when Fred started to stand up. "Don't let me interrupt. Just tell me where you put my coat and I'll let myself out."

"Don't go yet," said Fred. "Sit down." He pushed a chair out for her with his foot. "Give me a minute to let Aunt Jenny clean up on me."

"You're too easy," said Jenny. "You don't fight back. You need to put your desire for mayhem into it, the way I do."

Fred put his z on the triple letter score after Jennie's "sit" to make "sitz." "Thirty-three points, please," he said triumphantly, then almost without a hitch, he added his s, to make zs, the plural, in the other direction. "Excuse me, sixty-six points." He batted his eyes at Jenny. "What was that about mayhem?"

"Pretty good house rules," said Claire. "At our house, we can't pluralize letters that way."

Jenny was pretending to scowl at her letters. "Drat," she said, playing little old lady. "I thought I had you." She studied the board. "Maybe I can eke out a little something up here." She laid down her letters. The word covered the triple word score. "We all have our 'reverses,' don't we? Let's see, that's twelve times three, thirty-six, plus fifty. Eighty six points, if I'm adding correctly." There were only five letters left. She picked them up.

The game wound down now, with both Fred and Jenny just trying to keep from getting stuck with high-count letters. Fred still had the q when it was over, and Jenny's desire for mayhem paid off.

Fred walked Claire to the car. On the way she felt her Claire Pearlman image slipping away again, and before it left her entirely and she was back in the plaintive stance she hated so much, she asked him, in the most neutral manner she could summon, "How's the magazine story coming along?"

"It's not." His tone was brusque.

She stepped carefully over the rough ground. Fred's cat appeared, a dark meow at her feet.

"Look," he said, "I got principles against breaking a promise, but I just can't write it."

She stumbled. He caught her arm. "Careful," he said. "The tree roots stick up here."

Somehow it was worse having him tell her he couldn't do it than it would have been to tell him not to. That way he might have argued and done it anyway. As though to make this possible, she said, quickly, "I was just about to tell you not to bother. What's going to happen is going to happen. It wasn't very realistic of me to think a magazine story would save Corky."

As soon as she heard herself say this, she knew it was true.

She went on. "And to have him be the object of public attention would probably make it worse. There would be people with sick minds who wouldn't believe the truth."

"Yeah, and come knocking at your door." Fred was not above fueling this train of thought, which led away from his failure.

"What's been knocking at our door lately has been pretty ugly," said Claire. The phone calls. The news from Neil. "The more I think about it, the wiser it seems to call as little attention to ourselves as possible."

At the car she said, "See you in the morning." He was still in the driveway stroking the cat when she looked back from the street. He had turned out to be a disappointment, but what can you expect? At least the disappointment was over. She knew where she stood.

LAZARUS

Corky had gone out while Claire was away. Nancy was at Heather's for the night, and when Claire got home from her visit to Sara, the house seemed forsaken. Grimy. Dimly lighted. Sparsely furnished, yet still crowded. Uneasy.

Claire did not like being alone this way. There was comfort in having Corky somewhere under the same roof, even when he was physically in a different part of the house and mentally in a different part of the universe. He could be sought out. He was there, approachable, even if she didn't approach him.

When he was there, the mess was partly his, in fact mostly his, but now, alone in the house, Claire was responsible for it all. She went to the kitchen. The dirty dishes had been piling up for several days. She put on an apron and scoured the sink to wash them.

What would it be like without Corky?

She sometimes rehearsed this possibility. She would climb the stairs and imagine that no one was up there. If he was out, she would imagine that he was not coming back. She would cook a meal and pretend that half of it would be saved for another night.

She had lived mostly alone for two years before she married him. But that had been quite different, being so busy at the university, and then too he was there for her emotionally even though they did not share a house. Now the tables were turned and she had to be there for him emotionally whenever he needed her, day or night.

While the first sink full of dishes soaked, she wiped the table and the countertops and swept the floor. What a disgrace! Her mother had swept the kitchen floor every evening after dinner, every evening of her life. And here was a dustpan full of dirt balls, scraps of lettuce and corn kernels, two bottle caps, a blue puzzle piece, a twist tie, a Barbie shoe. She put the shoe aside for Nancy and tackled the dishes.

She had almost finished when Corky came home. She heard the front door open and close. The uncharacteristic quietness of the closing made her dry her hands on her apron and go to the living room.

Since they rarely used the room, she had kept only one lamp in there, a grubby, yellow-shaded floor lamp that stood by the front door, its single 60 watt bulb demonstrating failure of light. Corky was bundled up in overcoat and muffler. When Claire appeared, he hastily dropped the Lazarus shopping bag he'd been carrying and pushed at it with the side of his foot.

"Have you been shopping? I thought you'd gone for a walk," she said in surprise. "The car was here." His attempt to hide the Lazarus bag had failed. In fact, the shove had only served to open it, and what Claire saw there terrified her. "What is that? What are you doing with that?"

His drawn, blue face seemed to crumple. Tears came to his eyes. "I'm not going to do it, Claire." His voice cracked. "I promise."

Quickly she picked up the bag and folded the handles down over the top to cover the coiled rope.

He sat down heavily on the couch and put his face in his hands. "I feel so guilty," he said. "It's almost unbearable."

While his eyes were behind his hands, she stuffed the bag of rope behind the couch, then quickly sat down and put her arm around the thin, hunched shoulders. His coat was still cold from the outdoors. "Tell me," she said. "Just remember that you're not guilty just because they say you are."

His head shook.

She squeezed his shoulders comfortingly. "Tell me what happened."

He straightened out of her embrace and looked at her distractedly. "I had an appointment with Neil today."

Claire felt as though slapped. So Neil was trying to influence Corky behind her back! This could be very bad. Her thoughts flew around. The prosecutor was collecting written testimony. She had already heard some of it. The woodwork. People had been coming out of the woodwork to say terrible things about Corky. People from the past. People she had always thought of as friends!

"I went to Neil's office." Corky smiled a wintry smile. "I knew something was up when he asked me to come there instead of coming here."

"Oh, this makes me so angry!"

"I finally got to hear the tape of Josie's accusation," he said. "Neil played it for me to show me what I'm up against. They call it 'discovery,' showing the defendant what the evidence is against him."

"But you don't get to ask her any questions! She can lie all she wants to when she doesn't have to look you in the eye and do it. Oh Corky, they're going to crucify you." With her anger to fortify her, Claire stiffened and said, "I believe in you. I know you're innocent, no matter what they say. You mustn't let them make you feel guilty. You have to defend yourself."

He looked at her strangely.

"I'm sorry," she said. "I interrupted you. Here, let me take your coat. You don't have to sit here with your coat on." She pulled the muffler from around his neck and helped him out of the overcoat. But as she bustled nervously, she remembered the rope. There was more to the story. She'd better hear it. She squelched her rising fear and summoned professional skills. Instead of sitting back down beside him, she pushed the cluttered coffee table aside and drew up her rocking chair to face him, almost knee to knee. She took his hands in hers. "You heard the tape," she said gently. "Tell me what you heard. I wish Neil had let me in on it too."

"No you don't." He looked sick. "She's not lying," he said. "What she told was true." He hesitated.

Claire gripped his hands and clenched her teeth.

"Oh God," he said. "I had no idea she would feel so bad. I just had no idea. I thought she liked playing games with me. I feel so guilty."

This time Claire held back her automatic defense and let him continue.

"I can't deny what's on that tape."

"Are you sure you know what you're doing?" Claire cried. "Neil purposely had you listen to that tape without me. He's your attorney, but he doesn't believe in you the way I do. How can he really defend you?"

"He's defending me. He says the worst thing I could do would be to go up against a jury. He's got a couple of strategies in mind. If worst

399

comes to worst I can plea bargain and not have to go through a trial. But he's going to do what he can to get it thrown out altogether."

Corky paused as though recollecting his thoughts. "Actually, he says it might not come to anything, but we'd better prepare for the worst."

Claire seized on this small hope and tried to force its growth. "Then why are you talking about a plea bargain? Doesn't that mean saying you're guilty?"

"I *am* guilty. I did what she said I did. I feel terrible. If we plea bargain, I wouldn't have to go in front of a jury. And Neil would do what he can to see that it's in Judge Hamilton's court for sentencing."

"Oh Corky, you know as well as I do that you can *feel* guilty over all kinds of little things, but to really *be* guilty in a case like this, you have to have done something terrible!" She gripped his hands as though to send him faith. "You're simply not the kind of person who would harm anyone. You have to believe that, or you'll start admitting all kinds of things just because you're accused of them."

"Claire, I'm trying to tell you that this is not nearly as bad as it could be. The statute includes 'intent.' That's what Neil's plea for leniency is going to center around. There's nothing in the tape that accuses me of intent."

Claire's head bowed

Corky's hands moved helplessly.

Claire's thoughts went back to the rope. She swallowed, and then swallowed again, to ease the pressure in her throat. "But you thought about ending it." She tried to sound as supportive as she would to a client, but the voice was all wrong, she could tell. It was bitter, and as she heard it, ugly emotions bubbled up, a horrible stew of rage and grief, threatening to boil over. She rocked herself in the chair, hard little jerks back and forth. Her breathing huffed. She didn't see how she could get through this. She opened her mouth. A huff of breath flew out.

Corky shook her shoulders again. "I'm sorry," he said. "I was hoping I could make things easier for you."

"Being sorry doesn't help," she cried. "It doesn't help it doesn't help."

"Let me tell you what happened. It might make you feel better. It did me."

It wouldn't. Nothing would ever make her feel better. "Tell me," she whispered, with her eyes closed.

"I did decide to end it," he said. "I've been writing and writing, trying to sort out all the confusion, and it only got worse. I would think I had an idea, and I'd write it down, thinking it would lead somewhere, and it would lead to a blank wall. The kind of wall that's smooth. It rises right out of the earth."

Claire hated it when Corky tried to describe things like that. She nodded impatiently. "You need a therapist instead of trying to deal with this by yourself. It humanly impossible."

"There aren't any therapists for what ails me. Anyway, it got so that I knew the wall was there, no matter how promising the idea was. It got hopeless. I was blocked no matter where I turned. And all the time, the man who fell on Wolf's car kept coming to my mind."

Claire's body jerked convulsively.

"I wrote you a letter. It's up there, and thank God you'll never have to read it. But I wrote you a letter and I decided to go to the bridge and hang myself. It seemed right. It seemed like that was the right way to do it. Get it over with. End the suffering. Let you find a new life. Don't ask me why. It doesn't make sense, I know, but it doesn't have to make sense. That's just the way it was. It was as though the man Wolf hit had hung himself so that I would know to do it too." He shushed her. "I know, I'm being melodramatic, but that's how it seemed, as though it was *meant*." He began talking more rapidly. "And in a way, it was. I carried the rope in the Lazarus bag because I thought it would really look awfully strange to walk down the street with a coil of rope over my shoulder like a lynch mob." He swallowed. "And I got to the bridge."

"I can't stand this."

"Wait, let me finish. It has a happy ending."

A terrible laugh started to come from Claire's throat, but she held it back.

"I laid the bag on the bridge rail and looked for a place to tie the rope. Any place would do, of course, but with something this important, you want to choose the *right* place. And I had the place all picked out and went back to get the rope."

"Back where?"

"Back to the place I'd left it on the railing. And there was the

Lazarus bag. And the whole Lazarus story came to my mind. It was as though something called to me, the way Jesus called for Lazarus to come out of the tomb. The word 'Lazarus' no longer meant a department store. It seemed filled with meaning. I remembered that raising Lazarus from the dead was one of the last things Christ did. And Claire, you know that Jesus did not shrink from his fate. He could have avoided the cross, but he didn't. So when all this came to me, it was like an admonition to come out of the tomb and be a man and see it through. As though I had both been raised from the dead and given the courage to live." As he finished this story, he seemed relieved, almost refreshed. "It was a powerful experience, Claire. And telling you has brought it back. I feel better, as though it all means something, you know, not just happenstance misery that rains down on people. As though I'm supposed to stay alive and go through this purgatory for a reason."

"Any idea what the reason might be?" She had become interested enough to move a little way out of her wretchedness.

He shook his head. "There's only one reason possible. It's ineluctable. This near the end of my life, with no prospects left to accomplish anything worldly, the only reason to go on struggling is to strengthen my soul."

Claire sat quietly. She didn't really believe in a soul. But if Corky found some comfort in strengthening his, she had to agree that, for him, anyway, it was important. It kept him alive.

That night in bed Corky was the comforter.

JOSIE'S CHRISTMAS GIFTS

Miracle of miracles, Christmas had come and gone, and Dunk and Eve had yielded to Josie's longing for a dog. The girl had since spent every possible hour of the day or night, awake and asleep, in the dog's company.

For the adult Flannerys, the decision had not been easy. "It'll just get itself killed," prophesied Dunk, "out in the street chasing cars." "Dogs shed all over the house," complained Eve. "You could keep it shaved," said Dunk, being jovial, trying for Christmas cheer. "Duncan!" Eve replied, ever humorless. "Don't be ridiculous."

But the letter to Santa, with its carefully thought-out compliments, along with the evident loneliness their daughter displayed, roused their sympathy. She was their only child, after all, and they shared a dedication to what they felt was her welfare, even though they seldom agreed about what that was.

Josie had also embarked on further strategies to get in their good graces. In the days before Christmas she practiced her music lessons when both parents were at home to hear her, playing "Tumbleweed" several times each evening because Duncan liked it. She was invited to perform Christmas music for the residents of Portvillage and accompany their singing of carols. This pleased Eve, she knew. It also pleased Duncan, though he wouldn't let on. But Josie had had enough experience to recognize when his criticism was fueled by anger and therefore dangerous and when it was just his habit. She saw how his sharp features could soften with pride, even as he told her not to gasp for air when she sang "Fall on your knees," and not to hold the sustaining pedal down when she played "Fa la la la la".

She had also lost six pounds. How she did it was a secret, of course. Her mother credited LOVELY YOU, without noticing how rapidly the weight came off, and Josie kept her own counsel. She made it a point to pick over her plate at dinner, refusing first one kind of food, then the next, so much so that even Eve began to urge her to eat.

"You can have the potato," Eve said, "as long as you don't put butter on it." Josie shuddered. "No thanks," she would say when dessert was served. It gave her vindictive joy to think to herself, "You want me to lose weight. Okay. I'll lose weight." She ate no popcorn when they made strings for the Christmas tree. She watched Eve nibble on lebkuchen, marzipan and meringue kisses while displaying her own superior control and enjoying Eve's perplexity.

She had contributed more than popcorn and cranberry strings for the tree. Her friend Bess Kingman at Portvillage had helped her make ornaments: silver and white snowflakes, origami birds, and a kneeling camel made of plastic clay painted a realistic tan.

All this had its effect on her parents' behavior. Instead of putting all their efforts into whipping her into shape, they took advantage of the season to pamper her a little.

Eve persuaded Dunk to buy the tree a few days ahead rather than wait for the mark-downs late on Christmas Eve. They shopped the lots together with Josie in tow, awkward as it was, trying to act like a better family. This got them through the selection of a noble fir and the placing it on top of the car to carry home. Dunk had a system to hold it on by rolling the windows up tight against the ends of the ropes that secured it.

But Josie was not really aware of the system. Only half-listening, she had been reading *The Constant Tin Soldier* while he worked on it. The story was so beautiful and so sad that it completely absorbed her. At the end she had to put it down to keep from crying. She saw a group of carolers on the corner at a stop light and opened a back window, glad to take her mind off the story. The tree then escaped from the ropes, slid down the side of the car, and landed in a slush-filled gutter.

Dunk limited his fury to a burning glare toward the back seat, got out and replaced the tree and its securing ropes. He was trying hard. He breathed deeply instead of yelling. He even managed a joke, calling the tree an "ignoble" fir and chiding it for running away.

The dog did not appear under the Christmas tree in person, only a small stuffed model. But with the model came the promise to let Josie choose the real thing, subject to reasonable restrictions.

A few days later, after a morning at the animal shelter, Josie took the new dog, temporarily named Tippy, to visit Bess Kingman at Portvillage. Wearing a chain collar attached to a red leash, Tippy stepped smartly around puddles of melting snow as they approached the facility. Josie imagined envious gazes from every pedestrian she met, from every passing car. Inside the building, she introduced the dog to white-haired men and ladies in the lobby. The room was still decorated for Christmas in the jolly style of such places. Many of the residents were comparing gifts and Christmas visits with family, sitting in small clusters around the spacious room, but several interrupted their conversations to pet the new dog and congratulate Josie. On the way to Bess's room Tippy skittered on the gleaming hall floor, her toenails noisy as they sought traction. "I hear clicking!" Josie chided. This was what her piano teacher always said if the fingernails she was so proud of got too long.

She found Bess in her wheel chair at the window, reading. "Look at you!" Bess cried, when Josie hesitated at the door. "Come in!"

Bess was not shy around dogs. Soon Tippy was off her leash, nose to the floor, inspecting the room. Josie recounted the selection process. They discussed good names for dogs – Brownie, Rover, even Matilda – but neither of them thought that there was a better dog name than Tippy.

"Daddy wanted to name her Collara because of her ruff but Mama said it sounded like a disease."

Josie had brought with her in a tote bag the Christmas gifts she had not had time to deliver earlier. She pulled out two packages, one a tin of home made cookies, the other a generous red bow attached to a much smaller rectangular box wrapped in gold paper. She put the cookies on the table and handed the gift to Bess. "I hope you like it," she said. "It's my favorite."

Bess opened it eagerly to find a bar of Yardley Roses soap. She held it to her nose and breathed deeply. "No wonder it's your favorite. Thank you so much, Josie. I'll really enjoy bathing with this." She backed her chair a little way to reach the shelf under her table. "Here's something for you too."

This gift also had a red bow. Josie opened it carefully to save the ribbon. "Colors!" she exclaimed. "Twenty-four colors."

Bess explained that these were water-soluble oil pastels that she could use like paint as well as like crayons. "Bring them next time you come and I'll show you some tricks."

"I'm going to be here pretty often," Josie said. "They want me to play the hymns on Sunday afternoons." She was talking about the non-denominational services that Portvillage held on Sunday afternoon to give the rotating ministers a chance to do the morning service with their own congregations. "I'll come over to do art too." Then they said their goodbyes and Josie started for home with Tippy leading the way.

No one knew Tippy's ancestry. She was young and frisky but no longer a puppy. One of the Flannerys' restrictions had been no puppy to housebreak. She had dark pointed ears with white rims, black markings that looked like eyebrows, a long muzzle and movie star eyes. And of course the white ruff like a collar. Her coat was red and brown and blond and her tail feathery. The feature that led to her being chosen from all the eager dogs at the animal shelter was her personality. She acted interested but reserved. The adult Flannerys refused to consider a dog that jumped all over them. Josie's main requirement was a good smile, which Tippy displayed, panting slightly, along with a delicious little wiggle and discreet wags of the tail.

Signing a promise to have the dog spayed did not trouble the Flannerys, who for once agreed on something: an ounce of prevention was worth a pound of cure.

Most of Dunk's gift of Christmas quarters went for a snug, insulated doghouse, which now sat on the back porch in a sheltered corner. Tippy had to live outdoors during the day when no one was home. But as soon as Josie got out of school in the afternoon, the dog was her constant companion.

SARA'S EYES OPEN

The snowy gray days of the Portville winter were trudging along. Mr. Rochester's sneer dripped more and more acid as gray ice melted into gray slush and Sara refused to put on her pharmacist's jacket and climb back in the cage. It was still Charlie who was working double shifts, while Mr. Rochester reigned over the newly created Manager's Office in the back room with Claire. He had requested that Fred bring his Supreme Court Justice chair from his den at home. Seated regally he could boss his small domain.

"Sara's over the edge," he reported to Claire. "She's never going to get herself back in harness now. She's been lying around for weeks, since before Christmas."

"That must be a concern for you," Claire answered with sympathy.

"I can't afford to waste any more concern on her."

Mr. Rochester's concern for Sara (or anyone else) was in short supply. Of course he couldn't afford to waste it. But outrage he had in abundance, and he spread it around freely. His face flushed and his working arm shook over the stock orders and the inventory sheets and the invoices as he spit out his scorn for people who took every little hangnail of a bad experience to a support group.

"What she needs to do is reach around and give herself a kick in the rear end."

"You can throw your back out that way." Claire's tone was mild. Her job was listening, not arguing. Still, there were times she couldn't resist a word here and there.

"It's better to throw your back out than go sniveling off to a group where you 'share'." His tone assigned "sharing" to the pit under the outhouse. "Backs heal. But once you start 'sharing'," he came up for air and directed a stern glare at a stack of boxes as though they were the offending parties, "it can go on forever. You never get yourself back on track."

He had finally given in to necessity and begun the search for another pharmacist, demanding the best but certain that only the worst would apply. Why, after all, would anyone who could do better want to work at a drugstore on its way to oblivion? If he found someone he could tolerate, albeit fresh faced and right out of school, he would be forced to offer a competitive salary. He had already been forced to give Charlie the raise he had long deserved – and then pay the salary twice to cover the double shifts. What really rankled was that even with another pharmacist on the payroll, he still wouldn't be able to compete with Walgreens. The chains had too many advantages: quantity purchasing, advertising, and of course more parking space than was decent. He would grumble to Claire about Walgreens in an angry monotone, the same way he used to grumble to Fred and Sara. Back in the store and immersed in business, Mr. Rochester would have relished the prospect of competing with Walgreens if only he could.

"It's amazing that Sara did so well with a two-person job, isn't it, doing the managing as well as the pharmacy?"

"Never a night went by but what she had to bring it all home and hand it to me."

Sara would have been furious to hear the slant he put on her good-daughter policy of keeping him included and informed. But she didn't hear it. He was at the store now in the tiny office carved out of stock cartons in the windowless back room. She was absorbed in herself and her future, not in being his good daughter. In his presence she assumed a quiet, imperturbable mantle of self-communion. She smiled faint, enigmatic smiles. She allowed herself to gaze at her father in wonderment. She would actually look at him, as though for the first time, look at *him*, as though he were at a sufficient distance that she couldn't feel the weight of his anger and scorn.

Frequently she thought to herself, "I don't have to live like that." It's what Fred had been telling her for months, for *years* even, but now she was telling herself. "I don't have to live like that." It was true, now that the words were her own.

The robbers had not been caught. But Sara had been sent to Velma Winters, Friend of the Victim. She had enrolled in a support group of eight Victims, all of them women. They met Wednesday evenings and sat on the colorful beanbags under Velma's cheerful posters. Sara did not mind "sharing" one bit. That's what people did in support groups, and even though she hadn't warmed to it right off, she discovered that it was better than feeling so alone with her burden.

"It's not that my husband doesn't care how I feel," she told the others, when it was her turn to share. "It's not that he doesn't listen. He listens, and he cares. He even helps me – a lot. But he doesn't *understand* why I need to be a good daughter." There were nods from several of the women sitting or lounging on the brightly colored beanbags. They were talking about being good daughters in relation to being victims. "Maybe it's not so strange that he doesn't understand," she added. "I don't either."

"Do you want to understand?" asked Velma.

Sara stared at her. So did the others. "Actually, I don't care." She hesitated. "What I really care about is using this interlude to change direction." She glanced at Velma. "When I saw that my father didn't care what happened to *me*, only about what happened to the store, I felt relieved. Since then, I've begun to realize that it's okay for me not to love him. He doesn't love me, and that means I don't have to love him, or to be a good daughter."

Velma's face was a study of moderation, impossible to read.

"Maybe this doesn't make sense," said Sara.

Velma gave her an encouraging smile.

"It's the practical consideration I'm thinking about now. He lives with us. He can't live alone. I'm going to have a hard time going my own way with him right there at the dinner table every night. I can get another job, but his company is going to be pretty unpleasant." After a moment she added, "But so what else is new?"

"Have you looked for a job?" asked Velma.

"Not yet. I'm still reading trashy novels."

"Make it last!" exclaimed Sophie, whose lovely curves, violated by the man next door, were buried in the peach colored beanbag. "You may never get another chance."

The chorus of laughter lifted Sara's spirits. So did hearing the absurd lengths to which Clarissa took being a good daughter, reporting to her mother every detail of her life, enduring inspection and criticism couched as helpful suggestions. She sat upright, her legs folded semi-lotus off the edge of the beanbag. "My mother wants to know what everything costs, who I have lunch with, what we talk about, you name it. She buys bargains for me at yard sales, and then I'm stuck with a house full of stuff I don't want. She thinks talking on the phone every day is what *I* want to do." Clarissa had been robbed at gunpoint, and though her purse full of personal items was recovered from a curbside trash can, the wallet full of money, both paper and plastic, was gone forever.

When the meeting ended, Sara lingered until the others had gone, then asked Velma if she'd had anything particular in mind with her question about wanting to understand.

"As a matter of fact, yes," Velma answered. "Sometime clients want badly to understand why they feel or act the way they do, and I try to refer them to someone who specializes in depth psychology. I know some very good therapists in that line. Other folks don't have the need or the interest. They want most of all to change the behavior that's plaguing them. Still others just want what we offer here, some support to help get through a tough time."

Sara nodded. "I see. I think I'm probably in that last category. Only it's funny. I don't feel like a victim at all. The hold up scared me, but it also brought me out of the rut I was in. Did I ever tell you that one of the men who tied me up called out "Merry Christmas" as they left the store? I thought it was cruel at the time."

Velma enfolded Sara's slim body in a large hug and stood back, saying, "You're one tough lady. You're going to be just fine."

On the way home Sara processed the remark with enjoyment but decided to maintain her status as a delicate flower for a while longer. Being one tough lady could wait.

She had wakened with a frightening dream last night. Her crying out roused Fred into a semiconscious state, and he rolled over and held her while she told him the dream.

"There was a teeter-totter in the dream. It had an old man on one end, an old man dressed in black clothes that were just rags, tattered, you know, like a homeless man. He looked like a panhandler, really, the kind that pushes right up in your face and demands that you give him money. He was sitting on one end, holding the end down, and there was a little girl on the other end. She was only three or four years old, and this old man was holding the teeter-totter down so that she was stranded up in the air." Sara's breath came in gasps.

"Ummm, and then what happened?"

"The wind is blowing and his clothes blow around him in strings, like tatters, you know. He looks really malicious. He's got great big red thumbs you can see sticking up where he's holding on. What he does is, he mashes those red thumbs down on the handles and then slides off the end of the teeter-totter and lets the little girl crash to the ground."

Fred held her tighter. "It's just a dream, baby, it's just a dream."

"I know." But she cried anyway.

Being one tough lady could wait. It would take practice, lots of practice.

SOLUTIONS

One evening late in January the phone rang at the Bekin/Rochester house. Fred answered. It was Scott Pearce, an old associate from Powkin, one of the salesmen who claimed to spend his life in airports. Scott, with his hayseed good looks and rowdy sense of humor, was as capable of selling himself as he was selling products. He had not lingered jobless for long. "You still looking for work?" was the question after the hey-how-ya-doing was complete.

"I gave it up," Fred answered. "I was getting résumé sickness."

"You know anything about computers?"

"I know they're a pain in the ass."

"Get over it," said Scott. "You're just the person this outfit I know about needs."

"What outfit is that?"

"It's a place that makes computer programs for local companies. 'Solutions', they call it. They need somebody who can write manuals."

"What else do I hafta know besides how to write?"

"How to recognize a pain in the ass as the hottest thing since sliced bread."

"Oh that. I can pretend," Fred said. "But I don't know doodley-squat about how to use a computer, let alone how to teach the unwashed masses."

"Not a problem. The programmers show you how to use it, hands on. Then you teach the unwashed masses."

"How come they can't write their own manuals?"

"They can, but nobody understands them. Take a look in a computer store next time you're at the mall. The manuals are written in a second language by somebody who doesn't have a first. We can just be grateful that Solutions recognizes the problem. Maybe some of the others will catch on."

"So how do I connect with them?"

Scott gave him a name and phone number. "Tell him you're the guy Scott Pearce recommended."

"That'll sour the deal."

But it didn't sour the deal.

On the contrary, Ron at Solutions remembered Scott Pearce right away and set up an appointment for an interview.

Meanwhile Fred had continued helping out at the store mornings before going to the library for the afternoon. Claire's presence sweetened the grim prospect of being at Mr. Rochester's beck and call for four hours a day, but even without her he would have felt obliged to contribute some effort there, considering how much of the family income came from the store.

He set up the appointment at Solutions for an afternoon hour, telling no one that he was not going to the library.

Getting dressed secretly took some doing. Fred's business suits now hung at the back of the closet. His starched shirts were still in their plastic laundry covers folded around cardboard. With both Aunt Jenny and Sara at home, he could hardly escape notice changing clothes. It was not his regular practice to leave the house looking spiffy, shoes shined, carrying his briefcase.

It wouldn't do to get anybody's hopes up, his own least of all. Finding a job was not high on the possibilities list. Fred wanted his almost certain disappointment to be a private matter.

So he managed to put the suit coat and briefcase in the car well ahead of time. The good crease in the pant legs worried him, but he couldn't very well change pants in the car. So he entered the house quietly after finishing up at the store, timing his arrival to coincide with Jenny's nap. He couldn't predict what Sara would be doing, but here he got lucky. She was absorbed in her book and paid little attention when he arrived. She put her face up for a kiss and that was about it. When he was dressed for business with a big sloppy pullover covering his shirt and tie, he sidled to her chair, kissed her again, and sidled out, with only Marigold to watch him leave.

The Solutions office was housed in a new office park near the toll road. One of the buildings was still under construction. The others had vacancy signs that stressed affordability. Fred found Solutions on the fourth floor of a six floor building. To make himself feel fit, he climbed the stairs rather than use the elevator.

The office secretary doubled as a receptionist. "Hello," she said warmly. "You must be Mr. Bekin." She swiveled her chair and called, "Ron, Mr. Bekin is here."

Casual, Fred thought. The office was an undecorated workplace with four desks and two doors leading to private offices. The secretary/receptionist pointed him to one of these.

He found himself overdressed for the occasion. Ron wore tan corduroy pants, a royal blue sweater and a straggly brown beard that tried to counteract a tendency to premature baldness. He rose from his cluttered desk and offered Fred a long, loose-fingered hand. "Sit here," he suggested, indicating the only other chair that wasn't piled with stacks of paper. "Sorry it's such a mess."

"I'm used to mess," Fred said. He would admit to being used to mess, but he was careful not to relax into the sloppy speech that Aunt Jenny called "mobster talk."

Ron, however, did most of the talking. Solutions was a small outfit, he told Fred, but hoped to grow. They had three programmers and a salesman. They wrote specific programs for local businesses.

"It would save us a lot of time to have instructions that are easy enough to understand that people don't keep calling us to come over and show them what to do."

Fred opened his briefcase. He set out, on top of Ron's mess, manuals he had written for Powkin as well as magazines that featured his articles. "My problem is that I have never used a computer," he confessed. "Scott told me that I would be taught how. We would have to have that straight if I came to work here." He added, "I don't want to mislead you."

"Actually, that's an advantage," Ron said. "The programmers know too much. They can't get down to the user's level." He hastened to add, "But they can show you what you'll need to know."

Fred nodded. He had taken Scott's advice and checked out what the computer stores had to offer. Nobody could learn how to run the damn things if they didn't even tell you how to turn them on.

"I never take it for granted that the user knows anything," he said. "I always start with a section for the beginner who doesn't even know where the on/off switch is."

It did not take long before Ron offered Fred the job. "When can you come in and get started?" he asked. "We have a program almost finished for the dispatcher at the Columbia police station."

"I can be here Monday," Fred answered. He couldn't very well say "tomorrow" because tomorrow was Saturday.

His mood of secrecy vanished by the time he got home. Still wearing the suit and tie, he plopped himself down across from Sara and waited for her comment.

Her comment was a raised eyebrow. He remained silent but couldn't control the smile that threatened to turn into a grin.

"So what is it?" she finally said. "Your whiskers are dripping cream."

Although bursting with news he said calmly, "I start work Monday." She still didn't get it. "I gotta job, babe," he said, "I gotta job, a real go-to-the-office job." The drawbacks – the meager salary, the start-up business with its lack of amenities – did not diminish his joy. He and Sara stood up simultaneously to grab each other and hug, swaying together, for a long time.

At the dinner table Aunt Jenny, too, shone with pleasure. "I knew you could do it, Freddy," she exclaimed. "Just think how much better life is going to be for all those poor people who haven't had a Fred Bekin instruction book!"

Mr. Rochester's first comment was, "I hope I can get Ben to come back afternoons and work a couple of hours between his shifts at the school," he said. "Another pair of hands gone isn't going to help."

Sara shook her head faintly as she gazed almost unbelieving at her father, seeing him as he really was.

The next day she phoned the hospital to see if by chance they were looking for someone.

DRESSED FOR SUCCESS

The morning Corky's case was to come before the judge Claire took off work at the drugstore in order to accompany him to court. She had sent him to a barber the day before. She had made his clothing as near perfect as possible, laid out matching socks, a freshly dry-cleaned tie with diagonal gray and burgundy stripes, and an ironed handkerchief for his pocket. Carefully outfitted, he looked guilty of no felony, no misdemeanor, not even an indiscretion.

She took care with her own toilette as well, choosing a blue-gray fitted wool suit with a Miro scarf from the art museum and dressy boots purchased when they still had money. She would present the two of them as a respectable older couple of the same social class as the judge.

Their outerwear, however, was chosen for warmth, not style. Three inches of fresh snow threatened their footing on the walk to Claire's old VW van. The van was an unspoken choice. It had more tread left on the tires than Corky's even older Chevrolet. Claire had to rock the van, shifting from first to reverse and back again several times before she built up enough momentum to pull away from the curb. Clover Street had not been plowed. Fortunately there was no traffic. She drove slowly, but the rear end fishtailed slightly at every modification of speed. Traffic picked up when they turned onto Osborne. Here and on Euclid Avenue the street was grainy with salt and sand. Driving kept Claire occupied while Corky, belted into the passenger seat, sat with his head bowed. She hoped he was praying, not sleeping. It could be either. She never knew. Downtown, instead of trying to find street parking, she took a ticket and circled up and up to the fourth level of the courthouse parking garage.

They slopped across the wet street to meet Neil for breakfast in a booth at More Waffles 4 U. Neil, of course, outshone them sartorially, with his tailored suit, winter tan, fitness club physique, and hair not only coiffed but colored and silvered as well.

"You've had your eyelids done!" Claire exclaimed.

Neil chose to take this as a compliment, nodding modestly. "I think we'll do well today," he said.

Claire was not at all sure what Neil meant by doing well. Did he mean Corky would leave court a free man, which would indicate that Neil had done well as an attorney, or did he, as Claire's ex-husband, think it well that Corky go to prison for the rest of his life? The way he had glanced at Corky, then dropped his gaze to the menu, indicated the latter.

Before he could explain what he meant, the waiter appeared with hot coffee and took their orders. More Waffles prided itself on its many varieties of pancakes as well as traditional waffles. Claire stuck with blueberry, but Corky decided on peanut butter topped with wild grape syrup. Neil ordered yogurt, granola and half a grapefruit.

The restaurant was full: defendants indistinguishable from witnesses and victims, humanity en masse. Well-dressed attorneys nodded to each other and to Neil. A bail bondsman breakfasted across from what had to be a runner with muscles threatening to burst his sleeves. The two leaned together over a small corner table, conversing earnestly under a line drawing of the new jail, one of the several drawings of Portville's landmarks that decorated More Waffles' walls.

"Tuck your napkin," Claire instructed Corky. "You don't need syrup on your tie." He obeyed. She swiped a second napkin from the unused fourth place setting at their booth and laid it on his lap.

After a few bites of granola, Neil began filling them in on what would happen in court. "Judge Hamilton may put you off, but he's reasonable," said Neil. "And he's a stickler for the law. I do all the talking except when you're asked a direct question. Keep you answers down to Yes Sir or No Sir whenever possible. And Claire," he gave her a sharp look, "you can't hold Corky's hand. You sit where you're told and don't make waves."

She couldn't have stayed with Corky or made waves anyway. Claire sat in the part of the courtroom reserved for spectators. The seats were in rows like bleachers, their old oak arms deeply grooved by years of nervous thumbnails digging into the grain. She was not alone.

The families and friends of three other defendants awkwardly held hands or sat staring ahead with stony faces. Corky's was the third of the four cases before Judge Hamilton this morning.

Claire knew better than to get her hopes up for a dismissal. With Corky acting as he had been, shamed and grieving, she knew there was more than enough evidence to not only make a case but to win it.

In line with Neil's ambiguous prediction, she imagined going home without Corky, imagined visiting the prison where they would talk without touching through a steel mesh screen. She thought about the immense task of seeing that he had enough to read, of choosing books for him, of difficulties with the library. Although most of the books on Corky's card had been returned, thanks to Fred, the fine had not been paid. Her own card was good, but if he lost the books taken out on it, she wouldn't be able to use it for long.

She shook her head. Silly. How could a person lose books in a prison cell? She didn't know, but Corky would do it. He would turn himself and his cell into a lending library, and the books on her card would be scattered all over the prison.

Why can't I laugh at this? she asked herself. It's funny.

It's not funny to me, she answered. It's not funny when I can't get books back to the library on time. It's not funny when he prevents me from doing my civic duty. What if I too lose library privileges?

Then she left the luxury of thinking about books and libraries and turned her attention to the scene at hand. The principals did not use microphones; thus the proceedings were not easily audible in the spectators' gallery. Even straining her ears, Claire could make out very little of what was going on.

What a pathetic bunch of people these were, she thought. The man in front of the judge now wore a straggling ponytail down his skinny back and jiggled from one foot to the other. His offense had something to do with a borrowed car running into something. Was his driver's license being taken away? If so, she felt sorry for him. How would he hold down a job, earn money, pay restitution?

The power here is so unevenly divided, she thought. Little people don't stand a chance. If you're poor, you will be even poorer after the law gets through with you. The Lord giveth and the Law taketh away.

Claire felt disloyal in her Miro scarf, trying to place herself above the usual suspects.

But what could she do? She couldn't let Corky appear less than he was.

The man with the ponytail was escorted out of the courtroom. A blowsy woman left the spectators' area, her heavy bag bumping the backs of seats as she hurried to join him.

The second case involved a man's violating probation and went very quickly. Another year was added to the length of probation time with the warning of jail time if there was another violation. The judge's stern tone had made this warning audible.

And now Corky and Neil went forward. Claire slumped in her seat. There was Corky, tripping over an untied shoelace.

Although she had listened and tried to understand, Claire could comprehend neither the law nor Neil's defense. She didn't even know just what the event she was witnessing was called or what it would decide. She had never been able to follow Neil when he talked law, and she was particularly unable to take in and absorb what he said about Corky. This kind of information simply flew out of her mind: it was like the size of the national debt or the contents of Roberts' Rules, incomprehensible. But what she did know sounded bad. Corky had said he would plead guilty if he had to. A tape existed that described the crime. People from the past were burying Portville in letters accusing him of fondling little girls ten and twenty years ago. And then there was the other case last spring. Neil had mentioned something about intent, but why would a person do all this fondling for no reason and without any sexual feeling? With all this against him, Corky would surely go to prison for years. Child molesting had turned into the crime of the year. She could picture the judge picking up a heavy book, the Bible, perhaps, and slamming it down on Corky's bowed head.

All she could hear were voices, not words. Prosecutor Bayer talked first. Then it was Neil talking, nodding, emphasizing his words with little chops of the hand. With a flush of animosity, she remembered the way he used to practice this performance in front of a mirror back when he was still a student, working as much on presentation as on points of law. A flurry of argument arose. The prosecutor continued to talk while Neil shook his head and pointed to papers. And then the judge rapped his gavel. "Case dismissed," he said. Looking straight at Corky, he added, this time loudly enough for the whole courtroom to hear, "I never want to see or hear of you again."

Neil beckoned for Claire to join them in the hall outside. "What happened?" she asked anxiously, looking from Corky's still-bowed head to Neil's look of contempt and back again.

"There wasn't a case," Neil said. "What the girl admitted to doesn't constitute a crime. It's slimy as hell, but the law doesn't cover slime."

Corky winced.

"Does this mean it's over?" Claire asked.

Neil nodded. "It's over. We can all go home now."

The tears started in Claire's eyes.

Ahead on the left was the men's restroom. Corky excused himself.

"Neil, please tell me what happened," Claire asked. "How can there have been all this trouble if nothing happened?"

"I didn't say nothing happened. It happened all right. But the judge decided that what the girl told did not meet the criterion of 'with intent to arouse'. There was no touching of genitals. Bayer tried to make a case, but it didn't wash with this judge. Guilty as hell, but no case."

"I still don't understand. If there wasn't a case, why didn't you tell us?"

"Look, Claire," Neil said, taking her arm and moving her toward the wall out of the straggle of persons entering and exiting the courtroom. "Face it, Corky's a pervert, a pedophile. If they catch him, he'll go to prison. What you need to do is send Romy's girl back to her mother and keep Corky on a short leash."

Claire's tears crept down her cheeks.

Neil leaned closer. "I still care about you," he said. "But I could care less for Corky. He deserved to stew in his own juice for a while."

"You mean you let him think he might go to prison when you knew he wouldn't?"

"There had to be some consequence for what he's done. If he spent some time worrying, maybe he'll think twice about the way he acts." Neil put his arm around her shoulders. "You don't deserve this mess. I wish I could do more to help."

Claire was silent. Her thoughts jangled with her feelings for a while before some words came out. "You've already done more than anyone could ask for." She saw Corky come out of the men's room and look around for them. "Why don't you go on ahead. I'll wait for Corky. And thanks, Neil, thanks for everything." She hugged him.

He bent down and kissed her, then turned away and headed for the stairs.

When Corky joined her, he had more color in his face than Claire had seen for a long time. His hair and cheeks were damp, as was his collar, as though he had splashed away his grayness and ran it down the courthouse drain.

She felt herself grow hot as anger coursed through her body. How could he shed months of misery with a handful of water? Rather than show how she felt, however, she took Corky's arm and steered him past a knot of men in earnest conversation. They proceeded without talking out to the grubby sidewalk of downtown Portville. Half a block later she ventured a question. "Were you surprised?"

"Relieved," he answered. "Neil told me this might happen, but I didn't have much hope. I'm just terribly relieved."

"If he told you this, why didn't you tell me?"

"I did," he answered. "I told you that I had done what Josie said I did. I told you the tape didn't prove intent of a criminal act."

Claire stared up at him in amazement. "If you told me this, you must have buried it in a lot of other talk, because I sure never heard it. Here I've been worrying myself sick over nothing! Couldn't you see that?"

"I've been pretty worried too, Claire. I thought there was cause for worry and it didn't seem strange that you'd be concerned."

"So what are we going to do now?" As she said this, Claire realized that she really had been looking forward to Corky's absence. She'd been thinking she could get her life back together if she were relieved of having to take care of him. "Don't answer that," she said. "We need some time to settle into a new reality."

"Yes, now that we're no longer under the sword of Damocles, we can attend to smaller problems, like the fate of the world."

"Fate of the Pearlmans. Let's consider little details like where we're going to live."

"And on what."

"Well, in that regard we're no worse off today than we were yesterday."

Feeling guilty over wishing Corky were behind bars and off her hands, Claire suggested stopping for hot chocolate. "We've got almost another hour left on our parking."

But Corky shook his head. "I don't feel celebratory. Relieved, yes, but not exactly joyous." With his head down, he was just about to bump into a lamp post. Claire pulled him away just in time. He jerked his head up. "Yes, thanks!" he said.

"Tie your shoe!" Claire hissed. Obediently Corky stooped and fumbled with the laces.

In the van Claire turned on the heater while it was still cold, just to have the noise of the blower fill the silence with frigid air between them. They were almost home before Corky heaved a great sigh and said, "I'm only partly relieved. I wasn't looking forward to being treated like a criminal, but being where I didn't have any responsibilities had its appeal. If I *couldn't* take any action in my own behalf, or find work, I wouldn't have to try."

Claire's lips pressed together. It was okay for him to say this but not for her. He could tell her it was too bad that he didn't go to prison, but she couldn't agree. She was so intent on controlling herself that she missed the turn off Osborne.

"Go to jail. Go straight to jail. Do not pass GO," said Corky.

It was a relief for her to laugh.

Claire intended to take the whole day off from the drugstore. Mr. Rochester had grumbled but yielded, as he must. She opened a can of tomato soup and made tuna sandwiches for lunch.

They sat in the kitchen to eat. The dining room was still cluttered even while being bare. Claire had sent so much furniture to Bloomington with Romy that the house looked like a slovenly transient, grubby, bewhiskered with cobwebs, carrying too much stuff and too few possessions. There were fewer chairs to pile with papers and books. Now the books and papers were piled on the floor or on boxes, with an aisle allowing movement from one room to the other. The dining table was gone.

Claire swallowed her soup without being hungry. Even this liquid seemed to meet resistance from her knotted stomach. She had girded up her loins for disaster. The disaster had dribbled away, but ungirding for an anticlimax was going to take time. Also, Neil's advice was still with her: Send Nancy away. It echoed something she herself had begun to realize. Why was it that she had arranged her hours at the drugstore so as to be at home when Nancy arrived from school? Why was it that she managed to be present when Corky and Nancy were together?

Oh, this was intolerable! How could she possibly police her own home? And how could she possibly not?

"I think I'll go in to the store for a couple of hours," she told Corky. "Let the old man blow off some steam. He wasn't happy about my taking the morning off."

Corky was already reading. He nodded absently.

"Do you have any plans?" she asked. "What are you going to do this afternoon?"

His glance up at her was wondering. "How could I have plans? I suppose I'll stay in and read."

Again Claire held her tongue. He was right. A man doesn't make plans on the day his freedom is up for grabs. But it would be nice if he considered being useful.

As though reading her mind he asked, "Is there anything you'd like me to do? I've been a bit distracted from chores lately, to say the least."

"Look around you," she answered. "If you see anything that needs doing, any mess that needs picking up, anything broken that needs mending..... Oh Corky, pay some attention!" Her gaze took in the accumulated dirt and disorder of many dysfunctional months.

"Of course," he said. Standing quickly, he picked up their soup bowls and sandwich plates and carried them to the kitchen sink. "I'll go through the mail. That'll be an all day job." No one had thrown away junk mail for weeks.

"Be careful," Claire said in alarm. "Don't throw away anything we might need." If he tossed the electric bill, they would be in trouble.

He picked up the colorful, oversized junk card that lay on top of one pile. "We might need to buy waterfront property," he said. "Maybe I ought to save this." His voice was dry.

"You're hopeless," she said. "I'm going to work."

Mr. Rochester's scowl did not lessen at Claire's approach. "Look what we have to take this time," he grumbled. "What kind of pharmacy sells cat food and Spanish olives?"

Claire stuffed her scarf in her sleeve and hung her coat on the rack in the back room. She knew not to answer. Let him continue.

"This isn't a grocery. Or a pet boutique."

He was complaining again about the ad service that required him to deal with unwelcome merchandise. Rochester's needed the ads. But the old man's pride was at stake. "Cat food!" he repeated. "I never met a cat worth feeding."

Claire saw that the day's boxes from UPS had not been opened. Without Fred's help the work piled up. She rummaged through the crate that served as her desk drawer for the box cutter and busied herself opening cartons, checking inventory lists and stocking shelves. She had not expected Mr. Rochester to inquire after Corky. His lack of interest was just as well. If he even knew about Corky's trouble, Claire wasn't aware of it.

It was Charlie, the pharmacist, who asked, "How did it go?"

Struck by the concern in his voice, so at odds with Mr. Rochester's lack of it, Claire felt a surge of tears. "It's over," she said. "There was no evidence. No case."

"What a relief!"

She nodded. Relief was the sensible thing to feel. She tried.

Charlie did not ask for details and Claire did not provide them. She came to work this afternoon to get away from the situation, not to offer it up as gossip.

Claire had made friends with Charlie as soon as she began coming to the store. She admired his willingness to work, his cheerful attitude. Along with the sales clerks, Lenora and Christabel, they shared jokes about Mr. Rochester and the outrageous things he said.

But Charlie had more on his mind than the outcome of Corky's legal problems. "I have a favor to ask of you," he said. "I could do this myself, but it would be better, strategically, if I didn't." His face opened into a beaming smile. "Would you hand deliver this to the old man?" He held out a sealed envelope.

"Well, sure," Claire answered. She left the question unspoken.

He answered it anyway. "I'm making an offer to buy the store," he said. "I want to give him time to think about it before he talks to me."

With her attention caught, Claire's mouth fell open. "Wow!"

"Hold on to this until he's in the midst of something that drives him crazy."

She nodded. "That could be almost any time. He's crazy right now about having to sell cat food."

"You pick a time. I'm pretty well removed from what he's doing unless he comes up here to set me straight on something."

"What prompted you to decide to do this?"

"I've been working here for so long that it feels like it's mine. Actually, I like it. I think I could do more with it than he does. Sara's not going to come back; you know that as well as I do. She tells me she's checking out the HMO that's going up out on the east side."

"That's good news."

"Once he realizes he's going to have to manage the place till the cows come home, you can never tell, maybe he'll be glad to get it off his hands. He keeps putting off hiring another pharmacist, but I can put the squeeze on him. All it would take is for me to have another sore throat." He cleared his throat and faked a cough. "He doesn't appreciate the place anyway."

Claire nodded. "True. He's so stuck in the past he can't see anything good up ahead."

"It's time to bring some of the past back into the store," Charlie told her. "An old-fashioned corner drugstore with a soda fountain and some nostalgia items would bring people in. There are a lot of retired folks living around here."

A customer came to the pharmacy cage. Claire pocketed Charlie's offer to buy. "I'll get this to him at the right time," she promised.

Charlie was already with the customer. "What can I do for you?"

Claire went back to setting out inventory. She removed what was left of last month's sale items to the back room and filled the prominent sale shelves with the new ones, careful to stack the cat food cans artfully and the olive jars safely. Already several cans of cat food were in the hands of shoppers and Lenora was telling a customer that it was her own cat's favorite brand.

It would take more than unwanted merchandise, however, to provide sufficient dismay for Mr. Rochester to be in the mood to sell. Claire tucked Charlie's envelope in her purse.

Heaps of paper littering the floor greeted Claire when she arrived home later that afternoon. Corky had been busy with the piles of mail. A wastebasket sat empty in the corner. An unreasonable surge of anger washed over her. She tried to calm herself and ignore the litter. She recognized how trivial the mess of junk mail was, compared to what she was *really* angry about. She stood still for a moment. I don't have to deal with the issue now, she thought. A few deep breaths calmed her a bit. She hung up her coat.

Corky had been cooking as well as sorting mail. She could smell it as soon as she walked in the door but could not identify the odor. She found him in the kitchen. The odor was delicious and the kitchen windows steamed up.

She eyed him cautiously and sniffed. "What's cooking?"

Corky had changed out of his go-to-court clothing and covered his old green sweater with an oversized white apron. The ties were wrapped around and tied in front. He had not cooked anything for months.

"A mess of slumgullion," he answered. "I cleaned out the fridge."

"You also worked over the junk mail. Was there anything interesting?"

"I'm afraid to look," he answered. "A letter for you from Betty Nichols."

Betty Nichols was a former parishioner from years ago, from when Corky was still a Methodist minister in Indianapolis. She had faithfully taught Sunday School while her two little girls went through the ranks.

Claire's eyes closed for a moment as she steeled herself. So it wasn't over after all. How much longer would this hell go on? With her loyalty to him in tatters, she crossed the room to Corky standing at the sink and put her arm around him. "It's brave of you to save it for me."

"Believe me, I wanted to burn it up without letting you open it. But it's a federal offence to interfere with the mail." His voice was dry.

Claire accepted his attempt at humor. She rolled her eyes and changed the subject. "What's the difference between a mess of slumgullion and a mess of pottage?"

He replied instantly. ""Slumgullion has more broth. It was slim pickings in the fridge. I had to throw a lot of stuff out. So I put in the rest of the red wine." He turned to the stove and stirred the pot. "Esau probably wouldn't have sold his birthright for slumgullion," he reflected. "Not enough substance."

Claire heaved a sigh. "Corky, I sometimes wonder why I put up with you." Her tone asked the real question in a lighthearted way.

"I wonder that too."

And well he should, she thought. Why would anyone put up with a pervert? But this was not the time to address the issue. Nancy would come home soon. They would have to wait until there was time to talk. "Because you're fun to be around. Sometimes," she added. "But no one is fun to be around when he's depressed."

"My mood miraculously lifted today. I'm downright ebullient."

"I can tell." He was at least awake and on his feet.

"There's still trouble ahead. We still have Betty Nichols to contend with." Corky's tone turned serious. "I escaped going to prison, but not by much."

Prison would have settled it. As it was, it was still left hanging for them to deal with.

"And you got a letter from Elizabeth."

"I did?" Claire quickly found the small stack of real mail in the dining room amidst the flurry of junk. With the two letters and a couple of bills was her monthly settlement check from Neil's law firm. She smiled at the coincidence and felt grateful once again that Neil was a decent person and that their divorce had not been filled with the kind of rancor that so often eats up a couple's assets and makes satisfactory settlement impossible. She and Corky were poor, living on this check, some dividends from his father's stocks, and her pittance from the drug store, but they wouldn't starve.

She read Elizabeth's letter quickly, then called out to Corky, "She's coming home!" Carrying the scribbled sheets she went back to the kitchen. "She's taking leave and coming home."

"Wonderful! We'll kill the old red rooster! Think of it, two blessings in a single day!"

"We're due for some blessings."

"There'll be a third, wait and see. Things like that always come in threes."

Claire remembered the envelope in her purse. "It's already happened," she said. "Charlie's making the old man an offer to buy the store."

But Corky was reaching for Elizabeth's letter. "That's nice," he said. "When is she coming?"

"It doesn't say, but sometime soon."

"We'd better get busy. If she sees this house, she'll spend her vacation working on it."

Here their conversation was interrupted. The front door closed. "I'm home!" It was Nancy.

Claire glanced at the clock. "Where have you been?" She realized that she should have been worried. "It's almost five o'clock."

"I went to the library. I told you. You're the one who said I had to go today."

"That's right, you did tell me." Claire bent to hug the little girl. "I'm sorry I've been so hard-nosed about the library," she said. "But we have a horrible example right here of what happens when you don't pay attention to returning books on time."

Corky took a sheepish bow. "Do I get a hug?"

Claire's stomach knotted.

But Nancy had already flung off her coat and was heading for the stairs.

Corky slumped back into dejection before the meal was over, despite Nancy's joy at hearing the good news. "I would really miss you if you went to jail," she told him. "It's like you and Aunt Claire fit together. If you weren't here, she'd be lopsided." She fished a piece of turnip from the soup and laid it on the edge of her salad plate. "I prayed for you," she said. "I don't really believe in miracles, but I prayed for one anyway."

Corky's startled hand spilled soup, staining the apron he still wore. "Thank you," he said formally.

"Does this mean you can go back to church?" she asked.

He shook his head. "I'm afraid not. It only means I don't have to go to prison."

"I was hoping you would be the minister again," she said. "People are nicer if you're the minister."

His smile looked more like a grimace. "That all depends," he answered. "That all depends."

"What kind of homework do you have tonight?" Claire interjected.

"Language arts," Nancy answered. "We have to read the next chapter and answer questions. Answering the questions is the hard part."

"Let's read it out loud together," said Claire. "We can talk about it. It'll be easier then."

Corky gave her a grateful glance. They would have plenty of time to make plans and solve problems. To read or not read Betty Nichols' letter. Tonight they could do homework.

A BETTER HOUSE

Aunt Jenny now had the free run of the house. She could approach the kitchen without tiptoeing. Mr. Rochester no longer lurked in his den nearby, ready to lecture her on whatever she might cook or eat. She could nibble on sweets, butter her toast, fry an egg and salt it generously without bringing down his monotone of righteousness. She could even slip Marigold a bite now and then.

She no longer had to listen to him grumble about Sara and the store, at least during the day, and no longer had to close her ears to the fulsome tones of the televangelists he favored.

It was altogether a better house without him. Her small, slippered footsteps pattered quietly from room to room, up the front stairs and down the back, as she took her exercise several times a day. Her route did not include the downstairs part of the wing where Mr. Rochester and Fred had their dens and Sara had her sewing room, but she did walk the unused, chilly upstairs hall above with its three closed-off bedrooms. Sometimes she stopped, but not for long, at the double windows in the large bedroom at the end where she watched the chickadees and juncos flit about in the maple trees outside. Determined to keep herself mobile, she covered her miles indoors during the snowy Portville winter.

And thank heavens for the good reverend! Corky showed up faithfully on Friday afternoons to take her out in the car, or, if the streets were too icy, to join her in cocoa and cookies in front of the fire that Fred was always kind enough to lay for her on Thursday night. Corky would sit in a wing chair, Jenny in her small rocker, Marigold lying near the coffee table with her nose quivering toward the plate of goodies.

Sometimes Sara would leave the couch in her sewing room and pull up the other wing chair to join them. She was still sticking it out at home, determined not to go back to the store, no matter how much she pitied poor Charlie. There was no work for her at the hospital, but she had been promised a pharmacy position with the new HMO when it opened next summer.

Jenny still wanted spiritual direction from Corky to guide her in her waning years, as well as his companionship. She had urged him to give her assignments, and she read the books he brought her. Sara listened quietly to their exploration of late-life issues, occasionally joining the conversation. She wasn't at the late-life stage yet, but she would be one day.

Jenny wasn't really there yet either, in her own opinion. Yes, she was getting on in years, but she still had her health and her faculties – at least some of them.

"One of the important issues as we age," Corky advised her, "is to take stock of what we have left and how we want to use it."

Sara nodded, and Jenny sat up straighter to say, "I want to use it in self indulgence!" She folded her hands and assumed a prim expression.

"You don't want to save the world?" asked Corky. His doggy smile was teasing, his sparse, sandy hair sticking out in tufts like a scarecrow's.

"I know better. My efforts went to the children I taught all those years. Saving the world is their job now. Not that I believe they can do it."

"That's sounds pretty negative," said Sara. "They can at least try."

Jenny nodded. "It makes people feel better to try. I'm not so sure that it does much good." With Corky's encouraging attention, she continued. "I've watched people try to change the big things for many years. You can't do it until something else happens. The tide has to turn. There has to be some unexpected event or development in technology. Until it happens, you're better off biding your time and working on the small changes at hand."

"Actually, *healing* the world, I believe, is a better goal than trying to save it," said Corky. "Saving it, like curing something, implies once and for all. But healing takes place everywhere all the time, as new rips and tears and wounds occur." He nodded toward Sara. "You know all about that."

"Yes," she answered. "Your customers come in with their prescriptions and you think, 'What now?' They have diabetes and arteriosclerosis and God knows what else that are more or less controlled with drugs. They aren't going to be cured. But they also get rashes and cuts and infections that can be healed even while the big problems are still there. What I'm saying is that we stave off death with the one hand while we use the other to tend wounds."

Jenny frowned. "Are you suggesting that self-indulgence isn't enough?"

"What do *you* think?" Corky asked. "Does it feel like enough?"

"Not really," she replied. "But I'm limited in what I can do."

"What do you *like* to do? The best healing of the world is done by people doing what they really like to do."

Jenny sat silent, thinking. "I miss the children," she said, finally. "I'd still like to be teaching." She sighed. "Maybe I'm closer to late-life issues than I want to think I am. I'm elderly, and I'm just trying to stave off being frail-elderly."

"You can still do some teaching," said Corky. "There's a practical way and a spiritual way."

Jenny's glance was skeptical. "Tell me the practical way."

"You could mentor a child. Help with homework, be a confidante."

"Yes, of course." Jenny nodded. Her eyes brightened. "Oh, I'd love that! Good works and self indulgence both at the same time! But how would I hook up with a child?"

"I'll have Claire look into it. I'd do it myself, but…," he hesitated.

Jenny, who had no doubt of Corky's innocence, steered the conversation away from troublesome topics. "What about the spiritual way? What did you mean by a spiritual way of teaching?"

He answered slowly. "It's not that easy, at least for most of us. It means going inside. You sit quietly with your eyes closed and breathe attentively until you are relaxed. Then you imagine yourself in a place where you might meet with a child. You picture it as completely as you can, fill in as many details as possible. You might even set out a treat or a toy for the child. Then you wait. Perhaps a child will come, maybe a child you know or knew in the past, maybe someone you've never seen before. You remain quiet but welcoming. Let the child handle the action. In other words you watch, and you respond to whatever the child does, rather than initiate things yourself."

Jenny was listening carefully. She nodded. "I think maybe I could do that. But in addition to, not in place of, meeting with a real child."

Corky went on. "The thing is to make this an intentional activity. Do it every day, maybe even at the same time every day."

"Well, yes, but why is that so important?"

"You wouldn't stand up a real child, would you?"

Jenny shook her head. "Of course not."

"The child in your imagination doesn't want to be stood up either. He or she would be disappointed, and would lose interest if you didn't show up. This is the spiritual practice part of it: you have to take it seriously and do it regularly. You don't know what will happen, but whatever does happen, you need to pay attention."

"I've never heard of such a thing," said Sara. "You make it sound almost like prayer or meditation."

"It's very much like prayer or meditation," said Corky. "When you pray, you are initiating a conversation with God. Sometimes God will meet you halfway and converse. This is the same thing. You go there, and you attend to what happens. It's also like a guided meditation, only you are letting your own imagination do the guiding. You respect the aspect of God that is within you, who can meet you halfway."

"I would probably make up a script for God congratulating me on my good works," said Jenny.

Corky shook his head. "You don't make up anything. You don't write the script and you don't direct the play. You just let it happen."

"What if nothing happens?"

"That's what people are afraid of. That's why most people avoid this practice. But if nothing happens it's no worse than having a friend call and cancel a meeting. That doesn't make you give up on having friends, does it? You don't quit making arrangements to get together, do you?"

"If a friend cancels a date, you can always do something else," said Sara. "Here you're stuck just sitting."

"True. But you might just sit and wait for your friend if she's late. Just sitting isn't the worst way to spend an hour."

After Corky had gone, Jenny returned to her room and sat in her small rocking chair. An hour seemed like a very long time. Her mind was full of words, incomplete sentences, partial conversations, arguments, explanations. What a babble!

This isn't for me, she thought. I'll have to do it the practical way. At that, her mind's eye opened. She saw herself waiting downstairs. There was a knock at the door. She answered it, and there was a child, a girl child. Clear as a picture, the girl wiped her feet on the coco mat outside. "Come in, my dear," said Jenny. The girl entered. She looked around the room shyly. "Why I know you!" Jenny exclaimed. She was the girl who had run away from the party at the ice cream parlor.

SARA'S ART PROJECT

Sara's interest in trashy novels had waned. The bodice-rippers had served her well while she was more or less inert and trying to stay that way. They required enough attention to divert her thoughts from her father and the store but not enough to strain her.

But now that she had a new job lined up, she felt sufficiently removed from the pharmacy to take on a project that had been waiting for years. "Frittering her time away," was how Mr. Rochester described what she was doing. She agreed. How long had it been since she'd had any time to fritter? A vacation? A few days off? Because he was a perfection addict who worked day and night and tolerated no errors, he believed that this was the appropriate standard for others to emulate. Time-frittering had no place in the plans of a responsible person. She had lived with this standard all her life.

Sara's support group helped counter her father's decree. Time-frittering was the most appropriate thing she could do right now, they told her. It was going to take a while for her to reorder her priorities, and a vacation from priorities was the best way to shake them up and winnow them. "You'll be surprised," Velma advised her, "what the winds of change will send to the pile of chaff."

The pharmacy wasn't exactly chaff. Sara's work was still a high priority. She would go back to work as soon as the new HMO opened. But that was a while off, and for now, pharmacy could stay in a separate compartment, on hold.

In her cheerful room at the end of the south wing she spread out the materials of her project on the floor: pictures cut from old magazines, bits of colored, textured paper, scissors and a paste made of paper glue and water.

Back in the days when cigars were sold at the drugstore, her father had saved the wooden boxes the cigars came in. Stacks of them. They were too good to throw away. And now Sara was indulging the fantasy she'd had for years of making attractive containers covered with paper collage: pictures, bits of color, even words.

She had chosen lesser boxes to practice on at first, the ones without hinges or clasps, the lids held on by their paper covering. There were only a few of these; they weren't really worth saving. But she cut paper shapes and brushed them with thin paste. On some of the paper she used pinking or scalloping scissors. She learned how to smooth out wrinkles, how to miter corners and bind edges. After several tries her boxes were looking good.

The conversations with Corky and Aunt Jenny gave her food for thought. She tried to imagine the process Corky had described, conjuring up an imaginary person and giving it credence and dignity. Was this person an "it"? Perhaps dignity required the pronouns "him" or "her".

But she couldn't do it. Her mind fell naturally into thinking, not imagining. And what she thought was that this was much too woo-woo for her. It was out of her ken. Maybe it worked for some people, but it didn't work for her.

Maybe it was what Corky did when he couldn't get his hands on a flesh and blood child.

This was a chilling picture. How could she, or anyone, for that matter, reconcile it with the Corky she was coming to know, rescuer of robbery victims, companion to the elderly, spiritual advisor?

She and Fred had talked about this. "It's a matter of tolerance," Fred maintained. "If I'm going to listen to somebody's story, I have to tolerate what I'm told."

But Sara was not obliged to listen to Corky's story. And neither was Fred, not now. Nevertheless, Corky was in their lives, part of their milieu, and his story had to be contained in it somehow.

Neither of them, however, knew the latest developments in the story. Fred's days no longer included contact with either Corky or Claire. And Sara saw Corky only when he came to visit Aunt Jenny. His legal events were not part of their discussions.

"We're not the kind of people to write somebody off completely," Fred insisted. "The man has good qualities too."

"I know that," Sara answered. "But how can you see the good qualities when the awful scene of him molesting a little girl rises up in your mind? How can you get past the bad when it's that bad?"

"For one thing, we don't know how bad it is. He's innocent until found guilty," said Fred. "Who are we to take on the responsibility of the court?"

"Where there's smoke there's fire," said Sara. "I just can't believe that he would have been arrested twice unless there was something to it."

"I can't either," Fred agreed. "Here's where I have to rely on another old saying. Who is so lily white as to cast the first stone?"

This was not entirely comfortable for Sara. Even murderers cast stones at a child molester. If we waited for someone without sin to come along, no one would be punished for anything. But at this point she couldn't condemn Corky and bar him from her life, and she needed a way to accommodate his presence without approving of whatever he did to that little girl.

After all, she tolerated her father. She'd had plenty of practice in tolerating. Making a home for a person who treated you as badly as her father treated her required quite a bit of tolerance.

The thing was not to condemn Corky, it was to keep him away from children. That would not be hard for her. There weren't any children to keep him away from. He wasn't going to molest Aunt Jenny, was he?

The work her hands did pasting up the boxes allowed her thoughts to chew over the situation again and again, and every time she chewed, she digested a little more.

But frittering was not the only work in which Sara's hands were occupied. It hadn't been long after quitting the drugstore that she began to notice all that needed doing in the house, *her* house. There was dirt everywhere, the dirt an old house not only gathers but produces, as its paint and plaster and even its wood slowly disintegrate into powder.

She and Fred had shared housework as well as cooking all the time they had lived here. His cleaning was not as thorough as hers, but for the sake of domestic tranquility she refrained from criticism.

Her first step was to secure the proper tools for cleaning. She replaced everyone's toothbrush with a new one and began using the old ones to get into the cracks and crevices where dirt tries to hide. Because cracks and crevices were everywhere, it seemed almost as though dirt was the mortar that held the house together. "You get it clean enough, it'll fall down," Fred advised.

"It'll fall down clean and shining then," she replied. "There's a lot to be said for going out in glory."

Toothbrushes couldn't get all the dirt. Certain edges, like where the floors met the baseboards and the baseboards met the walls, required prying out little black chunks of crud with the tip of a sharp knife. The woodwork in these old rooms had cracks filled with more than a century of dirt.

Sara enjoyed taking possession of her house in this way. She liked the smells of Murphy's Oil Soap and Johnson's wax. Cleaning it inch by inch made it hers in a way it had never been when she just lived here.

Aunt Jenny turned out to be a help, too. She didn't trust herself on a ladder anymore, and Sara couldn't bear to see her with a scrub brush, but she liked to sit at the big kitchen table and polish the silver painstakingly with Wrights Silver Cream, attacking tarnish in the crevices with a cotton swab or a rag on the end of a toothpick, rubbing each piece until it shone.

Between the two of them the old house was getting a new lease on life.

WORKING AT SOLUTIONS

Working at the cutting edge was suiting Fred to a T. Here was an outfit looking ahead, finding ways to make things work, rather than looking back and assigning blame for things that didn't work.

"Thank God I'm no older and more decrepit than I am," he had told Sara. "I'm not gonna know all this computer stuff the way the youngsters will, growing up with it, but I still have the smarts to learn what I need to know."

He didn't rate one of the private offices at Solutions but rather had been settled at the corner desk where he at least had a window. When he looked out it, which was not very often, he could see the nearby building projects that had halted during the impossible weather. The two offices went to Ron, who was the owner and CEO of Solutions, and to Frank Wiggins, the smooth-talking salesman. The other three desks, arranged as a unit within a large cubicle, were inhabited by the programmers.

"Actually, the word processing alone beats using a typewriter all to hell. No eraser crumbs gumming up the works. No cutting and pasting and endless retyping. I'm gonna buy one for myself."

Fred had been settling in, but not the way he'd settled in at Powkin. It was a different world now. You didn't take a job thinking you'd stay until time for Social Security and the gold watch. You thought of the present job as training for the next. As résumé building. If Solutions made it big, Ron might sell it and Fred could be unemployed again, just as easily as if Solutions went down the tubes.

He did not personalize the wall of his corner. Nothing of his remained there when he went home at night. He vowed he would never again have to clean out his desk. Even the framed photograph that sat daytimes on the corner of the desk went into his briefcase in the evening. It was his favorite photo, of himself and Sara, younger, with Marigold as a puppy, in front of the big old house they had just bought. His family.

Learning how to use the word processor required both patience and self-restraint. Muttering "Oh shit!" every time he hit a key that caused something unexpected to happen was not the way he wanted to present himself at this new job. He kept his mouth shut and acted like a man on top of things. The biggest frustration was the one he'd been hired to overcome: the paucity of easy instruction. There was no manual at all for the program he was learning, only the so-called "help" within the program itself. How could anyone benefit from "help" that you couldn't get to when you needed it most? When you'd been typing along and hit the control key instead of the shift and everything disappeared? The yellow tablet beside the keyboard was in constant use, its pages filling up with notes to himself. There was something counterintuitive about an object that, when it didn't work, was supposed to tell you how to make it work.

And of course it wasn't even the word processor that he was working on. He was learning the language of a 911 dispatcher and putting it together with instructions on how to use the program. Translating computer jargon into dispatcher jargon. It was coming along.

On the way home he still listened to *All Things Considered* and tape recorded notes for his blame book. He noticed the way more and more euphemisms came into being. "Hold accountable" was the phrase they were using now. "Blame" sounded worse than ever and had to be blunted with a polysyllabic euphemism: "responsible" was to "blame" as "inappropriate" was to "bad" and "hold accountable" was to "punish".

He also planned a chapter on the watered down language that allowed the politicians not only to avoid responsibility for what was going on but even to place the blame elsewhere. With a Teflon president promoting a "trickle-down" economy that was getting worse and worse even while booming, with tax cuts for the richest and job losses for the poorest and money being poured into MX missiles instead of Headstart, people were being suckered by slick language into thinking it was still "morning in America," even as the "homeless problem" grew. The only issue where blame was not euphemized was the frightening new disease, AIDS. It was okay to blame homosexuals outright for killing themselves and each other with their dirty sex. No slick language here.

It was sickening, but Fred used his outrage to fuel notes for the blame book.

WINTER'S LAST BLAST

March came in like a lion. The wind sweeping down from Canada enveloped Portville in a chill factor of $-20\,°$F. New snow continued to compact into thick layers of ice, making streets and sidewalks treacherous. Fred had to order another heating oil delivery before getting a bill for the last one.

It was the extremity of the cold that brought Claire's hesitant phone call. Fred answered.

"I have to ask a great favor," said Claire. "Our furnace quit again this evening, and we can't keep it warm enough over here to get by. Could Corky and Nancy and I bring our sleeping bags and spend the night on your living room floor?"

"Of course you can," he answered instantly, even happily. He missed Claire, now that he spent his mornings at Solutions instead of Rochester's. "We got lotsa space. You don't hafta sleep on the floor." Without waiting for her reply, he called out to Sara, "Open up the spare rooms, honey, we got company coming."

The spare rooms were not decked out for guests. Fred and Sara never had overnight guests. There were beds, old beds with old mattresses left over from Sara's childhood and kept for just-in-case, but that was about all.

There was plenty of clutter, however. Christmas decorations, on the way back up to the attic. Mr. Rochester's summer clothing that he insisted be removed from his closet when October came. Battered packages of paper goods from the store – napkins, towels, toilet tissue – bought in bulk and left unsold, unsightly but perfectly usable. The cigar boxes, packed in grocery bags. Chocolates from Valentine's Day. (Aunt Jenny had found these and was nibbling her way through the dark creams, leaving the nuts and fruits and milk chocolate untouched.) Old linens, too ragged to use, but too good to throw out. They came in handy for cleaning rags. Because of all this extra space in the house, there was no incentive to part with anything, and because the attic was hard to reach, with its pull-down stairs, the spare rooms filled up.

Sara was not quite as pleased as Fred to have the Pearlmans visiting overnight. She was the lady of the house and responsible, even though she had very little control over this aspect of housekeeping. With her father's watchful eye all too present, even with him out of the house daytimes, she had been unable to assert her responsibility and lay claim to the storage spaces. Anything he wanted kept, they kept. Not in his bedroom or his den, of course, which had to be rigorously tidy, but in the spare rooms that he considered free for all and especially free for him.

As Sara opened the radiators and made up the beds, she mentally set aside items to take to the Goodwill, while in the here-and-now she made the room as pleasant as possible. She unfolded sheets, laid them out and tucked them in, making neat hospital corners. I'll do it, she thought. This time I'll really do it. I can consider it part of my therapy. Then she fluffed a pillow and frowned at her subversive thinking. He won't have to know, she admitted. She wasn't ready to load the car right in front of him, to flaunt the disposal of cartons of display-sale Mandarin oranges and Windex. But maybe I should, she thought. Let him watch. It might give him a heart attack. The rooms smelled dusty and dry, like ancient wallpaper or fragile old clothes that would fall apart at a touch, but it was much too cold to open the windows and air them out.

The Pearlmans were subdued when they arrived with Nancy already in pajamas and robe under her coat and bunny slippers under her boots. They had brought their forest green sleeping bags, unwilling to impose by causing extra laundry. "This is so embarrassing," said Claire. "I just couldn't call anyone from Freethinkers. We're trying to keep as low a profile as possible." Her milky skin looked pasty with fatigue. "But we can't possibly buy a new furnace, especially for a house that isn't even ours."

"You're welcome to stay as long as you like. We're glad to have you." Sara had become more enthusiastic about the idea. Her father was still one fourth of the dinner table, a large fourth, his presence dictating endless, boring, repetitive, one-sided conversation about the store. One seventh would be a better proportion. How many people does it take, she wondered, to dilute one spoiler? She imagined a long, linen-covered table in a banquet hall. The head and the foot had to converse by means of walkie-talkies. "We would really love to have you stay. The weather's not going to change any time soon."

Aunt Jenny had heated a kettle of water and now offered spice tea or instant cocoa. "Freddy, why don't you light a fire?"

"No, no, please don't go to any trouble," begged Claire. "It's time for Nancy to get some sleep."

The little girl tried to scowl but yawned instead. "Heather gets to stay up till nine thirty."

"It's almost nine thirty now," said Claire. "Come along." She and Nancy followed Sara upstairs. "What a house! I knew it was big, but I didn't know it was *this* big. They sure didn't skimp, back in the old days, did they?"

The hallway in the south wing was more narrow than that of the main house. It was obvious that when the wing was created, the idea had been to add three extra rooms on each floor as simply and cheaply as possible. This hallway was separated from the main house by a door that served to close it off, and it ran along two of the rooms, ending at the door of the third. With two windows in the hall and no radiator, it was a chilly trek to bed.

"It'll warm up pretty quickly," said Sara. She led them into the first bedroom. The radiator was hissing already. "Nancy can sleep here and I'll put you and Corky in the big room at the end." She had made up the single bed with a colorful patchwork quilt. "This used to be my bed when I was a little girl," she said. "I hope you sleep well here."

After a moment of Nancy's silence, Claire gave her a nudge. "Thank you," she said at last. Then she turned to Claire and asked in an anguished tone, "Can I stay at Heather's tomorrow night?"

Claire sat down on the edge of the bed and embraced the little girl. "I'll talk to Heather's mother," she said, smoothing back the yellow curls that fell in Nancy's face. "I think we can work something out. You sleep here tonight and we'll think of something. This won't last forever." She kissed the child's forehead. "Would you like to be tucked in?"

Nancy nodded. Oftentimes she insisted that she was too old to be tucked in, but tonight was different.

"I'll be down in a few minutes," said Claire to Sara. "Sometimes we sing for a while at bedtime."

A loud, metallic clank from the radiator punctuated the hissing and sent Nancy even closer to Claire. "It's the heat, honey, nothing to be afraid of."

"Turn it down before you leave," said Sara. "See, here's the knob." She stooped to the valve at the end of the radiator. "About halfway should do it. If you leave it all the way open, it will get too hot."

"Such luxury!" exclaimed Claire. "Think of it, too hot!"

"I'm just glad we had all the radiators worked on. This is an old system."

Claire sat on the side of the bed with Nancy snuggled under the covers. She sang "Waltzing Matilda" and "Danny Boy". At the end of "Comin' Around the Mountain" she asked Nancy if they shouldn't have chicken and dumplings when Elizabeth came home.

"We don't have an old red rooster. You'll have to buy the chicken at the store," said Nancy, giggling. "Tell me again where Elizabeth lives."

"She lives on a fruit farm down in Panama where it's very hot," Claire began. "She went there a long time ago on a job with the Peace Corps and she liked it so well that she went back and stayed." Claire could only tell Nancy about the farm secondhand; she had never been there. "They do experimental farming, combining the old local methods with new science." There had been talk about a visit, but it had never come about. "Your mama will come up for a weekend while Elizabeth is here. That'll be fun, won't it?" But Nancy did not answer. She had already dozed off.

When Claire joined the others downstairs, Corky was explaining how they had heated the parsonage during the furnace's several lapses. "The space heater works as long as you stay in one place. In the kitchen we can turn the oven on too. It's when you move to a different room that you realize just how cold it is," he said. "But when the furnace stopped working this evening, we knew we couldn't stay there. It's colder now than it's been all winter. We left all the water faucets open and the water running so the pipes won't freeze."

Mr. Rochester had emerged from his den during the commotion.

"I suppose moving into your own place will be easier after the weather breaks."

Claire set him straight. "Enduring the chill at the parsonage will be easier after the weather breaks. We want to postpone moving as long as possible. The parsonage is at least free." She allowed her dimples to flash briefly. "And free is good."

Fred spoke up. "You have a home away from home, here, until the weather breaks. Our pleasure."

"We'll be out of your hair during the day," said Corky. Claire nodded. He could busy himself at the parsonage while she was at the drugstore. He could manage in the kitchen with the space heater during the day. Imposing on the folks here at night was bad enough.

The three of them left early the next morning, a Sunday, not staying for breakfast. "We'll come back tonight, if it's all right with you." Claire's voice held an inquiry in spite of continued reassurances from Fred and Sara.

Nancy would not be with them again, however. She had been spending a lot of time at Heather's anyway, and Celia Merchant told Claire that having her there kept Heather occupied and happy. At the parsonage Claire supervised the packing of Nancy's suitcase and drove her to Heather's house through deserted, snowy streets. "You know how to act," she told Nancy. "Help Celia in the kitchen. Pick up after yourself."

"I know," Nancy rolled her eyes. "I know."

"I'll call this evening to see how things are going. But if you want to come back with us, you call me." Claire had written Fred's phone number in Nancy's homework assignment book. "Be sure to call, now, if you need anything." Although she knew the Merchants well enough to know that Nancy would be well cared for, she still fretted at having to hand her over. The poor child had already been handed over once, had lost not only her father but her home as well. Between goodbye kisses she reminded Nancy, "Get your homework done early and be quiet after lights out."

Back at the parsonage Corky was wrapped in a blanket in the kitchen, reading. Claire went straight to the telephone answering machine. Elizabeth might call any day now to tell them when she would be home. Eagerness to see her daughter was balanced, however, by hoping she wouldn't come until the weather warmed up and the parsonage was habitable.

She kept the volume low, listening to the phone messages. Corky didn't have to hear all of this. It would only depress him. The hate messages had not stopped coming with the dismissal of his case. She herself tried not to listen any more than was necessary to hear if a legitimate call had come in. The others she deleted right away.

The religious poison had to have been organized by somebody. The voices were different but the message was the same, and the calls came every day. Corky would burn in hell. Only by getting right with God could he be saved. The wording changed from day to day. One day it would stress accepting Jesus as his personal savior. Another day doing penance and washing his sins away was part of it. When Corky did hear it, he would shake his head and say, "If only it were that easy."

Other messages were pornographic. The child rental agency called from time to time offering juicy little bottoms. And there would be women's voices telling him that men like him had ruined their lives. Evidently a women's group had gotten his number, too, and its members used it to practice what they couldn't say to their own abusers. Neither Claire nor Corky actually answered the phone any longer. They waited to hear what the message was going to be and would pick up only for callers they knew. Today Claire erased everything.

DINNER FOR SIX

It was Aunt Jenny who persuaded Claire and Corky to come early Monday evening and have dinner. With Mr. Rochester out of the way, Fred at work, and Sara only too glad to be relieved of the responsibility, Jenny had again taken on much of the meal preparation. She put on a big apron and opened *The Joy of Cooking*. After salivating over several recipes, she realized that she'd better check the larder. Sara would no doubt go to the grocery if asked, but Jenny prided herself on not asking.

The freezer was well stocked. Jenny settled on pork medallions in a mustard marinade, baked potatoes, creamed spinach, and a salad of canned apricot halves with cottage cheese, Cavendish food, easy to set up early and prepare effortlessly. Freddy would love it, and the old puke wouldn't get home in time to interfere.

That's what she called him to herself, an old puke. Moving around the kitchen, greasing the potatoes, setting the apricots in the fridge to chill, nudging Marigold out of the way, she felt downright victorious. He was gone and she had the kitchen to herself.

At dinner, however, he managed to suggest that apricots were expensive, especially when they had all those cans of Mandarin oranges to be used.

Jenny spoke right up. "There are other considerations in menu planning besides using up the surplus canned goods that *Someone* had the poor judgment to buy." Out loud in company she did not call him an old puke, she criticized him as "*Someone*" with a capital S.

He shook his head at her dim-wittedness and gave her a wilting glance.

Claire asked, "Have you always had display ad stuff left over?"

"All too often." Mr. Rochester looked around for Marigold. "I suppose we can get rid of the cat food here. Dog food, cat food, what's the difference?" That led into fretful complaints directed at Sara about his poor health's forcing him to leave the store with just Christabel and Charlie evenings. He was convinced that they only stayed open until ten because they knew he would phone to check on them at five till.

Since talking with Charlie, Claire had been making it a policy to remind the old man of the store's problems. She tried heighten his dissatisfaction and encourage his grumbling. It would be a blessing for everyone when he finally gave it up. "I can't imagine them having any business on a night like this." The side street gutters were rutted with ice.

"A pharmacist has an obligation," he said. "You can't just walk off willy-nilly. I used to be able to manage things myself. You can't really count on hired help to do it right."

Claire interjected, "That reminds me!" Her face was all innocence. "Charlie asked me to give you this." She pushed her chair back to go get her purse.

Mr. Rochester examined the envelope front and back and glared at it as though it might contain poison. He fumbled under the spinach-stained towel pinned around his neck and rummaged for his pocket knife. His hand refused to move for a long moment, then he opened the knife and jerkily slit the envelope.

Everyone knew to refrain from offering help.

Enclosed was not only a short note from Charlie but also the legal document, an offer to purchase the drugstore, with Charlie's signature witnessed and everything.

Claire watched him read while Fred, not knowing what was up, was telling the others about the manual he was working on at Solutions. "The dispatcher can key in all the information on each call separately," he said. "With the old system using a voice recording, everything was recorded just as it came in. If there was more than one call at once, the voices would be jumbled together. Now the calls are sequenced, but handled very quickly." In answer to Sara's question, he went on. "Of course the dispatcher has to be trained. This stuff is new. Nobody really knows how to use it yet."

"The question is, do *you* know how to use it yet?"

"I'm learning, I'm learning."

Mr. Rochester interrupted, accusing either Claire or Sara or both. "How much do you know about all this?" Sara regarded him calmly, in spite of his stern stare, and Claire kept her expression of innocence. Neither answered.

He read over Charlie's note again. "Charlie wants to buy the store."

"He does?" Sara could not maintain dispassion in the face of this. "He does?"

"Evidently," said Mr. Rochester. "He's made an offer to give me $180,000 for it. Where he's going to get money like that he doesn't say. He'd be hard put to it if I accepted."

Astonishment silenced the room. Marigold, sensing an opportunity, heaved herself up and clicked her toenails over to the table to lay her muzzle on Jenny's knee.

It was Corky who spoke. "Isn't it amazing how we can worry and pray over a problem for years, and then the solution appears from some totally unexpected place?"

Mr. Rochester regarded him respectfully, still silent and thoughtful. "It *would* be a relief," he said, finally. Then he straightened his shoulders and stuck his chin out. "I don't know what Charlie thinks he can do with it. He's not going to want to work as hard as it takes to run the place."

Sara laughed out loud. "Charlie's been working both shifts for weeks now. He surely knows what it takes."

"It takes gumption," her father shot back. "It takes a spine stiff enough not to lie down on the job."

Sara took a deep breath and resumed her placid demeanor. With him around, deep breaths abounded. She smiled at him encouragingly while unclenching her teeth.

Again Corky spoke. "There comes a time to rest from the labor and enjoy the fruits." He went on before Mr. Rochester could argue the point. "Of course labor itself is often rewarding, especially when it uses a lifetime of learning and skill-building."

"I haven't been able to use my skills since my hands stopped working right. Maybe you don't know this, but I was diagnosed with Parkinson's five years ago. It's no picnic."

"I'm sure it's not." Corky inquired about the treatment, and Mr. Rochester filled him in on the benefits and disappointments of L-dopa.

Claire added her bit of persuasion to the talk. "You've probably had lots of offers." It wouldn't hurt to remind him how limited his options were.

"Hardly," he huffed. "The store was ruined when Grogan sold out to Walgreens and Bill Fletcher got them to turn Osborne Avenue into a one-way race track."

Claire nodded vigorously to remind him that she had heard about these abominations already, several times, in fact.

"Ecclesiastes had it right," said Corky. "There's a time for everything under the sun. It's just recognizing it when it comes."

"I don't know." Mr. Rochester reread Charlie's documents. "I'll have to study it. There's sure to be a hitch somewhere."

Fred and Sara exchanged glances as Corky pointedly approved of Mr. Rochester's acumen. "You'd want everything to turn out right."

"There's another $50,000 worth of stock. Where does he think he's going to get the money to replace it? Or maybe he wouldn't replace it. Maybe he'd turn the store into some New Age place with crystals in the window and incense stinking it up to high heaven. You never know what somebody else might want to do." He grumbled and growled, but he didn't tear the offer up and throw it away.

Jenny was the only one dismayed by the possibility. How many more meals would she cook in peace? How much longer before she would have to abandon her freedom of the house to hide out in her room again? Silently she dished out warm bread pudding and handed it around the table.

A BATHTUB IN THE KITCHEN

On Friday, after Corky's customary visit, Jenny found her access to the kitchen blocked. The swinging door was closed, the "Private" sign hanging on the driven nail. She could hear water running in the bathtub. So Sara must have come home and decided to take a bath. She was the only one who used the tub for this purpose, and only occasionally. The shower upstairs was much more convenient.

But no. It was not Sara's humming that Jenny heard. It was a male voice, two of them, in fact. She listened. "It's not only unnecessary but counterproductive."

"What about the shock value? I would think you'd want to drive something like this home."

It was Corky and Mr. Rochester there in the kitchen running bath water. What on earth! Jenny pushed the swinging door a little and put her ear to the crack.

Water splashed. "A little warmer. It should be just above body temperature. There's no value in shocking yourself with cold water. And with that cough you have, we need to be careful not to make it worse."

"I'm afraid I need help with the buttons."

Jenny pushed the door a little more, not much, and very quietly, just so that she could see. What she saw was Corky unbuttoning the old man's shirt. His sweater was already draped on the back of the chair beside the bath, where there was a set of new underwear still in its plastic wrap.

Well, to each his own, she thought. Mr. Rochester always used the shower, but if he decided to get in the tub for a change, it was no skin off her nose. But why would he ask for help from Corky? He could wait till evening and Fred would help him. She shrugged. She could hardly expect to understand this man. And what difference did it make, anyway?

The only thing was that she had a chicken in the oven. If the door was still closed when her timer went off, she would have no qualms about interrupting. It wouldn't be the first pair of skinny old shanks she had seen in her life. She had cared for her own father as he neared death, fed him with a spoon, dressed him and changed his diapers.

Jenny's fears about Mr. Rochester's presence had come to pass more quickly than she imagined. It was not that he had abandoned the drugstore to Charlie, oh no. He was home with a cold. His nose ran, his voice croaked and his choler waxed hot. Too sick to go to work, he had spent Wednesday and Thursday in his den with the TV blaring religion. Not in comfort, because his Supreme Court Justice chair was now housed in the back room at the drugstore. Instead, he sat upright and stiff on uncushioned wood as though punishing his buttocks for the cold in his head.

His presence in the house affected Jenny like the wrong end of a magnet. Although she refused to give up her exercise routine of walking the house, she tried to avoid meeting up with him, not always successfully. He could appear in the kitchen at any moment to refresh the hot whiskey / glycerin / lemonade he sipped to relieve the symptoms of his cold.

Over the weeks since Christmas, Jenny and Sara had adapted to each other's lunch times and learned how to stay out of each other's way, but with all three present, the kitchen seemed too small to contain them. "Can I make you a sandwich?" Sara had asked her father the first day he was home. "What sounds good to you?"

"Nothing sounds good to me, but I have to eat," he replied. "I'll make my own sandwich." He stood at the counter not only to prepare the sandwich but to eat it as well, blocking access to the bread box behind him.

But Jenny no longer let him intimidate her. "Excuse me," she said, pressing her shoulder against him, not quite shoving him out of the way.

On Friday she made her sandwich at the table and was already eating when he appeared. She spoke forthrightly to make it clear that he would not be welcome in the living room that afternoon. "I have an appointment for spiritual counseling," she announced. "Can I have privacy in the living room, or do I have to meet with Corky upstairs in my bedroom?"

It was Sara who answered. "I won't be here today. I'm going to visit a friend." She glanced at her father. Visiting a friend was a new activity for her. "One of the women in my group invited me over."

He made no comment.

Nor, when Corky came, did he interrupt Jenny's conversation. But she noticed that when the conversation ended, instead of going to the coat hooks in the hall, Corky went down the hall and turned to the door of the old man's den and knocked. "Come in." He entered and closed the door. The TV voices went suddenly silent.

Jenny had then prepared the chicken for slow roasting, its cavity stuffed with chopped onions, its skin well oiled and salted. She would dispose of both onions and skin before serving. Another old Cavendish recipe, and the moist, tasty chicken would melt in their mouths.

With the chicken in the oven, she lay on her bed for a few minutes' rest, then began her exercise routine, walking up the front stairs, through the hall and down the back. That was when she found the kitchen door closed. She could bypass the kitchen, of course, and walk through the downstairs hall instead, but she heard Corky's voice and was curious enough to stay a moment longer and listen.

"Have you ever witnessed a baptism?"

"I haven't been a churchgoer. Never had the time. Never had the inclination. But the Parkinson's has brought up the issue of mortality for me." He coughed heavily. "All I know is that you go under water and that whatever sins you've done are washed away. They say that without it, you won't get into heaven. I don't know that I've had the time to do much sinning, but I thought that perhaps since you were here anyway…"

"Please understand that I have not baptized anyone since I left the Methodist church years ago, and that even then it was done by sprinkling, not by immersion. Are you sure you really want to be immersed?"

"I'm sure," he said. "Sprinkling sounds trivial to me. I want the real thing." He coughed again, this time longer. "What's this?"

Jenny pushed the door a little wider. He was standing beside the tub staring at the shelf on the wall above where Sara kept her bubble bath and everyone else kept other necessities.

"Surely she doesn't bathe in washing soda. That's a caustic."

"I'm sure she doesn't. You should take off your glasses. Here, let me set them on the table so they won't get knocked around."

Jenny smothered a little snort of laughter. She had many a time put the roasting pan to soak in hot water and washing soda. The tub was the only place big enough for this procedure.

The old man clung to his glasses while he investigated the shelf further. "Dog shampoo!"

"The water is clean," said Corky. "I checked to make sure the tub had been well scrubbed."

"I suppose it is, if Sara bathes here. She's fairly careful about dirt most of the time." He handed Corky the glasses. Water was still running into the tub.

This ritual must already be having its effect. Jenny had never heard him speak so well of Sara before.

"What happens next?" he asked. "I don't know how I'm going to get myself into the tub."

"I'll help you," said Corky. "You can sit on the rim and I'll lift your legs over. Then you can slide into the water. Don't worry, I'll help you out. You're perfectly safe."

"I appreciate this very much," said the old man humbly. "Getting into a church for it would have been difficult."

As Jenny watched and listened from the other side of the swinging door, she began to realize that what she was witnessing was not a joke. The mechanics were funny indeed, but the intent was quite serious. Here was a man considering his own mortality and his prospects for immortality. She wouldn't have thought that Mr. Rochester ever considered that he had a soul, far less that he would try to save it.

With the old man sitting naked on the rim of the tub as the water ran in, Corky picked up a small black book and opened it.

"We come in humility to seek forgiveness for the wrongs we have committed in our lives. We ask for God's grace to be upon us now and forever more.

This water that we enter is holy. All waters are holy, God's gift to humankind. In the water of God's gift, what has hardened around us becomes soft, what has burdened us floats away, what has poisoned us dissolves."

He was only pretending to read. Jenny could see that the book was just a prop.

He put the book back on the table. "We go into this holy water to wash away what is hard, what is burdensome, what is toxic." He bent to the tub and braced himself to hold the old man steady. His sleeves were rolled up high. "We go into this holy water that fills the womb of our Mother Earth, from whom we came and upon whom we are dependent. Here we become like a newborn, ready to see the world afresh as one of God's people." With Mr. Rochester clutching his torso, he lifted first one bony white leg and then the other and placed them in the tub. Then, gripping him under the arms, he slid the penitent into the water, pushing him forward and lowering him at the same time. As his upper body and head went under, his knobby knees appeared and water sloshed over the rim of the tub. Corky flinched as it drenched his shoes but did not release his hold. His voice showed strain as he pulled the old man back up, saying, "You are now born new again, cleansed of all wrong, a baby in the eyes of God."

Mr. Rochester wiped his eyes and slicked back the long hairs at the side of his head. "Do I get out now?"

"Not yet." Corky turned the hot water slightly back on to refresh the bath and keep the old man from chilling. He went to the cupboard nearest the dining room door and brought out a half empty bottle of red wine. From a second cupboard he took a glass and filled it. From the breadbox he took a loaf and tore off a morsel of crust. "Here," he said. "I want you to remain in the water while you take in the symbolism of communion."

Mr. Rochester swallowed the bread and sipped from the glass.

Corky picked up the little black book. "As the water refers to the fluid womb of Mother Earth, so does the bread symbolize the newborn's embodiment and the wine refer to the Spirit that infuses him as he comes into being.

Under the water we are made small, relieved of our structure. We become as an invertebrate, taking naturally to the amniotic environment."

Jenny listened eagerly. This was no ordinary baptism. Would Mr. Rochester notice?

"Consider the octopus. Without a spine its structure is majestic. How far its tentacles reach! Can a man reach so far as this? In the water we increase our reach even after we allow our spine to soften."

Mr. Rochester continued to sip from the glass of wine as Corky pretended to read. "But reaching is not all there is to it. The octopus can suddenly gather in its tentacles and with this motion shoot rapidly through the water to a new place. In the water we learn new ways to move. Throughout evolution we have learned new ways to move, first swimming, then crawling, then standing upright and walking, as the Spirit enters us and guides our life."

Corky replaced the book on the table. "From the solemn rituals of immersion and ingestion, we emerge both blessed and rejuvenated into the life that is ahead. Ready to meet our death, we embrace our new life."

He dug in his pocket for a small vial from which he poured a few drops on the old man's head, then rubbed lightly with his fingertips. "With this oil you become consecrated to a higher purpose in life."

The sound of the front door opening drew Jenny away from her listening post. She scurried down the hall to intercept Sara. "Shhh!" she whispered. "We mustn't interrupt what's going on."

"What is it?" Sara stopped in her tracks. She looked stricken.

"Nothing terrible," Jenny hastened to assure her. "Your father is being baptized."

"What?"

"Corky is baptizing your father in the bathtub. I think they're almost finished. We really shouldn't interrupt."

Sara shook her head. "My father would never allow himself to be baptized. That's going much too far. He watches to the TV preachers, but it's only to sneer at them. He has had nothing but scorn for religion all his life."

"You've got a surprise in store for you." As Jenny spoke the piercing sound of the timer began to shrill forth from the kitchen. "Uh oh," she said, "the chicken's done." She stood, irresolute, then moved slowly toward the hall. Sara followed.

The noise ceased. Back at the door Jenny peered again through the crack. Corky was opening the oven door. "It's okay," she mouthed to Sara. She backed up, and the two of them returned to the living room.

"Let's give them a chance to finish up."

"Will wonders never cease!" Sara sat down and pulled off first one boot, then the other. "Are you sure that's what's happening?"

Jenny nodded. "I'm sure. I have to admit that I've been eavesdropping. I couldn't resist."

"Well, I don't blame you. I'd have eavesdropped too."

Jenny beckoned her toward the hall. "You still can. It's not over." They proceeded to the swinging door. Together they huddled as the ritual in the kitchen continued.

Mr. Rochester was being helped out of the bath now and into a towel. As he dried himself, Corky went on speaking. "Early Christians saw baptism as a solemn renunciation of their old habits. Even now, when young people receive the sacrament, they vow to give up their reckless, sinful ways and channel their energy into serving God."

"Whatever reckless ways I ever had are long gone," said the old man. "I don't know about serving God. I don't really believe in God."

Corky continued, unperturbed. "We serve God by serving humankind, where the image of God resides in every person on earth. It is not necessary to believe in a particular definition of God, only to contemplate the image of God you carry and to treat others with respect for their holiness. Have you read the Bible?"

"No. I've never had time to sit around and read."

Corky ignored the implicit criticism. "In the Christian religion one is instructed to love God – that is, the image of divinity within yourself and all others – and to love all others as you do yourself. One is charged with treating all others with compassion."

Mr. Rochester stood silently as Corky opened the plastic packages of underwear.

"We clothe ourselves in new garments as we come into the world anew. Here, can you get this on yourself or would you like help?"

"I can do everything but buttons. And thank you for bringing me these. You must let me pay for them." With Corky at his elbow he stepped into the new briefs.

Corky shook his head. "You pay for these garments not with money but with acts of compassion. As you receive a gift, you give to others."

Sara shook her head in wonderment.

"Do you think there's really a heaven?" The new undershirt clung to the old man's chest where it was still damp.

"I have never been privileged to glimpse the afterlife," Corky replied. "Some people have visions. Sometimes people who are near death recover and tell that they saw the gates of heaven."

"Well, but visions...," said Mr. Rochester, his distaste evident.

"I myself believe that humans have an *idea* of heaven. Because ultimate goodness can be imagined, people are obliged to make it as real as possible. Many Christians concern themselves with Jesus' teachings about how to live toward this goodness on earth rather than what might happen after they die.

Striving toward compassion in all we do is at the center of Jesus' teachings. One passage that sums it up goes like this: 'For I was hungry and you gave me food, I was thirsty and you gave me drink. I was a stranger and you welcomed me, I was naked and you clothed me, I was sick and you visited me, I was in prison and you came to me....Truly, I say to you, as you did it to one of the least of these my brethren, you did it to me.'

So you see, it is the image of God lying within every person that commands our respect and compassion. That is what you have taken on yourself today."

After Mr. Rochester had struggled into his shirt, Corky buttoned it for him.

"You have certainly given me something to think about," said the old man. "I appreciate your taking the time."

"Time is something I have plenty of," Corky answered.

With the event in the kitchen coming to a close, Sara and Jenny parted, Sara to her sewing room in the south wing, Jenny to the living room where she sat at the window looking out.

Was this the first time the old man had heard such words, she wondered. And if so, what might be their effect? She herself had tried sporadically to live according with these teachings, but it never hurt to be reminded once again.

After a time Corky appeared, shrugging himself into his overcoat.

"Thank you for taking the chicken out of the oven," said Jenny.

"You were listening."

She nodded. "How could you stand to minister to that hateful old man?"

His head bent back and his eyes closed while he was summoning his thoughts. "The worse we are, the more we need ministering to," he said wistfully. "And the harder it is to find anyone willing to minister." He buttoned his coat. "There are worse things than being a hateful old man." He opened the door. "I'll see you again tonight." A rush of cold air blew in before he could get the door closed.

CORKY'S CONFESSION

Claire found Corky steeped in gloom when she came home from the drugstore that evening. The house was dark. Just inside the front door she switched on the lamp, and discovered him slumped in his favorite chair with the space heater beside him, his head bowed. Only when she closed the door did he look up and nod hello.

There was no mail on the table. She went back to the porch and found two ads in the box, one for a housecleaning service, the other for a new credit card. Still no word from Elizabeth.

Whatever healing had taken place since Corky's court appearance seemed to have vanished. Other evenings she had found him in a lighted kitchen with the oven door open, the space heater turned on, and something cooking on the stove. She had begun to hope that their life might mend. But the wound was so large and the new skin so tender that one dark room could break it open and expose it again, raw and oozing.

"I'm sorry I haven't started dinner," he said. "I didn't realize it was this late. I just got home a little while ago." He rose and turned off the heater. He wheeled it along with him as he backed toward the kitchen.

Still wearing her coat, Claire went ahead of him to turn on the light. "Let's get it warmed up in here." He plugged in the heater, turned it on, and closed the kitchen door. "So where have you been?" she asked, trying to sound offhand while wondering what fresh hells awaited her. She turned on the stove burners and opened the oven door.

Corky's expression was bemused. He answered, "I've been ministering."

"That's right. It's Friday." But a session with Jenny Cavendish couldn't account for his demeanor. There was something else, she knew it.

He offered no more information. Instead he busied himself, first at the fridge and then at the table, making a salad. Claire warmed the stew left over from a previous meal. They had been eating soups and stews lately, making enough to last more than one evening. While it was heating up, she took the opportunity to leave the kitchen and check the phone messages. As usual there were two messages that filled the tape, and as usual, neither message was from Elizabeth. Shivering in the cold, almost-dark living room, she deleted first the one, then the other, as soon as she recognized them for what they were.

Conversation is trivial indeed when the real issue is being avoided. Yes, Portville was having a wretched winter, but Hoosiers have only so many words for snow. Yes, it had been warming up some. Surely the snow would melt soon. Claire and Corky were more polite than usual, each hurrying to fetch the stew from the stove when the other's plate began to empty. Toward the end of the meal Claire noticed Corky giving her sideways glances and clearing his throat as though starting to say something. She set the dishes to soak, wiped the table and sat back down.

"Tell me, Corky. Please tell me. I can't stand this wall between us. I'd rather know, no matter how bad it is." She scooted her chair around to where she could reach his hand. It was warmer than hers; she curled her small fingers and snuggled them into his palm, then thought better and laid her hand on the table near him, palm up, available.

He laced his fingers together and leaned his forearms on the table. Contained inside himself he rocked forward and back several times. This seemed to unlock his voice. "I administered the sacraments today," he said. "I baptized Mr. Rochester and served him communion. I haven't a right to do this but I did it anyway."

"Of course you have a right!" Claire interrupted. "You're a minister."

He gestured to shush her. "I'm still a minister because there's no denomination to kick me out. And because I've kept myself invisible." He paused. "Mr. Rochester has asked me several times. He wanted to be baptized. I tried to discourage him, but he's nothing if not persistent."

Claire nodded.

"It's been so long since I've done this, and the circumstances were so unusual, that I pretty well made the whole thing up. I tried to offer what he needed, but you never really know. He's not joining a church, probably not even thinking of himself as Christian, but he's begun to think about religion, and he got it in his mind that he needed the ceremony in case there's an afterlife."

Here Corky lost his gloom for a moment. "There was a touch of the ridiculous about the whole thing," he said. "He insisted on immersion, as though going under water was what would make it take."

Claire winced. "And?"

"We used that big old bathtub there in the kitchen."

Claire, picturing the scene, started laughing.

"I have to tell you," he said, "that there are Christians who would consider my doctoring up the sacraments more of a sin than my arrest."

"Compassion is not a sin!"

"That's how I try to think. But having come to this puts my whole life in question. I have tried so *hard*," he said. "I always hoped that the good I might do in life would be greater than the trouble I caused."

Claire reached for his hand but he ignored her. "Corky, please tell me about the trouble. I know how much good you've done, but you've kept the trouble to yourself. I need to know, and you need to tell."

He turned suddenly and pounded the table with his fist. His face contorted. "Those stories are true," he cried. "I have done those things. I have brought distress that I never intended."

Quick to comfort, Claire said, "Intention counts for a lot. And I think the stories were exaggerated."

"You don't understand. I heard the tape of Josie Flannery telling what I did. I can't ignore that. She did not exaggerate.

And what have I done to you?" he went on. "I've put you through hell, you, the one I love best in all the world." He buried his face in his hands and sobbed.

Claire summoned her skills to get through this. She let him cry. It was what he needed.

Finally he looked up and groped for a handkerchief. Not finding one, he reached for a dish towel and blew his nose.

"Jenny asked me how I could stand to minister to someone as hateful as Mr. Rochester. I told her that the worst of us need ministry the most. I *envy* that old man! Who could I ask to give me the sacraments?"

He fell silent. The kitchen clock ticked loudly. Finally Claire spoke. "I can't give you the sacraments," she said, "even if you wanted them. But I can give you a hand."

He nodded and let her take his thin hot fingers between her cool palms.

"I went to seminary to overcome my wickedness. But it didn't work out that way. The wickedness never yielded. I've had to struggle against it every day of my life."

"I never forced anyone," he said. "I never had sex with a child. I could not overcome my desires, but I could restrain myself from acting on them. I thought I had done well, but it turns out not well enough. I was deluding myself all along, excusing what I did by reminding myself what I *didn't* do. What I wanted to do but didn't. I should have admitted to myself that *anything* done surreptitiously is suspect."

Now Claire's face was buried. What she had tried not to notice all along had finally been said. "What about me?" she cried from behind her fingers. "Where do I fit in here? If it's children you're attracted to, why did you marry me?"

"I love you, Claire. I love you almost more than life itself. In fact, the only reason I'm still alive is because of you."

"That's not enough! I need to know the truth. All our lovemaking. Was I there? Or were you fantasizing someone else?" Her voice came from a well of immense pain. "Did you marry me to cover what you really were?"

He pushed his chair back out of the way and knelt awkwardly beside her, one bony shoulder pressed under the table. "You were there," he murmured. "You're always there. You're not the kind of woman who can disappear into a man's fantasy."

Although she was primed to suspect that he would not tell her the truth, this statement seemed too improbable to be a lie. She stroked his cheek, prickly with stubble, as she allowed herself to lean in the direction of belief. And what would be the point of disbelieving, anyway? She was not going to divorce him. She clung to his words of love, the lifeline of their marriage.

When he rose, the knees of his pants were gray with dust. Claire brushed them off and fetched out the broom. Corky washed the dishes and set them to drain. A sense of cautious normalcy returned. The world around them had not changed. Maybe they could survive this without further injury.

A little later they turned off the lights and, leaving the kitchen closed and the space heater on low to preserve one warm space for tomorrow, they drove over to Fred's to spend the night. They parked as near the curb as the melting clods of ice would allow, and held each other steady on the walk. The welcome odor of wood smoke from the fireplace scented the air. Fred's cat was still in her sheltered woolen nest by the door. She would have to come inside soon, dog or no dog. It was still too cold for her to remain outdoors at night.

Marigold met them at the door, woofing and then wagging. Sara called her to the kitchen, where she shut the door, while Fred fetched the cat inside and carried her to his den. "Here we go, princess," he said. "See, there's no dog in this house." He had made her a winter home there, complete with dry food, water dish, litter box and a folded blanket on the desk chair.

Back in the living room Sara urged Claire and Corky to join them by the fire. "You need a sign over the front door," said Claire. "Shelter for Waifs." They hung their coats next to Fred's on hooks in the hall. Voices arguing could be heard from Mr. Rochester's room around the hall corner, the talking heads on the Friday night shows. Even before they had taken seats in the living room, Jenny came down the front stairs. She went straight to Corky and without a word held out her hand to shake.

"We all need to shake your hand," said Sara. "I hold you largely responsible."

This greeting was so incongruous with the conversation she had just had with Corky that Claire felt as though she had stepped into a different corner of the universe, far warmer and more welcoming.

Fred returned and rearranged chairs, opening space so that everyone could share the crackles and flicker from the fireplace.

"He's accepted Charlie's offer," said Sara. "He called the store just a bit ago and told him it was his now."

"Not just that," Fred added. "It's his: lock, stock, barrel, and pills."

"Well, almost his," said Sara. "They have to go through the legalities."

"Wow," said Claire. "I'd begun to think he'd never yield. Are you sure he'll go through with it?"

Sara nodded. "Once he sets his mind to something, he doesn't change it."

"What about his lawyer? Has he gotten advice?"

"He doesn't have a lawyer. I don't think this attitude change is going to include any softening toward lawyers."

Loyalty to Neil straightened Claire's posture. "He really ought to have someone look at the paperwork, just to make sure there aren't any errors to come back and haunt him later."

"You tell him that," said Sara. "He'll listen, if it comes from you."

"I will. I can probably even supply the lawyer." Neil himself didn't do contracts, but she thought that one of the partners did. "In fact, I'll call and see right now. Keep the momentum up. May I use your phone?"

"Of course."

In the dining room Claire spoke to Neil, telling him what was needed, asking if it was available. "Oh, and don't try to call me at home," she said. She explained and listened to his lecture, rolling her eyes as he talked. "We'll be all right, Neil. Okay? I'll call the office on Monday after I talk to the old man."

A wonderful odor wafted from the kitchen, and soon Jenny called Fred to carry in a tray with cups and a pitcher of mulled cider. "If we have to endure winter clear into spring, let's do it up right."

Snuggling next to Corky in the love seat, Claire whispered, "We have a lot to be grateful for." He nodded slowly. Both were sleepy from the warmth.

Fred, hearing this, nodded too. "I'd been thinking I might never have a job again. And here I am, at the cutting edge."

They sat quietly, sipping the hot cider, and let the fire die down. It was a night to turn in early.

RETURNS

While Claire and Corky were toasting their feet and sipping cider in the glow of Fred's warm fire, at the dark and empty parsonage on Clover Street something else was happening. A familiar station wagon slowed in front and parked at the curb. A familiar figure walked past the leafless maples to the porch, stomped snow off his shoes, and rang the bell. When no one came, and no one came, he shivered and dug in his pocket for his key chain. Surely they wouldn't mind if he went on in, cold as it was. They had probably gone to a movie.

Lucky he had forgotten to give back the key when he left. Or maybe he hadn't "forgotten". Maybe some part of him knew he would come back.

Inside, the house seemed deserted. No lights. Colder than a witch's tit. Colder than a well-digger's ass. It was very odd that no one was home. He couldn't remember a time when Claire, Corky and Romy were all away at once.

Turning on lights as he went, he walked through the house to the kitchen, noticing how much things had changed. Where was the furniture? Had they sold stuff to make ends meet?

Odd, too, that the kitchen door was closed. But inside the kitchen it was warmer, with the space heater blowing its discordant hiss. So the furnace had gone belly up. For a moment he pictured Corky burning the furniture to keep warm, but no, not in an oil furnace, an oil furnace that wouldn't even burn oil.

Looking further, he found the dinner dishes still wet in the drain rack. Dishes for two, not four.

Wolf had stayed in Flagstaff long enough to make peace with his parents. He had done carpentry work for his uncle so as not to sponge off the folks. His father's health was still poor, but in no way terminal.

There was a limit to how long he could stand to be back in the family, a child to his parents. observed, pampered, instructed.

Thoughts of Romy had pursued him. He must have gone to the phone a dozen times to call her, then backed off, remembering his rude, abrupt leave-taking spurred by her impossible mother. Knowing Romy, he was sure she would hang up on him, and that would be the end of it. Better to make amends face to face where there would be time iron things out.

Could they really all be asleep this early? In bed trying to keep warm, perhaps. He went back to the living room to the corner where Romy kept her computer. It was gone.

There was nothing to do but go upstairs. He walked softly, not knowing whether to avoid waking them or to call out to reassure them that he was not an intruder. But of course there was no one there. He glanced in all the bedrooms. Claire and Corky's room was just the same, as was Nancy's. But Romy's room was devoid of personality, and nearly bare of furniture. The fourth bedroom, where he had slept, had not changed since he was here.

So she went back to Bloomington and left Nancy to finish her school semester. He had wondered if there was any basis for Claudine's flamboyant accusation of Corky as a "known molester" on his way to prison. Not that she was believable in any way. But if Romy had allowed Nancy to stay here, even that niggling concern was soothed.

He would have to wait until tomorrow to see Romy.

In the meantime he was tired. He had driven from Flagstaff in two days and had slept last night in his station wagon, albeit with the back seat folded down. His body needed to stretch out and rest.

He decided against sleeping in the guest room. It was too cold, and besides, he wanted to be where he would wake up when they came home. So he carried his sleeping bag in from the car and unrolled it on the kitchen floor. He pushed a chair aside to make room, took off his shoes, and, with his head under the table away from the heater, he stretched out full length and fell almost instantly asleep.

He didn't know where he was or how little he'd slept when he was awakened by loud banging on the outside kitchen door. He sat up and whacked his head against the table. The banging continued.

He struggled out of the sleeping bag, fumbling in the faint light cast by the heater's coils. There was a chain on the door and a key in the lock, but he finally got it open, expecting to see Corky or Claire standing on the porch, chagrined because they'd forgotten their house key, happy that he was here to let them in.

Instead, the person on the porch was a woman he didn't know. "Hello!" she said. "I thought everybody must be dead in there." She picked up a suitcase and moved as though to enter.

"Who are you?" he asked.

"I'm Libby Gustaman. Who are you? Where's my mother?"

Wolf was groggy. It took him a moment. "You must be Claire's daughter. I remember she had a daughter," he said, hesitantly. "I'm Wolf Rausch. I don't know where Claire is. But come in. Come in and close the door." He turned on the overhead light.

He would never have recognized this woman as belonging to Claire. Her face was sun-browned, her long dark hair tied in a pony tail. And she was tall.

Still holding the doorknob as though maintaining an escape route, she put her suitcase down and looked around. The rasp of the heater filled the room. The clock said eleven-fifteen. "I thought they were still up, with all the lights on. But I rang and knocked and nobody answered."

Wolf turned and opened the door to the dining room a little way. "Oops," he said. "I did leave a lot of lights on. But there's nobody home." He kicked his sleeping bag under the table. "Except me, of course, and I don't actually live here."

Libby's gaze searched his face. "So why are you here?"

"It's a long story," he said "I'll tell you the short version. I'm not a house burglar or anything. I stayed with Claire and Corky for a while last fall, and I just came back tonight. Couldn't you take off your coat and I'll make some coffee or something and we could figure out where they are?"

Her light tan raincoat was totally inadequate for the weather. "I'll leave it on," she said. "But coffee sounds good. I rented a car at O'Hare and drove here, even though I would be late arriving. Mother knew I was coming and I didn't want her to worry. I'm surprised she would go out."

Wolf filled the kettle with water and set it on the stove to heat. "It's going to be instant. I don't think they drink real coffee."

"I'll have to do something about that," said Libby. She smiled, and Claire's dimples appeared in her brown cheeks. "Now tell me why you were sleeping under the kitchen table."

"Because the furnace is shot and it's too cold to sleep anywhere else." He held up his hands to fend off questions. "I don't know what the score is. I just arrived a little while ago. The heater was on in here, and it looks like they had dinner. I crashed out on the floor because I was too tired to do anything else."

Libby went into the dining room. "You're right. It's cold." He could hear her moving through the house and going upstairs as he found the cups and spoons. He opened the milk carton and sniffed, remembering the state of the refrigerator last time he saw it. The milk smelled okay, and he set it out on the table.

The kettle began whistling as she returned. "There's no heat at all up there," she said. "Maybe they went to a motel." She sat down and spooned coffee powder into her cup. "I can't imagine Mom spending the money."

"Look," said Wolf. "I don't have to stay here. You're welcome to the accommodations, such as they are. I can go to a motel for the night."

"You don't need to leave. I'm going to call my dad. I can stay with him. What I don't understand is why Mom didn't even leave a note on the door when she knew I was coming. That makes me think something's wrong." She cooled her coffee with milk. "And of course I wonder where she is."

When she had finished drinking, she went to the phone and called Neil. Wolf remained discreetly in the kitchen with the door closed. With Libby here, a family member, he felt more an intruder, especially since Romy, the one he'd actually come to see, was no longer around. What he hoped for now was simply to sleep under the table until morning and then find out where she was.

Libby returned to the kitchen. "Dad says they're staying the night with friends," she said. "Because of the furnace. He gave me the phone number but I think I'll wait till morning to call. It's pretty late to call a stranger's house."

"Could I have the number too?" asked Wolf. "I need to talk to them before I leave town."

Libby found a scratch pad and wrote down Fred's phone number. "I'll get out of your way now," she said. "My dad has room for me." She rinsed her cup. "Go back to sleep. If I talk to Mom first, I'll tell her you're here, and if you do, you can tell her I'm at Dad's."

When she had gone, Wolf gratefully slid back into his sleeping bag and rested his tired bones on the floor.

A <u>REAL</u> BREAKFAST

Because it was Saturday and Fred wouldn't be going to work, Aunt Jenny went to the kitchen early, poured a cup of kibbles in Marigold's bowl, and started breakfast. A *real* breakfast, none of those cardboard flakes with nothing in them but fake vitamins. Fred liked oatmeal, and he liked bacon and eggs, and even though Sara might look at his waistline and frown, she would eat some too and enjoy it. Jenny didn't care whether Mr. Rochester ate any or not. He could subsist on dry toast for all she cared. When Marigold finished gulping her breakfast and searching the floor for anything she might have missed, she woofed at the door and Jenny let her out.

It gave her such pleasure to make food for people! She cooked the oatmeal in the double boiler to keep it hot, laid strips of bacon in a big iron skillet and set it on the stove, put butter and jam on the table, counted the eggs. There would be enough to feed the Pearlmans too.

Corky came downstairs next. Jenny poured him a cup of coffee. He held it up and breathed in its aroma. "Ummmm," he murmured. "Smells like the riches of foreign shores. No wonder the trade routes came into existence."

"Hawaii isn't foreign anymore," she replied. "This is kona, from Hawaii. Would you like cream?" She set out a paper carton of half & half.

He spooned in sugar as well and sipped. Glancing at the kitchen windows, he said, "I do believe I see some sunshine." He hummed the first few notes of "Morning Has Broken." The rising sun did not shine directly into these windows, but the gleam of its rays on the snow brought brightness to the room.

"It's about time," said Jenny. She sat down at the table with him to sip her coffee and wait for the others. The bacon was done now and wrapped in absorbent paper towels, the eggs cracked in a bowl, the first slices of bread ready to toast. She leaned toward Corky and said, in a lowered tone, "Was that a Freethinker baptism?"

He thought about it for a moment. "Perhaps it was. The first, most likely. And probably the last."

Jenny cocked her ear toward the hall doorway for the possible entrance of Mr. Rochester. "He was a different man last evening," she said. "Not a single complaint about the meal. Very quiet, for a change. And then he just announced that he was going to give Charlie the store."

"Give? Surely not give."

"No, no. He's going to get his money. But he said 'give' and I think he feels that he's giving it away. The biggest surprise was that he told Charlie he would have to take all the stock as part of the deal."

"That's quite a gift."

"He thinks it will make it harder for Charlie to change things. I even saw him crack a smile, something about cat food. Just about broke his jaw." She stood up suddenly. "Speaking of cats..." She left the room and went to Fred's den. "I'm putting Duck outside," she called to Corky. "It's easier when Marigold isn't around." She carried the cat to the front door.

Back in the kitchen she said, "That cat hates being in the house, but during this cold spell she's had to submit, especially at night."

"It's had its effect on all of us," said Corky.

"The thing is," she said slowly, resuming her story. "The thing is that he'll be here all the time again. I've gotten spoiled, having him gone. Being cooped up here in the house with him all day... the only way to avoid him is to stay in my room, and even then..." She sighed. "I've been enjoying myself."

Corky was paying close attention to her words. "Maybe this comes at just the right time for you," he said slowly. He sipped his coffee. "I think you're ready to buy a car. You've been out driving with me enough, now, that you know the streets, at least to where you're likely to go."

Jenny was too stunned to answer. She looked at him closely. Was he kidding her?

"Think about it," he said. "You need to reclaim your autonomy. You're elderly, but you're not frail elderly. It's too soon for you to let go. You're still able and healthy."

A door of hope opened in Jenny's mind. Her car would be small, something suitable to her own size. Might it have a racing stripe? For just a moment she pictured the racing stripe ending in painted flames. She had enough money, enough, at least, for a used model. In her own car she could go places without a chaperone, buy groceries without someone watching what she put in the cart, stay at the library as long as she wanted without hampering Fred. She could get to the beauty shop! Oh my. Asking for favors, especially transportation, was so humiliating.

Sounds of activity came from upstairs, and now they all descended at once, Claire and Sara, and then, more slowly, Mr. Rochester with his trembling hand on Fred's shoulder. Sara still wore a housecoat, though Claire and Mr. Rochester were dressed to go to the store.

Corky addressed Jenny. "As soon as the snow melts," he said in a meaningful tone. "As soon as the snow melts, we'll go shopping."

She held the thought of her car in one part of her mind like a treasure while turning her attention to the others.

"My God, it smells like heaven in here," said Fred.

"The fast track to heaven," said Sara. "I smell bacon."

"A little bacon now and then is not going to kill us."

Jenny indicated the table set for six and glanced back and forth at Claire and Corky. "I've made enough to persuade you good people to stay with us for breakfast. You wouldn't want it wasted, would you?"

Claire went behind Corky's chair and leaned on his shoulders. "We can't say no to that, can we?"

"How about if I just scramble all the eggs and you can take what you want?" Jenny asked.

Mr. Rochester investigated the stove. "I'll just have some oatmeal."

"Bring on the eggs," said Fred.

Claire and Corky exchanged glances at this byplay. How often family loyalties and hostilities are expressed through the language of food! "Supper, not dinner," Claire murmured. There had been a famous falling-out in Corky's family when a daughter got too uppity to call it "supper" any longer. It resulted in her parents refusal to "dine" at her house.

Sara poured everyone's coffee and made toast while Jenny beat the eggs with a fork, then poured them into a buttered frying pan. In a moment they were fluffed and ready to eat.

Claire congratulated Mr. Rochester. "What good luck that you could turn the store over to someone who respects its character!" she said.

But the virtuous glow of baptism had worn off by now. "There's sure to be a hitch somewhere," he growled. "The offer looks good on paper, but there are all kinds of ways to put one over on you."

"Don't worry," she said. "I know someone who does contracts all the time." She was careful not to use the word "lawyer". "I can have him look it over for you and make sure everything is the way it should be."

Fred had made a sandwich of his bacon and toast, which he ate bite for bite with his eggs before deigning to look at the oatmeal. "Brown sugar," he said. "That's what it needs." He was rummaging behind the salt and baking powder in the cupboard when the phone rang. "I'll get it," he said.

Mr. Rochester glanced anxiously at the kitchen clock. "Isn't it time for us to go?" he asked Claire.

She nodded. "Charlie and Lenora will have opened up by now. They can manage until we get there."

Returning from the phone Fred told Claire, "It's for you."

"That's odd," she said. Then, with alarm, "God, I hope they haven't found us here." She left the kitchen. The phone was in a wall alcove in the hall across from the coat hooks. "Hello," she said in a frosty voice, ready to hang up at the first word of the usual harangue.

"Mom?"

"Elizabeth? Is that you? Where are you?"

"I'm at Dad's. Where are *you*?"

Claire had to sit down. With no chair in the hall, she carried the phone to the living room, untangling the cord as she went. "It's a long story. Oh, Elizabeth, why didn't you tell me you were coming?"

"I did tell you. I left a message on your machine, two messages, actually. But that's water over the dam. I can't wait to see you."

"I'm on my way to work. No, I can't go to work today. I'll just drive Mr. Rochester to the store and come by Neil's."

"Hold on, Mom. Why don't we meet at your house?"

"It's cold at my house."

"Not in the kitchen it isn't."

This was more than Claire could comprehend. "Slow down, Elizabeth."

Her daughter laughed. "I thought that would get you. Mom, listen. There's somebody at your house who wants to see you. The man who stayed with you, Wolf. Couldn't we just meet there? We can all fit in the kitchen. I'll even bring some coffee." Then, in a lowered tone, she added, "I'm not too eager to stay here very long."

"Yes, of course," said Claire. She couldn't help feeling pleased that Elizabeth would rather come to the frigid parsonage than remain with her father and his young wife and second family. "This is a lot more than I expected for the day."

Back in the kitchen a wide smile overtook her. "Elizabeth's home!" she told Corky. To Mr. Rochester she said, "I'll drive you to the store but I can't stay. My daughter has come home from Central America." She sat back down and gazed at her half-eaten oatmeal. "Corky, hurry up."

Then the second piece of news soaked in. "She said that Wolf is at the house too!" To his wondering look she replied, "She didn't give me any details. We'll find out when we get there. Aren't you finished yet?"

"Three more bites," he answered. "I haven't had bacon for months." But he hurried, and soon they were moving along in the van, Corky in back, with Mr. Rochester belted into the front passenger seat.

"I'm sorry I've made you late," Claire told the old man. She knew what value he placed on timeliness. She also knew the strength of her own power with him. "Whatever needs doing I'll get to on Monday." They were almost to Osborne Avenue.

But he was staring ahead, straight as a statue. "Would you mind driving me back home?"

She slowed. "Are you well?"

"I'm as well as can be expected," he answered. After a long silence, while Claire pulled to the curb and stopped, he explained, reluctantly. "I'd prefer to stay away from the store. It's Charlie's now."

"You'll need to put things in order. And bring your chair home."

"Surely Sara can bestir herself long enough to do that for me." His chin was high, the picture of offended obstinacy. "When you cut something off, it's best not to hang around and pick over the remains. Make a clean cut. Like a surgeon."

Corky leaned forward. "Give yourself time, sir. This is a big transition for you."

But Mr. Rochester kept his chin in the air and did not reply. Claire drove around the block and headed back.

At Fred's, Corky helped the old man out of the van and up the sanded walk. Marigold came around to investigate, and when the front door was opened, she pushed between the two men and entered. "Thank you," said Mr. Rochester. "I can manage now." He stood frozen in place for a moment, then propelled himself through the doorway and fumbled with the knob to close the door.

Corky, now in the front seat, said, "I tried to help him soften his spine yesterday, but I suppose it's pretty well fused into place. At least he got through making the big decision."

She nodded. The sun was bright, and she groped at the mirror where her sunglasses hung by their Chums. "Here," said Corky, "I'll hand them to you."

They had talked some more in bed last night. "I won't blame you if you want to separate. It can't be easy, dealing with the mess I've brought you into." Corky lay at the far edge of the bed, careful not to intrude on Claire's space. He spoke softly even though their room was removed from the other bedrooms.

She had already thought about separating, thought about a solitary life without the incessant demand of caring for Corky. She'd been thinking about it in starts and fits for weeks. When there was still the possibility of prison hanging over him, she'd thought with some relief about the possibility of being alone.

But she realized that even if they separated, she would still have him on her mind. It wasn't that easy to end a relationship. She took her time replying.

"I feel so guilty," he said. "But I also feel unjustly accused. I've tried so hard. Surely what I *haven't done* ought to count for something. But as soon as I think about that side of it, the shame floods me and I feel like they made a mistake not sending me to prison. It's like running in a squirrel cage, this cycle of feeling. I can't make it stop."

Claire had never heard Corky describe his own feelings this fully before. Sometimes she had wondered if he even *had* feelings. But she had feelings too, and it was not *her* behavior that made them so painful, it was his.

"There's one thing I need to know," she answered finally. "Did you ever touch Elizabeth?" The thought of him molesting her own child under her own roof was the one thing, the one thing, she simply could not stand. And would she ever really know? Would he tell her if he had?

"I don't think so," he said slowly.

"What do you mean you don't think so?" she exclaimed. "Either you did or you didn't."

"That line may be clear to you, Claire, but it's not to me. I did not make sexual advances to her, if that's what you mean. But I've been learning that my definition of a sexual advance and other people's definitions aren't quite the same. All I can say with full honesty is that I don't think so."

What a bitter pill to swallow! Could it be that Elizabeth's choice to stay far from home was a result of his behavior? If she ever got a chance, she might ask her. But would she want to know the answer?

The same was true of Nancy. He would say the very same thing about Nancy. "I don't think so," he would say. Neil was right. Nancy was safe now, at the Merchants, but if they got tired of her, she would have to go home. Oh, the disruption!

But it was Nancy she was thinking of sending home. It was Nancy who should be removed from the house for her safety, not Corky. "Do I want to separate from you?" she murmured. "I don't think so."

He reached for her hand. She turned to let sheer animal comfort sooth the sore edges of the raw wound between them. Trust might never return, but the intent to try was the first step.

Now, in the glare of the morning sunlight, she put on her dark glasses and drove carefully. There was a sheen on the icy spots. Her eagerness to reunite with Elizabeth provided a reprieve from the intensity between herself and Corky.

But there was one necessary task to be done on the way. Claire drove to Osborne Avenue and parked down the block on Brewster. "I won't take a minute," she told Corky. "Do you have anything to read?"

He unbuckled the seat belt and dug in the pocket of his overcoat. "What do I have here?" he murmured. He pulled out a tattered paperback copy of *One Hundred Years of Solitude* book-marked two thirds of the way through. "Good," he said. "Take your time."

The drugstore was warm. The familiar aisles and displays, the mirrored pillars and old tiled floor, gave Claire a rush of yearning. She'd gotten accustomed to spending time here. What was she going to do now, shuffle around in a cold dark house with Corky? And the money wasn't much, but it certainly helped. She had hoped it would tide them over until the political pendulum swung over to decency again and social services were back in favor.

Lenora, the day shift clerk, was busy ringing up a stack of cat food cans for a customer. She glanced up and waved as Claire went to the pharmacy cage. Charlie, clean and bright as ever, in his starched white shirt and bow tie, welcomed her with a look of joy. Stepping down he grabbed her for a hug. "Thank you!" he said. "Thank you!"

"You have Corky to thank, not me," she said. She repeated what she'd heard about yesterday's kitchen baptism. "I can't help laughing," she said. "It must have been an ordeal, getting him in and out of the bathtub. It's not funny, but it *is*, you know?"

"Anyway, he's not going to come back. He says he'll send Sara in to wrap things up, and the paperwork can be done within a week, I'm sure."

"I can't get over it that he offered me the stock at no extra cost. That just doesn't sound like the Rochester we know and love."

"He's afraid you'll turn the place into a New Age supplements store and stink it up with incense. And sell crystals. Better cat food than crystals," she said. "That's why he wants you to have the stock."

"I'm not going to go New Age. My hope is to return it to its glory days. Put in a soda fountain. We have to be attractive to people on foot, the kids on their way home from school, the old people who remember how things used to be. It's going to take time, but that's my plan."

"It would relieve his mind if you told him," she said.

He nodded. "I can do that."

Claire hesitated. "Do you want me to stay on for a while until things are wrapped up?"

"I hope you'll be here longer than that," he answered. "I'm going to need a manager."

"Bless you!" Claire beamed her full-dimple smile. "You're a sweet-heart," she said. "I can't work today, I'm sorry – my daughter's just come home from Panama – but I'll be here on Monday."

REUNIONS

Wolf was still under the kitchen table when Claire and Corky arrived at the parsonage, but the house was too cold for them to stay out of the kitchen and let him sleep. Claire stepped carefully around his feet and around the heater, trying to keep quiet.

But their presence roused him, and he struggled to sit up.

"Watch your head," warned Corky.

This time he managed to open the sleeping bag and climb out less awkwardly. "I meant to call you," he croaked, with sleep in his voice. "I hope you don't mind that I'm here."

"Of course we don't mind," said Claire. She held him in a long hug. "It's wonderful to see you. But I admit that it's a surprise."

"I always thought you'd be back," said Corky. His gleeful, pebbly smile shone forth from the blue of his beard stubble. He drew Wolf close to shake hands.

"Premonition?"

"Precognition."

"Well at least nobody took a dive on my car this time."

A look passed between Claire and Corky.

"Actually, I was hoping to see Romy."

"Romy's in Bloomington. She took an apartment there for the time being," said Claire. "They will get their house back this summer. Oh, and Nancy's staying with her friend Heather while it's so cold and we don't have any heat. We're camping, really. We'll have to do something pretty soon. We can't impose on Fred and Sara forever."

When the greetings had subsided, Wolf said, "I don't suppose I could take a shower."

"We've done it," Corky replied. "There's plenty of hot water. If you close the bathroom door and run the shower for a while, the room warms up a little. It's not fun, but it's possible."

Claire said, "The trick is to have something warm to put on when you get out of the shower. Let me get Corky's bathrobe and I'll put it here in front of the oven."

Wolf shook his head. "I'll tough it out." He had had enough mothering in Flagstaff. It was embarrassing.

He was still in the shower when Elizabeth arrived. Claire had been watching from the living room, waiting to open the door, but Elizabeth went around to the back. Once inside, mother and daughter hugged, rocking together. Claire's eyes streamed.

"Let me look at you," she said, holding her at arm's length. "You're so brown!" She gave her another hug. "You're so beautiful!" Then she let go to wipe her eyes on her sweater sleeve.

"Mother, are you okay?" Claire's eyes were puffy and the skin on her face looked raw.

"I'm wonderful," Claire answered. "Your presence is a treasure."

Elizabeth turned to Corky and hugged him too. Claire's radar switched on automatically to an alert mode. There was nothing more than affection in the hug, at least that she could see. But would there be? Wouldn't he be careful now? She tried to disengage the radar, hating her thoughts, but with minimal success.

They bumped and fumbled around the kitchen while Claire searched for the coffee maker. "It has to be here somewhere," she muttered. When it was located, in plain sight on the counter, Elizabeth did the honors. "The trip was okay," she told them. "But I wasn't expecting it to be this cold. I know I've been away a while, but it's March, for God's sake!"

"The weather's changing," said Corky. "I smelled it. You can tell when the sunshine starts to mean something." He opened the kitchen door and breathed deeply in the cold air, making a display of his prophecy.

"Shut the door," Corky," said Claire. Reluctantly, he obeyed.

"The weather's not going to change fast enough for you to live without heat. What are you going to do?"

"We simply haven't faced that issue," Claire admitted. "We've had so much else to worry about that we avoided thinking about moving."

She hesitated. How long could she put off telling Elizabeth what the "so much else" had been? All this time, she had avoided what was most on her mind in her letters and phone calls.

"I've certainly thought about it," said Corky. His large head looked capable of a great deal of thought, but his moth-eaten appearance suggested that the thought did not lead to effective action.

"This isn't your house, is it? Doesn't it belong to the Freethinkers? Isn't it up to them to fix the furnace?"

"No it's not our house," said Claire quickly. "Oh Elizabeth, it's a complicated story. Couldn't we just enjoy each other for a little while before we start problem solving?"

Wolf's sure footsteps came tripping down the stairs. He entered the kitchen, clean-shaven, wearing his red sweater. "My cup runneth over," Claire murmured, "seeing you both." Their youth and vigor were in stark contrast to Corky's shadowy gauntness almost unto death.

Wolf accepted some brewed coffee and tasted it with a conspiratorial smile at Elizabeth. "Very good," he said. His sleeping bag was still on the floor. He rolled it up before sitting down at the table.

"Let's hear from you," said Corky. Unlike Claire, he showed nothing of whatever emotion he might be feeling, left over from the night before. Years of practiced control allowed him to project good cheer and simple affability. If he seemed a bit stiff, that was how he always seemed, unless there were children around. "What are you doing in these parts? What's the news from your father?"

"My father's doing well," he answered. "I just thought I'd drop by and say hello to Romy. And you too, of course."

"Are you on your way somewhere?"

"Not really." He took a moment to stir his coffee. "Okay. I finished up with a job helping my uncle, and I thought I'd take the time to come back and see her again. It was so rude, the way I left without even saying goodbye. I hope she'll open the door when I knock."

"You could phone her from here," said Corky.

Wolf shook his head. "She'll hang up on me."

"She won't hang up on me," said Claire. "I'll call and tell her you're on the way to Bloomington and she has to talk with you. At least that way she'll know you're coming and can be at home. She works all kinds of odd hours."

"She might be at work even as we speak," said Corky.

"I'll call her right now." Claire stood up decisively. She glanced a question at Wolf, who nodded. "I'll tell her you're already on the road. That way she can't invite you to the phone and then hang up on you."

"So Romy is still her same old self! What do you hear from Aunt Claudine?" asked Elizabeth.

"More than I like," Claire answered. "She's her same old self, too. But she's found a place to put her energy. She bought a clothing store, and she acts as manager and buyer both. It's just the thing for her. She's always been a clothes horse, you know." With two swift gestures she indicated Claudine's height and thinness.

Elizabeth offered more coffee to everyone. But Claire noticed Wolf glance at the clock. "I'd better call Romy. Let's get this poor man on his way. If she's home, you can go now, and if she's not, we can enjoy your company for a while longer."

Acting as a matchmaker was just what Claire needed right now. She remembered how suitable Wolf and Romy were for each other and what a disappointment it had been for their relationship to end. Going from the warm kitchen to the telephone she crossed her fingers and murmured, "Let her be home."

When Romy picked up the phone, Claire exclaimed, "What joy! You're home!"

"Aunt Claire? Of course I'm home. It's Saturday morning."

"Well, you always talked about people sleeping at the office. I didn't know but what you might be doing that too."

"I put my foot down. I'm willing to work late, and I'm willing to go in early – weekdays. But I won't work on weekends." She paused. "So what's up? I was hoping to come to Portville today, but from what I hear on the news, the roads are still bad. Maybe I ought to wait till next weekend."

"Romy, I have some news. Wolf's come back. He drove all the way from Flagstaff just to see you." Claire's voice was urgent, but she kept it low. "You have to agree to see him. He's on his way, but he's worried that you'll take one look at him and slam the door in his face."

There was a long silence. "That wouldn't be very smart, would it? Just as long as he knows how rude he was, leaving like that."

"He knows, Romy. And he's sorry. Just give him a chance, will you?" Claire continued, "There's more news, too. Elizabeth's here. She came in last night. You really do have to get up here next weekend."

Romy had kept in contact with Portville by phone, talking with Nancy frequently, and Claire too. She knew what was going on, knew that the furnace had given out and the family was staying at Fred and Sara's house. She had even talked with Celia Merchant several times, this past week, to make sure that Nancy was okay. Celia was more than glad for Nancy to stay: Heather was an only child, and having a friend with her was a great treat. It was delicately implied rather than spoken, also, that even though the accusations against Corky had to be false, her house might be safer for Nancy than the parsonage. Couldn't she just stay with them until summer? Romy supposed it was better having her happy with her friend than wretched at Fred and Sara's, though she refused to acknowledge any delicate implications about Corky. As for her weekend visits, she and Nancy could go to a motel for the night.

"Of course I'll come up," Romy replied. "I had made plans to take Nancy and Heather to Chicago for the weekend to go to the museums, but that can wait. I wish I was there right now!"

"No you don't," Claire answered. "You stay right where you are and get yourself dolled up. I think the man's serious."

Romy laughed. "If he's serious, I won't have to be dolled up!"

"At least make him welcome!"

"Aunt Claire, I'm a grown-up. I know how to act."

"Of course you do," said Claire. "I'm really happy for you," she whispered. She knew quite well that Romy would look beautiful when Wolf arrived.

Back in the kitchen, Claire, her tear-stained face beaming, told Wolf that the coast was clear. He could stop anticipating a slammed door or a hung-up phone.

"Tell her I can't wait to see her," Elizabeth instructed him.

It didn't take Wolf long to carry his bedroll and duffel bag to the car. Claire and Corky went out to see him off, see his happy grin and thumbs up sign out the window, see him drive away down Clover Street.

Claire hugged Corky and cried again for a moment. "Something good is happening," she said, with her wet face against his chest. He stroked her hair. "It's about time."

PROBLEM SOLVING

Elizabeth was not willing to put off problem solving for very long. "I'm not going to go back to Panama and leave you homeless," she said. "There's no reason we can't go house-hunting this very day."

"I told you she'd spend all her time taking care of us," murmured Corky.

"At least she's not doing the junk mail," Claire answered.

"I won't even ask what that's all about," said Elizabeth. "Where's the newspaper? We can check the classifieds and go look at houses."

"I'll let you take your mother on this excursion," said Corky. "Tomorrow's my day at Portvillage. I have to write a sermon."

"Couldn't you use a hand-me down? Surely you don't have to write a new sermon every Sunday."

"True. I should say, rather, that I *want* to write a sermon."

"Oh well, that's different. We'll get out of your way." Elizabeth set the cups in the sink and unplugged the coffee maker. Claire brought the newspaper in from the stack in the living room and found two columns in the Houses for Rent section.

"We really ought to wait till tomorrow. The Sunday paper has lots more ads."

"We can do that too, but if we go today as well, we'll have the jump on the Sunday paper."

Claire marked three ads that looked acceptable. "You're just what we've needed," she told Elizabeth. "We haven't had the energy to lift ourselves out of squalor. You're like an infusion." She went to the phone to make appointments to view the houses that afternoon.

Elizabeth asked Corky if he had a coat she could wear. "Mom's clothes are way too small."

"You're welcome to my overcoat," he said. "I'm not going any-where."

No one went anywhere until after lunch. They all tidied the kitchen and Corky put his typewriter back on the table. Elizabeth donned his overcoat, which was a little too long in the sleeves, but not much.

She and Claire were on their way out when the phone rang. "Aren't you going to answer it?"

"No." Claire switched on the message recorder's sound just long enough to know what, if not who, it was. At Elizabeth's questioning look, she said, "We don't answer the phone anymore. We've been get-ting hate calls. I won't give them the satisfaction of knowing that we hear them." She bustled Elizabeth out the door.

"Might as well take the rental car," said Elizabeth. "I have to pay for it whether I use it or not." Inside, the car was warm from the sun, and the warmth accentuated the rental car smell.

Elizabeth had refrained from asking the obvious questions, but she had been watching and listening. "Why would you get hate calls?"

Rather than answering, Claire stared as though seeing a ghost. "So *that's* why I never got your message! Those bastards fill up the tape with their poison and we don't receive our real messages." She broke into a sob. "Oh, Elizabeth, I hate to burden you with all this, but we've had such a terrible year." Noticing that the motor was idling, she looked out the window and said, "Don't sit here. I don't want Corky to see us."

Elizabeth drove slowly.

"Drive to the beach," suggested Claire. "We can park in the sun for a while until it's time to look at our two o'clock house." As Elizabeth drove, Claire alternately talked and sobbed. Once begun, the story could not be contained any longer.

"Corky doesn't have a job. We don't have a place to live. It's a lot worse than you can imagine," she cried. When Elizabeth broke in to mention Portvillage, Claire shook her head. "He only preaches there every few months. It's a rotating pulpit, with all the local ministers tak-ing turns. He hasn't been with Freethinkers since last fall. Even before that it was touch and go, they in search for another minister and Corky preaching week by week. The only thing that kept him on was that they couldn't find anyone nondenominational and radical enough to suit them. Evidently they still can't. Or maybe they don't want to."

She rattled on about the Freethinkers. "They do lay-led services or bring in guest ministers. I haven't had contact with any of them for quite a while, not even my friends. It's too stressful, what with their pity for me and their condemnation of Corky."

Effects but not causes. Claire would have to tell Elizabeth what brought about all this trouble, but she still couldn't bear to speak of it. She talked about how tenuous even the parsonage was, theirs only until the Freethinkers told them to go. "They may hate us, but having us in the house is better than having the place stand empty over the winter." Words flowed. Her own job at the children's shelter had ended with the cuts in social services – "but of course that's old news." She'd been working, but not in her own field – they were getting by on what she brought in plus the law firm money – the furniture was in Bloomington with Romy – the furnace had given them trouble all winter – on and on.

Elizabeth drove to the strip of parking along the beach that edged Lake Michigan. In the sunshine the water was blue and silver, the piles of plowed snow bright. Claire stopped talking and wiped her face. Seeing the stunning view through her daughter's eyes, she remained silent while Elizabeth drank it in.

Then Elizabeth turned sideways with her knee on the seat and her arm across the seat back. Claire burst into tears again.

"What's the matter with Corky?" asked Elizabeth. "Is he sick? He looks like an old man."

"He's sick at heart. Oh, Elizabeth, he barely escaped going to prison!" Again the words tumbled out. Arrested twice – beaten up the first time – dependent on Neil – in disgrace with the congregation – and their enemies in the congregation certainly didn't help any – accusations from the past – hate mail. "He came very close to suicide!"

When the torrent eased, Elizabeth spoke slowly. "He's a pedophile, isn't he," she said. "A candyman."

At last it was out. Claire's heart pounded. His shame was her shame. She nodded. Then she opened her eyes and looked directly at her daughter. "Was he ever – did he ever – did he do anything to you?"

"No," she said slowly. "He didn't. But he loved me too much. I only knew later. At the time I thought it was great, basking in all that attention. But he didn't molest me." She reached over the arm of her seat to hold Claire. "It's okay, Mother. You don't have to worry about that."

"Well, thank God for one blessed thing I don't have to worry about!" Claire straightened up and gazed at the scene outside, trying to bring herself back to her place on earth, rather than being tumbled around in her feelings. But it didn't work. She wasn't finished.

"I don't know what to think," she said. "I don't know what to do." She shielded her eyes from the glorious view with her wet handkerchief.

"Must you do anything? Right now, I mean. Other than finding a decent place to live."

Claire shook her head. "I don't know how I can go on with him knowing this. I've managed to deceive myself all these years, but looking back, I have to rearrange the whole marriage. It's all been a sham. I feel like I'm in little pieces on the floor. If I ever get put back together, I won't be the same person."

Elizabeth listened.

"I try to imagine what it must be like for him. What would it be like, knowing you would be feared and despised for something you can't help?"

When Elizabeth started to speak, Claire shook her head. "I know he can help what he does. It's no different from taking a vow of celibacy. But an ordinary celibate isn't drawn to something that he can't even think about without shame."

"What makes you think he's celibate? What did he do to get arrested?"

"I don't know. Neil wouldn't let me listen to the girl's accusation. All I know is that she took his playfulness amiss. But there wasn't really a case against him."

"You said he was arrested twice. What happened the other time?"

"It was the same thing. That time I believed that it was all part of a plot by a clique of the Freethinkers who didn't like him. But when it happened again, and the news got spread around somehow, and when people from the past started writing to the prosecutor – and even to *me* – about things he did years ago – how could I go on thinking there was nothing to it?"

"Did you ask him?"

Claire was silent. "I was afraid to ask him. I was too busy defending him. We didn't talk about it, not until this weekend, in fact. It all came to a head this weekend when he was asked to give someone the sacraments. That broke him down, believing there was no one to do the same for him. Not that he wanted it, of course, but that sense of being completely without the support of his peers. He told me he had never had sex with a child and that he had become a minister thinking it would help him control his impulses."

Here she began crying again. "You see how everything looks different, in the light of this? I feel so *cheated!*" She blew her nose loudly. "Don't you? Don't you feel cheated? He was a second father to you. How do *you* feel about this?"

"Mom, actually, I feel relieved. This confirms what I've come to realize, only I had to wonder if I was imagining things. I used to feel guilty, getting so much attention. It seemed like he ought to be paying attention to you, not me. But I couldn't help liking it, too. I felt like a princess. The problem for me, it's been that no one else has treated me like royalty, and none of my relationships ever work out. I think I expect too much, and then they get tired of trying to please me."

Claire heard her daughter describe a kind of damage, but it was so much less than the damage she feared that she reacted more with relief than indignation. "What time is it?" she asked. Suddenly, her flooding was finished – at least for now – and house-hunting took precedence.

"It's time," said Elizabeth. "Do you have a comb?"

Claire dug in her purse and handed it over.

"I mean for you," said Elizabeth. "You need a little powder and lipstick too."

Claire tidied herself and opened out her wet handkerchief on the dashboard to dry in the sun. "I've never cried so much in one day in my whole life. I feel dehydrated from shedding all those tears." She retrieved the handkerchief for one last wipe of her nose. "Thank you, sweetheart. I've needed to spill it all out. I'm just sorry you had to come home to this."

Elizabeth responded dryly, "Being useful isn't so bad."

Claire managed a laugh. "Same old Elizabeth."

The two o'clock house was in the same general neighborhood as the parsonage, between Euclid and Osborne Avenues, where the houses were fifty and sixty years old and rents were not sky high. Claire and Elizabeth were met there by the owners, an older couple.

"I'm Claire Pearlman, and this is my daughter, Elizabeth."

"Libby Gustaman," Elizabeth corrected.

The woman, Mrs. Blake, looked up at her husband and said, "Pearlman, that name sounds familiar. Who do we know named Pearlman?" He shook his head. "Well, come in and look around. Our last tenants have been gone since the end of January, and we've done some redecorating."

The house was typical of its era, two story, seven small rooms, with a breakfast nook in an alcove that looked out on the back yard. Bathroom upstairs. Washer and dryer in the basement. Small closets. Front and back porches. Narrow lot. A garage on the alley.

The Blakes had raised a family here. "We would have stayed, but when Sally here broke her leg, we realized that we were getting to the age where we needed a single story place," said Mr. Blake. "We refinished the floors," he continued proudly. "People are starting to appreciate these old hardwood floors nowadays." Their footsteps echoed as they walked through the downstairs. "All the appliances are here," he said. "There's even a freezer." In the dining room he pointed out the chandelier, hung all around with glass prisms. "And there's the coat closet, there under the steps. We thought about converting it to a powder room, but the plumbing would have been too expensive for what we'd get out of it."

They went out the back door, through the porch, which was enclosed. "You can see the garage if you don't mind going through the snow. I didn't get around to shoveling the back walk."

Claire didn't care to see the garage. She'd seen enough. It would do, but she wanted to look at the others as well. She thanked the Blakes for their time. "It's very nice," she said, adding that the hardwood floors made it especially attractive. "We have several more places to visit. I'll get in touch if we decide to take it."

"Don't wait too long," advised Mrs. Blake. "There's somebody else coming to look later this afternoon."

In the car Claire voiced her misgivings. "She'll figure out where she heard the name Pearlman. I'd rather not have to deal with that."

But the house was nice, not too different from the parsonage, though a little smaller. "Our furniture would fit."

"What furniture?" asked Elizabeth, dryly. When Claire started to explain, she said, "I know, I know."

The other two houses were also in the neighborhood, but neither was as clean and ready to move into as the Blakes' house. One did have a large downstairs den and a first floor powder room, but the kitchen had never been redone and was still redolent of the thirties with a smell of Dutch Cleanser and old glass knobs on all the cabinet doors.

"What do you think, Elizabeth?"

"If you really want to know, I think you ought to move farther away. Why should you stick around in the same neighborhood where you've had such a hard time? Why should you even stay in Portville? You could use this as an opportunity to make a new life in a new place."

Claire nodded. "It's not that I haven't thought of it. But what it comes down to is the fact that I do have a job here, and with things the way they are, it's not likely that I would find one easily if we went somewhere else. And Corky, he will never find another congregation, and he may never find another job at all."

"You still don't have to stay in the neighborhood. I sure wouldn't, if it were me. And why not buy a house, instead of pouring money into a rental?"

Claire shook her head. "No." She shook her head again, vigorously. "No. I just can't see making a commitment like that, especially now. There's every reason in the world not to. I'd have to borrow money for the down payment from Neil, for one thing. And neither Corky nor I are in any condition to enter into a big new project. Just moving is going to be hard enough."

"Okay, okay. But I still think you ought to get out of this neighborhood. It wouldn't be any harder to move across town than to move down the street, and you'd at least have a change of scene."

Claire struggled, trying to widen her vision beyond the box of the neighborhood. "You know, Elizabeth, I just can't picture us in the suburbs. I feel like I belong here, even if it's hard."

"I'm going to talk psycho-babble now, Mom. Give you a dose of your own medicine. I think you believe you don't *deserve* a better place to live. You've made your bed, now lie in it. Go down with the ship."

"You're probably right." Claire gave a forlorn sigh. "All of the above. I can't get in the mood to see new possibilities right now. But I'm willing to try. We can look in tomorrow's paper. Look for something outside the neighborhood. Just don't think too harshly of me, please. What we did this afternoon was a huge step. We should have taken it months ago."

The houses on Clover Street now looked dazed, as though struck with something more than a heavy winter. Elizabeth pulled up behind Claire's van. They sat for a moment, gazing out, and then she switched off the motor. The heater fan went suddenly silent. The roof of the parsonage seemed lower, like an old person losing height, the snow cover shaggy and drooping, like the thick, dirty wool on a sheep just before shearing time.

"To change the subject, what's a good restaurant? I'd like to take you and Corky to dinner."

Claire hung her head. "I haven't been out to dinner for so long that I don't know one restaurant from another." Then she brightened. "So it doesn't matter, does it? Any place we go will be the best!"

THE SERMON

While Claire and Elizabeth investigated houses, Corky attended to to-morrow's sermon as though it might be his last, as indeed it might. In his baggy old sweater, he hunched toward the typewriter, looking down to avoid the white glare from the window over the sink. The ticking of the wall clock accompanied the heater's blower, the two a rhythmic duet that picked up imaginary tones and blended into a dis-cordant symphony.

Corky had always used his sermons as possibilities for exploration, occasions for him to delve into questions that interested him, to talk to himself as well as to his audience – the best part of ministry. He and Claire had spent many a Sunday afternoon walking and talking about the issues he raised in the morning's sermon. He always said that he wrote in order to know what he thought. Sometimes people criticized this. These were the ones who wanted a neat little package with a neat little message. But others – and these were the ones he was talking to – liked it that he raised questions rather than giving answers. This one would open with a question. "Do you know who you are?" his words began. "Do you belong to yourself?"

"I am asking you, in your late years, to think about this question. Why, you might ask. What difference does it make?

If there is any meaning at all in an individual life, I believe it lies in becoming and acknowledging who you are, then acting in accordance with that knowledge. I say this, knowing it goes against common wis-dom. Most of us spend our lives trying to become what we *aren't*, try-ing to *over*come what we are, trying to be like someone else, someone we admire, someone whose fatal flaws and inner sorrows we're not aware of."

His fingers took naturally to the keyboard. The words, up till now, had come forth as though the sermon were fully formed. But here he hesitated, closed his eyes and sat quietly for some minutes with his hands in his lap and his head bowed. Then he continued, typing resolutely.

"Haven't we all had the experience of hearing someone say to us, 'Now I know what you really are!' This is usually said at a time when we've behaved badly and have found out. We're summed up, then. Our totality is contained in a single act.

That single act is certainly part of who and what we are, no question about it. We have to open ourselves to include our bad behavior in its proper place. But notice that I say "include" and I say "proper place". Our bad behavior is not the sum total of who we are.

I believe that when we get to the gate of Heaven, whether it's heaven here and now or a heaven later on, when we get to that gate, Saint Peter will already have a full description of us as God knows us, as we somehow know ourselves deep inside, who and what we are, complete. He'll have a scroll for each one of us with a full and accurate picture on it. We will be obliged to match that description with our own, and we won't enter heaven for keeps until we've fully realized every aspect of who we are and what we've done. Keeping part of ourselves hidden, not only from others but even from ourselves, is like trying to enter heaven with one of our feet missing. You just can't get there that way. You have to enter heaven whole, with all your parts gathered up and assembled.

If you come to the edge of Heaven, and you can see it waiting, if only you could get there, Saint Peter will look you over and listen to your account of who you are and what you've done with your attributes. If there are parts missing, he will send you out to gather them up. He'll say, "Go back and dig up that sullied hand you buried. That hand is part of you, and Heaven does not open to persons with parts missing."

He will notice how you have expressed who you are, too. What have you done with the hand, sullied or pure, that you were dealt? Have you found ways to put your talents to use and to keep rein on your flaws? We are accountable for our own lives. What have we done with the privilege of living?

I'm suggesting that those of you who are so inclined might review your lives with a thought to what would be on Saint Peter's scroll. You might write down your memories, the events and situations of your life and how you responded to them. The persons in your life and how you treated them. Your joyful memories. The work you did, what you've created. Your sorrows and disappointments, your tragedies. Your numinous moments, your intimations of the divine.

Some of us, to avoid the sin of pride, downplay the stars in our crown, others avoid shame, covering up the mistakes we've made. I'm suggesting that you use some of your hours here to write a full account. And if you're hesitant about writing, you know they have tape recorders here that are available for your use.

You might ask, how do we know that heaven will open to us when we do this? Well, of course I don't *know*. But I've done a fair amount of personal counseling during my years as a minister, and I've seen it happen. I know my own experience, too. Haven't you ever thought that you would truly be in heaven if only thus-and-such aspect of yourself were different? That, except for thus-and-such, you have everything you need for a happy life?

But it isn't that you need to *change* thus-and-such to find happiness in Heaven. It's that you need to acknowledge it as part and parcel of your life, of your place on earth. You need to *accept* who you are, not change it.

I want to make it clear that I am not advocating acting out bad behavior when I urge you to accept your undesirable traits. There's a vast difference between accepting who you are and using that as an excuse for sinfulness.

Sometimes you need to acknowledge a part of yourself that has to be kept closely in check. Suppose you are inclined to violence. Acknowledging it does not include acting violent. Suppose you yearn for material things. Acknowledging your desire does not excuse you for spending beyond your means. If you are crippled by a black heart, then you must take care to act with compassion *intentionally*, knowing that you can't count on spontaneous compassion.

When you feel the violence or the yearning arise in you, the thing to do is recognize it, name it to yourself – say "desire" to yourself several times, or "yearning", whatever word it takes to get it right – and then put it aside and go about your business.

This practice, followed faithfully, allows you to be who you are while acting responsibly in the world, and it carries you through the gate of Heaven."

He wrote slowly, nodding to himself from time to time.

"I'm talking about *salvation* here, my friends. Some of you are from churches that tell you salvation comes through belief. Others count on good works. I am discouraging neither beliefs nor good works. Beliefs can be comforting, and good works are one's obligations to life. I am only suggesting that, for me, salvation means gathering up all the pieces of myself and putting them together, like threads in a tapestry, like pieces of a jigsaw puzzle. There is no heaven, to me, like the heaven of fully belonging to myself, of being firmly rooted in my own soil.

Think of a tree. It reaches up, stretches its branches like arms to embrace heaven. But if it is not firmly rooted, it leans or even topples. When a tree is in its proper place, roots down and branches open, it touches heaven, and so do we. Have you not all experienced those moments when you are fully yourself and the thought comes to you: *this is what I'm here for*! I believe those moments constitute heaven. They are the precious jewels strung on the necklace of our life."

Corky read through what he had written. It would be enough to use as an outline. He could embellish it on the spot when he got a sense of people's response. He knew many of Portvillage's residents and could direct specific references and mention details that would make all of this meaningful to them.

To that end, he listed those he knew best and made notes at each name. He wasn't preaching in a cathedral, after all. This would be a small congregation assembled in the chapel. Intimacy was called for, in such a setting.

HELLO, GORGEOUS

The next day, Josie arrived at Portvillage at two-thirty, half an hour ahead of the worship service. With her was Tippy-the-dog, tugging on her red leash, sniffing every corner. Although Eve and Duncan approved of Josie's performances there, they rarely attended the service, having already gone to meeting with the Freethinkers in the morning. So this was what she had done the last two months, bring Tippy along for company and leave her in Bess Kingman's room during the service.

"Don't you look nice!" exclaimed Bess. "Is that a new dress?"

Josie was no longer chubby. Even though she knew she would never be pretty, she enjoyed the praise she got at LOVELY YOU and the petting she got from Eve.

"Mother gave it to me for my birthday." Josie turned, pretending to be a model. "But she let me help pick it out." A fitted jacket topped the cream and violet striped dress, the colors enhancing her complexion, which was much prettier than she imagined. "I love this color purple. It's exactly what I tried to make in that picture." She pointed.

The walls of Bess Kingman's room were decorated with several taped-up pictures that she and Josie had created together during the winter. First one would make some colorful marks on the paper, then the other would add to them, and so on, until the picture had grown into being. Josie liked making pictures this way much better than doing it alone, having to think of everything herself, not knowing what would be okay.

"Whatever you do is okay, dear," Bess had told her, but Josie couldn't accept this reassurance and take it in. Bess Kingman didn't really know, did she? No one did. And no one ever would. In her reading, Josie had come across the phrase, "the secret that would go with her to the grave," and she understood it perfectly, just as she understood, "My lips are sealed."

A folded blanket and a bowl of water were always out on the floor for Tippy. Josie unsnapped the leash and hung it over the back of a chair. The dog now nosed Bess's hand expectantly. "Guess again," said Bess. The dog biscuit was in her other hand. Tippy took no time at all finding it.

Josie, as the musician, chose the two hymns each Sunday. The repertoire was small. Neither Josie nor the residents were up to learning new songs every week, so they stuck to a few old favorites. There might be a different minister every week, but there was consistency in the hymns. Josie practiced them faithfully, so that she could play them without being afraid of making mistakes.

Bess wheeled herself out of the room now, with Josie beside her and Tippy left behind. It wouldn't do to have the dog running around, creating havoc, during the service. Once in the hall, Josie pushed the wheelchair.

The chapel was on the first floor of the far side of Portvillage from Bess's third floor corridor. They rode down in the cavernous elevator and passed the common room near the entrance, which was decorated in pastels, with matching pictures of flowers and landscapes on the walls. A gregarious woman, Bess stopped to greet people along the gleaming hallways, those old souls always well-dressed and tidy, thanks to the staff, with their personalities indrawn now and their voices a whisper. She took her time, listening to the whispers, reaching out to fragile old hands. Josie hid her impatience, leaning on the back of the chair, humming *A Mighty Fortress Is Our God,* which would be the closing hymn today. As she hummed, she thought the words to the parody she had made up, "A mighty huntress is our cat; All birds and mice are quailing." She hoped she could play it without giggling.

People were already gathered in the chapel when they arrived, some seated in chairs, others in their own wheelchairs. A picture of long-haired Jesus in a white robe adorned the front wall, and a crucifix hung between two windows. Josie left Bess and went to the piano, which stood against the side wall at the front of the room.

The piano was an old upright that must have once inhabited a cocktail lounge. Inlaid in the crazed black finish of the wood sides and front were mirrors, and a rim of colored glass chunks edged the lid. Scattered on the top were books of popular songs from decades past, some old sheet music, the Gray Book and the Golden Book of Favorite Songs. The piano itself was out of tune at both ends, but most likely no one noticed, since what was played here used only the middle of the keyboard.

Josie always arranged her music and the song books to cover the lower part of the front mirror so that she would not have to face herself as she played.

It was three o'clock now, time to begin the prelude.

Janice Beam, Josie's music teacher, believed in choosing music that her pupils could master, so that they would have the satisfaction of a good performance. She also required them to continue playing old pieces. "You want to have a repertoire," she told them. "When people ask you to play, you need to have things you can play well." Oftentimes during a lesson, she would ask Josie to play again something from months ago, and because Josie never knew what might be asked for, she had to keep everything up.

With her back to the room, she did not see Corky come in and walk to the lectern. It wasn't until she had finished the prelude that she looked up to the mirror above her music. She saw him watching her.

The worship service here at Portvillage followed a pattern that the various ministers agreed to, starting, after the prelude, with a reading, then a hymn, a prayer, spontaneous prayers from members of the congregation, Josie's solo, the sermon, another hymn and the closing words.

Josie's fingers gripped the edge of the piano bench. What if someone noticed that she was in the same room with him? What if the police came?

She had been warned repeatedly to stay away from him. Not that there was much chance of disobeying, with him no longer at the meetinghouse. Eve's warnings came as anxious reminders, Duncan's as a threatening order. There were the accusations of Nancy and Heather, too, that Corky's troubles were all her fault.

What could she do? He was right there behind her, reading something incomprehensible from a little book he held in one hand. It would be too embarrassing to leave. She *couldn't* leave. It was her job to provide music for the service.

Something stubborn arose in her. *She* was the one who belonged here, the one who came every Sunday afternoon. *He* was the intruder, not her. If anyone had to leave, it ought to be him, not her.

That was a bad thought. She smothered it. It was a thought that would not be revived and fleshed out until years later, in therapy. Corky was the minister. She was just the piano player.

The minister's incomprehensible reading came to an end. The piano player's hands went to the keyboard and played the introduction to *Come, thou Almighty King!* She hadn't known that this would be the first hymn – she had actually chosen *Faith of our Fathers* – but her hands played what they played, and it was a hymn that the congregation liked. "Come and reign o – ver us, An – cient of Days!" They sang along, a few voices strong, others wavering, twenty-five or thirty women, the dozen or so men who always came, the people Josie thought of as Ancient of Days.

Josie could not sing with them, her voice didn't work, but her hands had practiced enough to know the music no matter what.

Corky's voice came from behind her: "As we go about touching the lives of our fellows, may we be friends of all. May we be saved from blighting a heart by the spite of envy or the flare of hate. May we cheer the suffering by our sympathy, revive the disheartened by our hopefulness, look all people in the face with the clear gaze of fellowship."

During the prayer a part of her left her body. She felt it as a stillness, much like the blankness with which she endured her father's anger when it arose. It came to her what to do. She would pretend that Corky was just another minister she didn't know, one of the many who volunteered their services to Portvillage. She would exit the room immediately after the service. Maybe no one would notice that she was in the same room with him, and maybe no one would call the police.

With her feelings disengaged, she went into her solo. She was still unable to sing, so she played *Tumbleweed*. This was the piece she knew best, having played it every time Duncan was in the house when she was practicing. No mistakes. Her fingers worked even though her voice didn't.

When her solo ended, instead of leaving the piano bench to sit beside Bess until time for the closing hymn, she stayed where she was, with her back to Corky at the lectern, delivering his sermon.

The sermon was just words to her. She was not really present. She did not feel her own clenched hands, the agitation in her stomach. She could hear murmurs of agreement from the people around her, but it was just background noise. Time stood still.

Only when the quality of the background noise changed did she know it was time for *A Mighty Fortress is our God*. Again her fingers knew what to do. If ever she was glad she'd practiced more than she wanted to, it was now.

At the end of the closing words she stood up, preparing to bolt from the room. But Corky was too quick. He was right there, thanking her gallantly to the congregation for her music. Everyone clapped. Under cover of the noise, he bent down, gave her a big, doggy smile, and said, very quietly, "Hello, gorgeous!"

The turmoil in her stomach rose suddenly. With a strangled little sound, she tried to get around the piano bench. She almost made it before her stomach won and she found herself involuntarily upchucking her lunch right there in the chapel, spattering the piano bench on its way to the floor, where most of it landed on Corky's shoes.

Instantly Bess Kingman wheeled to her side. "It's okay, dear, it's okay. Sit down here." She called to the woman who'd been sitting next to her, "Go get a wet washrag, Suzie. This child needs some help."

Josie was crying now, humiliated. When the wet washrag arrived, it was Corky who wiped her face. Someone spread a newspaper over the mess on the floor until the janitor could be called. Someone else tried to hand Corky some paper towels to wipe his shoes. He ignored them.

When Josie looked up at him for just a moment, she was surprised to see tears on his face too. "I'm so sorry," he murmured. "I'm so sorry."

He was probably afraid, too.

She had to get out of here, and quickly. He would be in trouble all over again if someone noticed and called the police.

She pulled away from the hands that were holding her. "I want my dog!" she cried. She ran from the room and down the hall and up the stairs to the third floor. No waiting for the elevator. No stopping to talk to anyone.

In Bess Kingman's room she dropped to the floor. Tippy was all over her immediately. She held the dog tight for a moment. But she couldn't wait for Bess to come back. She hurried into her coat and snapped on the dog's leash. Then back down the stairs to the front foyer. Her fingers fumbled with the keypad combination that allowed the door to open, the device that kept Alzheimer's patients from wandering. Before she could get it right, Bess, wheeling through the common room, saw her there.

"Oh, here you are!"

"I have to hurry!"

Bess reached for Josie and embraced her, then leaned forward in her chair to pet Tippy. "Of course you do, dear. But promise me you'll come back tomorrow after school. We have to finish the blue picture. It's too beautiful to leave it half done. You promise?"

It would be okay to come back tomorrow. He wouldn't be here then. "I promise," she said. "Goodbye now." She keyed in the right numbers and pushed the door open.

"Be sure to bring Tippy," called Bess. "There's a dog biscuit waiting."

Josie hurried away from the block that held Portvillage, tugging hard on the leash. When she was out of sight, she slowed down. Tippy stopped, gratefully, to pee, choosing a spot where the snow was already yellow at a doggy bulletin board. The sun was still shining, making wet lace of the ice at the edge of the sidewalk.

Josie squatted down to hug her dog. Her coat dragged in a puddle. Tippy licked her face vigorously, as though enjoying the taste of her salty tears. Josie coughed, and the last bit of vomit that was in her throat flew from her mouth. Tippy found it and licked that up too. "You're my friend," Josie murmured into a silky ear. "You're the best dog in the world!"

She took the long way home. She listened, but there were no police sirens. He was probably safe. Everything would be okay.

ISBN 141209543-3

9 781412 095433